HEY, LIBERAL!

A NOVEL

SHAWN SHIFLETT

ACADEMY

CHICAGO

Copyright © 2016 by Shawn Shiflett
All rights reserved
Published by Chicago Review Press Incorporated
814 North Franklin Street
Chicago, Illinois 60610
ISBN 978-1-61373-560-2

Library of Congress Cataloging-in-Publication Data

Names: Shiflett, Shawn, author.
Title: Hey, liberal! / Shawn Shiflett.
Description: Chicago, Illinois: Chicago Review Press, [2016]
Identifiers: LCCN 2016003650 (print) | LCCN 2016010167 (ebook) | ISBN
    9781613735602 (pbk.: alk. paper) | ISBN 9781613735619 (pdf) | ISBN
    9781613735633 (epub) | ISBN 9781613735626 (Kindle)
Classification: LCC PS3619.H545 H49 2016 (print) | LCC PS3619.H545
    (ebook) | DDC 813/.6—dc23
LC record available at http://lccn.loc.gov/2016003650

Cover design: Joan Sommers
Typesetting: Nord Compo

Cover photo: Detail from a photo of Shawn Shiflett that appeared in
the author's high school yearbook. This book is a work of fiction in
its entirety, and neither the author nor any of the individuals who
are partially visible in the cover photo are depicted in any way in this
book. Any similarity between the fictional characters and settings of
this book and any real person or place is strictly coincidental. The
image is used only for purposes of evoking and commenting upon the
time period in which the fictional story is set.

Printed in the United States of America
5 4 3 2 1

For Sarah. You said yes, and my luck changed forever.

Be what you be.

—KOKO TAYLOR

CONTENTS

Part III: Return of the Riots

PROLOGUE

Chump Change

IN DEXTER HIGH'S MODERN WING, located at the north end of the block, a white boy named James Jeffrey came to his study hall class, held in the auditorium due to student overcrowding, with a loaded .22-caliber rifle tucked under his trench coat. He whipped out his weapon, calmly took potshots at students, and started a pell-mell stampede, with people ducking and dodging, sprinting, crab crawling, or even slithering for the exits. Cops hit the scene in a dozen or so paddy wagons and squad cars. After a little give-up-or-we'll-blow-your-ass-away persuasion, Jeffery surrendered without a fuss. Imagine, all those human targets at close range and no one killed or wounded.

The next day, Jeffrey was leading news in all the Chicago newspapers and on TV newscasts. It turned out he was the quiet loner type. Cops with a search warrant found neo-Nazi literature stashed under his bed at home. He told detectives down at the Eighteenth Precinct that he flipped out because he was sick and tired of gangbangers threatening to jump him if he didn't hand over his lunch money. No one seems to remember exactly how much time he spent in a jail for juvenile offenders, but within a year of the shooting spree, the Jeffrey family cleared out of the North Side Lincoln Park neighborhood, forwarding address unknown.

Classes, most of which were in Dexter's connecting "new" and "old" buildings—so called because the one in the middle of the block was built just after World War II, while its much older sibling with four ionic columns loomed like an ancient relic at the south end of the block—weren't even canceled on the day of Jeffrey's rampage, when daffodils and tulips in residential flower beds were already poking through the newly thawed earth. The way Dexter's principal, Dr. Donald Jursak, explained it on the ten o'clock *Eyewitness News*, he didn't want to "risk further racial violence by breaking routine."

Just a few weeks shy of a year passed. Whether in delayed reaction to James Jeffrey's attack, or to historical and present-day discrimination of all kinds, black kids at Dexter decided that it was Stomp Honky Day. It started in the lunchroom during fifth period. Someone gave the signal; they stood up from tables en masse and then proceeded to pummel, kick, trounce, fling, and body slam to the floor any white boy or girl within reach. For an overwhelming majority who felt righteously wronged, it wasn't hard to get the upper hand. They gave Hispanic students—no slouches in the gang department themselves—a pass. By 12:15, marauding bands of students were rampaging into classrooms and dragging white kids out of their seats. One teacher, either brave or stupid enough to try to stop an ass whupping, got his jaw cracked and nose broken.

Twenty-seven arrests and a few tense days later, things simmered down, but the damage was done. White kids transferred out of Dexter in droves, and the white student body plummeted overnight from 31 percent to 12 percent. The next thing you knew, the city got serious about enforcing its court-ordered desegregation plan. No more transfers to public schools outside the district you lived in. Talk about too little too late for Dexter; white flight had already happened.

A month later, Martin Luther King Jr. was assassinated on April 4. Within days, race riots erupted in 125 cities. In June, an assassin's bullet killed Bobby Kennedy. Come August, the Soviet Union reminded Czechoslovakia who was boss by storming it with troops and tanks. A week after that, the Democratic Convention lit one hell of a national spotlight on the City of Big Shoulders, with Vietnam antiwar demonstrators and police facing off and trading taunts for cracked skulls. No wonder people had all but forgotten about the white boy with a rifle who'd gone off the deep end at Dexter. Only a few plaster-chipped bullet holes in the auditorium ceiling and several others punched as big as silver dollars through the backs of wooden seats remained as Jeffrey's legacy. Students sitting in the auditorium seats found it irresistible to stick their fingers into the holes in front of them and trace the jagged edges.

Labor Day brought summer to a close, and Simon Fleming, the son of a civil rights activist minister, started high school at Dexter as a freshman. His sense of social mission—passed down from his parents—soon collided with the reality of gangbangers routinely shaking him down for chump change. There was a perverse etiquette to these petty robberies: fork over the dime or quarter demanded from you, and the gangbanger allowed you to keep whatever loose change remained in your pockets. But dare to risk saying, "I ain't got none," and the boy assumed the right to frisk you, keep all money found, and if in a nasty mood, coldcock you, or worse, for the uppity crime of forgetting your place.

Try as Simon might, he could do little to avoid these encounters. A combination of tall for his age and brooding did him no favors. The latest media hype about getting to the Space Race finish line before the Russians was a welcome distraction and put the impossible within his and humankind's reach. In just ten more months, man would set foot on the moon.

Part I

A Long Day

1

Demands

SIMON FELT SAFEST IN THE EARLY MORNING, always hoping that no one was awake enough to bother with a white boy. One of many students migrating across an asphalt playground that stretched for half a city block, he paced himself to blend in. Trampled snow crunched underfoot with each step, and he'd keep his chin buried in the collar of his wool peacoat to protect himself against the brutal December cold. Then after the first period bell rang, and everyone else had already crossed Orchard Street to surge toward the main front doors of the new building, he brought up the rear. For security reasons the outside door handles to Dexter's many entrances had been removed, so the crowd pressed against the doors until a teacher's aide opened one of them from inside. As Simon topped the concrete stairs, it was always the same dread—like volunteering to be swallowed alive.

He darted up a staircase in the old building, passed through sunlight cutting a bright path on steps and risers, and reached the second floor. He spotted Clyde Porter near the dead end of the hallway not far up ahead. The boy had beaten Simon to their shared locker, already worked the combination lock, and opened the door. A few days earlier, Clyde had been kind enough to adopt the white boy as a locker partner after Simon's first partner, Tommy, had kicked Simon out of their locker to make room for his new girlfriend.

Approaching Clyde from behind, Simon observed him shoving a baseball mitt onto the lower shelf. In a school where basketball reigned as the supreme sport, most students didn't even know that Dexter fielded a baseball team. For just that reason, Mr. Evans, the baseball coach, had called for an early winter tryout in the boys' gym to see how hard a recruiting job he would have come spring.

"Hey, Clyde."

"Hey."

"What's with the mitt? You trying out, too?"

"Yep." The gap between Clyde's front teeth both marred and enhanced his smile, on a face as dark as aged walnut.

Simon slid his baseball equipment rucksack off his shoulder and dumped it onto the locker's floor. As he began to snatch the folders and textbooks he would need for his morning classes, he asked, "Think us freshies stand a chance to make the team?"

"Hell yes!" Clyde said. "Chumps around here don't know nothing about playing no ball. We *make* our chance, ya dig?"

Simon noticed a button pinned to Clyde's ROTC jacket lapel, three fists superimposed on it. "What's with the fists?"

Clyde gave Simon a look and then shook his head. "Guess I'm going to have to educate your ass. The black fist mean power to the black folk, the brown one power to the Latino folk, and the white one power to the white folk. I'm a Black Assassin, but we ain't no gang no more; we's changed to a po-litical organization. You know—I help you, you help me, then we has ourselves a revolution and take over. We can't be letting no racism get in the way, ya dig?"

Simon nodded, Clyde's easy-bake recipe for revolution clear enough even for him to follow.

"Check this here out." The Black Assassin turned ROTC cadet turned junior revolutionary grabbed a mimeographed flyer from his shelf and handed it to Simon. The paper read:

BOYCOTT

We, the Coalition of Students, Faculty, and concerned Community at Dexter High School, demand the following:

1. An end to racism in the school administration and the dismissal of all racist faculty.
2. The hiring of more black, Latino, and Latina faculty.
3. A Black History Department directed and taught by black faculty.
4. An elected Community Board to which the school administration will be directly responsible.
5. The immediate dismissal of Principal Donald Jursak.

The time to unite is NOW! Help smash racism and boycott starting on January 10.
   POWER TO THE PEOPLE!

Simon didn't see a single demand in the list that he objected to, but any action that risked stirring up a rerun of last year's riots at Dexter gave him the willies.

"Keep it," Clyde said. "Teachers like Mr. Lange is helping us organize."

"Yeah, I got him for biology," Simon said.

"Man, you lucky. Mr. Lange one cool revolutionary dude. Now we best step on it. Can't get no tardy slips if we wants to stay eligible for the team, ya dig?"

As Clyde swung the door shut, its bang answered the staccato banging of other lockers near and far on all three floors of the old building. The boys started together through the labyrinth of hallways, Simon on his way to music class in the annex and Clyde to basic math in the new building. All around them, students were split into opposing flows of foot traffic. They rounded a bend, and through the library's glass doors, Simon saw a lone, twig-thin librarian stretching onto tiptoes to restock a book on a stack's shelf.

"Where do you live?" Simon asked, curious for the first time even though he had known Clyde for almost a semester.

"The Greens."

That meant Cabrini Green, the notorious public housing projects at the south end of the school district. The closest Simon dared get to Cabrini was either passing by its barren cluster of formidable high-rises in his family's Plymouth Fury on Larrabee Street or a bird's-eye view of it as he rode the Ravenswood El train to or from downtown.

"You want to come hang in the Greens sometime?" Clyde asked. "I'll show you around."

The deadpan humor flew right over Simon's head, and as he hesitated, his expression must have showed that his brain was scrambling for a polite excuse to decline the invitation. Clyde burst out laughing so hard, he staggered for a few steps. Then getting a grip just as he split away from Simon to take a flight of stairs down to the first floor, he tossed over his shoulder, "Man, you funny."

2

Death Knocks

THE MUSIC TEACHER, Mr. Egan, was rumored to be gay. Short, plump, with an oversized head and a leprechaun's bushy eyebrows, he liked to leave his music class watching a movie of Leonard Bernstein conducting the New York Philharmonic while he went to the teachers' lounge to drink coffee and grade papers. Pausing at the door, he'd hold his finger to his lips, look over his bifocals at kids scattered on the foldaway bleachers also used for chorus practice, and tell them in his honeyed, baritone voice, "I will be back in a few minutes. In the meantime, I want you all to be quiet like bumps on a pickle, like mice on ice, like sand on land."

Students stared at him dully. No sooner did Egan flip off the lights, shut the door behind him, and disappear down the hall past the rear exit of the lunchroom, than someone yelled, "Faggot!" and the class went up for grabs. In the dark room lit only by the flickering projector, a black boy on the third-row bench tuned in to the super soul sound of WGRT on his transistor radio. Then he called down to the projector boy in the first row, "Turn the gotdamn mothafuckin sound off, scrub, so we can hear us some for *real* music!" On a movie screen with COBRA STONE LOVE scrawled in thick Magic Marker lettering across the middle of it, Leonard Bernstein, dressed in tails, was working up a sweat as he conducted the New York Philharmonic through Beethoven's Fifth Symphony, but all anyone could hear was the radio playing:

I'm a girl watcher
I'm a girl watcher
Watchin' girls go by
My, my, my

From a huddle of blackjack players, someone yelled, "Hit me!" The cards in his hand must have busted the twenty-one-point limit— "Sheeeeit!"

A black girl popping her fingers and bobbing her head to the music stopped long enough to tell a trio of boys, "Well, if y'all think I looks like a cow, this be one cow y'all know you ain't never gonna lay your skanky-ass hands on."

"Oooooo-weeee!" another kid hooted, laughing and slapping five with his buddy.

By the windows, perched atop the highest bleacher with his back against the cinder block wall, Simon sat with his broad shoulders hunched, knees tucked, and gawky arms folded, like he was trying to reverse the biological process of growing. He'd already begun to day-dream, his glazed stare fixed on how he planned to snag grounders at the tryout, zip throws to first base, crack liners off a bat's sweet spot and—

He was snapped back to reality by the pounding of someone's work boots springing from bench to bench down the risers, shaking the entire structure. Louis Collins, the only other white boy in the class, stopped at the projector table and turned to face everyone front and center. Usually he cut music, a habit that Simon would later learn was responsible for Louis repeating that freshman class a fourth time as a senior, but on those rare occasions when he condescended to make an appearance, he mostly kept to himself and seemed content to doze. Between the World War II leather bomber jacket that he almost never bothered to hang in his locker and the stubble shadow that covered his square jaw, Louis could have passed for someone well beyond the age of a hulking seventeen-year-old. Once in a great while, he would wake, take a slow panoramic view of his barren surroundings in a way that insinuated he was double-checking on whether he should start to give a shit, only to reaffirm that he shouldn't, and doze off again.

Louis cranked the projector's volume knob to full blast, drowning out the soul music, and darted across the room toward the blackboard on the wall.

"Hey, what the fuck you think you doing, honky?"

Great, Simon thought. *Idiot's out to get his ass kicked.* Louis snatched the teacher's pointer off the chalk ledge, sidestepped Mr. Egan's desk, and scrambled back to the middle of the room, which was always cleared of chairs whenever the risers were used. He skidded to a stop right in front of the movie screen. Cracking the long pointer in two over his knee, he made a conductor's baton out of the top half and flipped the other half over his shoulder. Simon fidgeted, adjusting and re-adjusting his shoulder blades against the wall. *Sit the fuck down.* The last thing he needed was someone white making a scene. Louis's shadow blotted Bernstein's image out on the screen. Taking charge, he began conducting *his* orchestra through some serious Beethoven, the picture of stuck-up solemnity as he swung his arms in clean, precise, swooping strokes. Beethoven's Death knocked at the door:

Da-da-da-daaaaa

Da-da-da-daaaaaaaa

Cheeks trembling, eyes afire, Louis drove his left hand upward to command the strings to start cooking, while the baton in his right hand gingerly tamped the air to caution the horns to cool it. He was good, almost as good as Leonard. A black boy yelled, "It your thang, honky. Do what you wanna do!" Another kid stood up, clapping loudly and mimicking hoity-toity white folks—"Bravo, white boy, bravo!"

The class grew quiet. Like a raging god, Louis flung his arms high and then low, his entire body locking in a violent shudder, only to snap out of it and delicately thread, poke, and prod the baton through another glorious bar of symphony. He was pulling them all into the music, forcing students to break their safe, silent conspiracy not to learn: if no one tries, then no one fails.

The educational miracle didn't last more than thirty seconds before a girl on the third-level bench must have sensed the threat to the status quo.

"Sit your gotdamn honky-ass down!"

"Yeah, you heard Tina. Think you our motherfuckin teacher?"

Others chimed in, but Louis, thumbing his nose at majority rule, carried on without so much as a hitch in his performance. Finally, a boy got up from the fifth-row bench and came down the bleachers toward Louis. As was the fad, he wore an Afro pick stuck in the back of his hair, and his stretchy black Ban-Lon shirt advertised the pronounced muscle cords in his chest.

"Uh-oh," someone said. "You done made Ernie mad now."

Simon thought, *Satisfied, asshole?* He stopped his right leg from jiggling nervously, but it started up again. Ernie stood loose and ready in front of Louis, his stare theatrically cold.

"Now, honky, didn't you hear to sit your ass down?"

Louis went right on conducting, his eyes nearly lost in a mess of stringy hair the shade of baled hay.

"You deaf, honky?"

Still no response.

"Say, honky, I'm talking—"

Louis flipped his head up to reveal a snarling grin and stabbed the air with the baton directly under Ernie's nose:

Da-da-da-daaaaa

Da-da-da-daaaaaaaa

Taken off guard, Ernie backed up a step, then another. With Louis stalking toward him, he damn near tripped, the whole class hooting and howling. To save face, he laughed too, yelling, "Help! Help! This here white boy a crazy mothafucka!" He dashed up the bleachers, grabbed some bench again, and held out his hands in a show of mock fear, screaming, "Be cool, white boy! Be cool! I didn't know you was Frankenstein's mama!"

Louis slowly backpedaled until he was conducting in front of the screen again. His look of swooning rapture invited one and all to share in his bliss. *How the hell do you get away with it?* Simon wondered. *What do you got that I don't?*

Just then the sound of the classroom door shutting firmly signaled Egan's return. He must have forgotten his pen or grading book to come back so soon. In the course of the year, he had taught his pupils the difference between a major and minor chord, where to find middle C on the keyboard, and the lyrics to such oldie but goody classics as "Way Down upon the Swanee River" and "Eating Goober Peas." Puzzling over his bifocals at the white boy conducting in the center of the room, Egan stayed close to the door and further telegraphed his return with an "Ahem!"

Louis, not about to abandon his orchestra without damn good reason, continued on with his back to Egan. Everyone else, including Simon, smirked with an infectious *us against teacher* attitude, waiting to see what would happen next.

"Mr. Collins?"

No answer.

"*Mis*-ter Collins."

Still no answer.

"I'm talking to you, Mr. Collins. That pointer is public property and wasn't put here to be abused."

Arms swinging and jabbing in a flurry of dueling instructions, Bernstein's talented protégé seemed to have withdrawn all the more deeply into the music. Egan cautiously crept toward Louis, paused, crept closer, and then stopped a few feet behind the boy.

"Mr. Collins, I will not have you disrupting my class. Do you comprehend me, Mr. Collins?"

Louis worked and coaxed his musicians for all they were worth. The longer he ignored Egan, the more Simon wanted to burst out laughing. The teacher held out his open palm, his voice decidedly more stern.

"Hand me the pointer, Mr. Collins. I said, *hand* me—"

Louis flipped his head up, whirled around, and moved toward his victim, waving the baton like he wanted to cram the whole Philharmonic right down Egan's throat. The hapless man backtracked, his bushy eyebrows twitching and mouth forming a terrified *O*. As students laughed and whooped it up, Simon joined in, forgetting his fear of being white at Dexter.

"I think you'd better sit down, Mr. Collins. I think—oh my God— you're bucking for a suspension, young man—oh my God. If you don't sit down this instant and behave, I'm afraid I'll have no other choice than to—oh my God."

Each baritone *oh my God* entertained students to slaphappy greater heights. Louis cornered Egan up against the windows near Simon. Not missing a single beat with the baton, he used his other hand to pull on a shade. It rolled up with a final whip-like snap, sunlight flooding the room. He leaped onto a chair that stood beneath a window, his body silhouetted in an aura of light, and waved the baton through a final crescendo. Egan stared up at him, at a loss what to say or do next. With a flip of the wrist, Louis threw the broken pointer into the air, pushed open the hinged window, climbed out, and hopped down to the crusted snow on the yard outside—an easy feat since classrooms in the annex were built at ground level. He stuck his head back inside the room and wiggly-waved his fingers to one and all.

"Bye-bye."

He swung himself over the waist-high chain-link fence that encircled the small yard, crossed Dickens Street, and started trekking over the snow-covered, weedy field of vacant lots. There, urban renewal had recently evicted neighbors and torn down several blocks of their modest wood-frame houses to make room for a new high school.

Simon craned his neck as he and everyone else kept their eyes on Louis's diminishing figure. Thunderous applause erupting from the projector demanded that Leonard take a curtain call.

"Come back here, Mr. Collins!" Egan yelled out the window. "You're bucking for a suspension! Do you hear me?"

That kid's leaving, Simon thought, *really leaving*. He glanced around at other students, but they just looked back at him with the same astonishment. Walking with his loping, uncoordinated stride, Louis was already halfway across the field and would soon reach the DePaul Settlement House gym just to the west.

The excitement in the classroom faded into the distance with Louis. Still staring out the window, Egan reached his hands up to straighten and tighten the knot in his maroon knit tie. His tweed sport coat was in critical need of a good pressing on both sides of the rear vent. A few students giggled. Shaking his head, the teacher shut the window, locked both handles, and then began pulling up shades one by one. On Webster Avenue, running along the vacant lot's opposite border, a blue Corvair cruised eastbound toward the busy six-way intersection at Lincoln and Larrabee.

"A shame," Egan muttered. Looking at Simon directly above him on the top riser, he asked, "What was that all about, Mr. Fleming? Did Mr. Collins tell you?"

Simon's sullen headshake was intended to give the man not an ounce of pity. Egan picked up the half pointer that Louis had dropped on the floor. Then he looked out at his pupils, most of them slouched either coolly indifferent or as good as catatonic.

"Ladies and gentlemen, has anyone seen where the rest of my pointer is?"

No one jumped to volunteer any info. Egan, clearly on his own, went here and there about the room, hunting for the missing piece of stick. Soon he found where it had rolled close to his desk. He picked it up, tried to fit the pointer halves back together again, and said, "Maybe it can be glued."

Almost a year later and long after Simon and Louis had become fast friends, Simon was flipping through *One Flew over the Cuckoo's Nest*, a paperback from Louis's personal library. Wedged between pages 105 and 106, he found a letter written in a nearly illegible scrawl. Apparently Louis had never sent it.

December 18, 1969

Dear Gail,

So I'm walking across this field that wasn't a field when you were here because urban renewal tore down a shitload of houses, and I can still hear Egan yelling at me, when I decide why the fuck not come out to California and visit you? I mean, what am I doing here, anyway? In my mind I kept seeing you answer your front door that time your mom and dad were out of town, and all you had on was that red fishnet sweater that you could see right through. There was a sly grin on your face as you shook your hair out of your eyes and said "Hi," grabbing my crotch and pulling me inside. Gail, I swear to God, I haven't had a pair of tits to squeeze and suck as nice as yours since—honest injun. Even if I have to go all the way to California to cop another feel from you, it's worth it, and besides, I miss you a lot, you and that tight little pussy of yours. Yeah, yeah, yeah, I know what you're saying: "Can't you ever be serious, Louis?" Look, Pizza Face, the world isn't worth being serious about. But I don't want to argue about it right now, just let me tell you what happened. I'm crossing this field, see, and I'm so wasted on speed it's like . . . like I'm sure that if I just hurry up I can hitchhike from Chicago to San Francisco by late afternoon.

So I reach Webster, thumb a ride, get dropped off under a viaduct at Fullerton, and try to catch another ride onto the Kennedy Expressway. I'm still standing there an hour later— jagoffs in empty cars just whizzing by. This one dickhead even leans way over as he drives by and locks the passenger side of his car, like I might try and jump in while he's going thirty-five miles an hour. I mean, be honest. Do people do things like that in California? After a while my thumb feels heavy and my eyes start to stare at things, like my feet, or an empty potato chip bag blowing down the gutter. I notice all the dirt flying around in the air the way it always does under them stinking viaducts. I'm crashing. The realization that I'm not going to make it to California to see you is too fucking much—shit, this was the fourth straight time in a month I'd started out for California to see you, and only once did I barely make it beyond the suburbs. I could smell your hair the same way I could when we'd hug and the top of your head would tuck under my chin. I stare at drivers, trying to make them feel guilty for not picking me up, but no dice. The next thing I know I'm sitting on the curb with my legs stuck out in the street, and all these Republican-types in cars are honking for me to pull them in as they swerve around, but I can only hold my hands over my ears, close my eyes, and concentrate on your freckled face. I say to myself, Gail, please come get me. I'll do anything for you, and I know you can hear me so please ride by in your little VW and pick me up.

But when I opened my eyes, you weren't there and I wanted to die. Lots of times I think about wanting to die—yeah, yeah, yeah, you think I'm bullshitting, but I'm not. Sometimes I think I do speed just so I can think about dying when I crash. Before I forget, when I finally make it out there this summer, can we fuck on your living room floor like before with you wearing that fishnet sweater? Do your aunt and uncle have plush carpeting like at your mom and dad's house? If so, I hope you don't have your period again this time—ha-ha-ha. Did your mom or dad ever ask you about the stain, and if so, what did you tell them—that you stepped on a mouse while crossing the room to change channels on the TV? I can still see you on your hands and knees, scrubbing at it with a sponge, but no, Mr. Clean had met his match—ha-ha-ha.

So anyway, I'm sitting on the curb crashing my brains out. I don't know why it hit me so hard, maybe it's because it was the fifth straight day I'd been speeding, but what the fuck, I did the same thing last week and it hardly bothered me a bit.

I'm telling myself, Look, if you don't pull your legs in, some asshole's going to run over them, but I can't budge them, like they're not connected to my brain anymore. Did you ever have that happen? I mean, I party the hardest, I fuck the hardest, and I crash the hardest. I started feeling unbearably hot even though the weather's freezing. It took me a good five minutes before I managed to reach a hand up to unzip my jacket and another five to unbutton my shirt. The next thing I know all I got on is this itchy blanket and I'm down at the police station 'cause some pig arrested me for indecent exposure. He tells my ma he found me lying in the street under the viaduct "stark naked" with the traffic swerving around me and that I'm lucky he came by when he did or I'd have frozen to death.

So now my ma's been sending me to this dip-shit shrink once a week. I just sit there and talk. It's kind of stupid, but I act serious because it makes my ma happy and it costs her a lot and I figure I owe her that much with all the bullshit I cause her. Listen, Gail, I just wanted to say hi and tell you I really, really, really miss you and that even though I'm lonely I can understand why you moved out to California so that you could get away from me. I just wanted to tell you that I'm sorry for all the fucked-up things I did to you and that I really do love you, and I'm not going to lie to you again and say I'm getting my head screwed on straight, because we both know I'm not ever going to have my head screwed on straight. Hope to see you soon.

Louis the Terrible

3

Honky Love

WITH MUSIC CLASS AND ALGEBRA UNDER HIS BELT, Simon weaved down a crowded second-floor hallway in the new building, on his way to English. An overload of on-the-go conversations echoed off beige metal lockers and the tall, arched ceiling. Someone tapped him on the shoulder.

"Hey, Simon."

He whipped around, and there was Dia cradling a stack of books in her arms. Petite and doe-eyed, if she had tipped forward, she would have kissed him no higher than his sternum.

"You walked right by me."

There was a pause during which Simon almost swan-dived into her affectionately exclusive gaze, lost contact with time and space, and then reeled himself in.

"I Ii."

"Well, aren't *you* the shy one! Are you going to walk me to my world history class?" It was as if Dia, who had recently begun to single him out for special attention between classes in the hallways, felt that being white at Dexter were no more than an occasional inconvenience, probably because she attended honors classes enrolled primarily with middle-class students who came from the better grade schools in the district. Simon, one of the few whites tracked in "regular" classes, thought of honor students as members of an exclusive club. He watched these so-called gifted kids on the sly—small clutches of them in the

21

hallways or at a lunchroom table. The girls wore tight miniskirts with white blouses; the guys, button-down collar shirts with the tails hanging out of their bell-bottom pants. They were cool, of a dying breed at Dexter, and, by Simon's reckoning, off limits.

"I really don't have . . . I mean I've got to get—" A slap on Simon's shoulder packed a playful sting.

"I'm more important than risking a stupid tardy slip, aren't I?"

The girl's bold, pouty gamesmanship left him no options. *Shit!* He gently took hold of her arm just above the elbow and began escorting her down the hall. Within only a few steps, he felt a peculiar pride ballooning in his chest, gliding him forward.

A trip up a flight of stairs later, they came to a stop at a classroom doorway. Letting go of her, he realized that his palm had left a sweaty imprint on her cotton sleeve. *Now what?* As a couple of students filed past them into Dia's world history classroom, she seemed to be counting on him to jumpstart the conversation again, but all he could think to do was reach up and self-consciously brush his fingers through the wavy dip of hair on his forehead that never, when things really counted, behaved.

"So," Dia finally said, "how'd you end up in this lovely dump?"

"Umm . . ." Under pressure to impress, Simon simplified the complicated. "I used to live on the far Northwest Side—you know, everyone's white and lives in rinky-dink subdivision houses. My dad's a Presbyterian minister, and . . . like . . . he got involved in the civil rights movement and thrown in jail in Albany, Georgia, with a bunch of other northern clergymen. They went on this six-day hunger strike—you know, to keep protesting Jim Crow laws and all that jazz? Then he came home skinny as hell. Pissed off a lot of people in his congregation, so last year he quit and we moved here. Now he owns the Body Politic Theater."

"Hmm, interesting."

Simon rolled his eyes. *Blowing it!* Then horrified that Dia might take his eye-rolling as an opinion of her, he rambled on about other freedom marches his father had gone on—Montgomery, Washington, DC, where King gave his "I Have a Dream" speech. And as Dia listened, she snagged a piece of lint off his tan V-neck sweater, then rested her hand for a moment on one of his belt loops, touching, always touching, but with the nonchalance of someone oblivious of her own effect.

"Wow!" she said. "That's stuff you can tell your kids someday."

He looked away, then straight down, and scuffed the sole of his gym shoe against the checkered maroon-and-black tiled floor.

Dia singsonged, "*You're bluuush-ing.*"

"Am not."

"Yep."

"Will you stop?" Simon reached up and shook his fists—"Arrrrgh!" Dia was already giggling.

"S'okay." She rested her hand tenderly against his chest and let it linger for a moment before sliding it down, her index finger speed-bumping on shirt buttons underneath his sweater. "Just means you're sweet."

Simon's prick stirred in his Fruit of the Loom briefs. *Great.* The last thing he needed was a boner. Desperate for a distraction, he asked, "Say, do you know a kid named Louis Collins?"

Now it was Dia's turn to roll her eyes. "Yeah, I know him. A real nut case. Why do you ask?"

Simon quickly told her about Louis ditching music class via the window. "Funny as all shit! I bet Egan's still having a stroke."

"Yeah, that's Louis, all right . . . Mr. Drama," Dia said. "He used to go steady with my best friend, Gail, but then last summer he changes overnight from being a kid whose idea of fun is solving calculus problems on his slide rule to someone who smokes or pops every drug he can get his hands on. Gail says he even tried smoking catnip."

"Catnip?" Simon asked. "Gets people high, too?"

"Not unless you sprout long whiskers and start eating mice," she assured him. "One day, the doorbell rings at Gail's house. Good thing she opens the front door instead of her mom or dad, because there's

Louis on the porch wearing nothing but a blue-and-gold-striped tie, his underwear, and construction boots. *Yuck*, right? He rode there on his ten-speed. And it's late November, not exactly tanning weather. He shoves a bouquet of wilted red roses in her face and says, 'Will you marry me?' The next day at school, he's got the nerve to come up to her in the lunchroom and ask, 'Why'd you slam the door in my face, bitch?' Got to the point where she wasn't sure what the whacko would do next—kiss her, stalk her, or spike her orange juice with LSD—so she talked her parents into letting her go live with her aunt and uncle in San Francisco."

"Sounds fucked up," Simon said, trying to sound mature. "What's his problem?"

"Dunno. Maybe he smoked too much catnip? But I did hear something about his dad getting killed a few years back. Car accident? Not sure, really. Come to think of it, someone mentioned Louis's dad was a preacher, too."

"Then he's a PK—preacher's kid—just like me."

"PK, PB and J, whatever." Dia gave a dismissive wave. "All I know is the boy's definitely bonkers. Take my advice, Simon: he's nothing but a walking piece of bad news."

Simon was about to change the subject and ask Dia if she'd heard about the Community Boycott Coalition's list of demands or of Mr. Lange's involvement in organizing a student boycott. He wanted to feel her out as one white to another, to see if she shared his fear that any political rocking-the-boat at Dexter would quickly escalate and spiral into a replay of last year's riots, but before he could get a word in edgewise, she told him, "You have freaky eyes."

"Really?" He gave her the benefit of the doubt and assumed *freaky* was a compliment.

"And I suppose you're going to tell me you don't know you're one of the cutest boys at Dexter?"

Simon felt his already overheated face deepen a few more shades of red, a reaction that pleased Dia enough to make her giggle again. She asked, "Are you going to walk me to my classes from now on?"

"What for?" Simon, aware that he had just blundered, thought, *Because she likes you, idiot!* Not far away, a couple of black girls reached the top of the nearby staircase, and as they lollygagged through a crowded hallway intersection, one told the other, "I ain't lying. Sheila say she pregnant."

"Or maybe it's true what I've heard about you," Dia said. "That you're stuck up."

"*Me?* I'm not—"

"Prove it."

Dia's tactic was about to work like a charm on Simon when three Latino gangbangers came out of nowhere and stepped between them.

"Excuse me," the one in the middle said to Simon. Though the boy was short enough to qualify for a Napoleonic complex, his peach-fuzz mustache compensated him with a pubescent dash of manhood. "You don't mind if I interrupt, do you?" The flash of his smile drove home the message: *Beat it.* He and his taller buddies flanking him wore long, black knit cardigans with gold bands circling the shoulders—signature sweaters of the Latin Kings. Just the week before, members of that "club" had shot and killed a Dexter student who was part of the rival Harrison Gents in a drive-by on Halsted Street. Kings did that sometimes: killed people.

The beefy one on the left ran his eyes slowly up and down Simon. Then he shook his head sadly, the white boy failing inspection.

"*Do* you?" the middle King repeated, dropping all pretense of a smile. After a moment in which Simon showed neither the sense to retreat nor the balls to object, all three gangbangers about-faced so that he had nothing but the wall of their backs to stare at.

"Say, baby, your name?"

Dia, eye level with her new admirer, didn't miss a beat. "Who wants to know?"

"Hector, baby. I think you're a fine-ass *mamasita*. What say you and me—"

"My name," Dia said, sweet as punch, "is Good-bye." And with that she ducked inside her world history classroom just as the bell rang.

The King on the right laughed. "Put you *low!*" Narrow in the shoulders and extra long everywhere else, he slapped five with his stout friend. They found Hector's blown attempt to "lay the rap" so hilarious, they'd gone all wobbly.

"*Puta!*" Hector spat. Then he spun around, fists ready to strike, but the *maricon* white boy had vanished. At the other end of the corridor, a hall monitor clapped her hands and shouted at stragglers, "Let's move it, people!"

———

Simon hurried down the hallway toward the old building. *Like she'll ever talk to me again.* He hadn't yet learned that in some precarious situations at Dexter, white girls knew when to cut a boy slack. The halls were nearly cleared of students now, the second bell about to ring. *Coward!* He walked with his reed of a tall body bent and plowed forward. *Asshole Kings!*

———

English class brought on yet another confrontation between Miss Tettle—a woman diseased with negativity toward all things living or dead—and Mary, a student labeled "difficult." When Miss Tettle insisted three straight times that Mary stop napping, get her head off her desktop, and take her turn reading aloud from *Animal Farm*, Mary did indeed snap her head up and screamed, "I don't have to do nothing for no honky!"

After English came division, the midpoint in the school day when students went to their homerooms to hear announcements. Division teachers would also scold students for the class tardy and cut slips sent from the attendance office. "Will you look

at all of these?" Miss Temple yelled at Simon's class, holding a
three-inch stack of pink slips high over her head, shaking them at
everyone angrily. "These are just from yesterday alone! School is
not a vacation!"

In world history, as Miss Murphy lectured on the Dark Ages,
Simon imagined that historical period as one in short supply of sunlight. Come lunch in the cafeteria, a piece of chocolate cake that had
masqueraded as fresh behind the display counter window turned out to
be anything but. Simon rammed his fork into the dessert, then lifted
and twirled the entire piece like a lollipop without a single petrified
crumb coming unglued.

Spanish, a class in which Simon was either unable or unwilling
to retain a Romance language vocabulary much beyond the words
comer, *banjo*, and *la biblioteca*, kept him on the verge of a cold sweat.
Sooner or later, Miss Herta would call on him to conjugate a verb,
and shortly after that, the inevitable shoe would drop: a failure notice
that required a parent's signature. He banished the thought. *Finally!* It
was time to play ball.

4

Mira, Mira!

IN THE SUNNY BOYS' GYMNASIUM, the varnished wooden floor reflected light as though it were a pool of water. Eleven boys—just enough bodies to hold out hope of fielding a team—lined up at one end to take grounders from Mr. Evans, who, thin and prematurely hunched in his shoulders, also suffered from a bad case of adult acne.

"Garcia, catch for me." The gym teacher's voice went up at the end of sentences instead of down, making everyone feel that he thought they were all lazy bastards. A squat, built-like-a-bull Puerto Rican kid turned his Cardinals hat backward on his head and followed the coach until they were over near the pull-up bars, kitty-corner from the other boys. Evans motioned with a fungo bat for the first player to step away from the line. Then he tossed a rubber-coated league ball up and smacked a hard grounder. The ball skip-bounced across the slick floor and glanced off the boy's glove.

"Devon, get your ass back to the minors where you belong!" someone yelled. "You field like my grandmama when she tied up in a bag of laundry."

"Shut up!" Devon said, moping to the end of the line.

The boys continued taking turns fielding. The closer Simon got to the front of the line the more his hand sweated inside the pocket of his kangaroo-skin glove. When it was his turn, he stepped away from the line and got into a crouched position. *Stay on toes*, he coached himself, *glove down, set!* His eye zeroed in on the ball as it left Evans's hand with a measured toss, then the smack of the bat and a hot grounder coming at him. Without any fear that the ball might take a bad hop and hit him in the face, he *looked* the ball straight into his glove, scooped it cleanly, and in one fluid motion came up firing with enough zip on his throw so that the ball *popped* in Garcia's catcher's mitt. Relieved, he hustled to the back of the line. The next boy, a Cuban, yelled to Garcia, "*Mira, mira!*" He fielded a high chopper.

"*Mira, mira!*" Clyde said. Charging a grounder, he snagged it on the short hop.

The joke took hold, each boy yelling "Look, look!" in Spanish when it was his turn to field.

"*Mira, mira!*" Simon shouted. Being the only white boy trying out for the team, he got the biggest laugh.

A few successful turns later, Simon had gone from nervous to overly confident and bored. On his next fielding chance, he hardly bent his knees, lackadaisically caught the ball, and then flipped a lazy sidearm toss back to Garcia.

"Hold it right there, Hotdog!" Evans yelled at him. The pissed off look on his pale, spotted face stopped Simon in his tracks.

"Ooooo," someone yelled, "Evans gone teach the white boy a lesson."

Simon crouched low, game for any kind of challenge to his baseball skills, and got set for Evans to bring it on. He heard Clyde yell, "Show him what you got, Simon!"

The coach hit a ball so hard, it skip-darted past Simon before he could stab his mitt fast enough to his left. He heard the ball carom in the corner behind him and bang against the end of the bleachers, then saw it dribbling past him out onto the floor again.

Smack!

The next one handcuffed him, glancing off the heel of his glove.

"What's a matter, Hotdog?" Evans said. "Too hot for you?" Simon bounced on his toes in an effort to ready his reflexes.

Smack!

Stretching until he was fully extended, he snagged a smoking grounder, did a complete 180-degree turn, and whipped a perfect on-the-mark throw at Garcia.

Smack!

He dove, slid on the floor under the basketball hoop, backhanded a ball, and came up firing another strike at Garcia. The grounders kept coming, each one hit harder than the one before it.

"Evans ain't playing!" someone said.

Simon let his reflexes do his talking—darting, twisting, lunging, scooping, the gymnasium a blur, nothing but the ball, the ball, the ball, his glove like a fully tactile extension of his own flesh. And then that magical moment. He was already moving, reacting to where the ball would go a split second before it even left Evans's bat. The line drive whistled through the air with a *phfffft* and would have taken Simon's head off had he not gotten his mitt in front of his face out of sheer self-defense. He caught it. Fell back flat on his ass, but he caught it.

For a moment, the gym was silent. And then Clyde's voice echoed off the beige tiled walls, "My man, Simon. He *bad!*"

Simon picked himself up off the floor and zinged the ball to Garcia. Evans held the bat by his side and stared at him. Slowly, the stare changed into a grudging smile.

"Good with a glove, huh? What's your position?"

"Center field."

"More like shortstop," Evans said.

"Center field," Simon repeated.

"Forget it. L.D.'s got center nailed down. Fastest man on the team last year."

"I can beat him."

"Oooooo, you hear that, L.D.?" someone in line asked. "White boy say he be faster."

"Sheeeeit." This from the boy who looked all legs.

If Simon had been a year or two older, he would have recognized the expression on Evans's face. *No white boy can beat a black boy in a foot race.*

"You ever *see* L.D. run?" Evans asked Simon.

"No one see L.D. run," stated another boy. "That how fast he is."

"I can beat him," Simon said again, heading for the end of the line.

Perhaps intuitively sensing an opportunity to make some cash, Clyde challenged one and all: "Fifty cent say Hotdog can beat L.D." Then he strutted over to Simon, leaned in close to him, and whispered, "You sure? L.D. faster than a ho in heat."

The unanimous respect for L.D.'s speed was beginning to give Simon jitters, but he tried to display some low-ley confidence. "No problem."

"Make it a dollar," someone else returned.

"Hey, hey, cut that gambling out!" Evans warned. He paused and looked intrigued by the cocky freshy's challenge. "All right, Hotdog, L.D., get over here."

As the two boys went across the gym to Evans and the others took spectator seats on the bleachers, Simon heard Clyde's hushed voice. "Make it *two* dollar."

"You covered."

"All right, twice around the gym," Evans told the boys. "On the second lap, switch lanes so that it's an even distance."

He pointed to a red line painted on the floor next to the chin-up bars, and the two runners took their places. Simon shook his arms to stay loose.

"On your mark, get set, GO!"

L.D. exploded off the line and took a two-step lead. By the second turn, the gap hadn't changed an inch. Arms pumping, legs straining, Simon kicked it up a gear, thinking, *Dig! Dig! Dig!* They crossed lanes at the end of the first lap and were dead even.

"Go, Hotdog!" Clyde yelled.

"L.D! L.D! L.D!" another boy screamed.

Feet pounded the floorboards, neither boy able to shake the other. Simon felt his stamina start to give out, a clawing in his chest, and his calves and hamstrings tightening, on the verge of knotting up. With only half a lap to go, he reached for that something extra deep in his craw that he didn't know he had, sucked it in, and lunged across the finish line. He won by a nose.

"Ahhhh," someone laughed, "white boy beat L.D!"

Dizzy with exhaustion, not an ounce of effort left in him, Simon stumbled over to the bleachers and collapsed onto the lowest bench. He hung his head between his legs and took long, gasping breaths.

"Let's go again!" L.D. said, jumping up and down like a pogo stick, obviously not half as winded as Simon. He must not have wanted it badly enough.

"Boy, you lost!" Clyde yelled. "Hotdog beat your ass." He climbed down the bleachers and lifted Simon's arm, declaring him champion.

"Two dollar, sucker," Clyde told a boy farther up the bleachers. "Pay up." The moment Clyde let go of Simon's arm, it fell like a wet noodle to the bench.

"No betting!" Evans yelled.

"You heard Evans. Bet's off!" the boy called down at Clyde.

"Aww, scrub," Clyde said, and he headed up the bleachers to go argue with his friend. Someone passing by Simon patted him on the back, but he didn't bother looking to see who it was. *Get up*, he thought. *Walk it off.* He struggled to his feet and clasped his hands behind his head to open up the air passage to his raw lungs.

"Lucas! Jackson!" Evans said. "Let's go. Two laps around."

At the end of practice, the boys started trailing out of the gym to head down to the locker room. Evans stood in the double doorway leading to the stairs, and as Simon passed by, he held his arm out for him to stop. He gave Simon the once-over.

"I don't like hotdogs, especially ones like you with mustard to spare."

Simon looked at the floor. "Sorry." He made himself meet Evans's eye. "It won't happen again."

"Better not." Then, "Shouldn't be that fagged out after only two times around the gym. You don't eat your Wheaties or what?"

"I've always been like that. I'm fast, but I get tired easy."

"Not when I get through with you," Evans said. "I'm going to work your ass off." He smiled grudgingly again. "Official tryouts start in February. Be there."

"Thanks," Simon said, and feeling like he was floating more than walking down the short hallway toward the stairs, he shook a fist in the air. *Yes!*

5

Amoeba Politics

THE BIOLOGY ROOM, tucked away on the first floor in the southeast corner of the old building, smelled faintly of last week's fruit fly experiment. Two ranks of tables, all with black countertops, took up most of the room, and in front of them, just as the altar faces the pews of a church, stood a demonstration counter. High on the front wall and next to the blackboard, a life-sized anatomical poster of a man—his internal organs illustrated—looked down upon the scientific faithful. Recently, someone had taken liberties with a Magic Marker to draw a hard-on at the man's crotch and a balloon coming out of his mouth with the words BLOW ME.

Not long after Simon took his seat in the middle of the first row, Juan, his table partner, strutted bowlegged through the doorway wearing an ROTC uniform. His wide shoulders tapered sharply to his compact hips, and even though he was shorter than most boys, something about his low center of gravity seemed tightly wound, as though he were constantly on the prowl.

"What's happening, Simon?" Juan dropped his books on the table, kicked out his chair, and fell into it. Known as a kid who was good with his fists, he had taken a teasing shine to Simon.

"Nada," Simon said, only too happy to prove that, within limits, he could speak in grammatically correct Spanish. He tapped his fingers on the table and bobbed his head in time to the Isley Brothers coming from someone's transistor radio:

It's your thing
Do what you wanna do
I can't tell you
Who to sock it to

Julio, alone at his table directly in front of Juan, swiveled around in his seat to chat. A dense spattering of freckles made his cheeks equally two-toned. He noticed Simon jamming to the music and frowned.

"Oh, honky, don't be moving your head like you know how to dance. You're nothing but a wallflower. And who gave your honky ass permission to speak Spanish?"

The two Latino boys burst out laughing, each one stretching an arm across the table to slap five.

"Fuck yourself," Simon told Julio.

"Fuck your mama, honky."

"You wish you had a mama."

"Well, I'm sure glad you got a mama, 'cause last night I let her suck my dick. Bet she's still picking the hairs out of her teeth."

Seeing the desperate white boy stammer, "Well you, you, you . . ." only to have his wit fail him, Julio and Juan cracked up and slapped five again. Simon slouched in his seat, folded his arms across his chest, and stewed.

Mr. Lange entered the room and started toward his desk next to the demonstration counter. He yelled above the din of student chatter to a black boy at a table near the back of the room—"Harlow, turn that radio off."

Students moaned as Harlow obeyed his teacher.

"Jesus," Mr. Lange said, "you'd think you were all addicts or something. Can't WGRT wait for one period?"

Monroe, a beanpole of a boy seated at the first table in the second row, piped up in his falsetto, "Mr. Lange, we can't help it if we's some stone soul dudes."

The biology teacher laughed along with everyone else. Lanky, affable, but always firmly in control of his classes, he never gave students sufficient reason to challenge his authority. His long sideburns and mustache and the turtleneck sweaters that he wore instead of a sport coat and tie let students know he was hip.

After taking roll, Mr. Lange got up from his desk, jabbed a finger against his glasses, which had slid to a prominent bump midway down his nose, and turned to the blackboard. "OK, listen up. You were supposed to read unit twelve for homework on single-cell organisms, and today we're going to . . ." While pointing at a drawing of an amoeba on the blackboard, the anatomy poster, complete with its new "organ," caught Mr. Lange's eye.

"Oh, great, just great. Who the hell's the artist?"

With a hard slap to the back, Juan knocked Simon forward in his seat, prodding him to confess, and yelled, "Simon did it!"

A chorus of laughter drowned out the white boy's "No I didn't!"

From behind the demonstration counter, Mr. Lange held his disappointed expression until it silenced every one of his pupils. Then in a voice that started out softer than normal but would slowly grow in volume with his passion, he said, "Let me tell you what happens when you draw on school property. You give the school administration an excuse to say, 'We don't need new books; they just draw in them. We don't need new microscopes; they just break and steal them. We don't need to listen to what students say is important to them, because they're just a bunch of irresponsible hoodlums who lack self-control!' So take a look at this defaced poster, Mr. Principal. Take a look at all the desks with everyone's initials carved into them, Mrs. School Superintendent. See, you were right, Mr. Boss: they don't deserve any respect!"

Captivated just like everyone else, Simon, who had never drawn or carved graffiti on anything, felt as guilty as anyone else for the crippling *I don't give a damn* attitude that permeated the school.

"Look," Mr. Lange continued, his tone one of strict confidence, "if you don't like your environment and want to fight the system that put you there, learn how to use your anger in the right way, at the right time. Don't give bosses the easy way out."

A black girl, her skin nearly as fair as Simon's and her massive, peroxided red Afro as big as a beach ball, raised her hand. "Mr. Lange, ain't no one in here draw it. It be here before this class."

"It's not important to me *who* drew it, Sandra. What's important to me is that you educate other students who are playing into the school administration's hands, and begin to organize yourselves."

Monroe said, "I hear you." Then he finished off with the defiant black power slogan—"Right on!"

Students listened closely to their teacher's explanation of the day's assignment. They were to take stagnant, algae-green water from an aquarium with an eyedropper, squirt a couple of drops onto a slide, and then look for single-cell organisms under a microscope. Soon a pileup of students formed by the fish tank on the counter that ran along the windows, people fighting for a turn to use the only available eyedropper. Then after everyone had returned to their seats, the class settled into the work at hand. Simon focused his microscope and almost immediately found a squirming blob on his slide.

"Got one!"

"Me too!" Julio said.

But Juan groaned, "Man, I don't see shit on mine."

After a few minutes, Julio must have grown bored with observing his amoeba, because he wandered over to another table to lay the rap on a cute girl.

"Watch this," Juan said under his breath to Simon. He slunk over to Julio's microscope, exchanged his own slide for his friend's, and then brought the kidnapped organism back to his table.

When Julio, having struck out with the girl, returned to his seat, he peered once again into the lens of his microscope.

"Where'd that little fucker go?"

"Hey!" Juan yelled. "I found one!"

Julio eyeballed his friend. "Man, did you steal my amoeba?"

"Fuck no!"

"Honky, did Juan take my amoeba?"

"Your fucking mama stole it," Simon told Julio. "Come to think of it, your mama is an amoeba. She has to fucking fuck herself just to fucking reproduce." He beamed proudly.

"Ooooo, Simon, not bad." Juan raised both hands to double-high-five his white friend, while Julio, giving Simon the finger, let slip a grin that admitted he'd been had.

"Dang!" At the second table in the first row, Sandra waved her hand for anyone interested to come quick and check out her slide. "I got me so many amoebas here some of them must be on welfare, 'cause I know they ain't never gonna find jobs for all these suckers on just one drop a water."

"That's why my taxes so high," Monroe said. "All you niggas on welfare."

The whole class laughed, and then a boy across the aisle from Simon yelled, "Monroe, you a lie; you ain't pay no taxes."

"Damn straight. I ain't feeding you and your mama's other fifteen kids."

Mr. Lange had been making the rounds from one table to the next, but now he headed to the front of the room and asked, "How many of you in here really think taxes are high because of welfare?"

"That's what white folks say," Sandra said. "Ain't that right, Mr. Lange?" She seemed to differentiate between him and white folks.

"All right, let's see." Mr. Lange picked up a piece of chalk from the chalkboard ledge and wrote:

Total Federal Budget	$184.5 billion
Defense	$80.2 billion
Welfare	$14.6 billion
All other programs combined	$89.7 billion

"OK, everyone, take a look at this. Out of a total federal budget of $184.5 billion, 43.4 percent goes toward defense, about 15 percent goes toward social welfare programs, and the rest goes to all of the other federal programs combined. Now, you tell me, what is the single most logical reason taxes are so high?"

Shouts of "Defense!" came from several students.

"That's right. And since the overwhelming majority of defense contractors are conglomerate companies owned by the ruling class, it's easy to see that the rich take the biggest chunk of our tax dollars to line their own pockets. But what's really more important to working-class folks—that our country can blow up the world six times over, or that we have jobs?"

"Jobs," Sandra said emphatically. "We starve to death without no jobs."

"Right again. But to divert the working-class struggle for more jobs at fairer wages and better working conditions, the ruling class fills us with propaganda that says that the Russians are our real enemy, or blacks, or Latinos, or whites, or Jews—anyone but the industrialists who are economically sucking everyone else dry."

Juan leaned toward Simon and whispered, "What the fuck's this got to do with biology?" Simon shrugged, staying focused on his teacher. He wanted actual names and addresses of people in the ruling class. Couldn't Nixon have them arrested, or was even the president (and here Simon took into account Nixon's pro–Vietnam War stance and his conservative, "silent majority" rhetoric) in cahoots with the ruling class, too? *Probably.*

"What we really have in the world today," Mr. Lange continued, "are two superpowers controlled by small ruling classes who are constantly competing for world domination"—he raised and lowered his open hands to represent trays on a scale, neither of which could sustain an advantage in weight—"and who keep working people from uniting against them by using tactics like racism and nationalism. It's the age-old story of divide and conquer."

"Sounds like what we need is some power to the people," Monroe said. "Ain't that right?"

"Yep." Mr. Lange's smile reassured everyone that they were all on the same page. "Just remember, it takes a lot of time, effort, and money to brainwash us into believing blatant lies like how the poor are responsible for high taxes."

But exactly how did this brainwashing take place, Simon wondered. Had he, his parents, two sisters, friends, all of the people in the neighborhood, the city, country, and entire world been duped? Simon began to wonder if the threatened student boycott—the one that Clyde had said Mr. Lange was helping to organize—was in fact a united community stand against an enemy whose reach pushed the very limits of his comprehension. This was some serious shit!

For the remainder of ninth period, Mr. Lange used simple, concise, step-by-step logic to explain the simple need for the working class to overthrow the oppressive ruling class, and yet, with all that simplicity being thrown Simon's way, he began to see that the world was far more complicated than he had ever imagined.

6

Drivers' Education

"Sheeeeeeit, I'm moving my ass on over to the North Side."

"Damn straight. Fuck this shit! I ain't letting no P. Stones fuck with my ass."

"Man, I ain't coming to school till them mothafuckin Stones quit they mothafuckin drafting."

Three black boys whispered to each other during drivers' ed. in a third-floor room just off the stairs in the new building. The room always looked abandoned, candy wrappers and discarded mimeographed pages of homework assignments on the floor, and no books in the closets, since drivers' education and sex education were the only classes held in the room, both taught by the gym teachers.

In the back row of chairs with small desktops, Simon eavesdropped on the three black boys to his right more than he listened to Mr. Evans droning on about car safety.

"Man, I got this shit all worked out. When the mothafuckin P. Stones comes up to me, I say, 'Stone to the bone, brotha,' and when the mothafuckin Deuces comes up to me, I say, 'Deuces Wild, brotha, Deuces forever.' Sheeit, I got them mothafuckas thinking I'm in two clubs."

The tallest of the three, several seats down from Simon, snickered, wiping his runny nose with the sleeve of his tan fake cashmere overcoat, open in front, his soiled white ruffled shirt showing through. Bright red pants with slits at the cuffs were in need of pressing, yet his manner was that of a rich man showing off his riches. It was in the way he said *sheeit* or *mothafucka*. He'd pull his head back and stick out his chest, sprawling his pointed black shoes in front, with a drowsy look on his long face.

"Sheeeeeeit, they keep fuckin with me, I'm gone get my ass out of this shit," the second shorter, but stockier, one said, his chair between those of his friends.

"You take me with you, Leroy," joked the smallest of the three, seated in the chair right next to Simon. Neither his "gangster" overcoat nor the natural pick stuck defiantly in the back of his hair did much to toughen his round-faced look of a mama's boy.

"Oh, virgin! I ain't taking you no place," Leroy said.

The tall one laughed, saying, "Oooooo-weeee, *signified* your ass!"

The little one seemed to forget he was in class, looking like he wanted to jump to his feet and verbally defend himself. But he sat back in his chair and grinned sheepishly. Caught. He was a virgin.

"Moe, you mothafuckin fourteen! You might as well cut your mothafuckin dick off," Leroy said, snickering.

"Always fasten your seat belt," Mr. Evans lectured. "I know it's a bother, but it could be the difference between life and death, your life or your death. And remember, speed kills both ways." That upward lilt to his voice seemed to suggest to students that he wasn't too keen on any of them getting behind the wheel of a car.

"Say, man, you don't even mothafuckin deserve a 'fro, you a disgrace; fourteen and still no trim," Leroy said, making a playful grab at the comb in Moe's hair. The boy slapped Leroy's hand away. The tall one, who said nothing all the while, laughed again, giving support to Leroy, enjoying every minute of it.

"Man, the Stones don't want no mothafuckin virgin. Moe ain't got shit to worry about! Ain't that right, Conrad?"

"Oh man, leave the nigga alone," the tall one, Conrad, said, then laughed, his shoulders convulsing in a way that suggested he knew Leroy would do nothing of the kind. As they listened to Mr. Evans for a moment, Simon wondered if he, too, should feel ashamed for being fourteen and still a virgin.

"Always use your turn signal. I repeat, always," Mr. Evans said. "If you don't, the guy behind you isn't going to know what the hell you're doing."

"Oooooo, Mr. Evans, you ain't supposed to use pro-fanity around our virgin ears!" Leroy yelled, shaking his Bic pen at the teacher.

The whole class laughed while Evans tilted his head and slowly blinked, looking exhausted.

"Eat some shit, Leroy."

Everyone laughed again, Leroy the hardest; he'd gotten what he wanted. As soon as the class settled down, Simon heard Leroy say to Moe, "Hey, virgin, put your hands over your ears, nigga." And then Conrad, after laughing, touched Leroy's elbow softly, saying, "You hear what happened? Them mothafuckin Stones got Frank going home yesterday. Mothafuckin chased his ass all the way home and beat the shit out of him."

The look on Leroy's face said *No shit*, and Conrad nodded. "Damn straight." Then they both bent over snickering, Conrad flinging his arms back and forth like he was on top of someone and pummeling him with his fists.

"Frank say, 'I'll join! Stone love!' He a mothafuckin Stone now!"

Simon wondered how they could find something that they must have dreaded happening to themselves to be so hilariously funny.

"If you know you've got the right of way but some clown moves first, don't fight it; let him go by. There's no sense in getting yourself killed."

"Say, man," Conrad said to Leroy, and ignored Moe. "You know Charleen Thomas?"

"Everyone *know* her, man; she a *skank*."

"Jesse fucked her forty-nine times in one week."

Simon's eyes bugged out. *Forty-nine* times?

"Oh, man," Leroy said, "come on, ain't no one can fuck forty-nine times in one week, not even me."

"When there's a yellow line on a two-lane highway, you are not allowed to pass. Usually you'll find it when you're going around a turn or up a hill," Evans said, pointing to a diagram on the blackboard.

"Dig this, Leroy, dig *this*," Conrad said in a secretive tone that made even Moe lean forward and try once more to be accepted by the others. "He fucked her twice when they woke up, once after breakfast, once after lunch, once after dinner, and twice before they went to sleep. Man, he copped seven pieces of ass a day! That more than one man deserve."

"Jesse should have left some for old Moe here. Ain't that right, Moe?" Leroy said, snickering at his friend, who returned, "Kiss my sweet black ass, nigga!"

"Ooooo-weeee," Conrad said. "Here we go again. Nigga, you so bad, the Stones gonna want your ass for sure."

"Oh, man, Stones don't want no virgin," Leroy said again. "I bet Moe the only mothafuckin virgin in this room."

Simon quickly looked down at his *Rules of the Road* booklet. Other students close by turned around in their seats and laughed at Moe, some of them probably hiding the fact that they were virgins, too.

"You best cut that shit out, nigga," Moe said.

"Oh, boy, who you calling *nigga*? What you gone do, virgin?" Then for no apparent reason, Leroy looked around Moe and asked Simon, "Say, white boy, you ain't no virgin, are you?"

Simon suddenly got the same sheepish look Moe had gotten, and Moe perked up as the focus of fun switched to a honky, someone even he could not be put on the same level with.

"You virgin?" Leroy asked again.

Simon didn't even think of lying.

"Yeah." He instantly knew he should have lied. But what if they asked him for details—when he had taken her panties off or when he had shoved his dick in? *Screwed* either way.

"Oooooo-weeee! You really a virgin?" Conrad asked.

Simon painfully nodded *yes* and then looked straight ahead at Evans, hoping they would stop talking to him once he had broken eye contact.

"Say, white boy." Leroy drew Simon's attention back again. "How old are you?"

"Fourteen."

"Oooooo-weeee! Man, you fourteen and ain't never had no trim? Oooooo-weeee! Man, you's old as little Moe here. Don't white folk fuck? I mean, tell me how white folk fuck."

Leroy leaned forward and waited for an answer, like he really thought white folks might fuck differently. Simon didn't have any idea how white folks fucked, so he shrugged and tried to get his mind sunk into what Mr. Evans was saying.

"A car that cannot go faster than forty miles per hour cannot be allowed on the expressway."

"Man oh man, white boy, I can't believe you ain't never had no trim," Leroy said. "Why, I bet your dick ain't even got no hair on it."

"Sheeeeit, I bet this white boy got a hairy dick!" Conrad said, his skinny body shaking as he snickered and then wiped his nose with his coat sleeve. "I swear to God this white boy's so hairy under them drawers they call him Werewolf. Say, man, we'll give you five dollar if you show us which one is right, me or Leroy. What you say, Leroy? Two fifty apiece to see if the white boy gots a hairy dick."

Simon began to squirm in his seat, saw Moe's relieved smile, and then looked back down at his drivers' ed. booklet, trying to ignore the three of them.

"How about it, white boy?" Conrad asked.

"The law specifically states not more than three people will be legally allowed to sit in the front seat."

Simon glanced up at the clock high on the wall behind Evans. Three minutes to go.

"Ah-oooooo," Conrad said, his hand in front of his mouth so that the teacher couldn't hear him imitating a wolf. "Ah-oooooo, five dollar, white boy, ah-oooooo." And all the while Simon kept his eyes riveted on *Rules of the Road*, feeling trapped in his seat. Occasionally he'd force a chuckle that all but said, *Yeah, guys, ha-ha, very funny, but as you can see I'm trying to study.* He tried to engross himself in illustrations of cars stopping at red lights, moving on green, giving the right of way to pedestrians. *That's the way it should be,* he thought, *just like in the pictures.*

"Ah-oooooo."

"Never pass over a solid yellow line."

"Ah-oooooo. Say, white boy, ah-oooooo."

The bell rang. Simon bolted for the door, with Conrad yelling after him, "Five dollar, white boy! Five dollar! Buy your first piece a trim for five dollar!"

Simon kept moving, trying to ignore the laughter coming from the room behind him. The halls were full of screams and people laughing. He silently raced down the stairs in his gym shoes, two by two, all the way to the locker room. He had to bang on the door with his fist because the handle had been removed. Finally, Mr. Harrison, the school's only black gym teacher, let him in with a friendly "First bell ain't even hardly stopped ringing, son. What you got in them shoes, rockets?" Simon slipped past the bald-headed man to a locker in the middle of one of the rows. The windowpanes were broken so frequently, the janitors had given up replacing them, and frigid air poured through the holes, mixing with the smell of stale sweat. Shivering, Simon changed quickly.

Just as he got his gym uniform on—plain white T-shirt and baggy blue shorts that fit him like bloomers—a boy, about the same height as Simon but reed thin, rushed up and grabbed him by the neckband with both hands.

"Loan me a dime."

"I ain't got none," Simon said.

"Boy, what you mean you ain't got *none?*"

As the boy spoke, Simon noticed how the pink insides of his mouth contrasted with his rich, dark skin. He threw Simon up against the lockers and then began to dance like a boxer shadowboxing, his fists coming within a hair of his classmate's nose. Crouched down and pressed against the lockers, Simon held up a hand to protect his face—"Hey, come on, knock it off!" The kid ran up to another white boy and went through the exact same rigmarole, then tried his luck with a black boy who simply told him, "Turner, you crazy," and they both laughed. The boy, Turner, shot around the room asking for dimes, threatening whomever he thought he could get away with threatening. He had so much energy, never staying with one person too long, jumping up onto benches in between rows of lockers and running down to the end into a new aisle.

Simon joined the line of boys waiting to go upstairs to the gym. He kept an eye out for Turner and noticed other boys doing the same. Turner seemed hungry for something, *really* hungry, and it made him antsy, like he wanted to be mean.

The class was ready, and Mr. Evans unlocked the door and stood in front of it.

"No one's going up until you're all in a single file line and quiet."

People settled down, and Evans opened the door, but by the time three-fourths of the class had filed past him up the stairs, some of the remaining boys were yelling *fuck you*s and Tarzan calls, so he blocked the doorway again. Simon let out a long breath, wishing everyone would shut up and do things orderly for a change.

"We aren't going up before you guys learn how to behave, so it's up to you how much time you waste," Evans said, his arms stretched to either side, filling the open doorway.

"You gonna stop me?" a husky Japanese boy asked.

Evans looked surprised. Duane was usually the quiet type.

"Yeah, I'm going to stop you. Now get in line."

Duane swaggered over to the doorway and started to lean his shoulder into Evans. The teacher shoved him back, but Duane came at him again, this time harder, until finally Evans began to look as though he was using all of his strength to keep the student in the locker room. Duane would give up for a moment and then try again and again. Evans turned red. He couldn't lose face in front of the other boys, and as Duane paused, the teacher took a fast glance around at the audience that had collected from the rest of the locker room. Then he looked at Duane, grabbing him by the shoulders and acting tough.

"Come on, Duane! Cut it out. Get a hold of yourself!"

Halfway down the line, Simon felt sorry for Evans, but he grinned along with everyone else, watching to see who would win the power struggle. Finally, Duane smirked like he felt he had made his point, laughed, and sauntered out of sight back to his locker to change. Apparently he didn't even want to go upstairs. Evans let the rest of them go up and left Duane to himself. The color Simon noticed draining from his teacher's acne-scared cheeks told the story.

––––––––––––

Upstairs in the sunny gymnasium, twenty or so black boys gathered around a basketball hoop; the handful of Latino and white boys, including Simon, wandered over to the foldaway wooden bleachers along the sidelines and waited for Evans to come up and pass out the balls. Only one ball was out. A policeman, fully uniformed except for his hat, his handcuffs dangling out of his back pocket, shot the only basketball, with students watching, rebounding, and throwing the ball back to the cop. He was known to one and all as Officer Clark, and he'd been permanently stationed at Dexter ever since the school's riots the year before. Whenever Simon saw Clark patrolling the hallways, he'd notice the cop's steady gaze coming at him, and then as the man passed, the sight of those dangling hand-cuffs leaving.

A kid snared a rebound and started dribbling the ball to take it out beyond the free-throw line for a shot.

"Get your own ball, jagoff," Clark bellowed, and the boy smiled, throwing a soft pass to the cop, who took shot after shot while the class stood around and kept feeding the ball back to him. Soon the boys lost interest and started to fade away from the hoop.

"Sheeeeit, that mothafucka ain't gone let us do shit," someone said. "He ain't nothing but a mothafuckin pig." Then shouts of "Pig!" filled the gym and echoed off the tiled walls, coming from students with their backs turned toward the cop. As Simon lounged on a bleacher a few rows up, at midcourt, he spotted several black boys holding their hands over their mouths and pretending to sneeze or cough, except instead of saying "Ah-choo!" they'd say, "Ah-*pig!*" All the while Clark, remarkably agile for a man with a hefty gut, kept shooting his ball, not letting on that he was bothered by the insults. Suddenly he stopped and let the ball roll into a corner of the gym.

"Hey, you! Yeah, you. Get over here!" He slowly pointed with his finger to his feet. The gym grew quiet. A few black students snickered, and Simon heard someone say, "That pig gonna kill that mothafucka."

"Come on, get over here, clown."

Students filtered away and huddled in groups along the sidelines by the bleachers. Only one student remained on the floor, the cop ready to bust his face.

"Look at Slim. Fool gone get his ass *kicked*."

Slim pointed at himself and lifted his eyebrows in a way that asked, *Who, me?*

"Yeah, clown, get over here now."

The boy walked lazily toward the cop, his eyes cast humbly at the floor. A look of almost concealed satisfaction crept over Simon's face. It was payback time for every injustice gangbangers had inflicted on him.

"Call me a pig now, clown. I said call me a—hey, look at me when I'm talking to you, *boy!*"

Clark lifted Slim's chin, but the boy's chin dropped back as soon as it was released. All eyes were on them.

"If you're going to call me a pig, say it to my face, not under your breath."

The cop leaned on his hip with one hand resting on the handle of his gun.

"We can step outside and have it out if you don't like something about me, clown. I'm talking to you, boy. Look at me!"

He lifted Slim's head again, and again it dropped when released. The boy didn't say anything.

"Come on, clown, you want to fuck with me? Come on, Neee-gro. Goddamn you, look at me!" Clark slapped Slim lightly on the face, but the boy's eyes remained down, as though he were studying the cop's shiny black shoes.

"Come on, nigger, hit me. Come on, please hit me," Clark said, slapping Slim playfully across the cheek. Blacks along the sidelines snickered like they were finding it hard to watch, too embarrassing and too funny at the same time.

Clark asked Slim, "You a Cobra Stone, punk? That why you so brave?"

"Naw, I ain't no Cobra Stone."

"Disciple?"

"Naw."

"Deuces Wild?"

Slim shook his head. Through a closed door that connected the girls' gym to the boys' gym came the cheering of a team that must have just scored a run in a game of kickball. Clark humphed, his version of right and wrong the only one that counted.

"All right, clown. If I ever catch you calling me a pig again, I'll take you out back and beat the shit out of you. Understand?"

"Yeah, man, I understand."

"*Yeah, man*, what?"

Slim looked at him confused, and then he got it.

"Yeah, man, *sir*."

"Well all right, you motherfucking piece of chicken shit. Get outa here."

Clark went over to the bleacher where he had left his hat. Of all people, Turner held it delicately by the rim, leaned forward on one foot as the cop strutted toward him, and handed the hat over, his smile as respectful as it was uncomfortable.

They'll never take over, Simon thought. It had just slipped into his mind.

Slim faded into a group of friends by the bleachers on the opposite sideline. He wasn't going to leave; he wanted to play basketball. Clark walked to the door, slow and bold, tongue in cheek, looking at the basketball only a few feet away in the corner. He paused with his hand on the fire bar.

"Now you can have it," he told the crowd. And they dove for it, the quiet exploding into a basketball game, hiding Clark's laughter.

7

'Tis the Season to Be Jolly

EAGER TO GET TO HIS LOCKER, grab his coat and books, and escape for home, Simon ran up a short flight of stairs and slammed through one of several swinging doors into the old building's second floor. He couldn't stop dwelling on how he'd left Dia to fend for herself with those Latin Kings. *Fuck!* The walls changed from cream to powder blue, the lockers from beige to forest green. He careened past the library and then zigzagged two sharp hallway turns and passed the attendance office. On the wall next to a boys' bathroom door, a bulletin board decorated with cheesy silver tinsel and alternating green and red capital letters proclaimed MERRY CHRISTMAS.

He was closing in on his homeroom when, on a stairway not more than thirty feet up ahead, he heard the mad scramble of many feet coming up a flight. Then a terrified, doughy, fair-skinned boy lunged onto the floor with a pack of black boys in hot pursuit.

"Honky-ass motha—" A lucky hand clipped the white kid's heel and sent him sprawling to the floor. The five attackers, ranging in shapes and sizes from flyweight to bruiser, surrounded their prey and began to stomp, power-knee, gouge, and pummel the kid. He quickly curled up into a ball, but a well-aimed kick to the kidneys dug a pathetic "Ughhh" out of him. Simon frantically glanced around; not a hall monitor in sight, and other students already cleared out from their lockers and gone. At any second, the gangbangers would spot him and insist he join *their* party. The thrumming in his chest snatched his oxygen, making him woozy, the tendons behind his knees trembling. Then maybe it was one victim's *ughhh* too many, Simon's own shredded but not dead self-esteem, or just his will to do the right thing. He let the books and class folders under his arm spill to the floor, and charged.

The black boys never even saw him coming. He dove, made a snap decision in midflight to go for broke, and stretched his arms wide, soaring. Then he plowed into three of the boys, knocking them to the floor.

"Who the—"

With no phase two plan of attack, Simon found himself lying on top of a wriggling bed of shoulder blades, necks, torsos, elbows, and assorted other body parts. As he clawed at a wrist and pinned someone else's forearm, a blow to the back of his head rang in his ears. Footsteps were dashing up the staircase toward the third floor, and he caught a last glimpse of the other white boy, escaping.

"Get off—"

A group effort heave-ho sent Simon skidding on his hip across the tiles.

"*Brave* mothafucka, huh?"

Simon swiped at a set of ankles, but the feet they were attached to shook and tripped free of his grasp. Then certain that he was dead meat, something remarkably calm and even-keeled took hold in him. He flipped onto his back, hands and feet poised to block or strike.

"Hey!"

The jangling of handcuffs closed in fast from the direction of the attendance office.

"Hold it right there!"

No fools, the black boys did exactly the opposite of Officer Clark's order and took off, swarming down the stairs. When they reached the landing, one of the brawnier kids stopped long enough to look back

and fix Simon with a proud glare of unconquerable spirit. "Stone love!"
He beat his fist once against his chest and then extended it forward
with a straight arm—the Cobra Stone salute. All leaps and bounds,
he flew down the rest of the stairs to catch up with his bros on the
first floor. A moment later, the sound of a door slamming open onto
Orchard Street echoed throughout the old building.

"You OK?" Clark, hands on knees, bent low over Simon.

"Yeah."

Clamping a massive paw on Simon's arm, the officer hoisted him
to his feet.

"Sure?"

"Yeah," Simon repeated. He dabbed a hand against the back of
his scalp—no real damage done.

"Punks," Clark spat, making a friendly show of dusting off Simon's
shoulders. "Don't worry. Sooner or later I'll give them some *billy club*
love. Recognize any of them?"

Simon shook his head, grateful for the new company but also
afraid that being seen all buddy-buddy with a cop at Dexter wouldn't
win him any streetwise brownie points with black kids. The man's
bigger-than-life presence was making it difficult for Simon to meet
his steely eyes.

"They were jumping this kid, so I—"

"Another *white*, I'll bet," Clark said. "Where'd he go? Never mind,
I get the picture. Left you holding the fort, huh? He'll learn. Sooner
or later you got to stand up to them."

Them needed no explaining. Several classroom doors creaked open,
and teachers—all women of the mousey persuasion—peeped out into
the hall to check out what all the commotion was about.

"That's all, folks," Clark announced to one and all. "Nothing left
here but the happy ending starring yours truly, Officer Harry T. Clark."
As if he were enjoying having his own personal harem audience, he
reached a hand up and with humble aplomb tipped the brim of his
hat, adding, "I am available, ladies."

Doors began to close, but not before a giggle escaped through one near the end of the hall.

"I heard that, Miss Hadley. Just remember I'm a 100 percent all-beef patty ready to serve and protect."

When the last doorjamb clicked shut, Clark grinned and winked at Simon. "Don't know what they're missing." He lumbered down the hall, retrieved the messy heap of books and folders off the floor, quickly organized them according to size, and then brought them back over to Simon.

"Here you go, good as new. You're coming with me."

"But—"

"No *buts*." Clark gently gave the small of Simon's back a shove toward the stairs. "Got to fill out a report for your homeroom teacher." They started down the steps. "Who is she?" Before Simon could answer, Clark nudged him in the ribs with an elbow and whispered like a regular guy's guy, "Is she hot?"

Clark's office, deep in the bowels of the old building's basement and no bigger than a walk-in closet, barely fit a desk and a couple of chairs. Not a single picture or calendar decorated the institutional gray walls, and the desktop was whistle clean except for the cop's billy club, his hat with the famous checkerboard rim, and a black rotary phone—already dated compared to those newfangled touch-tone models.

Clark tipped back in his mission-style chair, put his feet up on the desk, and scrutinized his guest sitting across from him for a moment.

"Pretty cool digs I got here, huh? This is where I shove bamboo shoots under troublemakers' fingernails and stretch them on my rack if they don't tell me what I want to know."

Simon, anything but comfy in his plywood seat, kept his legs pressed close together to balance the stuff in his lap. He didn't even crack a smile.

"Kid, that was a joke. Lighten up, will ya? What's your name?

"Simon Fleming."

Clark did a double take on the boy.

"Wouldn't by any chance be *Reverend* Fleming's son?" The way Clark had loaded up on the word *reverend* didn't exactly put Simon at ease. Simon nodded, then glanced down and ran this thumb along the worn spine of his algebra textbook.

"Well I'll be a monkey's aunt."

"You know my dad?"

"*Know* can be a lot of things, but feel free to tell him hi from Officer Clark. In fact, do me a favor and let him know that I saved your ass from some of his poor, underprivileged Negroes."

Before Simon could come up with a clever way to deflect the obvious jab at his father's reputation as a liberal community activist, Clark asked, "How's that new theater of your old man's doing on Lincoln Avenue? What's it called—Body something-or-other?

"Body Politic," Simon corrected.

"Sorry, kid. Didn't mean nothing; I'm bad with names. Your dad sure is something, all right—preacher, arts entrepreneur, champion of the people. Problem is, I hear he rented space to a bunch of pinko riffraff. Now what kind of way is that to run a business? He might even be having a little trouble with"—and here Clark held his hand up to the side of his mouth, like someone keeping a confidence strictly between friends—"the law."

Simon, lost as to what the man was driving at, said, "I think my dad's trying to fix some fire code violations, but that's about—"

"Never mind, kid. Say, didn't I see you in the gym last period?"

"You saw *me*?" It shocked Simon that Clark had noticed a minor detail like him up on the bleachers. Through the walls of the claustrophobic office, he heard the low-key rumbling burn of what must have been a nearby industrial-sized boiler.

"I see everything. Got twenty-ten vision," Clark explained, "but it's also the peripheral vision that separates the chickens from the chicken hawks. Hell, during the convention riots last summer, I saw a rock that was practically aimed for the back of my head and ducked just in the nick of time. Draft-dodging scumbag commies. You can damn well bet I gave them better than I got." He let out a guffaw before continuing. "So how'd you like what I did to that smart-mouthed colored fuck in the gym?"

Simon rubbed the book's spine with his thumb a little harder. "Didn't think anything."

"Come on," Clark prodded. "Dares to call *me* a pig! Where's a fucking lynching when you need one?" He bellowed another laugh so demanding the fourteen-year-old boy across from him couldn't withstand the illogic of grinning himself. Clark feigned astonishment.

"He smiled! Quick, get a camera!" Then he said, "Say, you don't really think this thing between you and the Stones is over, do you?"

"What do you mean?"

"I *mean* you're a whitey sticking his nose into their business. Don't you know the Cobra Stones belong to the Peace Stone Nation? You just picked a fight with more than five thousand card-carrying gangbangers."

Slack-jawed, Simon waited for a signal from Clark that the five thousand figure was just another one of the cop's bad jokes.

"You heard me, and by next month it'll be six thousand. Maybe that's OK for watermelon farmers, but for you . . ."

A hot flash toasted Simon's cheeks, his stomach flip-flopping and turning sour.

"Think maybe you could use a little backup from yours truly, Officer Friendly?"

Saying yes to a man with so blatant a racist streak would have violated everything the name Fleming stood for, but the realist in Simon—the one stuck with going to Dexter five days a week—weighed the intriguing possibility. What about what Mr. Lange had taught him? Did cops attend secret meetings where they received direct orders from the ruling class? Clark must have read the boy's tongue-tied ambivalence.

"Tell you what, Simon. From now on, if anyone messes with you, they're messing with me, too. All I ask is that if you hear anything . . . you know, like who's who behind this rabble-rousing boycott bullshit I keep hearing rumors about, you come to your good friend Officer Clark with the info. Deal?"

As far as Simon was concerned, the slight nod he gave—no more than a temporary surrender to adult authority—still left his options open. Clark took his feet off the desk, tipped forward onto all four legs of his chair again, and folded his hands neatly together on the desktop. A model of professional decorum, he said, "OK, let's take it from the top. What happened?"

Later, on Simon's brisk walk home down Webster Avenue, he wondered what Clark's talk about the Body Politic had been referring to. *Pinko riffraff?* All Simon knew was that the fledgling business had turned his dad into a nonstop grump, one who Simon avoided being around whenever possible. *Should have kept his church,* Simon thought. *At least that job paid money. Fuck the Body Politic.*

8

The Body Politic

THE FIRST TIME ADAM TOOK SIMON to see his new not-for-profit business, he asked his son, "So what do you think?" They were watching a couple of sweaty, shirtless actors turned temporary carpenters use drills to power-screw a plywood riser into place on a stage. Preparations in the Big Theater—one of three venues under the Body Politic's roof—were behind schedule for an upcoming show. With the brutal honesty of a thirteen-year-old, Simon replied, "It's a dump."

Adam grinned patiently. "Sometimes to get to where you want to go in life, you have to try to see the potential in things."

"Yeah but, Dad . . ." The look on Simon's face implied that he couldn't get rid of a bitter taste. "A dump's a dump."

Renovations to the Body Politic—formerly a rundown bowling alley upstairs and a meatpacking plant downstairs—continued piecemeal, limited by budget. After ringing two sides of the Upstairs Theater with framing and drywall, Adam had studios and offices he could rent out to the Peggy Lemond Dance Company, the Chicago Muralists' Alliance, Phil's Marionette Workshop, the Clay Men Pottery School, and Rising-Up Rage, a radical left-wing political organization that appealed to his sense of community mission with their People's Free Healthcare clinic. On Mondays, Wednesdays, and Fridays, between the hours of 1:00 and 3:00 PM, interns from Northwestern Memorial Hospital donated their time and expertise to those in need of medical care. An illegal Mexican couple whose infant had strep throat.

"*No problemo. Aqui esta uno dosis de penicillina.*" A minimum-wage laborer who'd gashed his hand while working on a wrecking crew. "Some stitches, a tetanus shot, and you'll be good as new." A runaway from Baltimore who was hitchhiking cross-country to join the flower-child generation in San Francisco's Haight Ashbury district. "Here's enough asthma medication to last you through the month. Say, do you need a place to crash? Some better shoes than those Jesus sandals? Birth control pills? We can arrange that, too."

And as Adam observed the trickle of far-flung humanity paying a visit to Rising-Up Rage's no-frills office, he'd think, *Starting to come together—providing the arts along with other basic needs for the community.* Was his ministerial concept for the Community Arts Foundation really too avant-garde for people to grasp? *Nonsense.*

To help keep rents affordable at the Body Politic, he came up with the novel idea of having troupes share stages. Rainbow had dibs on the Big Theater Monday through Friday, and the Rock'n'Roll Cantata Singers ruled the roost on weekends. The Dingle Beats called the shots in the Little Theater for 7:00 PM shows and then passed the experimental baton to the Mime Sweepers at 9:00 PM. Dream Theater and Flying Onion split time upstairs, leaving the Children's Puppet Troupe to work the Saturday and Sunday matinee kiddie crowds. As productions closed, new companies rotated in: one happy revolving door of art and political liberation under the same rooftop.

That is, until Rising-Up Rage began to flex their territorial muscle by spray painting "educational" graffiti all over the Body Politic. In the downstairs lobby, a sandblasted brick wall got adorned with SMASH CAPITALISM, and in the center of the room, the front of the ticket-booth island proclaimed OFF THE PIGS. On each and every staircase riser, the people's power salute of a clenched fist, neatly stenciled in white, made sure that no customers lost their way from the downstairs bathrooms back to the Upstairs Theater after intermission. The radicals, a disparate band of eleven, many of whom had decided to forgo college to prepare for a workers' revolution, dressed in combat boots, double-cuffed 501 Levi's, and a seasonal rotation of dago Ts and flannel shirts. They further tried Adam's patience by dubbing him Abe, because the bearded six-foot-six reverend could have indeed passed for a robust version of the sixteenth president. Rage members believed that the slave emancipator was nothing more than an opportunistic racist given preferential treatment by sell-out historians. From a Rage member at a urinal next to the one Adam was using, he'd hear a snarky, "How's it hanging, Abe?" Or when the first of the month came around and Sam Paull—Rage's de facto leader among equals—dropped off a rent check in Adam's office, he got "Here's your money, Abe. Any chance of you freeing us?"

Adam, seated behind his desk, picked up the check that had just skidded his way across a felt blotter pad, folded it neatly in two, and tucked it into his shirt pocket. After several pats of his hand to that same pocket, he said, "Thanks, Karl."

"Karl?"

"Yeah, as in Marx. And can you and your band of merry revolutionaries please stop turning the Body Politic into a Lenin-Marxist shrine? Not all patrons of the arts believe in your brand of politics."

"Funny," Paull said. A young man who had been born of wealthy means, he'd toned down his fair-skinned, Nordic look of assumed privilege by turning flabby on a lower-class diet of junk food and Old Style. Moving toward the door with a sluggish contempt for *the man,* he let out a parting "Sure, Abe. You're the boss."

The next morning, Adam came to work and found his Community Arts Foundation office door spray painted with BAD VIBES. *Why that son of a . . .*

Evict Rising-Up Rage? All of those people seeking medical attention gave the Presbyterian minister reason to think carefully before he reacted. A graffiti problem is always fixable with a new coat of paint. But a seriously ill and dehydrated child who doesn't get intravenously fed fluids before it's too late? Not so fixable.

Keeping his landlord cool worked, and Rising-Up Rage members honored an unspoken truce by putting away their spray paint cans.

"Nothing personal, Abe," Paull told Adam a few days after the BAD VIBES incident. Passing each other on the stairs, they'd stopped midflight. With the self-proclaimed people's revolutionary on one step of higher ground than the tall reverend, the two men had a fair chance of seeing eye-to-eye. "I'll make sure your door gets repainted."

Problem solved? Hardly. In the aftermath of the '68 Democratic Convention in Chicago, and its nationally televised riots between antiwar demonstrators and cops, Mayor Richard J. Daley and his political machine didn't take kindly to anyone associating with "agitators," including landlords. Next thing Adam knew, it seemed like every municipal building inspector within the city limits was finding reasons to stop by the Body Politic and discover fire code violations. It didn't matter that the Big Theater had a puny 150-seat capacity, the Upstairs a measly 100, and the Little a laughable 60; the same stringent codes applied to them as to 2,000-seat venues. Only three exits instead of the required five? That's a $100 fine. Short one fire extinguisher? Ante up another hundred. And he could either upgrade the building's electrical system from top to bottom with one-hundred-amp service or pay a fine every week that it wasn't up to code. Sorry, Reverend. The law's the law. Welcome to "the city that works." Adam blew his opinion of that commonly held propaganda out the side of his mouth and thought, *Except for most of us.*

"But, Dad," Simon said at the dinner table one night, "can't someone just tell Mayor Daley that we're poor and can't afford to fix the stuff?"

"Son," Adam replied, "I doubt the man gives a darn. And how many times do I have to tell you that we're middle class?" Then he added with dark humor, "We just happen to be temporarily *poor-ish.*"

Several months and $3,600 in fines later, Adam put two and two together. In the eyes of city officials, he was in cahoots with people who had no problem with the violent overthrow of the government. *At least*

Rising-Up Rage pays its rent on time, Adam thought, which was more than he could say for a couple of his other tenants. *And screw city hall if no one there understands the First Amendment right to freedom of speech.* Meanwhile, Peggy Lemond was threatening to break her studio lease because when Phil, the lush marionette maker, got loaded on gin, he'd wander from his workshop over to her dance studio and interrupt rehearsals by inviting female modern dancers back to his studio for a private "puppet show." His added attraction? A new invention called a waterbed. In the Upstairs Theater, during performances by Dream Theater or the Mime Sweepers, mismatched chairs bought from the Salvation Army tended to collapse now and then with paying customers in them. Without giving notice, the Dingle Beats jumped ship by starting their own theater in a storefront several blocks north on Lincoln Avenue, leaving Adam scrambling for a new Little Theater tenant. Dream members were unanimously threatening to crash the Rock'n'Roll Cantata Singers' show and pull the plugs on their electric guitar amplifiers because the excessive hard-rock beat and volume coming from the Big Theater shook the upstairs stage from below and ruined the phantasmagoric, Kafkaesque ambiance of Dream performances. And through it all the government's assault on the Body Politic continued. Finally, Commonwealth Edison pulled the plug on the building's electricity for three months' nonpayment. While Adam scrambled to come up with a way to cover the debt, all shows were canceled for a night, except for the Mime Sweepers, who took the saying "The show must go on" to the extreme. They lined large candelabra complete with lit candles along their stage's three-sided perimeter. Talk about a *real* fire hazard.

One year after opening its doors, *crisis* had become the Body Politic's middle name.

9

Home Front

SLAM. Simon's footsteps pounded up the stairs. The Flemings lived on the top two spacious floors of the duplex graystone and rented out the first-floor apartment. Though it was a fixer-upper—what with its leaky roof, rusted-out plumbing, occasional attacks of termites, and rotten window sashes—its turn-of-the-century elegance was impossible to erase. When Simon had made his way through the living room, his father's office, and the dining room, he flung his rucksack into the cubbyhole closet tucked underneath the back stairs and began taking off his peacoat so that he could hang it on one of the hooks.

"Hi, Simon." Helen, beyond a doorway and in the kitchen, was already working on dinner at the stove, stirring a skillet full of chicken and rice with a spatula. She got no more than a huffed grunt from her teenaged son. To many, she was the silver-haired, green-eyed beauty with cheekbones that defined *high*, but to Simon she was just Mom.

"How was school?" Adam asked. At the kitchen table, he nursed a glass of cran-apple juice, his elbows spilling over a captain's chair.

"Fine." Simon assumed the conversation was over and slipped between his parents on his way to the refrigerator for a snack.

"Keep it small or you'll ruin your dinner," Adam said.

"I'm starving!"

"You heard your father."

From Simon's grip on the refrigerator door handle, he hung his weight like he was about to collapse from malnutrition. He grabbed a vacuum-packed tub of bologna and started opening it.

"One slice," Adam said.

"*One* lousy slice?"

Both parents knew full well that Simon could have eaten a McDonald's restaurant, golden arches and all, and still have room for dessert. "You'll just have to wait," Helen said. Then, attempting a lighter note, "Nothing at all you can tell us about school today?"

Yet another huffed grunt. Simon stuffed the slice of meat into his mouth, most of it already down his gullet by the time he'd swung the refrigerator door shut. He beelined across the kitchen to make his exit out the doorway, but just before he got there, Adam stretched his arm out like a tollgate.

"Whoa. Your mother asked you a question."

"Nothing happened. Oh, I think I've got a good shot at making the baseball team."

Responses of "Great!" and "Fantastic!" overlapped.

"Can I go now?"

Adam gave an exasperated sigh and let his arm drop.

"Set the table in ten minutes," Helen said.

Already scrambling up the back stairs, Simon called down, "Why can't Beth or Dawn do it?"

"Your sisters wash and dry the dishes," Adam reminded him.

Well, la-de-fucking-da, Simon thought as, with a stair-skipping bound, he reached the top of the flight. He was about to duck into his room at the end of the hallway when he heard guitar plucking and Beth singing a Joni Mitchell song from her room, to his right. *How can anyone stand that honky folk music?* He passed the bathroom and came to her closed oak door. Only thirteen months older than Simon, Beth's above-average smarts had earned her a full scholarship to Francis Parker, one of Chicago's most prestigious prep schools. A few days earlier, Simon had slipped into her room to try his hand at playing her guitar and then forgotten to take his sweater with him when he left. Not long afterward, Beth discovered the foreign garment in her territory and proceeded to open the window and toss the sweater out, whereupon it plummeted three stories down to the backyard and landed atop piles of dog shit—frozen, thankfully—left by the tenant's mutt, Bandit.

Time for payback. Simon knocked his knuckles in a drum roll on Beth's door, put his mouth near the crack, and in a whiny voice, sang:

I've looked at clouds from both sides now

The guitar plucking abruptly stopped. "Fuck off, asshole!"

From up and down and still somehow
I really don't give a shiiiiit

Wham. Beth had probably whipped a shoe at the door in the general vicinity of Simon's head. Cackling, he started down the hallway to the next closed door across from the walk-in ironing closet. He tormented Dawn for no reason other than sibling tradition, the origins of which were lost in the haze of his early childhood. A senior at Senn, she had already begun attending that predominately white high school before the board of education clamped down on students transferring out of the district they lived in. Simon leaned close to her door and in a falsetto, quasi-feminine voice said, "Oh, I'm sooooo beautiful. All the boys love me. Don Ishiwari worships the ground I—"

"Creep!"

That was it? He pounded the door three times with his fist—"Arrrrrrrgh!"

"Grow up, ya little turd!"

On his way back down the hallway to his room, he banged his fist against Beth's door just for good measure and an encore response.

"Loser! Get a fucking life!"

Inside his sanctuary, Simon locked the door. Through the floor-boards, he heard the muffled arguing of his parents below in the kitchen—*What else is new?*—then his father's raised voice, "Oh, forget it!" Every brick and beam in the house tensed, followed shortly by Adam's heavy footsteps descending the front stairs. *Slam!* Another dinner without him. The house relaxed again, the interrupted flow of oxygen resuming. *Good.* With less than two weeks to go till Christmas, the Flemings still hadn't bought a tree. *Why,* Simon wondered, *can't we get our act together?* He flipped the switch, and the fluorescent ceiling lights blinked on. Dark-brown corkboard covered the far wall, the other three paneled in cheap faux mahogany. Heaps of dirty clothes lay scattered on the floor along with assorted remnants of past snacks—a dried brown banana peel, an apple core, and a sticky circle where he had never cleaned up an overturned bowl of Jell-O by the foot of his bed. A closet, built by his father out of two wooden telephone booths, stood with folding doors open and shelves jammed with old toys Simon hadn't touched in ages—Mouse Trap, Kaboom, Creeple Peeple, Etch A Sketch, an electric football game. On the other side of the room, a sheet draped over a Ludwig drum set—an expensive relic from a former passion he'd given up—looked like a phantom ready to pounce. He stared into a full-length mirror clipped to the paneling next to the door. *Shit!* Another zit—in his opinion big enough to deserve its own address—had decided to grow just below his left nostril. He stroked his fingers over peach-fuzz side-burns, one a slightly darker shadow than the other. His cheeks seemed too sunken, his eyebrows too thick, his hair too incapable of lying flat. And the way his long nose spread at the nostrils, and spread some more. *Dia thinks I'm cute?* His own close-up encounter with him-self left him buried in lost hope.

He stepped over to the small mono radio on the floor next to the Jell-O stain, reached down, and clicked the volume dial. On WGRT, James Brown was gettin' down funky:

Whoa! I feel nice
Like sugar and spice

The godfather of soul could get funky better than Joni Mitchell any day. Simon went back to the mirror and began practicing the latest dance, the Four Corners. Swivel one hip, step out, swing and cross arms; swivel other hip, step out, swing and cross arms. Not bad. Maybe one day he'd get up the nerve to dance outside of his bedroom. He moved on to working on his pimp-walk—a laboriously stylized means of moving from one place to another, popular with black males. He strutted toward the mirror, exaggerating a dip in his knees with every other step, his right hand cupped and swinging low by his side. Then he stopped and glared at a reflection stupid enough to return his challenge.

"What you lookin' at, honky? Think you *bad*?" He slapped his hands off his chest. "Go ahead, mothafucka. If you so bad, jump in my chest!"

"Siiiiimon," his mother yelled up the back stairs, "set the table!"

He flipped the light switch again, illogically hoping that darkness would throw her off his trail, and tiptoed to his bed. He lay down carefully to try to prevent any bedsprings from creaking, and stared at the dropped-ceiling tiles, but their white perforated pattern offered zero entertainment. Maybe he could sneak down the front staircase to the living room and watch *The Three Stooges Show.* No matter how many times he'd seen their eye-poking, head-conking, face-slapping reruns, he found the Stooges' violent humor relaxing. *Nah*, his mom would hear him for sure. He dwelled on his blown chance with Dia. Did he dare to think of Clyde as his friend? Should he buddy up to a scary, in-your-face racist like Clark? Simon felt like he'd been snagged, jerked, and reeled in by the man's offer for protection. What about that crazy kid, Louis? Out to prove something? Why couldn't Simon be tough like Juan? The idea of a student boycott, no matter how well intentioned, stank of trouble. And to top everything off, according to Mr. Lange, the ruling class had the entire planet by the balls. The song on the radio changed to Marvin Gaye's "I Heard It Through the Grapevine."

I bet you're wonderin' how I knew
'Bout your plans to make me blue

Simon gazed out the window, past the gnarled branches of the grand cottonwood tree in the backyard, and over a neighborhood sea of tarred rooftops. A ribbon of brilliant red lay low on the horizon, textured with clouds ripped and fraying down from a sheet above. God must have tipped open a cauldron lid for a peek at the fiery lava within. Then before Simon's eyes, the indigo evening squeezed down and shut it.

Part II

Boycott

10

Happy New Year

DEVOTIONAL CANDLES FLICKERING ON WINDOWSILLS, *Amahl and the Night Visitors* on the stereo, and a cascading ring of presents and credit card debt under a tree smothered in tinsel. Then New Year's Eve, the Times Square countdown on TV, a tooted blast from party favors, and vacation is over. Welcome to second semester.

A freak January warm snap boosted the mercury into the low fifties. Simon decided to take advantage of the sun-drenched day by hustling three-quarters of a mile home for lunch. Once there, he would pit stop in the kitchen only long enough to inhale a chipped-beef and Miracle Whip sandwich, and then hightail it back to school again.

Lone whites sprinkled among the gaggles of blacks moved quicker than most to reach side streets. Already, the reverse tide of lunch students flowing into the building had bottlenecked at the main entrance, leaving most of the sidewalk to stragglers. Simon was about to step off the curb, free himself of Dexter's formidable shadow, when he heard, "Say, honky!" Turning around, at first he didn't recognize the boy only a few feet away, leaning back against the tall chain-link fence that enclosed one of Dexter's small lawns. The boy's tan gangster overcoat doubled his hefty appearance and complemented his flawless toffee skin. Then something familiar about the kid's long-lashed, placidly bitter eyes wiped a chill across Simon's cheeks. It was the Cobra Stone who, not at all pleased with Simon diving to the rescue of another white kid getting jumped, had paused on the stair landing long enough to give his gang's chest-pounding salute.

The boy bounced off the fence and beckoned with a finger that Simon now knew flexed the street authority of five thousand Stones.

"What's up, man?" Trying to play stupid, Simon lagged a step behind the boy, following him down the sidewalk. "Something wrong?"

Without so much as a glance back, the Cobra Stone beckoned again. Simon's father had told him, "Black kids won't respect you if you don't defend yourself." *Against a whole army?*

Not a single teacher or school administrator ever patrolled outside the school. If Simon ran, he knew that even more Stones would track him down sooner rather than later. Fear made him lightheaded. A paper cup blew past him in the gutter, its scratchy tumbling against the asphalt as distant to his ear as the clank of a basketball hitting a bent rim on the court across the playground.

They reached the corner, crossed Dickens Street to the vacant lots, and then descended into a shallow dirt trench where city workers had recently dug up the abandoned two-block span of Orchard, sewer lines and all. The gangbanger stopped and abruptly squared off with his reluctant partner.

"I'm sorry, OK? Can't we just—" Before Simon could think *Duck*, a furious roundhouse punch slammed against his temple and knocked him sideways, his feet scuffling for steady ground. In the instant it took for his peripheral vision to go from fuzzy to clear, the other boy had already slipped out of his coat and let it drop on the dirt in a fake cashmere heap.

"Think you *bad*, honky?"

A right cross connected flush against Simon's jaw, snapped his neck, and sent him reeling again.

"Fire on me!"

The open invitation for Simon to throw his best punch only sharpened the dry swelling in his throat, his hands poised to block instead of strike.

"Sissy-ass honky mothafucka!"

Despite more blows, Simon heard the trampling of feet, a crowd of thirty or so students swarming off the playground to cross Dickens and gather ringside. The gangbanger hauled him out of the trench by the collar of his coat and manhandled him toward the rear of a boarded-up six-flat—the last building left standing in the lots. Stumbling, Simon slipped on a torn sheet of pink linoleum left from someone's demolished kitchen, and as he lurched forward, the weedy field's melting patchwork of snow tilted one way while the line of flat and peaked rooftops way over on Webster Avenue slanted the other way. He caught his center of gravity again, his gym shoe kicking at a rusty door hinge that sailed through the air, ringing like a tuning fork. Then an uppercut plowed into his diaphragm, and he doubled over, dry heaving for breath.

"Gone kill that white boy," someone said.

Then someone else: "Dang!"

Behind the six-flat, out of view from Dexter or the playground, the boy shoved Simon up against the brick wall. The corner of Simon's split lower lip throbbed. To either side of him, battleship-gray back porches and stairs stacked three floors high looked remarkably well kept and more ready for tenants' barbecues than for a wrecking ball.

"Move, I'll kill your fucking ass!"

Directly above, Simon noticed a fleet of magnificent cumulus clouds in the dazzling blue, their fast-moving shadows sweeping the reclaimed prairie below. It didn't take the Cobra Stone long to find something handy—a two-by-six board easily recognizable as having once been the crossbar on a yellow Streets and Sanitation sawhorse. He picked up the piece of lumber and started back toward Simon.

"Uh-oh." This from a girl lost among the spectators. Then a boy, as unassuming in size as he was hip in his granny sunglasses, stepped forward and blocked the gangbanger's path.

"Brother, this ain't right. You need to cool out."

"Get the fuck out my way!"

One end of the board was placed with a narrow side resting on top of Simon's head.

"Naw, brother, don't."

The plank was lifted, and Simon, too afraid to move, heard himself think, *Tomorrow, I will still be alive.* Then in a piece of luck too perfectly timed to believe, a mars light flashed, followed by the screech of car brakes, and the gangbanger quickly tossed his board to the ground. In the trench that used to be Orchard Street, a squad's door flew open—"Hey!" Clark lunged from behind the wheel and hit the ground running. "Hold it right there!"

Simon obeyed the order and kept still, but the billy club poised for action in the cop's hand didn't exactly encourage the black kids to do the same. They fled around the six-flat toward the playground, the entire crowd vanishing in the few seconds it took for Clark to reach the white boy.

"Punk motherfuckers!" Winded by the sprint, Clark bent over with hands on knees, wolfing deep breaths. When he came back up, the flushed color of his bloated face began to return to normal.

"You OK?"

Simon nodded but kept his eyes fixed on a dried clump of weed brush a few feet in front of him.

"See something special down there?" Reaching out, Clark lifted Simon's chin with a firm finger. "That's one hell of a shiner and busted lip. Guess you won't be winning any beauty contests for a while. Know any of them?"

Flinching away from the cop's touch, Simon shook his head. He gazed across the field toward the DePaul Settlement House gym, imagining where he should have been right about then—a half-mile farther due west, in the foyer of his home and unlocking the front door with his key. Exhaling heavily, he slumped into his own self-loathing.

"Good thing I noticed there wasn't the usual crowd of spooks cutting class on the playground," Clark said. "Always a sure sign something's up, so I figured I'd better do a little snooping. Nearly cracked an axle driving into that ditch. Come on, you've had enough school for one day. I'll give you a ride home."

Before Simon could say *No thanks*, Clark gave him a good-old-boy slap to the back that jolted him forward a step. His other foot followed without the same excuse, and he went with the cop to the squad car.

"This field gets any more wild, I'll have to bring my shotgun and bag a buck. You ever hunt?"

"No," Simon muttered. He ran his tongue back and forth over his raw, puffy lip.

"Oh, yeah, I forgot. Reverends probably aren't big on teaching their kids how to kill Bambi. Don't know the fun you're missing."

At almost the same instant, Clark and Simon noticed a flattened heap of camel-colored fabric on the ground just behind the squad's rear bumper. Judging from the dirty tire-tread mark across the coat, the car must have run right over it.

"Well, what have we here?" Clark picked up the garment and inspected it at arm's length. Almost immediately he discovered a white patch hand-stitched into the silky lining right below the Squires brand-name tag. "Bingo. Somebody's mama is worried about him losing his prized possession." There was carefully printed felt-tipped pen handwriting on the patch, and Clark read it out loud. "Frank Tucker, 1567 North Orleans Street, Chicago, Illinois, MO4-7992."

11

Détente

"You're sure they were black?"

"Unless I'm colored-blind, Reverend. They all took off like a bunch of Wilma Rudolphs."

Officer Harry Clark grinned at his own witty comparison. From a living room chair across the coffee table, Adam Fleming didn't so much as crack a smile. He wanted answers, the exact details as to why his son had just come home a bruised and bloody mess. Elbows propped on the arms of the chair, hands folded together with the teepee of his index fingers pressed under his lower lip, his grave pose reflected his mood. "A friendly chat" is the phrase the cop had used to get an invitation to sit on the Flemings' couch. From upstairs, down the hallway, and through the closed bathroom door, Adam heard water running in the sink, Helen's, "Hold still," and then Simon's snotty, "I'll do it myself!"

"Happens to white kids every day at Dexter," Clark said.

"Not to my son, ever again. I'd like a word with this Frank Tucker and his folks."

"Makes two of us, Reverend. Jeez, now there's a dumb thug—leaves his coat for a calling card."

Clark's massive hands, toying with the checkerboard rim of the hat in his lap, reminded Adam of extrathick meat cleavers. He watched the cop glance around at the mismatched antique furniture bought on the cheap at Goodwill and the Salvation Army, or even scavenged from alleys, and walls that were replastered and sanded in places but still in need of primer and paint.

"Interesting place you got here, Reverend. A work in progress, huh?" Clark's jovial expression dropped a notch. "Not that it's any of my business, but I just got to ask, why would you send your kid to a school like Dexter?"

Adam leaned back into his chair to gain a few more inches between himself and his guest. "That's the school district we live in."

"Yeah, but your kid seems awfully bright to me. Why not send him to Lane?"

"An all-boys vocational school?" Adam asked. Lane was the only other public school option still left open by the board of education. "Those military-strict rules at Lane— getting suspended just for having hair too long or because your shirttails weren't tucked in—aren't my family's educational style. Besides, Helen and I like the diversity at . . . listen, I really do appreciate you giving my son a ride home."

"To serve and protect," Clark said.

"So I'm told," Adam returned. He'd gotten clubbed over the head by a cop at an antiwar demonstration in Lincoln Park during the Democratic Convention—nothing four stitches in Grant Hospital's emergency room couldn't fix.

"I'll drop in on Dr. Jursak over at Dexter, let him know what happened, and ask what he intends to do about it," Adam said.

Clark humphed. "You think a principal who's got that much trouble on his plate can track down and punish every Tom, Dick, and gangbanger? Lots of these punks don't even go to their classes, so finding them at school is like looking for a missing needle in a haystack. Besides, we're talking a two-day suspension for Mr. Poor Underprivileged, tops. That your idea of justice, Reverend?"

"Wrong is wrong, underprivileged or not."

"Exactly!" Clark said. "So how's about another option?"

"Such as?"

"Mine. I'll see to it that Tucker gets an extracurricular lesson in cause and effect—*his* cause and *my* effect. Not like your boy couldn't use some looking after. You do understand that Dexter is sort of a dangerous place for a white kid, don't you?"

"Let's call it a school that's definitely a work in progress," Adam said. As he and Helen could almost never pry a word about Dexter out of Simon, and their son had never come home from school visibly harmed until that very day, Adam wasn't about to let an obvious racist sway his opinion one way or the other.

"And why would you do that, take such special interest in Simon?"

"Like I told you, to serve and protect."

"I'm sure Simon can look out for himself just fine."

"Like he did today?"

"Look," Adam said, "I'm not at all interested in making a bad situation worse. Don't forget, Tucker's just a boy, too."

"Yep, just a misguided youth." Clark let his sarcasm hang between them for a moment, and then grinned. "OK. Your son, your call. Just remember, it's the scars that don't always show on a kid that can cause the most permanent damage."

"I'll keep that in mind, Officer." Adam watched Clark survey the room again with a keen eye.

"Yep, it's works in progress that keep us all so damn busy. I'll bet it takes a pretty penny to whip a big house like this into shape. How's business going for you over at"—Clark snapped his fingers a couple of times as though he was trying to jog his memory—"the Body Politic?"

How, Adam wondered, *does this cop know so much about me?*

"They tell me you've been having some legal problems over there lately."

"Who are *they?*"

"Oh, little birdies down at the Eighteenth Precinct."

Adam's stare turned guarded. "Is that right?"

"Yep, right as rain."

"Birdies in the Red Squad, I suppose?" Adam knew full well that the Red Squad, more officially known as the Subversive Section of Chicago Police Intelligence, kept a watch on any individuals or organizations that they deemed subversive. This included social activists like himself, religious and civil rights groups, artists, black power advocates, neighborhood organizations, and many others. Sometimes he suspected that his phone was tapped or maybe even the house was bugged.

"Red, blue, purple—I don't birdie discriminate," Clark said. "What's a smart guy like you doing renting to a bunch of idiots like Rising-Up Rage?"

"There's a law that says who I can and can't rent to? You'd think birdies would have more important things to do, like chasing criminals, than harassing a small not-for-profit businessman like me."

"That's one way of thinking." Clark's fair-minded tone insinuated that there were other ways of thinking, too. "I suppose you're going to tell me that you aren't friends with John Lange, either, that communist biology teacher over at Dexter?"

Adam hesitated. "I've crossed paths with John a few times. He's not any more thrilled than I am with Urban Renewal tearing down homes and pushing poor people out of the neighborhood."

"Can't stop progress, Reverend."

"What's so wrong with *humane* progress?"

"And how's about Bobo Rodriquez, leader of the Young Saints street gang? He a friend of yours, too?"

"The Saints have changed to a political organization," Adam corrected, and wondered, *Who the hell is this cop?* "I make it my business to know lots of community leaders, whether I always agree with them or not. Is there a problem with that?"

"And I suppose you cross paths with Fred Hampton, too?"

"The chairman of the Black Panther Party?" Adam asked. "Can't say I've ever had the pleasure."

Clark humphed again. "*The pleasure?* You know, if the Panthers want to shoot their mouths off about the violent overthrow of the government, the government might not turn the other cheek. Is that so complicated?"

"From what I hear," Adam said, "Hampton advocates the right to bear arms for self-defense. That's a hell of a lot different than . . . are we about done here?"

"There I go, wearing out my welcome. Bad habit, I'm afraid." Clark scootched forward on the couch, ready to leave. "Tell you what. I'm going to put in a good word for you to the birdies. Know why?"

"Haven't the foggiest."

"Because hard as it might be for you to believe, I respect you. The question is, can you keep an open enough mind to respect me?"

"Sure."

With an exaggerated wink, Clark continued, "And I will not under any circumstances look out for your son, fair enough?"

Adam felt a disturbing relief sneak into his tense shoulders. "Look out for him same as you would anyone else."

"Deal," Clark said, and offered his hand across the table. Adam politely grabbed it, but the cop's firm shake, bordering on painful, lasted longer than most.

12

Paranoia Will Destroy Ya

No sooner was Clark gone than Adam heard Helen's flats clacking through the dining room, his study, and into the living room, where the green carpeting muted her arrival. Her outfit of navy surplus bell-bottom jeans and muslin fuchsia blouse imported from India reminded Adam that his wife had gone fashionably hippy. She went over to the couch, sank into the same impression Clark had left in the feather cushions, and seemed at risk of crumpling under the weight of her own gloom.

"Good thing I took a sick day." An artist, Helen occasionally stole time from teaching in a public primary school to work on her latest charcoal drawing or acrylic painting in her basement studio.

"Is he all right?" Adam, having just escorted Clark to the stairs, now returned to the chair he'd been sitting in earlier.

"No, but he'll live. You ready for this? Simon told me that a black kid was about to hit him over the head with a board when that cop showed up."

"Hit him with a what?"

"B-O-A-R-D. That's all I could get out of him before he locked himself in his room."

Adam still didn't believe his ears. "A board?" Clark must have either forgotten to tell him that detail or missed it altogether.

"If you make me say it one more time . . ."

"I better go up there," Adam said.

Helen signaled with her hand *Not so fast.* "Trust me. He doesn't need anyone else interrogating him right now."

"You're right." Adam let a moment pass, then changing the subject—"Do you ever get the feeling that our house is, well . . . bugged?"

"Why on earth would you think—"

"That cop, that's why. I find it just a little too weird how much he knows about me—that I'm friends with John Lange and Bobo Rodriquez, and how the city's putting the screws to me at the Body Politic."

"It's not like you keep a low profile," Helen said. "Anyone could ask around and find out—"

"Maybe. All I'm saying is, I got the distinct feeling that this Clark fellow could have told me what color underwear I have on."

"Hmmm," Helen mused. "We did let a draft dodger spend the night here on his way to Canada, remember? That's aiding and abetting, but is it really the kind of crime that draws—"

"Shhhhhh!"

"Oh." Helen put her finger to her lips and checked herself. They listened to the silence listening back at them. Keeping her voice down, Helen asked, "So what are we going to do about Simon?"

"Don't know. Maybe we should reconsider sending him to Lane."

"Absolutely not." Helen's tone threw caution to the wind. "That school grooms boys for Vietnam."

———————

Adam drove to the Body Politic, spent the rest of the afternoon working, and returned home in the early evening. He skipped his usual routine of decompressing by reading the *Chicago Daily News* and instead took the back stairs straight up to his son's closed bedroom door. He knocked, got no answer, and then tried the knob.

"Simon, open up."

Still no answer.

"Let me in, please."

"I'm sleeping."

"I just want to talk to you."

A millennium seemed to pass before Adam heard the lock bolt slide, but in the instant it took him to swing the door open, Simon had sprinted back to bed. Adam saw the last jiggle of the settling mattress, the boy's curled back facing him.

"Starting to get dark in here, don't you think?" Adam thought about flipping on the lights, and then decided against it. He went around to the other side of the bed and sat down on the edge of it, his knee nearly touching the boy's chin.

"Rough day, huh? You want to tell me what happened?"

A glassy eye blinked.

"No?" Adam put his hand on Simon's shoulder and gave it a comforting squeeze. From deep within his son, he felt a subterranean ripple, but not a muscle on the boy moved. Was this the same kid who at the age of five had gone through an agonizing phase of asking, "Dad, you'd never leave me, right?"

Through the window looking out over the backyard's cottonwood tree and alley, Adam spotted a golden crescent moon, as sharp as a sickle blade, about to clear rooftops and start arching across the cobalt night. While staring at it, he suddenly reflected that the precious commodity of time seemed to be slipping away from him faster and faster. In September, he'd turn forty. He took a huge breath and then emptied his lungs.

"You can stay home from school tomorrow. Did you hear about the student boycott that starts on Monday? Your mother and I want you to be a part of it and meet with students at the Church of the Three Crosses. John Lange's volunteered to supervise. Maybe if the community can force the board of ed. to make a few changes at Dexter, black kids won't feel the need . . ." He gave Simon's shoulder another squeeze. He would never leave his son. "When Mom calls for you, I want you to come down and join us for dinner. I'll make sure that Beth and Dawn don't ask a lot of questions about what happened to your face."

Waiting a moment before he got up to leave, Adam took one last look at that blade of rising moon. High above, a handful of stars now seemed like they were trying to scatter away from it, on the run.

13

Demands

"OK, PEOPLE, LET'S GET STARTED." At the head of a table that almost filled the small church choir room, Mr. Lange waited for the thirteen white students to come to order.

"You may or may not have already heard that Assistant School Superintendent Betsey Stewart has rejected every one of the Community Boycott Coalition's demands."

Simon, keeping a low profile in his chair to delay the inevitable moment when someone would ask him how he'd gotten his shiner and scabby, bruised lip, heard groans. "In other words," Mr. Lange continued, "she's a bitch."

Groans switched to laughter, and Simon thought, *Tell it like it is! He's so cool!* Earlier, Simon had even overheard a couple of students chitchatting with Mr. Lange call him by his first name.

"As some of you already know, the CBC is organized into three caucuses: black, Latino, and white. Each one is meeting today to come up with new demands to add to our original list. Who wants to get the ball rolling?"

Directly across the table from Simon, Louis looked bored. *Crazy's here*, Simon thought. He watched Louis tilt back in his metal folding chair and take a deep drag off his cigarette. Then the boy began shooting smoke rings from the cannon of his lips, squinting as he watched each of the expanding halos play follow-the-leader on their doomed

journey to the ceiling. Give the manly stubble on his cleft chin another
couple of days' growth, and it would have qualified for a beard.

"How about study halls?" This came from a pasty-faced kid
squeezed between Mr. Lange and Louis at a table corner. He had an
odd nervous twitch that made him look like he was either cringing
or winking. "I say get rid of study halls so that we can get out of
school earlier."

"Or gym," a plump girl said. "Since when did jumping jacks have
anything to do with how prepared I am for college?"

Simon straightened up, felt himself blush, and said, "Why should
we have to take a foreign language? It's not like I plan on living in
Mexico or Paris."

"I disagree." This came from a girl sitting next to Louis. With her
appealing face wedged between sheets of limp red hair, she leveled a
dismissive look across the table at Simon. "Most Europeans can speak
several languages. No wonder they all think Americans are lazy."

Simon sank again and thought, *Eat my second language, puta.*

"Ann's right," another boy piped up. "It's a big world out there
beyond English." Someone else complained about the horrible cafeteria
food.

"OK, but if we demand better food, we should also demand that
the janitors get off their asses and start supplying bathrooms with
toilet paper." The kid cringe-winked. "Am I the only one here who's
had to go from class to class with his asshole caked shut?"

"Ewww!" Dia squealed from the far end of the table. "Gary, do
you mind sparing us the details?" Simon sneaked a peek at her and
noticed the downy fluff on her cheeks. He'd been avoiding her ever
since that day he'd chickened out in front of those Latin Kings.

"Folks!" Mr. Lange rapped his knuckles on the table. "I think we're
getting off track. Are these the kind of demands that prevent Stewart
and her board of education cronies from keeping our community
divided along lines of race?"

The girl who hated calisthenics said that a greater share of the curriculum in American history should be devoted to slavery. "Otherwise, we might as well rename the class what it really is—bogus white history."

"Hah!" Mr. Lange pitched forward. "Good one, Donna! I think we can all agree that slavery deserves to be treated like something more than a footnote."

"Exactly," Ann agreed. "I mean, what's more historically relevant: the genocide committed against black people in this country, or how a bunch of pilgrims were too dumb to survive the winter at Jamestown?"

Louis, looking bored as ever, spat more than blew out a stream of smoke.

"Now we're moving, folks." Mr. Lange nodded approvingly. "Will someone here volunteer to play secretary?"

The discussion shifted to composing demands on paper. Simon let his eyes wander to Dia again. He admired her socially confident manner and how she stayed engaged in the discussion by chipping in with an occasional "I agree" or "You got that right" or "Good one!" He swallowed hard, in love, and for a while heard only snippets of what anyone said as demands were debated, modified, voted up or voted down. High on the powder-blue wall behind Dia, a golden-framed portrait of Jesus stared down at him with a look of pure serenity.

"We should demand that the board of ed. stop using standardized tests that are culturally rigged to keep blacks and Latinos out of honors classes."

"Why not get rid of testing and grades all together? Pass/fail is the only fair way to go."

Louis landed with a bang on the front legs of his chair. "I got a demand, John."

"Let's hear it." A magnanimous sweep of the teacher's hand gave Louis the floor. "I was starting to think you only intended to communicate with the rest of us through smoke signals."

Louis quipped, "Better smoke signals than a forked tongue, ke-mo-sah-bee." He squished the last of his cigarette into the graveyard of butts already laid to rest in a glass ashtray on the table. "Here's the deal. I want someone to tell Jesse Wilks to stop stealing my lunch out of our locker every day."

A girl as thin as a waif sitting next to Simon hung her head, tried to hold in a laugh, and ended up snorting.

"He's not funny, Claudia," Ann said. "He's pathetic." Then to Louis on her right, "I'm tired of you always turning everything into a joke."

"Who's joking? List it as demand number one: Jesse Wilks will stop being a thief."

"I agree with Ann," said a girl next to Dia. Her lips, always slightly pursed, gave her a look of having been born indignant. "This is a serious meeting about serious issues."

Louis imitated a parrot: "*Proooock*, I agree with Ann, I agree with Ann, *prooooock*. Carla, why don't you just get it over with and lick Ann's clit."

"Fuck you!" both girls screamed.

"Oh, I get it. Siamese lesbians."

"Look," Mr. Lange said. "If you're just out to piss people off, I'm afraid—"

"What?" Louis asked innocently. "Clits, boycotts, and revolution don't mix? Personally, I think that's open for debate."

"Male chauvinist pig," Ann said. "Louis, why don't you do us all a favor? Take a few more drugs and OD."

"Now, now," Mr. Lange intervened. "Can we just get back to our demands?"

Louis rose from his seat and took a deep bow. "Certainly, my lord." From his overall gawkiness, Simon wondered if maybe a recent growth spurt had left Louis a stranger in his own body. Extending an arm out to assume the pose of a statesman, the boy began, "My fellow honkies, I demand that from this day forth, the Cobra Stones and Gangster Disciples stop shaking me down for free reefers. They can pay fifty cents apiece for them just like everyone else."

Some students groaned.

"Hey, what am I?" Louis asked. "Drug welfare?"

Claudia snort-laughed again, and a boy next to her haw-hawed. Then, noticing the glowering disapproval from Donna, Gary, Ann, and several others, he told everyone, "You got to admit that's funny."

"No, that's racist," Mr. Lange said. "Louis, you of all people should damn well know better."

"Should I?"

"Yeah, you should. I'm sick and tired of hearing black people and welfare mentioned in the same breath. They work hard for their money, when they can find work at all. And if you're stupid enough to deal dope, you better be smart enough to deal with the consequences. Now, I suggest you either get with what we're trying to accomplish here or stop wasting everyone's time and go on back to school."

"Back to school?" Louis repeated. He looked thunderstruck and fell into his seat. "Can you keep a secret, John?" He cupped a hand to his mouth and stage-whispered so that everyone could easily hear him. "It's really dangerous for us honky students at school."

"All the more reason to do whatever we can to let blacks know we're on their side," offered Gary.

"You're white, you got a weird-ass tic, and you can't play basketball for shit," Louis said. "Soul brothers aren't about to let you be on their side."

Gary flipped him the finger, but Louis had already turned away to look around the table at the other students. His eyes landed on Simon, and he let out a whistle.

"That's a mean-looking shiner. Lemme guess. You got it because you're on their side?"

Simon would much later in life come to think of this moment as having had far more destiny in its sails than chance. He went tongue-tied, braced himself, and then managed, "What's it to you?"

"Yeah," Dia said. "Leave Simon alone!" She snatched what looked like an empty pack of Kent cigarettes off the table, crumpled it into a ball, and whipped it at Louis from one end of the table to the other. As the paper and cellophane projectile flew several feet wide of its mark, Carla yelled, "Hey, I still had a couple of cigs in that pack!"

"Awww, what's a matter, Dia?" Louis asked. "You sweet on shiner-boy?"

"Better him than a loser like you."

Simon didn't know whether to preen or go hide in a hole. Louis trained his eyes on him.

"How about it, Romeo? Had a little misunderstanding with the Negroes?"

"The correct word is *black*," Mr. Lange said.

"*Colored, Negro, black*—bet'cha next year it'll be something else."

"At least I'm not a racist," Simon said.

"Maybe you should leave, Louis." Mr. Lange pointed his thumb over his shoulder at the open door. "Come back when you're ready to belong here."

"Yeah, or when you're ready to appreciate free speech," Louis returned.

"I'll give you some free speech." Ann raised her hand. "All those in favor of the male chauvinist racist pig leaving?"

Though the meaning of the word *chauvinist*—just then coming into feminist vogue—eluded Simon, he voted in lockstep with the over-whelming majority.

"Opposed?"

Simon saw Claudia's hand rise a few inches off her lap, hesitate, and then drop.

"Thirteen to zero." In Ann's capacity as secretary for the day, she picked up her pencil and dutifully recorded the tally in her spiral notebook. "See you around, pig."

Louis hung his head and shook it woefully. "This sure as shit isn't very white of you guys."

Mr. Lange rhetorically asked, "Like *white* ever meant *fair* in this country?"

Claudia cleared her throat. "I abstained."

"Fine." Ann noted the new tally in her spiral. "Eleven for, zero against, and one abstention. Big surprise there; everyone knows Claudia has the hots for Louis."

Timid or not, Claudia countered, "And you've practically let every boy at Dexter lick your clit."

"That's a fucking lie!"

"Ladies, please! I never lick and tell," Louis said. "However, I did once pleasure a piggette, two-faced, nameless bitch in this room."

"In your dreams, asshole."

"Folks, enough with the insults," John said. "We're wasting valuable time."

Louis popped up from his chair. "I'm outa here."

"Good riddance," Ann said.

"You don't have anyone but yourself to blame for getting kicked out," Gary added.

Louis bent down close to Gary so that they were practically nose to nose, and imitated the other boy's cringe-winked twitch. "I'll miss you, too, you spastic fuck."

"That's mean," someone said.

"We're better off without you."

"Yeah, get lost."

Louis zipped his coat in an easygoing manner that Simon interpreted as *Kiss my ass.*

"Before I leave, I got one last demand."

Ann folded her arms across her chest. "Save it for your next KKK meeting."

"It's a real humdinger," Louis said.

"Are you deaf *and* racist?" Carla asked.

"I'm going to have to ask you to respect the group's decision, Louis," Mr. Lange said.

"How about you, Simon?" Louis gave him a quick once-over. "With a mincemeat face like that, you just might want to cosponsor this demand with me."

Before Simon could distance himself with a curt *No thanks*, Louis slammed his fists on the table and sent coffee splashing out of Styrofoam cups. He raged, "I demand that the niggers stop fucking with us!"

In the stunned silence that followed, Simon glanced around to gauge people's reactions. More than a few students appeared pinned back in their chairs. Only Gary was hunched over the table, hands covering his ears like they refused to stop ringing. "Whoa," he said. "Not cool."

Mr. Lange, looking grim, told Louis, "Get out."

The boy snapped a heel-clicking salute. "It's been real." As he swaggered out of the room, his happy-go-lucky voice resonated off the sanctuary walls:

Racism, racism go away
Come again some other day

No one spoke, everyone listening to Louis's work boots pounding down the stairs. Soon one of the two heavy front doors squealed open on its hinges, then shut. Even the sharp click of the latch traveled up to the choir room.

"Wow," Mr. Lange said. "What's gotten into Louis? Last year, at student meetings we held to try and calm things down during the riots, he was so reasonable and articulate—a born leader. This year . . ."

"Drugs," Dia said. "He's always either stoned, tripping, or on speed. I'm really worried about him."

"Must be popping racism and chauvinism pills, too," Ann said.

"Maybe if your father had been—" Dia started to say.

"Uh-uh," Mr. Lange interrupted. "That's Louis's personal business."

Simon was dying for more details.

———

By eleven o'clock, the white caucus's list totaled eight demands. Ann hunt-and-peck typed them on a manual typewriter in the church office, and then Gary ran off five hundred copies on a mimeograph machine. At just past twelve, they broke for lunch with the "battle plan" to meet two hours later in front of Dexter and distribute leaflets to students attending classes, with the hope of educating them into joining the boycott.

Just as Simon was about to file out of the choir room behind several other students, Mr. Lange suddenly broke off a conversation he'd been having with Gary next to a bookcase lined with hymnals, and said, "Hey, Simon! I like what you had to say during the meeting. Tell your father hello for me."

"You know my dad?"

"Sure. He and I get around in the community. See you back here again tomorrow?"

"Yeah, see you . . . John."

When Simon reached the vestibule at the bottom of the stairs, he heard someone racing down after him.

"Wait up!"

He felt a shudder in his chest but turned around to meet Dia with a facade of cool indifference.

"Want to come over to my house for lunch?"

"Nah," Simon said. Just the idea of having to hold up his end of a conversation with Dia for two whole hours without somehow making a fool of himself . . . *No way.* "I'm taking the bus home." Immediately, he saw the disappointment in her eyes, watched it pool into hurt and then level off. She reached up, touched the bruise on his lip, and left her finger pressed to it for a moment. Heat flashed down his neck and got trapped under the broad collar of his olive-green shirt.

"What happened to your . . ." Then Dia must have reconsidered why she should give a damn and dropped her hand. "Yeah, OK, fine. Here." She shoved a folded, torn-off piece of notebook paper, one she must have already intended to give him, into his shirt pocket. Then with her head held high, she flounced toward the front doors and pushed one of them wide open. A cold breeze disturbed flyers posted on a bulletin board. She stormed out into the bright day, the door slowly shutting behind her. From outside on the church's cement steps, Simon heard her yell down the block, "Peter, wait up!" He leaned his forehead hard against the door. *Fucking blew it again.*

He lingered in the vestibule. Taking the piece of paper out of his shirt pocket, he unfolded the crease and then admired the clean lines of the penmanship. It was Dia's phone number.

14

Dynamite

SIMON STARTED UP the sidewalk on Sedgwick. Mounds of old snow along the curb glittered black with grime. He passed three flats and Connie's Bar and Grill, which had a neon Pabst Blue Ribbon sign in the window. Not until he heard the squeal of brake pads on tire rims did he notice Louis on his ten-speed pulling up right next to him at the curb. They both came to a halt.

"Hey." Louis dismounted with a smooth leg-lift over his saddle.

Simon thought, *What's he want?* He gave a quick wave and started up the block again. *Nothing I give shit about.* The next thing he knew, Louis had fallen into step beside him and was guiding his Schwinn along by its racing handlebars.

"Your dad runs the Body Politic, right?"

"Maybe," Simon said.

"That place is so cool! I saw the Rock Cantata there three times! And your dad's a Presbyterian minister, big into civil rights?"

"Maybe."

"And *maybe* I'm sorry I fucked with you at the meeting. I was just trying to make a point. By the way, I'm a PK, too."

"So Dia told me."

"Pres, same as you," Louis said. Then, moving on to Dia, "Man, she is hot. If I were you, I'd jump on that shit before she changes her mind."

"You really think she likes me?"

As the rapid clicking from Louis's bike kept time to their swift, in-sync pace, Louis gave Simon a sly smirk. "I think she's already got your sperm halfway up her pussy."

Simon took that for a yes. Then he wondered, *Is this kid glomming onto me or just being nice?* They passed Turin Bicycle Shop and Yashin's Corner Grocery, where a huge sign in the window advertised Glory milk for ninety-five cents a gallon. At the busy six-way intersection of Sedgwick, Armitage, and Lincoln avenues, they waited at a corner bus stop, Simon with his back against the sign pole.

"Say, wanna come over to my house for lunch? It's close enough to walk," Louis said. "You like ham and cheese?"

"I'm more of a chipped beef man."

"Make it bologna? Plus, I've got a new batch of homemade smoke bombs hot off the assembly line. We can have a war with them in my backyard."

Simon found himself staring across the intersection at the sliding glass door to the emergency room entrance of Augustana Hospital. He weighed Louis's generous bologna/pyromaniac offer against the boy's reputation for being crazy. *What the hell.*

Louis lived on the top floor of a two-flat on Mohawk Street. Not a blade of grass grew in his small backyard, and the frozen dirt had been trampled smooth as polished clay. Armed with arsenals of Louis's smoke bombs in their coat pockets, the boys took up opposite ends of the yard and reenacted last summer's Chicago Democratic Convention riots between police and antiwar demonstrators.

"Off the pigs!" Simon yelled. Using a cigarette lighter that Louis had lent him, he lit a bomb's fuse, which was wrapped tightly in electrical tape and only a couple of inches long. Then he cocked his arm and waited a moment for what Louis called his "secret recipe" of chemicals to ignite. When blue smoke began to furiously hiss and bellow, Simon lobbed the bomb sidearm like a hand grenade across the yard. "Take that, you Nazi pigs. The streets belong to the people!"

"Kill da hippies!" Louis screamed in a *dese* and *dose* Mayor Daley voice. "You's are all outside agitators come here to destroy our wunnerful city of Chicaga." Using his lighter on a bomb's fuse, he returned fire. In a cat-and-mouse pattern of charge and retreat, the boys whipped their ordnance at each other.

"Fucking draft dodgers!"

"Long live Students for a Democratic Society, and the Black Panthers!"

"Antiwar scum!"

"Nixon lover!"

"Longhair faggots!"

"Down with the establishment!"

"Love your country or leave it!"

"Ho Chi Minh for president!"

"The only good Viet Cong is a dead Viet Cong!"

The battle raged. Simon watched plume after plume of smoke drift out over a shed painted fire-engine red, the alley, adjacent backyards, and garages, through telephone wires, over rooftops, and into the great American beyond. Trying a change in tactics, he approached the understood demilitarized zone at the center of the yard, solemnly lifted his hand, and gave Louis the peace sign.

"Make love not war, my brother pigs. Can we not put aside our hatred and live as one?"

Louis, sticking close to the first-floor apartment's back porch, grabbed his crotch—"Suck on my love!"

The battle resumed, flared, ebbed with one or the other combatant succumbing to "tear gas" and collapsing to his knees next to a bomb. It would spin from the pressurized, spewing force of its smoke. After a fit of coughing and choking, Simon miraculously recovered, sprang to his feet, lit another bomb, and hurled it.

"Flower power!"

"Pinko!"

"Gestapo!"

"Kiss my silent majority ass!

"Hey, hey, LBJ, how many kids did you kill today?"

"The whole world's watching!"

"Drop the bomb! No more Nam!"

By the time the boys had exhausted their ammo, wads of burnt electrical tape lay scattered everywhere.

"That was fun!" Simon smelled the reek of chemicals in his clothes. "Got any more bombs?"

Louis slowly picked himself up from the ground after a ghastly performance that had ended with his own death rattle. He dusted himself off. "I was going to save what I have left of my stockpile for the fourth of July, but OK. Wait here."

He ran up the stairs to the second-floor porch, quietly cracked the door open, and slipped inside his apartment. It was the second time he had left Simon alone in the backyard. The first time, he'd gone inside to retrieve a paper bag full of his smoke bombs, the cigarette lighters, and a couple of sandwiches. He'd said that his mom, home with the flu, had forbidden him to let anyone into their apartment. Still, as Simon paced the yard to keep his toes warm inside his boots, he thought, *Like he's hiding something.*

A minute later, Louis tromped back down the stairs carrying a life-sized dummy.

"Whaddya think?" He held out his "friend" for Simon's inspection. A pair of old jeans and a ratty gray sweatshirt stuffed with wadded-up newspaper had no bendable joints, feet, and hands, but what the dummy lacked in anatomical features it made up for with its brawny chest. Two round scraps of sheet, stitched together by hand and also paper stuffed, served as a head with a face crudely drawn in black Magic Marker. What appeared to be a king-sized version of one of Louis's smoke bombs—as thick and long as a roll of quarters—was secured by a loop of twine at the throat.

"Cool!" Simon said. The dummy, complete with a full set of horsey teeth, kept leering at him with what seemed honest-to-God intelligence.

"Watch this." Louis carried his guinea pig pal over to the shed at the back of the yard and propped him up against the padlocked door. After one last wicked grin over his shoulder at Simon, he flipped opened his lighter, lit the bomb's fuse, and took off running. Just as Simon began to suspect a scheme far bigger than making smoke, Louis pulled up short next to him, crouched, and plugged each of his ears with a finger.

BA-LOOM!

The blast not only decapitated the dummy, it also blew a hole the size of a grapefruit in the door of the shed. Newspaper confetti rained down over the yard, birds squawked and scattered from trees, and a chorus of dogs barked from blocks around. The headless figure lay prone, the neckband and shoulders of its sweatshirt ripped to shreds and powder-burned. Simon held his hands over his ringing ears, in a mild state of shock. "You asshole," he said, but he knew the joke was on him.

Louis, doubled over laughing, caught his breath long enough to ask, "Did you shit your pants?" The storm door on the third-floor porch of the house next door flew open, and a man in a dago T-shirt, his shoulders every bit as hairy as his chest, charged out to the railing.

"Hey, how many times I gotta tell you? I'm going to call the cops you keep messing with that stuff! You'll blow up the whole damn neighborhood!"

Despite the ringing, Simon heard the doorknob up on Louis's porch jiggle.

"Shit!" Louis said. "My mom!"

As the boys fled toward the gangway between houses, Louis flipped his neighbor the finger.

"Louie?" It was the tired voice of a woman at her parental wit's end. "I told you not to make any more of those—"

"The cops!" the man shouted again. "Smart-ass punk!"

When the boys reached the front of the two-flat, Louis collapsed on the stairs and beat his fist against one of the wooden steps. "Was that the coolest or what?"

Simon paced the walkway that led from the stairs to the front yard gate and expected a squad car to come flying down the residential street any second.

"You better tell your mom I didn't know anything about that bomb." Then Simon's pyro curiosity got the better of him, and he asked, "Where'd you learn how to make it?"

"From a friend," Louis said, cagey. "Getting the chemicals is the tricky part, but if you know where to look through mail order . . . I'm pretty sure I can make a bomb that'll put a stick of dynamite to shame."

"Dynamite?" Simon let out a hard puff of air. "Better be careful."

Whether Louis decided to take the advice to heart or not, he cocked his ear and seemed alerted by an intuitive sixth sense for danger.

"Gotta go."

He bounded up the stairs, dug for a key in a pocket of his Levi bell-bottoms, and unlocked the front door to his apartment. Tiptoeing into the vestibule, he quietly shut the door behind him. It took Simon a moment to register that he was gone. Whether Louis intended to deny bomb culpability to his mother or simply get her wrath over and done with, Simon didn't know. He slung open the wrought-iron gate and started fast down the sidewalk, even though he had more than enough time to get to Dexter and rendezvous with the rest of the while student caucus. *Dynamite! Kid's definitely loony.* But no matter how hard Simon tried, he couldn't wipe the smile off his face.

15

Black Power

"MY NAME IS SHERI PHILLIPS, I'm a senior at Dexter, and the black caucus has elected me chair of this boycott meeting."

The girl's straight-shouldered poise reflected her militant tone. In the unfinished small basement of Saint Matthew's, a church just off Orleans Street and at the "doorstep" of the Cabrini Green Projects, people who were sprinkled about on rows of folding chairs came to order.

"First off, I would like to welcome the white caucus to our community this evening and to thank them for they support in what we all trying to accomplish—"

"Sheeeeit," came a voice from the back of the room. "Ain't no one ask them for no support!"

Everyone, including Simon and Adam, who were seated in the middle of the second row, turned. At the rear of the basement and close to one of the stone foundation walls, a man was leaning forward in his chair with his elbows on his knees and hands dangling between his legs, as one might casually sit playing a game of checkers. A severely widow-peaked hairline made his forehead look huge to Simon.

"Like I was saying, I want to welcome them and thank them for—"

"What you talking about *thank them*? We work hard to keep trash out of our community!" In the lenses of the man's glasses, the reflection of a naked light bulb from a ceiling fixture gave him two white-hot pupils.

Sheri rapped the soup spoon she was using for a gavel three sharp times against a table substituting for a lectern. "Order, Mr. Clayton.

You keep talking without me recognizing you. We into the second week of the boycott, and hardly no one boycotting no more. If the community going to beat the board of education at its own game, we gots to stick together."

"Sister," Clayton said, "you don't think I got something worth saying, then it high time get the house nigga out your mind."

Shouts of "Right on!" and "Tell it like it is, brother!" came from a scattering of Clayton supporters. Then a man in the front row, sapling lean and middle aged, told them, "Y'all shut up! Sheri running this here meeting like we agreed on yesterday!" Simon recognized him as a teacher's aide. He often monitored hallways at Dexter and shooed students to quit dawdling and get to class before the bell rang.

"Awww, what's a matter, Marcus?" Clayton asked. "You think maybe 'cause you conk your hair, the white man going to think you white and make you Dexter's principal? And even if he do, what you going to put on your office door—Principal Uncle Tom?"

"Nigga, you don't tell me where I should work or how I can wear my hair!"

"You shucking and jiving for the white man," Clayton returned, "but I'm the nigga?"

"Order!" Sheri smacked the spoon against the table again and seemed to brace her backbone for war. "Just 'cause you stacked this meeting with your friends don't make you chairman. We going to show the white caucus the same respect they showing us."

"*Respect?*" Clayton belly laughed.

Simon watched the man called Marcus start to his feet, but a woman next to him put a restraining hand on his shoulder and then got up herself.

"Horace Clayton, I've had to listen to you and your big mouth all of my life. You're not doing anything but making me ashamed of how we're treating our friends."

"Sister Rose, you damn right; I knew you when your mama used to wash your mouth out with soap every time you talked what she call 'ghetto.' Now here you is all grown up, wearing them fancy Marshall Field's clothes, putting that red rouge on your high-yellow skin, and talking white."

"I wasn't aware I had to apologize to you for the way I talk, the way I dress, the makeup I choose to wear, and certainly not for the way my mother saw fit to raise me."

"Sister, it's the black you so ashamed of that deserve your apology, not me."

"Y'all out of order!"

Clayton yelled at Sheri, "Who you calling out of order!" The loud scrape of metal chair legs against the cement floor told Simon that the man must have jumped to his feet. "It whitey who out of order! What they come here to talk about, anyway, some of their jive-ass nonviolence? They put us in chains and then preach nonviolence; rape our women and children, but can't get enough of that sweet nonviolence; lynch brothers from lampposts and tell us, 'Y'all better stick to nonviolence.' When is black folks going to take the *pretty-please* out our vocabulary and realize that the white man is the most violent, despicable devil who ever lived? He so dumb, he scratching he head going, 'Nigga, why you uppity?'"

"That's right!"

"Testify, brother!"

"Mmm-hmm."

"Not taking it no more!"

The anger all around Simon as well as the heat from a decrepit boiler tucked in a corner of the basement was causing his armpits to swim in sweat.

"Slavery over," Sheri told Clayton. "We talking about the boycott."

"You damn right, sister, and we don't need whitey to help us take what belongs to us. We march into Dexter as a community and tell all them honky teachers to go on home. We pull down a map of the world, point to the cradle of civilization, and say, 'Looky here, students. This be Africa. We going to talk about Africa today, we going to talk about Africa tomorrow, and we going to still be talking about Africa next month.' Then we tell the board of racist education, 'We's teaching, so where's our paychecks?'"

Sheri took a deep breath that insinuated she was close to calling it quits. "Mr. Clayton, we going to listen to what folks in the white caucus got to say whether you like it or not."

"Oh, we is, huh? OK, you the boss." Simon heard Clayton's chair rattle as the man must have sat in it again. "Whitey got something new to say? Let him say it."

Simon watched as eye contact darted around between whites in the audience to see who would answer Clayton's call. And then Ann, in an act of adolescent bravery that would forever earn her Simon's respect, slowly got up from her chair and said, "We really didn't come here tonight with a prepared statement. We just wanted to show our solidarity with the black and Latino caucuses and to see if we couldn't come up with ideas for how we can get more students to join in our fight against—"

"Honey," Clayton interrupted, "ain't no one here want your solidarity. It time for the black man to solidarity with hisself."

During another angry chorus of people shouting "Right on!" John Lange stood up.

"Look, we're just as interested in fighting racism as you are. Can't we focus on our common goals instead of stereotypes and beliefs that keep working-class people divided?"

"What I care about," Clayton said, "is the black class, not no working class."

Adam got up to speak, his head grazing the low basement ceiling.

"We're here in good faith to join with all those who feel that the board of education should be accountable to the needs of—"

"Ain't no good faith about it." The changed angle of Clayton's voice told Simon—without him daring to so much as look over his shoulder—that the black nationalist was on his feet again. People in the audience laughed derisively, applauded, or shouted out "Black power!"

"All right, forget good faith," Adam told Clayton. "Forget solidarity, the working class, the boycott, white or black. I'm asking you here tonight to talk to me as one man to another."

A hush fell over the meeting. It was the moment of statesmanship that Simon had been waiting for from his father. Clayton let out a "Hah!"

"Can't we at least do that?" Adam asked. "As a starting point? Talk to each other as equal human beings?"

Simon heard the boiler click off, and wind rattled a small window high on a wall. Finally, Clayton said, "I don't make deals with no guilt-ridden racist."

"You damn right!" someone yelled. "Sit your Abraham Lincoln ass down."

Adam gave Clayton a moment to reconsider. Then, with a shrug of disappointment, he took his seat. Sheri pounded with her spoon.

"Order! Y'all have to start following the rules and get recognized!"

Simon felt his father's defeat so strongly, it might as well have been his own.

————————

Soon the meeting broke up amid shouting and finger pointing. There hadn't been a single mutually agreed upon demand drafted to present to the school administration. In the cold night air, under the glow of a floodlight that lit the sidewalk from above the church's front doors, a faction from the meeting rehashed the failure of the CBC to unite. John Lange insisted Clayton was playing right into the ruling class's hands, Adam predicted that the man would eventually wear out his appeal to the black community, and Marcus Herns complained, "Every time we try to get something positive going, that son of a bitch got his own agenda." Someone else reported that the Latino caucus hadn't come to the meeting because they were still arguing about what their demands should be. Among the handful of white coalition students who had showed up for the meeting, Gary, Ann, and Donna, all hatless, looked close to shivering right out of their shoes. Simon was disappointed that Dia hadn't shown up or been to the Church of the Three Crosses for the last several days. After a week and a half without any tangible concessions from the board of education, many students were throwing in the boycott towel and returning to school. He put on his earmuffs and looked around at his foreign surroundings. That block of Monarch Street was lined with more vacant lots than houses and dead-ended against the deserted, snow-covered grounds of the Cabrini Green high-rises, ominous to him by reputation alone. Stacked rows of drawn shades, many of them backlit, served as the only clue that hundreds of tenants were at home.

"It's so frustrating," Ann said, and took a drag off her cigarette. Rose put her arm around the girl's shoulders.

"Don't go and let a fool like Horace Clayton give a strong young woman like you reason to quit fighting for what's right. You did good in there! And sister Sheri . . . whoa Jesus! Where is that girl? Must have gone home all hangdogged before I could tell her how proud I am of the way she wielded that spoon." Rose turned to Adam. "Just like old times, huh, Reverend? How long has it been?"

"Operation Encouragement," Adam said. It was a federally funded summer youth program that Adam had coordinated almost three years earlier. "I still remember kids raving about your improvisational theater class."

"My, but we had so much fun in Operation Encouragement, didn't we?" Rose asked. "All of those kids doing photography, creative writing, theater, dance, and drawing. They ate art up! Then Congress has the audacity to cut funds for a program that keeps our young folks off the streets. Since when is it good government to discourage encouragement?"

A minute or so later, Simon wandered over to the curb. Just above the labyrinth of project buildings, a half-moon looked close enough for him to grab and tuck inside the breast of his coat for safekeeping. Someone tapped him on the shoulder.

"Hotdog finally made it to the Greens, huh? I didn't know you was po-litical."

Happy to see Clyde's familiar, crooked smile, Simon raised his clenched fist. "Hell yes, I'm political. Were you at the meeting, too?"

"Got there late. Don't seem like I missed much. I used to hate all white folks just like Clayton do, but then I educated myself. They's good white folks, and they's bad. Mostly they bad, but that ain't no fault of yours, right?"

Clyde held out his palms, and Simon, appreciating that Clyde counted him among the few "good" whites, slapped him double-five.

"You know, us Black Assassins trying to be strictly po-litical, but we still end up gangbanging when someone mess with us or our associates." Giving Simon a long, baffled once-over, he shook his head. "Hotdog in the projects. Now I seen everything. You hip that when this boycott over, they going to be trouble at Dexter, right?"

"Who says?"

"I do. If the community can't get it together, you best believe the clubs—or, as you call them, *gangs*—has theirs together. And ain't no Disciple, Cobra Stone, or Deuces Wild give a gotdamn if you's po-litical. To them you just white."

"I can take care of myself," Simon said.

"Yeah, you po-litical, all right, and dumb, too. What you out to prove? Take my advice: when the shit go down at school, get your ass on home. What good you to the baseball team dead?"

"I'll be OK." Simon looked north out over blocks of vacant lots where concrete foundations and the skeletal frames for expensive town houses and condos had already begun to change the neighborhood landscape. People like his parents, John Lange, the white caucus members, Rose, Marcus Herns, and the entire working class were counting on him to tough it out at Dexter.

"Suit yourself," Clyde said. "Your funeral."

16

Baby and Me

"WHY THE HELL are you boycotting?"

"Why the hell are you not?"

Coming home from the Church of the Three Crosses, Simon had stopped off at Juan's house—a third-floor apartment in a six-flat on Racine. Atop a bunk bed that took up nearly half of the tiny room, they sat facing each other. From the ceiling fixture, the bluish glow of a black-light bulb (Juan said it made everything psychedelic) reflected off the whites of their eyes and teeth, and even the dust on Simon's V-neck wool sweater.

"I hope you're not expecting me to bring you up to speed in biology. And what's with Mr. Lange?" Juan asked. "If he's not blabbing about the ruling class, he's off boycotting with the niggers. Those of us who show up for class get stuck with a sub. You think that bow-tie-wearing motherfucker knows the first thing about photosynthesis? Dude's so geeky, I doubt he can find his own dick."

"The boycott's for the good of the entire community," Simon explained, "not just—"

A souped-up car thundered down Racine and drowned him out. Juan sprang off the bunk, landed cat-like on the floor, and lifted an edge of the window shade. The revving roar was already fading fast toward Oscar Mayer Elementary School on the next block north.

"There goes Donnie. I'd recognize the sound of that Hemi in his Road Runner anywhere—baddest set of wheels in Chicago."

Simon noticed that the sun had already dipped below a jagged line of crowded rooftops. Juan, bathed in a wedge of impending twilight, scanned the residential artery below. He'd long since changed out of his ROTC uniform and into his after-school "greaser" clothes—tight dago tee and green workpants, commonly referred to as baggies. To Simon, his friend's sculpted upper body seemed to be putting enough stress on his short, bowed legs to make them appear on the verge of snapping. The shade slipped from Juan's fingers, and the room turned ghostly again.

"Yeah, just yesterday I was sitting on my front steps with Donnie and my older brother when this Rican comes up and asks me for a quarter. That's how stupid Ricans are—thinks he can shake me down for chump change when there's three of us, only one of him, and I got a baseball bat in my hand. I told him to go fuck himself, so he pulled a switchblade and started dancing around, jabbing the blade at me. I'm like, OK, have it your way, took my bat and *BAM!* Cracked his skull open. Rican blood everywhere. It was cool."

Juan always acted out his stories: the Puerto Rican hot footing it back and forth with a knife in his hand; how Juan raised the bat with a two-handed grip over his head and slammed it down; then he switched into his victim and collapsed onto the oval throw rug, his eyes crossed and tongue hanging out the corner of his mouth.

"Give me a break." Simon needed proof. "You didn't crack anyone's head open."

"Fuckin'-A if I didn't!" Juan held out his little finger to bet. "How much?"

Before Simon could decide whether to pinky shake on a quarter or fifty cents, or go for broke on a dollar, Juan stooped down, pulled out a baseball bat from under the lower bunk, and held it up for his friend's inspection.

"See the blood?"

Simon scootched to the edge of the bed. In the darkness, he barely made out a reddish-brown stain on the bat's meaty end, better known to Simon in baseball lingo as the "sweet spot." *Real blood?* He was still debating when Juan raised the Louisville Slugger high like a club, swung it down, and stopped just short of smashing Simon's head— *"BAM!"* The near miss made Simon flinch and quickly draw back on the bedspread, printed with lassoing cowboys and pony-riding Indians. He pinned himself flat against the wall.

"Will you fucking knock it off?"

"Shhhh! My ma's in the kitchen. She hears you swearing like that, she'll kill me. Here." Juan slid the bat onto Simon's lap. "Take a good look."

Simon traced his fingertips over the stain. Then he asked, "Are you in a gang?"

"Yeah, Corps."

"You're kidding." Corps was a white gang, most of whose members went to Saint Michael's, a Catholic school, to avoid the outnumbered odds they would have faced against black and Latino gangs at Dexter. "Shouldn't you be in the Kings or Harrison Gents?"

"Why, because I'm Mexican? Too many Ricans in those gangs. I stick by my friends."

"But"—a Mexican in a white gang went against Simon's concept of gang rules and regulations—"Spanish is Spanish, right? What's the difference?"

Juan snatched the bat away from Simon. "A Latin King shot my friend Chucky for no reason last summer. A bunch of us were just hanging out in front of Pete's—you know, that little grocery store on the corner of Kenmore and Dickens? This car drove by and *Blam! Blam!* Got Chucky right in the neck and chest. Put him in the hospital for six weeks."

"Really?" The corner of Kenmore and Dickens was only a block away from where Simon lived.

"Really," Juan said. The next day, I was with five carloads of Corps dudes that pulled up in front of that Methodist church on Armitage where the Kings have their meetings. The do-gooder minister there lets them use a room in the basement for their headquarters; thinks he can change the Kings from a gang and into responsible citizens. Dumbfuck. A couple of our guys who just got back from Nam had AK-47 rifles sticking out windows like in the gangster movies. It was cool. They elected me and Baker to go inside and scope out the situation. I had Baby, and Baker had his zip gun."

"Baby?"

"Yeah, that's my sawed-off shotgun. You should have seen them Ricans when Baker and me kicked in the door to their meeting room. They about shit their pants. Twinkie's their leader, and he said, 'Hey, man, we don't want no trouble, man. How come you dudes is vamping on us, man?'"

Whenever Juan imitated Puerto Ricans, he'd draw out his words like he was mentally challenged. "So I said, 'Twinkie, you shot Chucky when we hadn't done shit to you!' Twinkie's face got all red, but he couldn't do nothing 'cause I had Baby pointed right between his eyes. It was me and Baker holding off about fifty Kings when Bobo, leader of the Young Saints, comes into the room. See, the Saints got their headquarters up on the second floor. Bobo's such a fucking hypocrite—claims the Young Saints have changed from a gang and into revolutionaries."

"It's true!" Simon had heard his parents speak of Bobo with respect on many occasions. "They're fighting to stop Urban Renewal from pushing poor people—"

"Trust me," Juan interrupted. "Strip away Bobo's bullshit revolutionary rap, and he's nothing but a Rican gangbanger. He tried to talk the Kings into joining the boycott, and they told him that the Saints could shove those purple berets they wear up their asses."

"At least Bobo tried," Simon said. He thought about defending Bobo and the Young Saints further but decided, *Why bother?* He'd gotten used to the contradictions between his parents' political views and his everyday reality in the neighborhood. "So what happened next?"

"Bobo must have seen my friends parked outside with all them AK-47s sticking out car windows," Juan continued. "So he said to me, 'How come you're in a white club when you're Mexican? You should be ashamed.' Like I'm going to let some blue-eyed, red-haired Rican tell me that he's more Latino than I am? I just ignored his ass and told Twinkie that if he ever fucks with Corps again, I'd personally blow his brains all over his Latin Kings sweater. Message delivered, me and Baker back out of that church real slow. Once we'd climbed into the backseat of Donnie's Road Runner, the dudes with AKs shot a round at the church as a good-bye gift. It was cool."

"You're full of shit," Simon said.

"Don't believe me? Walk by that church with me tomorrow and I'll show you the bullet holes in the bricks. Corps don't back down from nobody. This one time, some Cobra Stones jumped a couple of our dudes on North Avenue near Old Town. No big deal, until they decided to shoot each one in the head. A dude bled out on the spot, and the other one ended up a vegetable for life. Really pissed us off. So we arranged a rumble with the Stones, and a few days later, there was about ten carloads of us heading right into the middle of Cabrini Greens. We went to this playground surrounded on three sides by these tall ghetto projects, hopped out, and waited for the Stones. After a while, we figured they'd chickened out, but then someone opened fire on us from a first-floor window just beyond the teeter-totters. All I could see was a rifle sticking out a white curtain. We hit the dirt and started shooting back—*BOOSH! BOOSH! BOOSH!* That Cobra Stone must have been either high or crazy, 'cause there was only one of him against all of us. Then someone yelled 'Pigs!' and we ceased fire. I looked over my shoulder just in time to see this squad car pulling up at the curb. I was like already imagining life in Cook County Jail when the driver's window rolls down. What do you know? It was none other than Corps' very own personal Officer Friendly, Clark."

Simon leaned forward. "You mean the Clark who's always at Dexter?"

"Yep. He took one look at the situation and said, 'Got a report there's some shooting going on around here, boys. Seen any people with guns?' We all stood up by the swings, monkey bars, and merry-go-round and pretended the cops couldn't see us hiding our weapons behind our backs. We were like, 'No guns around here, sir.' Clark and his partner just laughed their fucking asses off. Then he did something that really cracked me up. He kept nodding *yes* the whole time he was saying, 'I do not under any circumstances want you boys shooting at Negroes. Have I made myself perfectly clear?'

'Yes, sir, Officer sir.' Those cops just drove off."

Simon asked, "How come I didn't hear about this rumble between Corps and the Stones on the news?"

"Because lots of things don't get on the news. Are you just slow or what? Anyway, after Clark and his partner split, everyone in the playground hit the dirt again and started trading shots with the Cobra Stone just like it was fucking World War II. Finally, one of our dudes decided to make a suicide run at the window with his shotgun, and *BA-LOOM!* All we could see was this limp nigger hand sticking through the curtain. It was cool."

In Simon's mind, he was all in—lying flat on his belly and shooting Baby, the suicide dash, and the lifeless Cobra Stone hand.

"But lots of Corps guys can't afford to live in the neighborhood no more, so they're moving out. It's getting harder to get enough dudes together to rumble. Even my family might have to move, 'cause our landlord's been talking about selling the building, and you know what that means. The new owner will kick us out, jack up the rent, and find some rich fuck dumb enough to pay it. Say, you want to see Baby?"

"Sure." Simon hoped that Juan would let him hold the gun, maybe even let him put his finger on the trigger. The boy rested the bat against his closed bedroom door, stepped over to a dresser at the foot of the bunks, and yanked open the top drawer. For a moment, he rummaged with his hand through assorted pairs of socks and underwear.

"Shit, it's gone. My brother must have hid it with his pistol in the garage. I'll show it to you some other time."

"Tomorrow?"

"Yeah, if my dad's not around. He sees Baby, I'm in deep shit."

Simon stretched his arms over his head. "I got to get home." He slid over to the edge of the bunk and jumped down. Before he could reach for his gym shoes, Juan began to use him for a sparring dummy, always stopping within an inch of landing blows. A couple of jabs to the face—"*BAM! BAM!*" A knee to the balls—"*BOOM!*" Karate chops to both sides of the neck—"*BOOSH!*" Simon retreated a step, felt his shoulder blades press against the top bunk, turned his face away, but couldn't stop flinching—"*BOOSH! BOOM! BAM!*"

"Cut it out!" Before he realized the power of his own shove, he saw Juan stumble backward and then catch his balance just in time to keep from crashing into the drawn window shade.

"What the . . . shhhhh!" Juan's blacklit expression looked more startled than angry. "Calm the fuck down! You want my mom to come in here and ground me?"

———————

A freezing wind slapped Simon's cheeks and leaked through the buttoned collar of his coat. He headed home fast the way he always did, avoiding the cracks in the sidewalk for good luck. Up and down the block, sandblasted and renovated brick and graystone houses stood out smartly from those that had not been gentrified. Even a fourteen-year-old boy couldn't help but notice the upscale transformation taking place in Lincoln Park. The trickle of white professionals moving into the neighborhood had changed into a torrent. In the desolate indigo sky, a few faint stars challenged the city's lights below. Simon thought, *Probably made up half those stories and exaggerated the rest. And I'll believe Baby when I see it.* As much as he wanted to think it mattered to him where Juan's truth ended and his fiction began, he knew he really didn't care. He wished he had been the one who had broken the Rican's head open with a baseball bat. He wished he owned a gun named Baby and had the guts to blow the head off the next Cobra Stone who fucked with him. He wished he were a gangbanger like Juan.

17

Nazi Nuts

SIMON GRAVITATED TOWARD LOUIS. On Sunday, they decided to head down to the lakefront. Reaching Lincoln Park, they passed by the muddy field of baseball diamonds, crossed the pedestrian bridge over the six lanes of heavy traffic on Lake Shore Drive, and strolled on the wide cement path that runs along the North Avenue and Fullerton beaches. Lake Michigan stretched to the east, its snow-crusted moonscape divided into huge ice slabs with jagged, irregular borders that fit together like the pieces of a puzzle. The ice cap, nearly melted, dipped and swelled on a gentle current, and in the sky above, puffball clouds reflected pink from the dying sunset in the west over the city.

"Pretty cool looking, huh?" Louis commented, gazing out at the lake.

Simon, imagining himself trying to nimbly hop and balance from one wobbling ice chunk to another until he'd crossed the lake to the sand dune shoreline in Michigan, said, "Yeah, cool." Where the white expanse met the horizon, a thin ribbon of blue-black night already stretched tight as a rubber band.

"Wish we had a joint," Louis said.

"No thanks." Simon had been dutifully taking in John's political doctrine at boycott meetings. "Drugs and revolution don't mix."

Louis tilted his head back and laughed, spitting out gobs of cigarette smoke. "Well, la dee da da for revolution. If you're going to make the jump from being a liberal to a radical, just remember, Che preferred combat boots over your penny loafers any day."

"Fine," Simon said. "Rot your brain for all I care." As he stared out over the lake again, his daydream took on a new twist, one where he skidded off a frozen slab and plunged into the icy waters, never to surface again.

"You know," Louis said, "Dexter wasn't always such a shit hole. By no means perfect, but people basically got along. Then last year, that Jeffrey kid went ape-shit in the auditorium with his .22."

"I heard about that. Must have been crazy. Where were you?"

"In the auditorium."

"You're kidding," Simon said.

"Nope. Saw the whole thing. We're talking over two hundred students there for study hall. About five minutes into it, Jeffrey gets up from his seat, goes down an aisle to in front of the stage, and whips out his rifle from under his trench coat. He starts squeezing off shots just as calm as you please, spraying the whole goddamn auditorium. The next thing I know, I'm in the middle of this mad dash for the exits. The weird thing is no one got shot, not even scratched. I mean, with that many targets, he could have closed his eyes and still killed someone."

Simon theorized, "Maybe Jeffrey was a lousy shot."

"Yeah, maybe," Louis said, "but my hunch is he just wanted to send blacks a message."

"Such as?"

"*Leave me the fuck alone.* You can push people too far. Look at what blacks did when King got assassinated last year—coast-to-coast rioting. Come to think of it, it's been open season on us honkies at Dexter ever since."

"But Jeffrey had to have been nuts," Simon said. "I read in the newspaper that cops found Nazi pamphlets in his bedroom."

"What drove him nuts?" Louis asked. "That's the question."

At a snail's pace, they continued on, each lost in his own thoughts. By the time they reached the boarded-up refreshment stand at Fullerton, night had descended, and on the other side of the park, windows lit up in high-rise apartment buildings. To the south, the nearly completed John Hancock Building jutted head and shoulders above the downtown skyline, its observation deck still only girders. They waited for a break in the Lakeshore Drive traffic coming off the exit ramp, then crossed it and passed under a viaduct. A block later, as they went by the fenced-in rookery of the Lincoln Park Zoo, Simon imagined a third version to his daydream, one where he saw himself balancing on a shrinking ice floe out in the middle of the lake, water lapping up to his ankles. If the wind picked up, maybe it would blow him to land.

––––––––––––

Half an hour later, they were on Dickens Street and passing right by Dexter's music rooms. In the gloom, the huge building with its graffiti-scarred walls looked like an abandoned fortress that had once withstood a prolonged siege.

"Watch this, Liberal."

Louis swung himself over the waist-high chain-link fence and into the yard that ran along the north end of the school, then tiptoed like a prowler over the soggy lawn to a boarded-up window on the wall of Mr. Egan's music room. He must have loosened the nails sometime previously, because when he yanked on the sheet of plywood, it pulled free from the window frame. He climbed inside the classroom and looked back at Simon, his arms resting nonchalantly on the sill.

"Wanna drop acid with me in the principal's office?"

Simon glanced around, ready to take off down the sidewalk, but with nothing more than the overgrown vacant lots on one side of the street and the slumbering school on the other, there wasn't a soul or car coming either way down the block.

"Are you fucking insane? Get outa there!"

"Relax," Louis said. "I do this all the time." Holding out his open palm, he revealed two small pills. "How about it? Up for a magic carpet ride?"

Simon didn't know what to be more afraid of, the acid or that
someone might come around a corner at any second and make a
citizen's arrest. He started to hurry away, only to abruptly stop a
few steps later, and gave Louis one last chance to come to his senses.
"Will you quit fucking around? You're committing some serious shit!"
Louis leaned out the window, picked up the sheet of plywood he
had rested against the brick wall, and fitted it neatly back into the
window frame so that no passerby would suspect the break-in. Through
other windows, Simon watched him slink across the room and into
the engulfing darkness. Louis opened the door, waved so long, and
disappeared down the hallway. For a moment, Simon expected his
friend to still chicken out and reappear. Then he realized that *gone*
meant exactly that. *Unbelievable.* He headed home fast.

"Simon!" Beth, yelling from upstairs, sounded pissed at her brother
out of habit. "Get the phone!"
He picked up at the desk in the study. "Hello?"
Nothing but giggles on the other end.
"Who is this?
More giggles. Then, "Liberal, it's me."
"You're making me miss *Star Trek*. What do you want?"
"I'm in Jursak's office," Louis said. "Used my mom's expired credit
card to slip the lock."
"You mean right now? In the principal's office? Tripping?" For
some reason, Simon had thought Louis wouldn't go through with it,
just wander around Dexter for a while before getting bored and going
home. There was even more giggling on the other end of the line until
Louis got a grip.
"I can feel my lungs . . . breathing . . . through hallways . . . pumping
oxygen into the gyms . . . classrooms . . . aaaall the way to—"
"You're loony. Gotta go."

"No wait!" The touch of desperation in Louis's voice did nothing to put Simon at ease. "I saved your tab. You can still come back and drop—"

"Bye."

In the living room, Simon collapsed onto the couch. Having adopted his parents' paranoia about bugging devices, which included phone taps, he thought, *Fucker could get me arrested.* He heard the thud of his father's feet hitting the floor in the bedroom above as Adam got up from his nap. On the TV screen, Captain Kirk's body had just been invaded by a diabolical alien life-form out to take over the starship *Enterprise.* Like someone swearing off a vice, Simon thought, *No more Louis.*

18

Payback

THE DAY'S BRILLIANCE TEASED FOR SPRING, but its freezing cold argued, *Not a chance.* Simon had just left the Church of the Three Crosses when a blue-and-white squad car did a squealing U-turn on Sedgwick, skidded to a halt at the curb, and nearly made him jump out of his skin. Clark rolled down the driver's window and peered out with a grin that said, *Gotcha good.*

"Need a ride?"

Through a salt-grimed backseat window, Simon saw a black boy with his hands cuffed and in his lap. Slouched low in the middle of the backseat shadows, he stared sullenly back at Simon. Then the boy looked away and gazed dismissively, like one who holds no illusions about fair play, at Connie's Bar and Grill across the street. Something as hard as the Cobra Stone's fist seemed to slam against the bridge of Simon's nose all over again. Clark reached across the front seat and opened the door.

"Hop in."

"You remember my good friend Simon, don'tcha, Frank?"

Not one word came from the backseat. Simon, riding shotgun next to Clark, hugged close to the passenger door. Despite his obvious advantage over Tucker, shame chewed at his insides. Clark edged the squad car into the middle of a busy six-way intersection and flipped a toggle switch on the dashboard. The mars light started flashing from the roof, and the driver of an oncoming Dodge Charger braked to let the Law wheel sharply onto Armitage Avenue.

"What's a matter, Frankie?" Clark flipped the toggle switch off again. "Nigger got your tongue?"

As the car sped well over the thirty-mile-an-hour limit past a Gas for Less station, Simon spotted a pop machine advertising 7Up, the "uncola." Then suddenly he was imagining himself floating up through the squad car's roof, ascending higher and higher until he reached jet-liner cruising altitude. There, he hovered, looked down, and pinpointed the squad car, gliding like a speck in an artery fed by a vast grid of side-street capillaries.

"Gee, tough guy sure is being quiet," Clark said. Simon crashed to earth, the springs in the bench seat doing little to cushion his fall.

"I guess he's upset that a buddy of his chose option number one—telling me I could find dumb-shit in Dexter's lunch room—over option number two—having a billy club shoved a foot up his ass. And speaking of Dexter, have you dropped in, lately, Simon? Can't say I'm seeing many Ne-groes boycotting, so I got to ask, why the fuck should you?"

With the boycott well into its third week, and boycotters increasingly nonexistent, there was no denying the logic to the question. Simon shrugged, staring down at his shoes on the dirty rubber floor mat.

"So when I get to the lunchroom," Clark continued, "who do you think I find at a table all by his gangbanger lonesome? I know it's him because I dug up his mug shot in a yearbook. He takes one look at me and nearly chokes on his cheeseburger. I say, 'Excuse me, Frank Tucker of 1567 North Orleans, why is it that every time I go to your apartment in Cabrini and knock on the door, your sister, mama, cousin, brother, auntie, or whoever the fuck else you got crammed in there tells me you're not home? Let's play racial harmony together and

go get your coat out of my squad car.' Maybe I'm wrong, but I think
that's right about the time he turned into a mute."

Simon asked, "Where are we going?"

"To party, kid. Just you, me, and Mr. Afro Sheen."

Simon couldn't stop the almost imperceptible trembling in his
hands no matter where he rested them. He wondered, *Shouldn't I want
this?* And what would happen once the army of Cobra Stones at Dexter
found out that he'd gone with a cop on a revenge ride that ended
badly for one of their own? Maybe the cop only intended to throw
a scare into Tucker. The silence from behind Simon drummed in his
ears. They crossed Larrabee Street, where for blocks in either direction,
those skeletal townhouse and condominium frames signaled that the
community's battle against urban renewal was as good as finished. A
couple of blocks later, they swept by Dexter's old building, the paint
peeling on all of its classroom window frames. A quick look down
Orchard to the sidewalk in front of the new building, and the huge
crowd of milling students waiting for the fifth-period bell to ring
told Simon that the boycott didn't stand a chance in hell of winning.

At Halsted, they started through a gauntlet of small businesses.
Light foot traffic went in and out of Rexall Drugs, Armitage Fish
Market, True Value hardware store, Spin Records, and a Five and
Dime. The sign on the front door of a trendy boutique known for
its perfumed soaps, candles, and incense read OPEN, while across the
street, a revolutionary banner with a portrait of Che Guevara hung
from a second-floor windowsill on the Armitage Avenue Methodist
Church, headquarters for the militant Young Saints. As Simon flew
past, Che's looming eyes followed and judged him.

"You look like you're having your teeth pulled out," Clark told
Simon. "Will you relax? I figured you could use a little boycott break.
Tell me something. What the hell is your old man doing making you
hang out at that church every day with a scumbag like John Pinko
Lange?" Then Clark's expression changed to one of putting two and
two together. "Oh, I get it. Just playing along to keep the old man

happy, huh?" He punched Simon in the shoulder hard enough to make him sway and hit the window with his other shoulder. "Smart boy!"

Simon looked straight ahead through the windshield and cracked a smile to keep Clark at bay. He worried that the cop may not have been too far off the mark about him boycotting just to please his parents.

They passed into shade under the rusted steel girders supporting the Armitage El platform fifty feet above. Dappled light filtered down through the railroad ties and danced across the car's white hood. Then the car burst into the blinding day again. From the dashboard police radio, Simon heard a squawky dispatcher's voice instructing another patrol car to proceed to an accident at Belden and Seminary. As they passed Kenmore, he peered in the direction of his house, which was only two and a half blocks out of reach.

"You know what Lange's problem is? He thinks niggers aren't responsible for their own goddamn actions. He fucking loves them so much he married one. I mean, they say she's hot-looking and all, but *married* her?" Clark glanced at the rearview mirror. "How about it, Frank? You think you're owed something? That because your great-great-granddaddy was a slave, you had an excuse to do what you did to my friend here?"

From Simon's angle, he couldn't see Tucker's reaction in the mirror, only heard a brief metallic jangling of handcuffs as the boy shifted his weight.

"Answer me, you fucking piece of shit!"

The rage in Clark's voice stuffed Simon down in the seat. Bracing his hands flat on the slick vinyl to either side of himself, he stared out his window at a mailman rolling a three-wheeled cart loaded with letters and boxes down the sidewalk. Then, trying to collect himself, he said, "I'd really like to just go home. I can walk from—"

"And miss the party? Who the hell do you think I'm doing this for, me? Think again. Now buck up or shut up."

They blew by a stop sign, took a right onto the residential street of Racine, and headed north past Juan's apartment. The trembling that Simon kept trying to suppress had moved to the tendons behind his knees.

"How about it, Cobra Stone? You feeling Stone to the bone and ready to party?" Clark guffawed, and then broke into a lighthearted whistled rendition of Elvis Presley's "Hound Dog."

They turned left onto Webster by a deserted muddy baseball diamond, where the summer before Simon had hit many a home run over the left-field chain-link fence and into Oscar Mayer School's playground. They tore by a string of store fronts converted into artists' studios and then crossed Magnolia Street. The squad car bumpity-bumped over railroad tracks, came to an industrial area, and passed a tire dump with a mountain of black rubber donuts rising high above a corrugated metal fence topped with three strands of barbed wire. Simon had ridden his Raleigh ten-speed past the dump many times before, but now as he stared up at those thorny wires, he wondered if they'd been strung for the purpose of keeping him alone on the outside looking in. After a left onto Wayne and another quick right into an alley lined with the brick walls, rusted doors, and barred windows of two-story factories, they stopped midway down the block.

Clark pantomimed pulling the cord on a steam locomotive whistle— "*Woooooo-woooooo!* End of the line, folks. Everyone out."

Simon wanted no part of whatever Clark had in mind. *Not my fault!* The cop flung open his door and rocked the chassis getting out of the car. The rear door clicked open next. Simon heard Tucker getting yanked across vinyl, the thump of his combat boot catching on the car's middle hump and the other one scraping to find footing on the alley's paving bricks.

"*Everyone,*" Clark repeated.

Simon's last-ditch hope for staying in the car by himself evaporated. *Fuck!* He reached for the metal door handle, grasped it with his sweaty fingers, and hesitated. Then he pulled.

———————

"Hit him."

Simon flexed his fist inside the washcloth that Clark had taken from the squad car's trunk and wrapped around Simon's hand. He raised his fist belt-high, then left it poised, as if the gears in his body had suddenly jammed. In front of him, Tucker stood with his arms awkwardly pulled back around a telephone pole. The handcuffs kept him shackled to it.

"I don't . . ." As Simon dropped his fist, Clark let out a disgusted "Pfffft." He reached over, grabbed Simon by the wrist, and jerked the boy's hand back into striking position. "Do it."

"But I don't . . ."

"Fuck *don't!* If you want me protecting your white ass at that nigger school, show me what you got."

Now Tucker, chin on his chest, seemed to have accepted his fate every bit as passively as Simon had accepted his that day in the vacant lots.

"Hit him as hard as he hit you!"

Not fair, Simon thought. Tucker even looked smaller in his nylon jacket than he had in Simon's memory. "I just . . ." He turned to give Clark back his washcloth, but before he could start unwrapping it, the cop grabbed him roughly by the shoulders and faced him toward Tucker again.

"You want this nigger's respect? Do it!"

From somewhere down the alley in one of the buildings, Simon heard the faint, repetitive clack and roll of what sounded like a printing press. The alley's red paving bricks began to swirl in his vision, while the cloudless, rich blue above seemed permanently stuck.

"What's wrong with you?"

Tucker lifted his head and nailed Simon with a look of contempt that seemed to ask the same question.

"Be a man!" Clark cuffed Simon on the back of the head hard enough to sting his scalp. He winced.

"Hit him!"

Desperate for a compromise, Simon threw a feeble punch to Tucker's mouth. The impact barely made the boy flinch.

"That's all you got?"

Simon's taut arms grew feather light, his wrapped fist tightening, loosening, and tightening again. *Like I should feel sorry for him?* A second punch, crisper and surprisingly more accurate than the first, buried his knuckles into the soft tissue below Tucker's cheekbone.

"He thinks you're a pussy!"

Starting with the balls of his feet, Simon uncoiled his full weight and momentum into an uppercut, drove his fist at Tucker's nose, and snapped the boy's head back so that his skull hit the telephone pole with a wicked thud. Grimacing, the Cobra Stone spat, blood already rimming a nostril.

"Cocksucker!" Simon hissed. He unleashed a two-fisted flurry using his unprotected left as much as he did his washcloth-padded right, but as he whaled on a face that was trying to slip blows, renewed shame and a scary thrill overwhelmed him to the brink of tears.

"That's it! I quit!" He yanked the rag from his hand and threw it past Clark to the squad car's open trunk, where it landed on top of the spare tire. Backing off, his feet didn't stop moving until he'd gone around to the other side of the blue-and-white car, putting the vehicle between him and what he'd just done. He stayed put by the front passenger door, tempted to crouch down and pretend that he could hide behind it.

Clark called to him across the car's roof, "Good job!" He took Simon's place in front of Tucker. "Guess it's my bats." One of the boy's caramel-colored cheeks had begun to puff. "Look at me, punk."

Whether out of submission or defiance, Tucker kept staring at his boots.

"I said look at me!"

Tucker's silent refusal to obey seemed to put the finishing touch on Clark's justification. The cop cut loose with a mighty swing. There was an awful *crack*, and as Simon watched Tucker's head spin from a blow flush to his jaw, a vicarious jolt rocked him, too.

"Uhhhhh!" Tucker slid partway down the pole, but his arms and the cuffs hung him up.

"That loosen your tongue, Frankie?"

Panting heavily, Tucker slurred, "Please."

"Please give it to me some more, or please I'm a dumb-shit who got what he deserved?" Not waiting for an answer, Clark unsnapped the safety strap from his revolver holster, pulled out his gun, and rubbed the tip of the barrel along the boy's ballooning jaw and up to his temple. He cocked the hammer. The sudden catch in Simon's dry throat told him that Clark wasn't bluffing.

"If you ever so much as look at Simon again, much less fuck with him, I'll blow your head off and say that you were resisting arrest. That goes for all of your gangbanger buddies, too, so pass the word. Do you understand me?"

Tucker nodded, his eyes straining to see the weapon in his peripheral view.

"You sure?"

Tucker's lips barely moved. "I'm sure."

It was the answer that let Simon know he could go back to school without getting killed, maybe. Clark dragged out the moment. Then he released the hammer with his thumb and holstered the gun. Digging a small key from his pants pocket, he unlocked the cuffs. *We're even*, Simon thought, but somehow he knew perfectly well that he and Tucker would never find *even*.

"Have a nice walk to Cabrini, Frankie. Too bad you'll have to go through Corps territory to get there. With any luck, you'll only get your ass kicked twice on the way home." Clark reached down, grabbed Tucker underneath both of his armpits, and helped him get fully to his feet, a gesture that years later Simon would remember as strangely kind. The boy hadn't stumbled more than a few yards down the alley before Clark called out to him, "Hey, wait up! Jesus, what the hell's wrong with me?" He went over to the car, retrieved the fake cashmere coat from the trunk, and slammed the lid shut. He winked across the car's roof at Simon, who, with a couple of fingers already on the front passenger door handle, quickly looked away. He couldn't stop grinding his teeth.

Clark brought Tucker's coat over to him. "This yours?"

The boy slowly reached for the garment, but Clark snatched it back. He felt around for the vent, grabbed either side of the fabric slit with his hands, and in a show of brute strength, ripped the coat, lining and all, straight up a seam to just a few inches shy of the collar.

"Here, you go, Frankie." As Clark threw the incriminating evidence at the boy, Tucker lurched to catch it. Ruined or not, the coat apparently still held value for him. Simon pushed his thumb on the handle's button, opened the car door, and hoped that climbing inside would send Clark the signal *That's enough.*

"Wear your fucking cashmere proudly, punk. Adios."

———————————

The squad car rumbled over the railroad tracks on Webster Avenue and once again passed through sleepy residential side streets. To Simon, the neighborhood appeared disturbingly unchanged. He rubbed the already sore knuckles of his left hand inside the palm of his right, then looked down and noticed that a huge area of his coat had been marked with chalky salt that must have rubbed off the squad car door. When they passed the baseball diamond again, he stared across it and the playground, to Oscar Mayer's gymnasium wall. He remembered the fun games of dodgeball he'd played in that gym during eighth grade. Friends from Mayer had all gone to Lane or Catholic high schools.

"Got a little hairy for you back there, huh?" Clark shattered the wall of silence that had hung between them ever since they'd peeled out of the alley. From the way he was tightly gripping either side of the steering wheel, it seemed to Simon that the officer were making doubly sure that no one could accuse him of being on the wrong side of far more than just the road. Soon they passed Kenmore Street, Simon's house less than half a block down on the left.

"I live right—"

"I know where the fuck you live!" Clark said.

Simon heard the irritation in the cop's voice more than he did the worry. They tore past Saint Vincent Church, with its twin bell towers; on the other side of the street, the red-and-white-striped pole of Earl's barber shop twirled hypnotically.

"Doing what you got to do isn't always easy. Before you go blabbing to Mommy and Daddy, we better have ourselves a talk."

Simon kept his eyes on the passing neighborhood. He knew he would eventually have to confess to his parents about what had happened in the alley, but not anytime soon. At the corner of Sheffield Avenue, Clark braked for a stop sign in front of Roma's Pizzeria. Then he stepped on the gas, and the squad lunged forward again. He reached over and gave Simon's thigh a couple of hard *Everything's going to be all right* pats.

"Welcome to a man's world. Hungry? Lunch is on me."

Simon hunkered down until his line of vision barely cleared the dashboard. He could still see in a straight shot a mile down Webster to where the city's tall buildings left off and the sky opened up over the park and lakefront. They were closing a huge loop through the neighborhood. Kenmore fell away block after block behind them. And Simon was thinking, *I am a long way from home.*

19

The Good Old Days

SIMON AND CLARK MUST HAVE JUST missed the last of the student rush at Nick's, a Vienna hot dog stand directly across Armitage Avenue from Dexter. Seated on bar stools at a counter along the back wall, they ate their Polish sausages and home-cut fries. Nick, a man who Simon imagined changed his greasy apron even less often than he shaved, puttered about in the steamy heat of his cramped kitchen, dripping sweat. Whether dicing onions or scraping fat from the grill with a spatula, his expression seemed to say, *It's a living.*

Clark took another huge bite out of his Polish smothered in hot peppers. "Mmm. Hits the spot, don't it?"

"Yeah," Simon mumbled. Perpetually hungry since birth, eating had always comforted him. He dipped a couple of fries into a puddle of ketchup on his meal's tissue wrapping. "How come Nick didn't make you pay?"

"I guess you might say that Nick and I have an understanding," Clark said. "He keeps me fat, and I keep an eye out. Amazing how a peek at my badge makes scum think twice about treating Nick like he's *their* slave." Clark hollered, "Isn't that right, Nick? Us old coots scratch each other's backs."

"Sure, Harry." Nick grabbed the handle on one of his deep fryer baskets and shook it to speed the process of crisping. "And seeing as you're a homo, it's more like you keep wanting to scratch me."

"Easy there, Nicky. You're the one playing with sausages all day."

The men guffawed, and then Clark leaned into Simon with an elbow nudge and said, "I've known Nick since dinosaurs roamed the earth and I was a student at Dexter. Didn't allow no spooks back then. If one of them showed up for class, my friends and me used to sic our T-Rex pets on him. Yep, everyone understood their place—Dexter for whites, and Cooley High for the shines. And now there's all the Ricans and Mexicans playing both sides of the fence. What's wrong with staying in their own countries?"

"Puerto Rico's not a country." Simon said. "It's a US territory."

"Fuck that territory bullshit," Clark said. "Declare Puerto Rico a country again and order every single spic to swim home. Just think of all the tax revenue we'd save on welfare."

Welfare, Simon thought, amazed at how often that subject came up, but he kept his John Lange–aligned opinion to himself, saying, "Your average Puerto Rican might not appreciate dodging sharks for hundreds of miles in exchange for their US citizenship."

"No?" Clark shrugged. "Too bad. My sorry-ass family never stooped to taking a handout—not one single fucking food stamp. Whatever happened to pulling yourself up by the bootstraps?"

"You were poor?"

"Yeah, kid. So fucking poor, the mice in our house signed a petition demanding that my old man bring home some groceries. He may have been a lush, but he sure as shit had his pride and would rather have choked on his Schlitz than live off the government. With him always loaded and my ma practically living at the racetrack . . . I'm telling you, their idea of feeding us three kids was a box of Cheerios—the cereal for breakfast and lunch, and the empty cardboard box for dinner."

"You ate cardboard?" There were limits to Simon's gullibility.

"Tastes yummy with mayonnaise," Clark said, grinning. "Look, my point is this: Nick's gotten me through some tough times. He'd give me a hot dog for sweeping out this place, emptying the trash—stuff like that. Later, I graduated to flipping burgers. He drummed it into my thick skull that just because my folks are trash, that don't mean

I have to be. If my grades started to slip, Nick always kicked me out of here until I got them up to snuff. Fucker even drove me to the police academy so that I couldn't chicken out of taking the entrance exam. And when the shit hit the fan with the Democratic Convention last summer, he fed me a quick meal or two so I could keep up my strength bashing hippie heads. For such an ugly bohunk, he has a heart of gold."

Simon thought, *Could have been my dad's busted head,* but he kept that to himself, too, and shoved another fry into his mouth. Then, peeking around the broad shoulders of Clark's police leather, Simon watched Nick stocking cans of Sprite onto a top shelf in a cooler. Under the fluorescent lighting, the man's coloring took on the hue of one of his hot dogs gone bad. "I suppose looks can be deceiving," he said, trying to sound adult.

"You got that right, kid. And I stand by my friends. The question is, are you going to stand by yours?"

Simon picked up the remaining nub of his Polish and bun. As he fretted over coming up with an answer that would pass for loyalty to all concerned in his life, he pressed it hard enough into his puddle of ketchup to rip the soggy tissue paper. Just then Nick called out, "How's your mom, Harry?"

Clark kept drilling Simon with a stare. "Happy as a clam, Nick, so long as she gets to bingo nights over at Saint Mike's." Then, lowering his voice, "How about it, kid? You going to tattle to Mommy and Daddy? Who's really taking care of you out here in the big bad world, huh? Don't like my methods? Tough titty. Maybe if the good reverend spent a few days in your shoes . . . and just remember that this bullshit boycott run by lefties like Lange isn't going to last much longer. I'm counting on you to help me keep tabs on that prick. Can you do that?"

Simon shrugged.

"What the fuck's that mean? You'll be back at school in no time, praying for someone to protect your skinny butt."

Simon finished off his fries, avoiding the cop's eyes. The image of
Tucker stumbling away on the cobblestones and clutching his ruined
coat kept replaying in his mind. But would the stupidity of blowing
a chance to have a cop for a bodyguard at Dexter be any less wrong?
A tinkling bell on the front door announced the arrival of a couple of
black boys, and Simon, grateful for the distraction, swiveled around
on his stool, watching them enter. In their oversized "Jew Town"
gangster coats, they looked like they'd physically shrunk overnight
and hadn't yet realized it.

"What'll it be?" Nick asked.

"Tamale and a Coke," one said, and began fishing deep in his coat
pocket for some change.

"All out of tamales, but if you come back *tamale*, I'll have them."

Clark bellowed out a laugh at Nick's lame joke, drawing the boys'
attention. Their awkward smiles made it clear that they somehow
hadn't noticed the cop tucked in a corner only a few feet away
from them. For a moment, as they studied the menu board above
the counter, Simon felt a palpable thickening of the black-and-white
divide. Finally, the second boy signaled to the other with a nod
toward the door.

"Come on."

When they were gone, Nick shook his spatula at Clark. "There
you go scaring off my loyal customers. They looked like big spend-
ers to me."

"Hey, is it my fault that soul brothers consider me *the man*? Probably up to no good, anyway."

"Maybe they just wanted to buy some food," Simon said.

"Maybe," Clark admitted. "But the way I see it, niggers are guilty
until they prove themselves innocent. You know what that philosophy makes me 99.9 percent of the time?" Clark leaned in closer to
Simon. "Right. Now I got a city to protect. Think you can get back
to that lefty church on your own? No point in me blowing your
commie cover."

Not until the door had finished closing behind Clark did Simon turn around and face the counter again. He began batting his Coke cup back and forth on it, listening to the shifting ice cubes. He wanted to make sure he'd given Clark sufficient time to be long gone before he got off his stool and started back to the Church of the Three Crosses. He stopped the cup in one of his hands and squeezed his grip on it just enough to feel how easily the waxed paper would crush. *Is it really so bad to want a cop on my side?*

This close to Dexter, Simon knew that he'd have to stay on his toes for a few blocks to avoid gangbangers on the prowl for chump change. Nick, stuffing napkins into the dispenser on the counter, yelled out, "Want something to go for a snack later? It's on me. Any friend a Harry's is a friend a mine."

20

Radicalism for Beginners

THE FOLLOWING MONDAY, Simon was rushing home on Webster Avenue after leaving the Church of the Three Crosses when a red VW Bug came tearing down the street. The driver slammed on the brakes, did an eighty-degree spin, and jumped the high curb right next to him, somehow without busting an axle. The car trenched someone's parkway grass, stopped just inches in front of Simon on the sidewalk, and pinned him against a tall wrought-iron fence. He stood there with his arms stretched out to either side like Jesus Christ on the cross, and with the screech of tires still in his ears and his heart pounding up into his throat, he looked to see who the hell the madman was behind the wheel. Louis leaned out the window grinning and, just like Bugs Bunny, held his hand up to his mouth like he was chomping on a carrot.

"Ahhhhh, what's up, Doc?" Louis revved the engine a couple of times. "Come on, Liberal, I ain't got all day. Hop in."

Maybe Simon had to obey that order from Clark, but from Louis? "Get outa here!" He noticed that a few neighbors were peering out the windows of their houses and apartments to see if there had been a wreck. Squeezing past the car's bumper, he hurried on his way. Louis backed up the VW, shifted to drive, and idled along right behind Simon. The car's left tires rolled along the sidewalk while the right ones stay-pressed home owners' yards.

"Wanna ride with me to California?"

Without looking up from the sidewalk, Simon waved his hand low by his side, trying to shoo the car as he would a pesky stray dog. He came to the end of the block and crossed the street, but Louis followed right along in the VW, the car bouncing on its shock absorbers as it rolled off the high curb of one block and back up the high curb of the next block, continuing down the sidewalk.

"You're getting me mad, Liberal, and do you know what happens when I'm mad? I do crazy things. Now, for the last time, in the name of Martin Luther King, get in this goddamn car!"

As Simon's frantic pace slackened to a standstill, the VW obediently heeled. He looked every which way, searching for what to do next.

"Hey!"

Simon saw a bearded man leaning out a second-floor window of his home. "Get the hell off my lawn before I call the cops!"

This again? Simon was about to proclaim his innocence and disassociate himself with the guilty party behind the wheel, but Louis crawled halfway out of the car window and pointed at him, shouting, "The liberal in the penny loafers made me do it!"

"Jail! That's where you're going!"

"Fine, Harvey." Louis sounded unfazed. "Now go suck your mama's dick. She's the one with tits on her back and hair on her ass."

Seconds later, the front door of the house burst open, and the offended neighbor stormed down the stairs to the front gate. Dark bags under his eyes made him look sucked dry by his own misery. "You two want trouble, huh?"

Two? Simon panicked, threw open the car's passenger door, and jumped inside. Before he could shut it, Louis had already peeled rubber on the sidewalk with one back tire and dug a hole in the lawn with the other. The car banged down over the curb, darted between two parked cars, and zigzagged along the street for half a block, nearly causing two wrecks and two Simon Fleming heart attacks before Louis finally seemed to come to the enlightened conclusion that maybe he should stay on the right-hand side of the road. Simon sank in his seat, his arm braced against the dashboard.

"Crazy fuck! Will you watch where you're going? I bet that guy wrote down your license plate."

"So." Louis calmly lit a cigarette with the lighter from the dashboard and hung a right onto Sheffield. "Not like it's my car."

"Whose is it?"

"Beats me. I stole it."

"You what?"

"Shit, I don't even have a license," Louis said. That's when Simon noticed there was no key in the ignition. The car was hot-wired.

"Oh fuck, just let me off—ohhhh fuck!"

"Don't have a cow," Louis said. "I've been doing this since I was thirteen. Cops never pull me over, 'cause I look old for my age. And is it my fault Beetles are easy to hot-wire? Besides, after I've taken it for a spin, I always park within a few blocks from where I borrowed it. No harm, no foul."

They passed tennis courts, a Catholic retirement home for the elderly, the Lincoln Park Branch Library, then hung a left on Fullerton and closed in on Kenmore.

"Pull over. I can walk—"

"Relax, Liberal."

This one *Liberal* too many snapped Simon out of his panic, and he yelled, "Quit calling me that!"

Louis melodramatically slapped his hand over his chest. "Oh! I beg your pardon! What exactly are you then?"

Simon stared straight ahead out the windshield, trying to achieve an expression of adult seriousness even though he knew that Louis would make fun of him for what he was about to say. "I'm a radical." Then, not at all appreciating the other boy's fit of snickering, he went on, "And feel free to blow your shit-doesn't-stink attitude out your ass. You think you're something special because you ride around on your bicycle in your fucking underwear delivering flowers? That's what I heard anyway."

Louis just shook his head and let out a long, smoke-filled breath.

"I don't know what I do to start these scandalous rumors about me, but the fact is, I was not in my underwear; it was my bathing suit. OK, so maybe that's a little weird when it's almost winter, but if you take into consideration that I had just smoked a nickel bag of grass, done a tab of pure Owsley acid, and been speeding my ass off for five straight days . . ."

Simon launched into a nearly verbatim John Lange lecture on the evils of drugs and how dedicated radicals should stay away from them. He didn't realize that Louis's exaggerated responses of "Really? No shit . . . you don't say . . . how about that" were his way of mocking him, and by the time he caught on, he felt had.

"Prick."

They continued down Fullerton past shops, a Sinclair gas station with a poster of Dino the Dinosaur in a window, factories, greasy spoon restaurants, a National grocery store, and then crossed a bridge over the murky Chicago River. After a few more blocks, they passed under the same viaduct where Louis had once been arrested for indecent exposure, took a right, and climbed the ramp leading to the I-90 Kennedy Expressway. As they accelerated to merge with the three lanes of fast-moving traffic heading northwest, Simon asked, "Are you serious? The fucking expressway?"

Louis burst out singing:

We are liberals
We are fearless
We will talk a good game
But are really very tame

At the chorus to his original song, he tossed his head from side to side like a jolly buccaneer.

Ha-ha-ha-ha-ha-ha-ha

They swerved from lane to lane through heavy traffic, darting in and out around cars. Simon clutched at either side of his seat cushion, yelling, "Will you knock it off?" Louis ignored him, keeping time by pounding the heel of his hand against the steering wheel.

We are liberals
We are fearless
If you look the other way
We will really make you pay

"I already told you, *I'm a radical!*"

Louis stared at Simon, his eyes off the road for what seemed to his passenger an awfully long time.

"You really think you're a radical?"

"Yeah, asshole, I really do."

"Then here, you drive for a while." Louis let go of the steering wheel. The car started to veer over into the next lane toward a white Buick that looked like a luxury liner next to the Beetle. Simon's eyes bugged out, and he threw up his hands, covering his face from the oncoming doom.

"Are you crazy?"

The man in the Buick let out a long blast from his horn.

"Grab the fucking wheel, Liberal!"

Just before the two cars collided, Simon lunged over and grabbed the wheel with both hands. He was practically lying in Louis's lap as he steered the car back into the middle lane. Louis floored the gas pedal, the VW catching up to cars in front of it so fast, Simon had to swerve all over the highway in order to avoid driving right up someone else's exhaust pipe. He weaved around slower-moving cars, a Wonder Bread truck, a huge semi, steering as best he could from his awkward position.

"Louis, I don't know how to drive!"

The speedometer read 60 . . . 65 . . . 70, and the chassis started to shimmy. Each time Simon let go of the wheel, challenging his friend to either take control or let them crash, Louis would do nothing but grin or sing, the car drifting and forcing Simon to lunge for the wheel again. Not a cop car in sight. *We're going to die,* Simon thought, cutting in front of cars and zipping by others. Drivers honked at them from all sides. His arms grew tired and his back ached.

"Please, I can't do this anymore."

Louis eased his foot up on the gas and grabbed the wheel. The engine wound down. Simon collapsed back into his seat, feeling woozy and breathing hard. They cruised along for a while.

"Now that's what it feels like to be a radical."

Simon stared vacantly out his window. The city had thinned into modest cookie-cutter homes. As they skirted Oriole Park—his old house, before his family moved to Lincoln Park, only three blocks away—he wondered what his life would have been like if they had never left. He watched jets coming to and from nearby O'Hare Airport, one roaring and descending low enough for him to make out the shadowy silhouettes of passengers in windows. When they hit a tollbooth, Louis sped right by one of the automatic money takers without paying, and Simon didn't even have enough fight left in him to think of protesting. The whine of the car's engine lulled him. They passed suburb after suburb—Elk Grove, Schaumburg, Hoffman Estates, South Barrington—then on out into farmland, the brown, stubby stalks from last year's corn crop scattered like broken bones over fields.

Lost in his own thoughts, he didn't notice that an hour had gone by, only that Louis had become as silent as he was. The sun was low and blinding. They started up a ramp, a hopeful sign that Louis was about to call it quits and head for home, when, for some reason, he failed to cut the wheels sharp enough to stay with the banked turn, and the car ran off the road. There was no guardrail, and in a matter of seconds, the right front tire hooked over the outer edge of the dirt shoulder. Louis tried to correct himself too quickly, and the car flipped, tumbling down a steep, grassy embankment. To Simon it all seemed to happen in a dreamy slow motion, the car tossing and knocking him every which way until it finally came to an upside-down stop. He found himself sitting on the back of his head and shoulder, his chin digging into his chest and his feet wedged up against the floor. It took him a moment to orient himself enough to find the door handle and then a moment longer to figure out how to use it upside down and push the door open. He crawled out, rolled onto his back in the tall, dry grass, and lay there staring up at a sky streaked by trails of wispy clouds. It all seemed so peaceful—sparrows chirping in a grove of trees on the other side of a field and the sun about to set, casting a deepening amber hue over a flat, rural landscape dotted with silos far and wide. A chilly, persistent wind off the Great Plains brushed his cheeks. Then he remembered Louis and bolted to his feet. His head ached as the blood rushed out of it. He stumbled around to the other side of the car. Its bubble roof was slightly caved in, the windshield shattered but still intact. A chrome hubcap lay in the grass not far away. He flung open the driver's door and found Louis upside down in a tangled heap.

"Hey, you all right?"

Louis just blinked, grimaced, and slowly lolled his head around. Simon pulled him out of the car by his ankles, then yanked him up with a bear hug and leaned him against a fender.

"Say something!"

Still grimacing, Louis dropped his chin and stared at the ground. "Get me home," he said. "I'm crashing."

"Whaddya mean? We already crashed. Are you hurt?"

"On speed. I'm crashing on speed."

"You mean on drugs?"

Louis didn't answer. The embankment blocked their view of the expressway, but just then a car winding up the ramp slowed to a crawl, the driver gawking at the wreck down below. Simon, peering over his shoulder at the new arrival, couldn't decide whether he should feel rescued or trapped. When the Good Samaritan saw that no one was seriously hurt, he continued on without stopping. Simon paced back and forth, shaking his head. He threw his hands up in the air and thought, *Oh fuck, sooner or later someone's going to stop and I'm going to be arrested for stealing a car and it'll be on my permanent record.* He went over to Louis and yelled in his face, "Come on, I've got to get home! You're the one with all the bright ideas! How the hell should I know how to get us back?"

Finally, Louis glanced up at Simon, his eyes empty and strangely as gray as they were brown. "Don't think; just do it."

The thumping in Simon's chest settled. "OK." He gently took his friend by the arm. "Just leave everything to me."

It was like helping a blind man. Simon held onto that arm and led Louis up the embankment, along the ramp, over the bridge, and back down the ramp to the other side of the highway. They stood on the shoulder, and Simon stuck out his thumb to hitch a ride back to Chicago, just as he'd seen it done in the movies. He had always thought of himself as much shorter than Louis, but now he noticed for the first time that the difference between them was maybe an inch. Within minutes, a Mercury Cougar pulled over and a middle-aged man, wearing a plaid blazer that Simon considered *square*, offered to give them a ride.

Upbeat and chatty, the driver said that he worked in sales for IBM. He talked about the wonders of the dawning computer age, how "bleeding hearts" who outlawed the death penalty deserved to fry right alongside Charles Manson, and that the United States should stop "pussyfooting" around and drop the bomb on North Vietnam. Simon, keeping close to his door in the front seat, knew how to recognize a lost-cause argument before he got into one. He wished he could let his mind go blank instead of having to hold up his end of the conversation with "Uh-huh," "Yeah," "Sure," "You really think so?" "Hmm, I guess that's one way of looking at it." When he wasn't smiling uncomfortably at his host, he was watching the day give way to dusk. The long strands of glowing taillights directly in front of him, along with the blaze of oncoming headlights from across the grassy median strip, had already begun to turn the meandering four-lane expressway into an electrified ribbon that had no beginning or end. Once, he glanced at the backseat, where Louis sat glassy-eyed, his head and shoulders rocking in tandem to the car's swaying feel of the road. When Simon turned forward again, he saw that the man was studying Louis in the rearview mirror.

"Awfully quiet back there. No offense, but you're looking a little on the peaked side. You wouldn't be getting carsick on me now, would you?"

"Nah," Louis mustered. "Just tired is all."

"Well, holler if you need me to pull over on the shoulder so you can lean out and let her rip. Man oh man. I once had a friend who couldn't hold his liquor. Puked all over the Pontiac I owned at the time. I must have shampooed that upholstery a hundred and one times, but I'm telling you that stink was there to stay." As the man shook his head at the bitter memory of it all, his face took on the godforsaken droopy look of a hound. "Yep, good cars, Pontiacs, but barf-proof they definitely are not. Say, you sure you're all right back there?"

"He's fine," Simon cut in. Then, changing the subject, "It was awfully nice of you to give us a ride."

"Aw, what the hell." The man's fixed gaze on the road softened to wistful. "I was young once."

When they reached the suburb of Schaumburg again, four lanes turned into six. The closer they got to Chicago, the more Simon noticed subdivisions, office buildings, and billboards competing for space along either side of the highway. On one sign, a woman with a black eye held a Tareyton cigarette, the bubble of words next to her mouth reading, I'D RATHER FIGHT THAN SWITCH. Another billboard advised, PRACTICE BREATH CONTROL. LISTERINE. A Volkswagen Beetle ad proclaimed, IT MAKES YOUR HOUSE LOOK BIGGER. And a sexy

United Airlines stewardess in a micro-miniskirt teased Simon with the slogan COME FLY WITH ME.

"You said Fullerton, right?" the salesman asked Simon.

"Yeah, we can take a bus from there."

A few minutes later, they were coasting down a southbound off-ramp.

Louis, propped against a Fullerton Avenue bus sign pole, slid straight down and smacked the sidewalk hard with his ass. One of his scuffed-up work boots dangled over the curb, its rawhide shoelace untied. "My ma said that if she ever saw me like this again, she'd send me to military school."

"Guess you better get used to saluting and spit-shining shoes," Simon said. Towering over his friend, he had a bird's-eye view of the cowlick corkscrewing out the top of the boy's scalp. Louis shut his eyes and pinched the bridge of his nose between his thumb and index finger.

"Getting a migraine."

"Un-get it," Simon said, starting to lose patience. "You plan on crawling onto the bus from down there?"

"Can't move."

"Can't or won't? First you kidnap me out to the middle of—should just leave your sorry-ass here to rot."

The muddy vacancy in Louis's bloodshot eyes troubled Simon, but then he thought, *Since when is this nut-job my responsibility?* In the small window of a dive bar right next to them on the sidewalk, he noticed a Falstaff beer sign blinking erratically, on the fritz. Worried that a cop driving by would mistake Louis for a drunk, pull over, and arrest them both, Simon reached down, grabbed the other boy by his armpits, and tried to hoist him to his feet. It took only a few seconds for the deadweight strain on Simon's arms to make him realize there was no way, and he let Louis drop again. He watched Louis rest his forehead on his kneecaps.

For the next twenty minutes or so, Simon kept stepping off and on the curb to scan Fullerton's heavy traffic for as far as he could see due west. Finally, he spotted a bus emerging from a slight dip in the road, no bigger than a jellybean at that distance and easily recognizable by the trolley rods atop its roof. They looked like insect antennas attached to the electrical power cables strung over the street.

"It's coming."

Louis didn't respond, his head still on his knees. Simon was about to shake his friend by the shoulders when he heard someone call from down the block, "Hotdog!" He spun around. *Can't be,* he thought. Coming toward him on the sidewalk with a jaunty dip and bounce, Clyde Porter raised his clenched fist in the power salute. A McDonald's cap, cocked hard to the right on his poufy Afro, must have been bobby-pinned in place to keep it from falling off.

"Awful long ways from Cabrini, aren't you?"

"Just got off work," Clyde said. "I's king of the all-beef patty. How's about you?"

"Long story."

Clyde looked at Louis and shook his head. "Don't tell me. He be the damn lead character in your story."

"You know him?"

"Hell yes. Used to cop weed off Louis before I turned po-litical. Can't be no revolutionary if you high all the time, you dig?"

"Yeah, sure," Simon said, "I dig." The hip word felt even more foreign to his tongue than Spanish.

"I seen my man here toasted around school lots of times. Maybe if he learned how to handle his high better, people would stop calling him crazy." Clyde gently nudged Louis in the elbow with the toe of his gym shoe. "Yeah, he out like a light."

"Simon considered letting Louis sleep at his house for the night, but then he thought, *Can't exactly introduce him to Mom and Dad in his zombie condition.* Then a long shot popped into Simon's head. *Worth a try?*

"Say, can you stay here with Louis for just a minute? I gotta make a quick phone call." And before Clyde had a chance to say no, Simon was already dodging through two-way traffic to cross Fullerton. When he got to the other side, he slipped through the door of a Duds and Suds Laundromat, went over to a payphone next to a row of dryers, and dialed a number written on the crumpled piece of paper in his hand. He'd been carrying it around in the breast pocket of his coat like a precious good luck charm for three weeks. It took several rings before someone finally answered.

"Hello?"

Thank God it wasn't one of her parents. "Hey, it's me, Simon. I got a problem."

Why Dia, after only a little hemming and hawing, agreed to let Simon bring Louis to her house was not something he had time to question. "Thanks!" and he hung up. He made a second call and told his mother that he was eating dinner at a friend's house.

"Fine," Helen told him, "but make sure you're home by nine."

Now if he could just talk Clyde into helping him get Louis to Dia's house. *Beg him?* Simon was out the door and dodging through traffic again.

21

Come Together

HOTDOG LUCKY WE'S TEAMMATES. That the only reason I help him with Louis. Had that speed freak's arms slung over our shoulders like he some kind a Vietnam wounded and carried him three damn blocks from where we got off the bus to Dia's house. Heavy mothafucka, too, even though Simon had him by his other side. When we get here on Belden Avenue, I about busted a nut. This place so big it make that millionaire comic book dude Richie Rich look like he live in a shack. It got a wraparound front porch and a yard on the side that big enough to build another mansion. Dia already sneak us in a basement door. This den ain't nothing fancy—walls paneled in knotty pine, and the place got that funky sewer gas smell. Somebody upstairs watching TV, 'cause I hear the music to that cop show *Dragnet* coming through the ceiling. Dia say Louis can crash here all night, and no one in her family ever find out. That's right, the girl be bold. She say her mama only come down here to do laundry on the weekends, her baby brother scared a spiders, and when her artist daddy ain't off teaching college, he mostly in his studio on the third floor, working on one of his paintings. What the fuck a stu-dee-o?

Dia take us into the laundry room at the back of the basement, where she got a sleeping bag laid out in front of the washer and dryer. We dump Louis, and I swear he already snoring before his head hit the pillow.

"Nighty night, idiot."

Dia call Louis idiot, but then why she kneel down and give that boy a kiss on the cheek? Why Simon care so much about somebody he say damn near got him killed in a car crash? Sheeit, you ask me, a druggy mothafucka ain't nothing but a druggy mothafucka.

Dia shut the laundry room door behind us. Then she grab Hotdog by the hand and start leading him across the den, past a La-Z-Boy recliner, Zenith TV, a coffee table with one of them new component stereos on it, and a couch that so beat up, it begging to go to Goodwill. I follow at first but stop in the middle of the room by the La-Z-Boy soon as I see they heading for a twin bed over in a corner. Think I's dumb? Hotdog gone get him some—hee-hee-hee. He acting scared of pussy, making her tug him along, saying, "Are you crazy? What if your mom and dad—" She tell him "Shhhh" and push him down on that bed like she the one gots the dick. I'm thinking maybe I should leave, but then Dia whisper over to me, "Make yourself at home, Clyde. Why don't you try the headphones on the stereo?"

"Cool."

Dia flick a switch on the wall, and out go the fluorescent ceiling lights. I guess her and Hotdog do they thang over there while I do mine over here. Through the door closed at the top of the stairs, I hear silverware clinking like someone setting a table. Then just as I'm feeling in the dark to where I know a stack of record albums and forty-fives is leaned against a leg on that table, it must be Dia's mama upstairs, who sound loud, clear, and very white, "Don't forget, Stanley, forks on the left, knives on the right."

Bet I looks like a pilot wearing these headphones, flying the friendly skies of United. They *bad*, like John Lennon right inside my head singing:

He got hair down to his knee
Got to be a joker, he just do what he please

How the hell did the sissy Beatles ever go from *She loves you yeah, yeah,* to writing a song us brothers dig? The cement underneath this carpet a little hard on my ass. Lemme go check if the cord on these headphones long enough to stretch to the couch. Nope. How about to the La-Z-Boy right over . . . Sheeit, won't stretch far enough for a nigga, anyway. Fine, I just sit on the floor again and jam. It cool the way the blue glow from the tuner dial show my shadow rocking across the Armstrong tiles on the ceiling. And above this basement is three more floors? What white folks need so much house for—hide a mothafuckin baseball stadium? If my mama, three brothers, and me live here, she never have to whup one of us ever again. We break curfew, mouth off, or come home high, she just say, "Get your black ass up to the third floor, do your homework, and don't come down again till you twenty-one and ready to act like a man." Seem like all white folks do is snap they fingers, and *poof,* they living in a mansion. Snap again, and *poof,* now they got a stereo, headphones, a color TV, and a mothafuckin Corvette that come complete with a garage. Where can I get me a white hand that snap like that?

I ain't a peeper, but now that my eyes is adjusted to the dark, I just . . . Hotdog and Dia making out. Even though they mostly underneath a quilt, ain't nothing look like a bootie bouncing on top a cootchie. Maybe Hotdog should treat pussy the way he do center field. A few weeks ago, it so warm for a day that coach Evans take us outside to practice on a diamond in Lincoln Park. Had us an inner-squad game. Think Evans give a shit they wet patches big as lakes on the infield and we getting our cleats full a mud? Hotdog happy as a clam out there in center, shouting like he some kind of outfield captain, "Pull hitter! Play the line!" "Lefty up! Shift!" "Look alive! One down, play's at two!" Mothafucka never shuts up. The brothers in left and right field be like, "Is this honky for real?" It hard for them to argue when somebody always right. The way that boy get a jump on the ball before it even leave a batter's bat, he must got ESP. And Hotdog sneaky-fast with that long, smooth stride, like he gliding over the grass. He chase down flies so far into the gaps, he technically outa position. Maybe he stop wasting time and let Dia pop his cherry, he be able to run even faster from now on and cover all three fields by hisself. He want to stay a virgin so bad, he should move over and let his teammate . . . like they say: "Once you go black you never go back"—hee-hee-hee.

Hotdog already told me he lie to his mama about where he at. Louis best wake up soon and call home, too, or his mama going to think there something wrong and sic the po-lice, FBI, and National Guard on his ass. My mama don't care if I late for dinner, long as I don't mind my brothers ate up all my food. Not like I's poor and going to starve to death. Me and Ray Kroc business partners. I fry his french fries, box up his apple pies, flip his all-beef patties on the grill, and smile every time I say, "May I take your order?" Ray pay me twenty-two dollar a week, remember me someday, and then give me my own McDonald's franchise. Brothers keep telling me, "Ray ain't gonna help no nigga." How the fuck they know what Ray do? Brothers ask why I sometimes hang with whitey at school, tell me I'm an Oreo—white on the inside and the black on the outside. They got this thang about *Can't play both sides of the fence.* Sheeit, I be the fence. It Ronald McDonald by day and Black Assassin by night.

He say, "I know you, you know me"
One thing I can tell you is you got to be free

I'm going to stop off at Sammy's Vienna on my way home and buy me two cheese Polish. I bet Louis not even hungry in his dreams, 'cause that speed trick your stomach into going on a diet. Dia say he can use the bathroom down here, even take a shower before he slip out the door in the morning and go to school. I try hiding Louis in my family's two-bedroom apartment in Cabrini, my mama know right away that something up, and ask, "Where this new son come from?" Then she probably say, "It fine with me if he want to stay, long as he don't *stay* white."

Somebody crack the door open at the top of the stairs. Light shoot straight down and land on me. I yank off the phones and so scared, my heart forget how to beat.

"Diiiiiia."

"Yeah, Mom?"

I'm trying not to breathe and keep quiet as a nun's pussy. Who Dia's mama gonna shoot first—her daughter, the boy all up in her daughter's titties, the druggy using her laundry room for a hotel, or the nigga minding his own business? First scream that white lady make, and I'm going to be all the way to Sammy's on North Avenue.

"Time for dinner, honey."

"OK, be right up."

Everything go dark again. Dia's mama must not have even bothered to look where she yelling before she shut the door. Hotdog start freaking, whispering, "Where's my shoes?" He spring outa bed and ain't got nothing on but his white jockeys. They a little tight on his boner. And he worried about his shoes first? Next thing I know, he done fished his pants out from under the quilt and start hopping around on one leg, trying to slip them back on. Talk about skinny. That boy ain't nothing but bone on bone and must have been behind the door when God passed out the muscles. Dia taking her sweet time under the cover, probably fixing her bra, pulling down her sweater, and straightening that miniskirt that don't hardly hide her pussy nohow. She got herself together by the time she hop outa bed. Hotdog buttoning his shirt, scrambling around looking for his second high-top, and zipping his pants like he wish he had three hands. Sound like he about to cry when he say, "This is all Louis's fault! If he hadn't—I wouldn't even—"

"Shhhh." Dia put her finger on Hotdog's lips. "Relax, silly. Mom probably thinks I'm down here talking on the phone. My parents respect my privacy."

Dang! Didn't anyone ever explain to her mama and daddy the difference between privacy and a horny pussy? My mama ever suspect I copping some trim at home, she throw me out one of our high-rise windows. Hotdog and Dia not paying me no mind. They arguing—she begging him to wait for her to come back down here after dinner, and he saying he gone. She hug him like she not ever letting go.

"Pleeeease."

Must have squeezed some of the scared right outa that boy, 'cause now he hugging her, too. She so small compared to him, the top of her head don't come close to reaching the bottom of his chin, and it look like he a little afraid he might break her if he squeeze too hard. Long as everything back to normal, I'm going to slip on the phones again. During all the fuss, the automatic arm on the turntable must have lifted the needle off the forty-five. My hand a little shaky, so as I puts the needle back on the record, it scratch and do a *errrrrp.*

Dia already upstairs, and Hotdog on the edge of that bed, elbows on his knees while he keep tapping the fingertips of his hands together. He even got on his coat and stocking hat. He shoot me a look with all that virgin worry on his face, and I think he either going to bolt across the room for the door we came in off the backyard or piss hisself. It obvious my man in need a some advice, so I tell him, "Depend on how bad you want the pussy." I'm hearing the Beatles more than I do myself. Them fingertips come to a stop, and it seem like Hotdog thinking over his options real hard. Finally, he start slowly unbuttoning his coat. I gives him the *power to the people* salute with my fist. "Right on!" Then he point at my head and start laughing 'cause it must look funny the way these headphones fuckin' with my 'fro. Don't bother me none. I just smile at him and groove on the bass.

Dia must eat fast when she horny, 'cause it ain't ten minutes before she back and making out with Hotdog under that quilt same as before.

He say "One and one and one is three"
Got to be good-looking 'cause he's so hard to see

My mama always say that since I the oldest boy in the family, I'm going to be the first Porter ever go to college. Hamburger University sound fine to me. Don't laugh, mothafucka; it a real place owned by McDonald's. Day after I graduate, I make an appointment to see Ray at corporate headquarters. I look him square in the eye across his desk and say, "My smiling and *May I take your order?* days is over. Here my diploma, now where my franchise? If he prove the brothers right by throwing me outa his office, I go to plan B: revolution. See how much Ray like it when Huey P. Newton, chairman of the Black Panther Party, become president of the United States. Once we in power, we take over all the McDonald's restaurants and rename the Big Mac, the Big Black. Every honky who want to order fries, Coke, and a Big Black got to let anyone darker than him cut in line. Honkies pay double for everything on the menu, and if any one of them gets uppity or forget to say please and thank you, we throw his ass in jail. He keep acting the fool behind bars, he get the electric chair.

Somebody tap me on my shoulder. Hotdog standing over me, all dressed and ready to split with his coat and hat on again.

"Let's go."

Who am I to argue with my teammate? While I'm picking my ski jacket off the couch, Dia making it hard for Hotdog to button his peacoat, kissing and pawing all over that boy. Then she put a hand on his shoulder and rest the other one on his hip like she expecting him to lead her in a dance.

"You better call me," she say. Hotdog "promise" that he will. Now that he got a whiff of pussy, there something new underneath his grin, something hard to read that he keeping to hisself. Maybe he realizing the world just one big center field. That a little scary, if you ask me.

They go to Frenching again, not caring that I close enough to stick my tongue in Dia's mouth, too. Lucky for them, I ain't no sick mothafucka. When they done, Dia notice me all of a sudden and say, "Thanks for helping with Louis, Clyde. You're a real trooper."

Trooper? Who this crazy bitch think I am? I let it slide, give her a two-finger Boy Scout salute, and say, "No big thang." Hotdog want to check on Louis one last time before we leave, so the three of us go back into the laundry room. It dark in here, too, but I can make out that boy flat on his back. He snoring loud as the goofy Three Stooges do when they asleep in one of their movies.

"I feel like I'm abandoning him," Hotdog say. Dia tell him that Louis "sucks everyone into thinking that he's their responsibility." Then she say that she'll bring Louis a piece of toast in the morning, but after that, "he can go on his fucked-up, merry way."

I about to shut the door behind us when I realize something very funny. *Caring* infectious around here. The dude out cold on that sleeping bag, but I give him the peace sign anyway and whisper, "Later."

On the sidewalk out in front of Dia's house, Hotdog and me stop for a moment to take in the spooky quiet. Even though it only just past eight o'clock, the white folks that live around here either gone to bed or be hiding. A few streetlights casting circles up and down the block, and cars parked so bumper to bumper, it'd take a can opener to pry one free from the others. Across the street, somebody gutting a three-story apartment building during the day, cause a demolition shoot run from a busted-out window on the top floor down to a Dumpster in the alley. That Dumpster full to the top with broken-up plaster and even a toilet that still in good enough shape to take a shit in. Hotdog smiling big as you please and looking straight up through the tree branches at the night sky. What the fuck so special up there, all them small clouds coming in fast off the lake? They in lots of separate packs like they afraid to mix. Hotdog so happy, he must be seeing *special* where no one else do.

"So, you get you some?"

Hotdog take his head out the sky. "Maybe, maybe not." Then he look straight up again and yell like he don't care who the fuck hear him, "I'm in loooooove!"

"Yeah, love cool and everythang, but did you get you some? Cop a feel? Suck some titty?"

"That's for me to know and for you to—"

"Awwww, don't do me like that, Hotdog."

Any white folks live around here sleeping, they awake now 'cause Hotdog hold out his arms and sing at the top a his lungs, "*Figaro, Figaro, Fig-a-ro!* I'm in loooooove with Dia Grossinger!"

I'm about to remind him that teammates shouldn't keep no secrets about pussy from each other, when he get this expression that say he doing me a big favor.

"No, I didn't get some. Satisfied?"

"Dang, Hotdog! Why you no . . . that girl act like . . ." Then I catch myself. "Don't worry." I hold out my hands for Hotdog to slap me some skin, and he do it so hard, my palms sting. Then he give me this look like I's crazy and ask, "Who's worrying?"

"That's my man! You don't put your dick in her soon, she rip your pants off and put it in for you. Meantime, you best get your ass to Harold's Gas Station on the corner of Division and Clybourn. Buy you a Trojan out the machine in the men's bathroom. Every smart dude at Dexter pretend he got to go piss when he pass by Harold's."

It like there suddenly all this seriousness in Hotdog's eyebrows, and he want to know, "Where's Clybourn?"

Soon he go his way down Belden, and I go mine. I's hungry, Sammy's over a mile away, and I'm moving fast. Someday, I'll own headphones, a component stereo, and a house with a third floor and a studio. So I's slick, I'll learn my manner rules like where the knife and fork go next to a plate. I'll take my politics and pussy from any side the fence I choose. Have me lots of privacy, too. Mama say that hate, the kind you can't never shake, don't do nothing but shorten your life. Look at me. I ain't no nigga. I want to live a long life. Now it up to Ray.

22

Passive Resistance

THE NEXT EVENING, Simon asked, "Dad, did you know a minister named Collins?"

Adam poked his head out from behind the Sports section of the *Chicago Daily News*. "Huh?" Too tall to fit stretched out on the couch, he'd made do by dangling his huge feet off a cushion. Then, noticing that Simon was tipped far back in the director's chair, he said, "How many times have I told you, you're going to break that—"

"Sorry." Simon landed forward with a heavy thud, lowered the funnies page to his lap, and repeated, "Collins. His son goes to Dexter."

Adam's expression changed from that of one stumped to that of one so deeply reflective, it bordered on weary.

"Strange, almost forgot. *Terrence Collins.* His family moved here from Pittsburg four or five years ago after . . . I met his wife and son once when I was filling in for a pastor on vacation at the Fullerton Avenue Church. Margaret was it? Skinny as a scarecrow and about as undone, too, like she'd tried out three different hairstyles that morning and ended up using parts of all three. Poor woman."

"And Louis."

The Sports slipped from Adam's hands, and a front-page photo of Bobby Hull winding up with a hockey stick to blast a 120-mile-an-hour slap shot toppled face down onto the minister's rumpled white shirt. "Yeah, Louis, I believe that was his name. A real pistol and couldn't have been more than ten or eleven at the time. Kind of rangy and with a big head that didn't quite fit the rest of him. Had this way of meeting your eye that seemed to say, *Here I am*. When he and his mom came through the receiving line at the back of the sanctuary, he kept shaking my hand, telling me how much he liked my sermon, especially the part where I acted out Goliath getting 'bonked.' I said, 'Yep, David *bonked* that bully good.' Louis just laughed and laughed. The kind of kid you instantly like. I haven't crossed paths with either him or his mother since. Must keep a low profile."

"Maybe she does," Simon said. Out of habit, he had slowly begun to tilt back in his chair again. "But I wouldn't exactly call Louis a low-profile type of guy."

"Why's that?" Adam asked. "And will you *please* stop ruining—"

"Oops." Simon landed forward again, the loud creaking from his chair's stressed joints warning him that he was indeed flirting with disaster. "For starters, Louis cuts class, takes drugs, and steals cars— you know, your run-of-the-mill juvenile delinquent." Then it occurred to Simon that he had flippantly just given his father reason to declare Louis off limits, so he quickly added, "Just kidding. Louis is reeeee- ally smart. I hear that colleges are already lining up to kiss his butt. Not that he ever brags about what an Einstein he is. His attitude is *Big whoop*. Do you know how his father died?"

"Yep. The way the national media—what was it, the spring of '62?"

The funnies slid to Simon's knees, teetered, and then swooped— Charlie Brown, Dick Tracy, Dotty, Pogo, *B.C.*, and all—to the carpet. That's when Adam told Simon about how Louis's father and other civil rights protesters had lain down in the middle of a construction site in Pittsburg because they didn't believe that high-income hous- ing should be built where it would push low-income families out of the neighborhood. Someone driving a bulldozer claimed he didn't see Terrence Collins on the ground behind him. He put his Caterpillar in reverse and crushed the minister under a tread. An official investigation ruled the incident an accident.

"You mean . . ." Simon sank into the white canvas straps of his chair. "Instead of getting out of the way, the man just laid there?"

"Yep, just lay there."

"Didn't scream or nothing?"

"Didn't scream or anything."

"But"—Simon let out a short, incredulous laugh—"that was a stupid way to die."

"Think so, huh?"

"Don't you?"

Adam gave a sober, noncommittal shake of his head. Then he asked, "Does Louis ever talk about his dad?"

"Not really."

"Seem angry?"

"Maybe once in a while."

"A blow like that to a boy. I can't even imagine."

"How's about *imagining* that Louis's dad was nuts."

"That's one opinion," Adam said. "Odds are you're in the majority, too. But me, personally . . . I don't feel qualified to judge the man. Sometimes there's a fine line between nuts and righteous."

"But not between crazy and coo-coo," Simon said. "He had a family. You just don't . . . hey, fuck him." The *fuck* had slipped out, and Simon braced for an immediate reprimand. Instead, he saw that reflective weariness return to his father's gaze, a weariness that reached in, hooked Simon, and dragged him floating along in a sorrowful undertow. He realized that he reserved his right to one day change his mind to the minority opinion.

"Do me a favor," Adam said. "Let Louis know that he's always welcome around here." He snatched the Sports off his chest and buried his face behind it again, only to lower it a few seconds later and add, "I do know this: I am not a nonviolent man. I can take on the discipline of nonviolence if I have to, but I am *not* a nonviolent man."

"Me neither." Simon looked away at the bay window across the room, unable to remember when or why it had become so embarrassing

for him to agree about anything with his father. He suddenly verged on
confessing to his dad how Clark had made him repeatedly hit Tucker in
the alley, and then he thought twice. He had only done what had been
done to him. *Tucker deserved it.* But it still felt wrong, and always would.

Across the street, under the halo reach of a street lamp, he saw the
dark row of tall windows along DePaul High School's second story.
Too bad it's Catholic, he thought. *Could have rolled right out of bed and into
class every morning.* From upstairs and behind closed bedroom doors,
musical tastes—psychedelic rock on Dawn's radio and lamenting folk
music on Beth's guitar—dueled to a draw. He knew that his mom was
probably down in her basement studio working on another charcoal
drawing. Everyone home, everything normal. He waited for his father
to start reading again before he slowly, so as to minimize any creaking, tilted far enough back to test the limits of his balance. He stared
straight up at the blank ceiling. In actuality, the bulldozer had rolled
over Terrence Collins from the side, killing him instantly, but Simon
imagined that the minister had watched the bulldozer come straight at
him, crushing his toes first, then his ankles, calves, testicles, the sides
of his stomach splitting open, lungs popping flat, blood rushing up
his throat and into his mouth, until finally the tread rolled right over
his head. And Simon thought, *Didn't even scream.*

He quietly lowered himself again. Then he lunged up from his chair,
stepped over to the portable TV, and clicked the on button. By the
time the picture tube had warmed up and flickered a black-and-white
image, he had returned to his seat again. Walter Cronkite, the *CBS
Evening News* anchorman, was announcing the day's body count. *I don't
get it,* Simon thought. *We always kill twice as many VC and North Vietnamese
as they do of our soldiers, so why are we losing the goddamn war?*

"How's things at the white caucus?" Adam asked.

"Umm, we're down to about five students."

"You're kidding. Only five? For how long?"

Simon didn't take his eyes off the screen. "Last couple of days."
In truth, it had been for double that, but hoping to stretch three and

a half weeks off school into four, he hadn't exactly kept his parents up to date on the white caucus's demise. "John thinks that the leaflets we pass out every day are starting to educate students over to our—"

"Son of a . . . just yesterday Lange told me on the phone that the boycott had the board of ed. shaking in their boots. Even a romantic communist knows the difference between optimistic, delusional, and just plain lying."

Stocks, Cronkite reported, were down with heavy trading. Simon suddenly felt like he was dissolving into his chair and would pass right on through to the floor. He braced for the inevitable.

"To hell with it." With a snap of the Sports section, Adam turned to the next page. "You're going back to school tomorrow."

Part III

Return of the Riots

23

Louis

"IF ONLY HE WOULD APPLY HIMSELF," teachers said. "If only he would stop playing the clown." The boy with an IQ of 137, whose achievement test scores rated among the top 2 percent in the nation. "What a pity," school administrators said. "What a waste." "What a Louis."

Like the time Simon and Louis stopped off at the A&P after school to buy a couple of bottles of pop. No sooner had they passed through the automatic front doors of the store than Louis was shoplifting. As they moved quickly up and down the aisles, he grabbed things off shelves and stuffed them inside his bomber jacket—bananas, apples, carrots, Campbell's Pork and Beans, Green Giant Creamed Corn, Jell-O.

Simon hissed, "Will you fucking cut it out!" He looked up at the huge mirrors that were high on the back wall above the meat counter and checked if anyone in another part of the store was keeping tabs on them. He tried to stay a few steps ahead of Louis, pretending they weren't together, but his shoplifting friend remained right on his heels. Whatever item Louis picked up, he held over Simon's shoulder for approval.

"Hey, Liberal, you want some Rice-a-Roni? You want some chicken wings?" They took a swing down the frozen food aisle. Louis snatched a box of peas from inside one of the open freezers and shoved it down the crotch of his khakis—said he wanted the peas thawed by dinnertime. Simon found the pop section, grabbed a bottle of Orange

Crush out of a display cooler, and headed straight to one of the checkout counters. As he waited in line, Louis sneaked out the front door and stood on the sidewalk in front of the store's tall windows. He pressed his nose flat against the glass, crossed his eyes, and smiled in at Simon. When he saw that his friend was still trying to ignore him, he reached into his jacket, tore loose a couple of chicken wings from inside a plastic-wrapped package, held them up to either side of his head like ears, and wiggled them.

Fucking crazy jagoff must want to get caught, Simon thought. In desperation he stared down at his Orange Crush on the conveyer belt, then over at the DAIRY sign high on the wall across the store—anything to keep from laughing. He fumbled getting the correct change from his palm to give to the gum-popping checkout girl, rushed out of the store, and started down the block. Louis stayed right on his tail and kept pulling out all kinds of food from inside his jacket.

"Hey, Liberal, you want some Bisquick? You want some mac and cheese? You want a navel orange?"

Meanwhile, the store manager finally realized he had been ripped off and ran out of the store after them—"Hey, you two! Bring that stuff back here before I call the cops!"

Simon stopped to give himself up, but Louis yanked him along by the arm and took off running, singing:

We are liberals
We are fearless

Lemons and apples and a can of pork and beans spilled out of Louis's jacket, a trail of food left behind the boys as they ditched the store manager. They didn't stop running until they were back at Louis's house sprawled out on the front steps.

"You crazy asshole!" Simon tried to catch his breath. "I swear to fucking God, you're a fucking banana. Now I'll never be able to go back to that store again."

Louis didn't seem to be listening. He patted his hands on his chest like he'd misplaced something, then reached down the crotch of his khakis, pulled out a soggy box of peas, and held it up for Simon's approval.

"How about some peas, Liberal. You want some peas?"

Or there was the time Simon took the El downtown to Wieboldt's to buy a pair of pants and Louis tagged along with him. First, Louis talked him into buying a pair of those bell-bottoms that all the hippies were wearing, and then he insisted Simon come with him down Wabash Avenue to a bookstore. One thing Simon couldn't stand was bookstores—something about all those rows of books and the fact that someone was going to read them and that someone wasn't going to be him. It took him six whole months just to read *Black Boy*, a book his mother had given him. So there he was in Kroch's and Brentano's—biggest goddamn bookstore in Chicago—and had only been downstairs in the paperback fiction section for a few minutes when he got the jitters and started tugging on Louis's arm.

"Come on, Louis, let's get the fuck out of here. I gotta get home, OK?" All around him customers browsed in the aisles.

Louis gently shook his arm free and continued to scan a wall of books. "Relax, Liberal. You're always in such a hurry." He picked books off the shelves: *The Electric Kool-Aid Acid Test*, *In the Penal Colony*, *One Flew over the Cuckoo's Nest*, *Moby Dick*. At least Simon recognized the last one because he'd seen the movie three times on the TV show *Family Classics*. Louis shoved every other book he picked up under his bomber jacket. "One for me and one for them; one for me and one for them."

Ohhh, fuck, Simon thought, but by now he knew better than to try to stop Louis. He ducked into another aisle, pretended to be searching for a book on the *G* shelves, and quickly continued on to books written by the *H* authors. His ankles felt as if they were swimming around inside his first-ever pair of bell-bottoms, and he was sure that everyone in the store was giving him dirty looks because he looked like a hippy. When he saw Louis head up front to the checkout counter, he shoved the copy of *Siddhartha* he'd been flipping through back on the shelf, made his way to the stairs, and stood with one foot on the bottom step so that he could dash out of the store just in case his friend got caught. Louis smiled at the prim black checkout woman, laid the books he was going to pay for on the counter, and in a sweet voice said, "Nice weather we're having, huh?"

She nodded, not even bothering to look at him as she rang up the books on the cash register. Louis paid for them, and just before he walked away, he slapped his hand over his heart—rather, over the stolen books—and with the same sweet voice said, "You have a nice day, now."

The woman, not biting on Louis's thickly laid charm, nodded again, already reaching for the next customer's books.

Simon thought, *Goofy fucker must want to get thrown in jail.* By the time he had reached the main floor and was passing by the world travel section, Louis had caught up with him.

"You know, Liberal, you're always in such a hurry. I mean, what's your problem, you beat your meat too much or what?"

Simon socked Louis in the shoulder. "Fuck you, motherfucker! I don't beat my meat!"

Louis stopped next to a man in the aisle who was looking at a display of discounted books. "Hey, mister, can you believe it? This kid says he don't beat his meat."

The man headed for another part of the store like he hadn't heard Louis or didn't want to hear. Simon socked Louis in the shoulder again—"Will you shut up?" They exited out of the store and onto the crowded sidewalk. Tall office buildings lined both sides of Wabash Avenue, and even though the El tracks ran plain as day above the middle of the street, Simon tried to change the subject by asking, "Which way to the El?"

"Which way do you think, fool?" And then right there on the sidewalk, Louis pointed at Simon, screaming, "Meatbeater! Meatbeater! Meatbeater!"

From the look of Simon's embarrassed grin, he might as well have been caught in the act, and he backed off a few steps, his hand clutching the Wieboldt's bag that contained his old jeans. He glanced around to see if anyone was listening to Louis, who now yelled like a carnival barker, "Yes, ladies and gentlemen, step right up and see the gen-u-ine meatbeater. All ya gotta do is give him a nickel, step back (so he don't get your pretty clothes all sticky), and watch him *beat that meat!*"

Before Simon could collect himself enough to be on his way, Louis yelled out a rhyme at the top of his lungs the way marines yell cadence when they march:

Eight, nine, twenty-one
Beat your meat, you've just begun, say

Beat your meat, baby
Beat your meat, baby

Eight, nine, twenty-two
Beat your meat till black 'n' blue, say

Beat your meat, baby
Beat your meat, baby

He bounced and shuffle-danced in place, and every time he hit the chorus, he'd stop long enough to eyeball an unsuspecting all-American citizen passing by. Some folks took a quick glance at him, but they all kept moving. Simon tugged on Louis's elbow—"Will ya knock it off?"

Eight, nine, twenty-four
Beat your meat right through the door

"Fuck this," Simon muttered, and started down the block toward the Randolph Street El station, but he couldn't seem to stop laughing as he heard Louis's voice rise above the crowd:

Eight, nine, twenty-eight
Beat your meat on roller skates

Once when they were on their way to Nick's for Vienna hot dogs and home-cut fries, as they crossed Armitage Avenue, a stylish blonde in Jackie O sunglasses whizzed by in a Mercedes convertible. Louis stopped in the middle of the street, his gaze following the long-gone Mercedes. In the solemn tone of a devout prayer, he said, "Oh, baby, let me suck your succulent titties; touch your tantalizing thighs; lick your delectable, bushy beaver; covet the hot, flowing juices of your fearless snatch; watch my hot cum succumb to your impatient tongue." Drivers honked, cursing out of their windows as they swerved around Louis, and black students hanging out on the corner in front of the school laughed and pointed at the white boy acting the fool. Simon pulled on Louis's arm, "Will you come on, Louis!" He was scared of the drivers, scared of the blacks, scared of the whole goddamn world, but laughing anyway. Louis wouldn't budge.

"Oh, baby, let me cultivate your fertile delta; nibble on your hard, rosy-red cherries; cop the tender, sweet feel of your round blossoming buttock; part your soft, silken cunt hairs so that I may thrust my hard, righteous rod into your unsuspecting honeypot."

On another occasion, Louis came over to Simon's house so that they could shoot their bows and arrows at a target in the backyard. Adam shook Louis's hand in the living room and told him how he'd grown at least three feet since the last time he'd seen him. "And how's your mom?"

Simon, already over near the stairs with his bow and rabbit-tip arrows in hand, couldn't help but notice that Louis looked about evasively and answered small talk questions with minimal replies of fine, no, yes, fine. *Like he's scared of my dad*, Simon thought.

Regardless of the senior counselor's warning, Louis continued to cut classes for days on end or show up at school so burnt out, he'd walk right by Simon in the hallway like they'd never met. When Simon found Louis sitting at a lunchroom table with that empty, ghostly gray in his eyes, he pulled up a chair across from him and with a dead-serious expression, which he figured all revolutionaries should wear, said, "Why do you mess with drugs, man? Drugs only help the ruling class to keep the proletariat masses in line." Louis's condescending look seemed to say, *Don't lay that commie shit on me*. Then he picked up his carton of chocolate milk and moved to another table, leaving Simon to wonder if maybe he was missing something more important altogether.

During Louis's long absences from school, Simon would get the addictive pangs of Louis withdrawal. So one day after school, he stopped off at his friend's house to find out why the boy hadn't been to school in three days. Louis's mother answered the clacking of the brass knocker.

"He's been in his room all day." Almost always dressed in a robe and slippers whenever Simon stopped by, she had the drained and pasty look of a woman who had next to nothing left in her emotional tank. Simon slipped past her and opened the door to Louis's bedroom. The shade was drawn, and a strobe light was flashing. On the stereo, Grace Slick sang about revolution, and the smell of cheap Indian incense burning in a brass bowl on the floor permeated everything. Louis, wearing wraparound sunglasses, lay flat on his back in bed, crashing his brains out, not moving a muscle. His face had grown gaunter over the last month or so, his clothes starting to bag on him.

Simon yelled above the music, "Hey, where you been?" With his hands extended in front of him, feeling his way through the flashes, he slowly crossed the room and turned down the volume knob on the stereo tuner. "Didn't your mom tell you I've been calling?"

Louis waited a moment before he got up from the bed, brushed past Simon, and turned the volume back up even louder than before. Without so much as looking at Simon, he moved past him again and collapsed onto the bed. As he lay on his side, the blue light of the strobe reflected wickedly off Louis's sunglasses with each flash. A surge of hurt quickly turned into anger and threatened to close Simon's windpipe. *Some friend.* His mind felt like it was dissipating into the strobe. *Got to get out of here.* He rushed out of the room and slammed the door shut behind him. *What the fuck do I care about that asshole?* He slunk by Louis's mother, who was wiping off the kitchen table with a sponge. "I don't know, Simon. Maybe when they throw him out of school, he'll shape up." She yelled at the closed bedroom door, "Louie, how many times do I have to tell you? *Turn that thing down!*"

"Bye," Simon mumbled. He opened the back door, shut it firmly behind him, and took the porch stairs down. He cut through the backyard, banged the gate open with his hand, and headed home fast through the alley. But soon he slowed his pace and wondered, *Why the hell do people always get tired of me?*

A few days later, Simon was zigzagging his way along a second-floor hallway in Dexter's new building to avoid any groups of gangbangers who might happen to be looking for something tall, white, and skinny to beat the shit out of. And then, just up ahead, he saw the shaggy back of Louis's head and his broad shoulders through the crowd. The way Louis walked in a lazy straight line seemed to announce to every gangbanger within ten miles, *Here I am, motherfuckers.* Simon wanted to yell, "Idiot! Don't you know how to play the game?"

What happened next happened fast. Simon watched as Louis refused to step aside for three gangbangers and instead tried to plow right through them. They threw him up against the lockers and were all over him, smacking him silly in the face and kicking him in the balls. Louis crouched off balance against the lockers and swung up at them wildly. He let loose God-awful screams: "Cocksuckers! Cocksuckers!"

Simon stopped, realized he'd let his mouth drop open, and snapped it shut. Black students ran past him and gathered around the fight. Someone yelled, "Hit him!" Already Simon saw another gangbanger frisking a white boy for chump change only a few feet away. *Should I help Louis?* Then overwhelming numerical odds swept Simon's first impulse aside. *Keep moving.* He started to backtrack, hoping that Louis hadn't spotted him. *His own fault; he asks for it.* But as Simon made his way down the stairs and through the first-floor corridor, he looked around, feeling that he wanted to explain something to someone, but didn't know to whom or what.

24

Black Friday

CLOSE TO 2,500 STUDENTS, teachers, and nonessential staff dropped whatever they were doing during division and began to evacuate Dexter. Under the ringing of fire alarm bells, they fetched coats from lockers, clogged corridors, jammed staircases, bottlenecked at exit doors, and then trailed out into the chilly, overcast morning that threatened rain. By the time the alarms shut off, everyone had pooled onto the playground.

Simon stuck close to Orchard and spotted none of his friends close by. All around him kids had subdivided into cliques, and teachers, sprinkled few and far between, kept glancing at their wristwatches, ready to get back to the unfinished business of division. He kept his eyes on the middle of the playground, where a few huddles of black students had quickly grown into a gathering of hundreds. The weird lack of noise from such a large mob of teenagers telegraphed trouble. In the weeks since the demise of the boycott, everyone had been expecting the riot-shoe to drop. *This is it?* The wail of a siren closing in from blocks away on Armitage Avenue told Simon it was not a drill.

A truckload of firemen came and hadn't even finished unrolling their hoses before they must have gotten the all-clear single from the principal's office. Just another prank false alarm. They restowed their gear and climbed on board the truck again. As it pulled away from the curb, a fireman clinging to a safety bar on the back of the vehicle glanced at the playground with an expression that Simon couldn't fail to read: *Damn niggers.*

The all-clear bell rang, and the mass march back across Orchard began. Simon had barely fallen into step behind Miss Temple, his division teacher, and a couple of Latino girls she'd been chatting with, when a shower of asphalt chunks—handy ammo from the crumbling blacktop—rained down all around him, bouncing and skittering across Orchard. Girls shrieked, and the mass surge toward Dexter turned into a stampede. In an instant, the entire student body parted into roughly equal thirds: those returning to classes, those high-tailing it for home, and those staying on the playground to riot. It was on.

"Everyone inside *now!*" No sooner did Miss Temple give the order than she tripped on one of her high heels, caught her balance just in time to avoid tumbling face-first in the middle of the street, and rushed on again. Simon galloped past her, reached the opposite curb, and heard an explosive *poosh* at his feet. Bits of glass from a shattered pop bottle nipped at the cuffs of his corduroy pants. He ran smack into the crowd jamming the walkway leading to the new building's doors, and didn't anticipate how fast others would pile up behind him until it was too late. Trapped. Hemmed in on either side by the tall chain-link fences encircling Dexter's small front yards, students crammed tighter toward the front, banging their fists on the locked doors—"Let us the fuck in!" In quick order, three windowpanes were shattered in a first-floor classroom. Amid screams, giddy laughter, and angry shouts of "Get off me!" Simon felt himself being lifted onto his tiptoes by bodies smashed against him from all sides. His neck started to break out in a clammy sweat. *Can't breathe!* He pried a hand free, but without any place to rest it except on top of someone else, he kept it held awkwardly high. With his chest and collarbone molded over the shoulders of the petite black girl in front of him, he vaguely registered her pleading in his ear, "You're hurting me!" The crushed mass of bodies began to sway as one and then tipped precariously forward.

"Stay calm, people!" That booming baritone command from a teacher stuck somewhere in the crowd behind Simon went ignored. *Poosh.*

In the yard to Simon's right and just shy of the drawn shades on Principal Jursak's office windows, a new splash of glittering bits decorated the brown lawn. Amazingly, he hadn't yet seen anyone get hit by a rock, bottle, or piece of asphalt. The farther he tipped, the more he panicked. *Going to get buried! Going to die!*

Finally, someone from within the school tried to shove open one of the middle doors, but the solid wall of bodies at the top of the stairs forced it shut again. On the next attempt, the door stayed ajar long enough for a few people to squirt through and into the entranceway. They pried open the other two sets of doors, and soon the crowd began to budge forward. Simon's feet only grazed the walkway: he had no other choice but to go with the flow. He got spun backward on his way up the stairs and caught a panoramic view of the riot: the first paddy wagon turning off Armitage Avenue and idling up Orchard with the rooftop mars light flashing; Mr. Lange bringing up the rear of the walkway pandemonium at a pace so deliberately calm, he seemed to be challenging mob rule even as he retreated from it; a volley of rocks and bottles reaching the tops of their high arcs; a swarm of gangbangers on the playground, all of them jockeying for a clean shot at someone with their fists. So thick was the curtain of flailing arms that Simon got only a snapshot of the staggering white boy's stunned and bloody-mouthed face. Then spun forward again, shunted through the middle doors, and released into the darkness of the tiled entryway, Simon thought, *Could have been me.*

With roughly ten minutes left for division, why, Simon wondered, should he run the risk of getting jumped by gangbangers on his way to and from Miss Temple's classroom in the old building? *No thanks.*

He decided instead to delay getting his books for afternoon classes—
left behind on his division room desk—or dropping off his coat at
his locker and skipped ahead in his schedule by going straight to his
fourth-period study hall. He peeled off from the students flooding into
the new building and raced up the closest staircase to the third floor.

The first to arrive, he had his pick of more than sixty wooden desks
bolted to the floor in four neat rows. After slinging his coat over one
of them in the back, he stepped over to a windowsill, rested his hands
against it, and felt cool air seeping through the sashes against his sweaty
palms. From his bird's-eye view, he saw the mob on the playground
below. A ring of gangbangers competing to get in licks looked like
the eye of a storm that drifted whichever way the trapped white kid
lurched, tripped, or got slammed or tossed. *Can't anyone do*—but before
Simon could finish his thought, a squad came out of nowhere, jumped
the curb on Burling, and ripped across the playground. A few black
kids on the outskirts of the mob saw the vehicle closing in and fled,
but everyone else, focused on the beating, didn't notice the car until
it slammed to a halt right by them. The driver's door flung open, and
the car's shock absorbers gave a mighty bounce as Clark leapt out. He
raised his billy club high overhead and roared loud enough for Simon
to hear him even through the closed window, "Get outa here!" Kids
scattered in all directions, many of them screaming in what sounded
like an awful mix of fear and delight. They left behind the white boy,
doubled over, sagging, but still on his feet. Blood, so rich in color it
looked theatrically fake, dripped off his chin, and a trouser leg, torn
straight up one seam to midthigh, had blown open like a tattered
sail. He straightened himself, teetered, spat, and finally shook off
what must have been Clark's offer for a ride home or to the hospital.
Then in a show of salvaging his dignity, he limped away on his own
power, favoring one shoulder higher than the other. As he disappeared
down a sidewalk and around the brick corner of Washington Upper
Grade School's cafeteria, the cop lumbered back to his squad car, got
in, and drove across the blacktop toward Orchard. There, the mob

had already regrouped, gained confidence, and begun to rove up and down the south end of the block between Washington and Dexter, throwing rocks, playing a cat-and-mouse game with police. The number of squad cars parked along the curbs had gone up to five and still counting. Cops, fresh on the scene and wearing baby-blue riot helmets, stood along the sidewalks and in the middle of the street, apparently content to duck or only threaten with their billy clubs until more reinforcements could arrive. All of Washington's first- and second-floor window shades had been pulled down to shield the seventh and eighth graders inside.

"Mmmm, mmm, mmm. Crazy niggas and pigs." Simon looked over to see Clyde leaning against the sill next to him. A total of only nine students had shown up for study hall. Sharing a window to Simon's right, a couple of white girls were looking particularly harried as they craned to see down the block toward Armitage. A few windows farther down from them, a Latina appeared every bit as engrossed in watching the riot as she had seemed on other days when Simon saw her sneak-reading one of her Spanish-language romance comic books. And at the corner window by the front of the room, a small white boy who hardly ever spoke to anyone was shifting his weight back and forth in an antsy show of indecision. Clyde stared at his teammate as if he were hoping the mirage before him would have enough common sense to vanish.

"Hotdog, why the fuck you still here instead of at your crib?"

"Excuse me?" The option of running home had never entered Simon's head.

"Every Cobra Stone, Gangster Disciple, and Deuces Wild out there. You think you so po-litically pure that Martin Luther King going to swoop down from heaven, take you under his wing, and start singing 'We Shall Overcome'? Ain't nothing sorrier than a white boy with a death wish."

"Death what?"

"Maybe you unaware that the brothers race rioting and you's a honky?"

Simon raised his hands to inspect his skin color, feigned shock, and said, "What the . . . when did *this* happen?"

"Funny, Hotdog. You a regular Three Stooges. Don't make no nevermind to me you get your ass killed. Hey, wait a goddamn second. You die, who play center field for us?"

"How's about Martin Luther King?" Simon said. "I mean, if he's got wings—"

"Yeah, a barrel a laughs, Hotdog. Now get your ass to the crib. That an order!"

"Yes, sir, Mr. President, sir," and Simon gave Clyde a snappy salute. Then he stared out the window again and counted up the new police vehicle total. Eight, including two paddy wagons. Teachers had long since disappeared from the street, probably returning to their class-rooms for their own safety. Even if Simon had listened to the buried voice that agreed with Clyde, he knew that his chance to leave school unscathed had passed. *Fucked.* He watched as three cops cornered a black boy up against the side of a parked squad and started whacking at him with their billy clubs. But with all the kid's ducking, weaving, and virtual shape-shifting, he proved to be as elusive as smoke, slipped their attempts to snatch at him, and managed to dart away unharmed. The officers had succeeded only in putting dents in the car's roof.

"Did you see that?" Simon couldn't help but admire the sheer athleticism of the gangbanger's escape.

"Pigs starting to vamp, all right." Clyde giggled. "That one lucky brother."

"And you can forget about me going home," Simon said. "Think I can't handle myself?"

"Suuuuuure you can, Hotdog." Then, lowering his voice to let Simon in on a secret, Clyde said, "Ain't no sin to run if you wants to live." He paused to give that advice a chance to sink into his friend's skull, and then changed the subject. "Say, if I's president, you can be my press secretary. Reporter ask, 'Mr. President, is it true you pass a law declaring anyone with an Afro get a Cadillac at half price?' You grabs the microphone and tell them, 'No comment.' Another one ask, 'Is it true, Mr. President, that you made a farmer who grow black-eyed peas and sweet potatoes your chief of soul food?' You grabs the mike again and tell them, 'No comment.' And if one of them uppity reporters ask, 'Is it true, Mr. President, that you threaten to drop an atomic bomb on Disneyland unless them mothafuckers start letting black folks into the Magic Kingdom for free?' you holler out, 'Damn straight!'"

Playing along, Simon asked, "What's press secretary pay?"

"Nothing." Clyde shrugged apologetically. "I forgot to mention that when I's running thangs, white folks don't get paid for work. Sound familiar?"

Before Simon had a chance to respectfully decline President Porter's generous job offer, the bell rang. Miss Cranston, running a little late, entered through the door at the front of the room and stepped onto the platform that raised her desk off the floor. As the study hall classroom ran twice the length of a normal-sized classroom, her elevated height allowed for a more commanding view of her pupils. She looked miniskirt contemporary from the waist down and Victorian retro from the waist up in her frilly white blouse pinned at the high collar with a cameo brooch.

"All right, people." She dropped her attendance book and folders stuffed with student homework papers on the desk and took her seat. "If rocks and bottles are the order of the day, I'm going to have to ask you to move away from the windows for safety's sake." Everyone let out a collective groan of disappointment and began to drift to seats of their choosing—everyone, that is, except Clyde.

"Awwwww, come on, Miss Cranston. It educational for us to watch a riot—teach us what not to do in life."

The teacher rolled her eyes and, with a huff, blew her platinum-blonde bangs off her forehead. Young and attractive, she compensated for these and other authority drawbacks with students by constantly flip-flopping between strict and kind.

"I'm not buying it, Mr. Porter. Since when do you sound like a TV commercial for the Boys Clubs of America? Now no shenanigans." Before Clyde or anyone else could challenge her final word on the matter, Miss Cranston opened one of her folders and got to work marking papers from geometry classes.

"Dang," Clyde said. "Boys Club . . . that cold." After a momentary display of mock pouting, he started to pimp-walk toward a desk near the back of the row that ran along the windows. It was a walk of the most unnatural and elaborate form of human locomotion—a combination of foot dragging, shoulder dipping, arm swooping, head bobbling, and other physical affectations that Clyde somehow managed to meld into a display of ultimate cool, or so Simon thought. When Clyde finally reached the desk where he had left his stack of folders, textbooks, and other supplies, he flipped a spiral notebook open to an unfinished drawing and went to work with a Bic Banana pen, keeping his tongue tucked into his cheek for extra concentration. Simon leaned across the aisle from his desk for a closer look at his friend's artwork.

"Nice. You sure are good at shading things." Then, further impressed by the perfectly proportioned anatomy of Clyde's muscle-bound character streaking through an outer space loaded with ringed planets and stars, he added, "Superman with an Afro, huh?

"This ain't no sissified Superman," Clyde said. "The *S* on his cape stands for Supersoul."

"Oh, I beg your pardon, Picasso. My mistake. And what's with the four doors in his path?"

"That for me to know and you to find out, Hotdog." For a moment, Clyde continued to expertly shade in Supersoul's sculpted calf muscle. Then he stopped. "OK, since we's teammates and you so interested—"

The sounds of yet another girl's hair-raising scream, more glass shattering, and a cop's stern "Move it!" reminded everyone in the study hall of the parallel reality just beyond the windows.

"See, Supersoul flying through a galaxy called Chaos. He got to hurry 'cause they be something nasty in the atmosphere that make him go crazy and crash-land on a planet full of zombies. He do that, they suck his blood, steal his superpowers, turn into an army of super-zombies, and rule the cosmos. You dig?"

"Kind of," Simon said. "I mean, the whole cosmos-chaos thing on top of zombies gets a little—"

"Science fiction some tricky-ass shit, Hotdog. Pay attention. Super-soul ain't nobody's fool. He flying at Mach 5 speed when he sees doors floating right up ahead. Each one big as a mothafucker and got its own label—PAST, PRESENT, FUTURE, and INFINITY. He thinking, Time dimensions? An evil sorcerer's trap? Maybe just some bullshit the zombies put up there with their cargo spaceships to confuse him? He choose the wrong door, the cosmos fucked. So tell me, Hotdog, if you Supersoul, which one you pick?"

"How should I know?"

"Don't you want to keep your blood and superpowers?"

"OK, the future."

"Uh-uh."

"The past?"

"Uhhhhhhh-uh."

"The fucking present?" Simon didn't know the definition of *infinity*, but he surmised, from the disappointed manner in which Clyde shook his head, that a dictionary might have come in handy.

"Congratulations, Hotdog. You done killed off mankind. Infinity be the past, present, and future all rolled into one. You best stick to baseball and leave science fiction to me." Clyde went back to shading in the contours of Supersoul's calf muscle.

"Still looks like a Superman rip-off to me," Simon said. "Besides the Afro, what's the difference?"

"*The difference?*" Clyde didn't even bother to stop drawing. "You mean beside the fact that Supersoul eat Kryptonite like it candy, don't need no signal from Jimmy Olsen's wristwatch to know when aliens about to atomize the earth, and sure as hell don't fall in love with no flat-ass bitch like Lois Lane?" He looked up at his friend with a subtle grin. "The difference be that Supersoul know how to dance."

———————

Not until later that evening, atop Juan's bunk bed and once again under his friend's eerie black light, would Simon get some of the gaps in his eyewitness account of the riot filled in for him.

"Yeah, me and Julio were over by the baseball backstop when the shit hit the fan. I mean, the way them niggers jumped poor Jerry Cutler on the playground. Know him? Skinny hillbilly kid who's got a bad stutter and always wears unironed shirts too short in the sleeves? Bet his mom shops for him at Good-fuckin'-will. Not like we could run over there and try to save his ass against half of Africa. If Clark hadn't shown up, wouldn't have been nothing left but pieces of hillbilly."

"Saw all that," Simon told Juan. As he marveled at how the blacklit dust particles clinging to his sweater looked as thick as the Milky Way, just thinking about what had happened to Jerry made his skin crawl.

"The niggers all run over to Orchard, so me and Julio decide to ditch class and follow after them. I mean, how often do you get to see a riot? We're walking nice and slow down the sidewalk past the auditorium, then the new building, minding our own damn business, when black dudes start coming up to us and asking, 'Honky or Rican?' Julio goes, 'Sheeeit, try Mexican.' They're like, 'Right on!' and give us the soul brother handshake. I start sweating bullets that someone's going to know I'm in a white gang, but I guess when it come to Corps, I'm still cruising below nigger radar."

"Lucky you," Simon said, hardly unaware that some people had different advantages than others at Dexter.

"Lots of dudes had rolls of pennies in their palms and ACE bandages wrapped around their fists. That way, if they go to dot some pig's eyes, they'll knock his eyeball clear out the backside of his skull. Nothing much happens for a while besides maybe a rock flying by a pig's nose or a gangbanger getting tossed by some pigs headfirst into a paddy wagon. Then this kid with a small baseball bat climbs over one of the tall chain-link fences in front of the new building, drops down in the yard, and runs along a row of classroom windows busting them out. A handful of pigs try climbing over the fence to arrest him, but their beer guts don't do them no favors and everyone on the street starts pelting their dumb asses with rocks. They can forget about arresting the dude with the bat, because friends of his inside the building pull him through an open window, give everyone the black power salute, and then disappear. Talk about pig-pissed. Those cops jump down to the sidewalk again and start chasing bangers around in circles, trying to clobber them with clubs. Things are looking a little hairy, so me and Julio duck into a doorway to the old building. The door's locked, but at least we can lay low from there."

"You call that laying low?" Simon asked. "If that had been me—"

"Hey, no one made you get born a honky," Juan said, and laughed. "Right around then, a busload of piglets from the police academy arrives on the scene all eager beaver and shit. There's enough pigs now for them to get organized, so they string out across the width of the street in two double-file lines, maybe fifty yards apart. Not like they're scaring nobody or nothing, 'cause the niggers trapped in between them are giving the finger and acting all *Bring it on!* Pretty soon, those blue lines start slowly marching toward each other. The pigs are all in lockstep and keep thrusting their billy clubs like battering rams, grunting, 'Huh! Huh! Huh!' Must be some goofy crowd-control shit they learned at the academy, the kind that looks and sounds good until some real rioters show up. This girl gets spooked and tries running across the hood of a parked squad so she can make a break for it down the sidewalk in front of Washington, but pigs gang-tackle her.

Really fuck up her leg—one long raspberry scrape that starts oozing blood and staining her bobby sock."

"I guess no one made her get born black," Simon cracked.

"Exactly." If Juan had picked up on Simon's sarcasm, he didn't show it. "And don't believe everything you hear, either. Contrary to popular belief, the niggers aren't stupid. They see what's up, don't much appreciate getting squeezed in, and charge the lines. It's a sea of hand-to-club combat. Maybe some genius lieutenant should have counted before he gave the order to go on the offensive, because there's ten niggers for every one oink. Not far from me, a cop and a banger trade punches to the jaw, nearly coldcock each other, and then stumble away. If pigs try to arrest someone, dudes swarm all over them like flies on blue turds. A rock ricochets around inside the doorway and drops at Julio's feet. Suicidal fucker picks it up and cocks his arm to throw, but before I can tell whether he's gone *pig* or *nigger* on me, I slap it out of his hand. I notice this dotted trail of blood that's stitched back and forth across the street, and it adds a touch of *for real* to the riot. So long as no one ups with a piece and starts shooting, most everybody's having fun."

"*Fun?*" Simon was incredulous. "You might want to ask Jerry Cutler about that."

"OK," Juan conceded. "Fun for everybody except hillbillies. That is, until half of Cooley High School shows up. Who the fuck invited them to our riot? They come pouring across Armitage and onto Orchard like an army of ghetto reinforcements from Cabrini Green. Maybe the pigs don't mind ten-to-one odds, but fifteen-to-one? And don't forget, even Dexter niggers consider Cooley niggers crazy. Can you blame a few doofus cops for putting their hands on their guns, ready for some target practice? Julio's about to pee himself and pounding on the door for someone to let us the fuck inside. God must have figured it was a good time to pass out a miracle, because the door clicks open and a kid who looks like a black version of the Nutty Professor in his thick, Coke-bottle glasses let's us push past him. Half the riot piles in right behind us, everyone scrambling up the stairs to the first-floor hallway. Fuck this bullshit. I decide to split up from Julio and head for my algebra class.

"It's guerilla warfare all around me: pigs chasing niggers, and niggers going all hit-and-run Viet Cong ambush. I smell smoke but don't see none. With three floors and staircases all over the place, how many escape routes does a decent rioter need? If the pigs chase them down one hallway, they scatter, regroup, and then sneak up behind those same cops with everything they got—Elmer's glue bottle, chunks of asphalt, a ruler. I even seen one cop get his helmet knocked off by a fucking boot. Funny as shit the way it slid down the hall like a spinning salad bowl.

"Above me on the second floor, I can hear the *boom* of someone kicking in a locker door. So that's where all the ammo's coming from, stealing stuff out of lockers. Something zings by overhead and—*Blam! Blam! Blam!* Must have been jars of tempera paint, because there's splatters of primary colors on the wall just above the attendance office window. Then the pigs notice that paint's fucked up their leathers, too, and they tear off toward the other end of the hallway to beat the shit out of whoever done it. And that pretty much sums up what them slowpokes will be doing for the rest of the afternoon—chasing ghosts."

"Some ghosts," Simon said. Growing irritated by how Juan's version of the riot contradicted his own terrifying experience, he left it at that.

"It's already pan-fuckin'-demonium when the fifth-period bell rings. Bad timing. Any honky stupid enough to step foot outside a classroom gets vamped on by gangbangers. Think the cops are swift enough to do anything about it? Sure, one fires a twenty-foot squirt from a can of mace, but the group of bangers he aimed at sees it coming, flattens themselves against some lockers, and watches the stream sail right past their noses. Then they scramble back around the corner they just came from, so all that mace ends up doing is stinking up the hallway and making everyone's eyes burn, including the cops'. Smart. There I am, almost blind from that nasty shit, but I still see Benny Foster getting jumped by a platoon of niggers on a staircase landing. He's that tall, red-haired kid who I seen in a garage band; fucker plays a guitar almost as good as Hendrix. Them bangers are all over him, and when this dude's fist connects with Benny's jaw, there ain't nothing left for that honky but a drop-and-roll down the stairs.

"I just keep moving past the library, through the swinging doors into the new building, and up that short flight of stairs to the second floor. The coast is clear in this hallway, but up ahead smoke is pouring out from under a bathroom door. Guess someone set a trashcan on fire. From down on the first floor, there's lots of screaming and Vice Principal Tanana yelling, 'Walk, girls! You will walk quietly or leave the premises!'

"'Fuck you, Uncle Tom!'

"So much for Tanana getting respect for being black. I hear that Ann chick down on the first floor, too—a real know-it-all who's always passing out leaflets and talking revolution?"

"We were in the white caucus together," Simon said. "Once you get to know her, she's OK."

"If you say so. She's whining, 'But I'm on your side!' Not today, bitch. Then there's a shriek."

"That's fucked up." Simon said. "Ann didn't deserve . . . she boycotted!"

"Think most niggers give a shit about that? All they see is *white*. I make it to algebra, and there's only us seven students and Mr. Lee. He's nice enough, but how'd he ever get hired to teach in America when can't nobody understand that Chink accent of his? They say he's got a black belt in judo, so that's probably why Immigration let him into the country—scared not to.

"We take our seats and start working on the first equations Mr. Lee had on the blackboard, when all of a sudden I hear feet running in the alley outside the windows and then, 'Keep your hands off me!' I go over with everyone else to see what's happening. Down below, four niggers got a honky chick surrounded near some garbage cans. What's her name . . . kinda short, has killer lips and big brown eyes."

Out of dread, Simon took a shot in the dark. "Dia?"

"Yeah, that's her. Always shaking her assets around school like she's the next Raquel Welch. One dude slaps her silly, another yanks her by the hair, and a third dude pops her in the mouth with his fist—*BAM-BAM!* Down she goes on the alley's bricks, her legs all twisted open and shit. You can see her white panties, and this pimply faced honky at the window next to me starts whooping like some kind of pervert getting his rocks off. Next thing you know, them niggers are all in a tight circle around Dia, two of them looking around, nervous and shit, like they want to call it quits, but this other dude starts unbuckling his belt. Yep, he wants some pussy, and I can tell from the tent in his pants that he already has a boner. I'm not into no rape, so I'm about to fly out of that room and go all Lone Ranger to Dia's rescue when Mr. Lee throws open a window and yells in that Chink accent of his, 'You boys stop that light now or I get police!'"

"So Dia didn't get—" Before Simon could shudder at the thought, Juan reassured him.

"Nah. Two niggers take off down the alley, a third gives Mr. Lee the finger, and the one with a boner . . . think he's happy? He yells up at Mr. Lee, 'Go ahead and get the po-lice, mothafucka!' Before you know it, him and his pal are reaching into one of those garbage cans for some Schlitz bottles, and it's bombs away. We all dive under desks just as glass from windows sprays everywhere. I'm combat-crawling for the door across the room, but by the time I get halfway there, it's all over, and the alley's left to the rats again. Mr. Lee pokes his head out from under his desk, fucking glasses cock-eyed, and says, 'Clazy boys!' For the rest of the period, he has us filling up the wastepaper basket with broken glass. Nice education, huh? So what happened to you during the riot today?"

What indeed. The fifth-period bell hadn't even stopped ringing before Simon was already up from his desk and trying the knob on the study hall's back door. Locked. *Damn.* To play it safe, he had wanted to get as close as he could to his world history classroom in the old building before the hallways filled up with students.

"Hold your horses." Miss Cranston stepped off her platform, key ring jangling in her hand as she moved quickly toward the back of the room. "People, if any of you want to stay here for the rest of the afternoon, I'm sure that your other teachers will more than understand." Amazingly, there were no takers on her offer, everyone clinging to their schedule routines.

Simon bolted into a hallway already crowded with people. He smelled smoke and heard Clyde calling after him, "The crib, Hotdog. That where you belong."

At a three-way intersection, the herdlike sound of trampling coming up the stairs on Simon's right told him to do an immediate about-face and backtrack. Moving at a steady pace that he hoped was neither too fast nor too slow to attract attention, he reached the northwest corner of the new building and descended another staircase. He'd just stepped foot onto the second floor when the streaking image of a figure holding himself as vertically straight as possible in the narrow airshaft between stair flights whizzed past him. An instant later, the sound of boots smacking hard on the first floor below was followed by someone moaning in excruciating pain. Simon peered down over the railing, saw a kid writhing on the tiles, clutching at his ankles, and immediately recognized Gary, the twitchy hippy kid from the white caucus. *Fell two stories?*

"Dang!"

The voice drew Simon's attention straight upward to where a row of heads was overlooking from the third-floor railing.

"Honky jumped!"

Move. And before Simon could allow himself the luxury of his own astonishment, he was heading at the same steady pace as before down a smoke-filled hallway. He wondered, *Jumped to avoid getting . . . jumped?* A prickly shiver on the nape of his neck put an end to his imagining what it must have been like to make such a drastic choice, and he switched to worrying about Dia. *Someplace safe?* Though he kept his eyes peeled for her, he hoped to God that she'd been smarter than him and gone home while the going was still good. And Louis? *Fucker's never around when you . . . probably ditched the riot to go steal another car.*

A teacher's aide carrying a fire extinguisher almost bumped into Simon as he rushed past on his way to where smoke poured out from the crack underneath a boys' bathroom door. Farther up ahead, a gangbanger dodging a couple of cops ran vertically straight up one of the tan lockers lining a wall and then did a backflip with height to spare over the swipe of a billy club. He nailed his landing and, unscathed, took off running with a couple of his buddies. Simon steered clear of the incident by hanging a hard left down another corridor.

Each detour he took further complicated his route to his world history class. Through the smoky haze, which stung his eyes and made them water, he thought he saw someone with Juan's distinctive bowlegged strut, but before he could positively identify his friend, the figure ducked inside Mr. Lee's algebra classroom. Along the wall on Simon's left, a kid emboldened enough to wear his red Cobra Stone beret inside the school was lighting a piece of loose-leaf paper with a cigarette lighter. Then after stuffing the burning sheet through the vent of a locker door, he produced a small metal can from his inside overcoat pocket, squirted a flammable stream through the grill, and *whoosh.* Tongues of flame shot out from inside the vent, took a licking peek around, and then vanished into their locker hideout again. Simon thought, *How's about a fire alarm when you need one?*

He reached the east end of the hall, took the stairs down, and had just gotten to the landing when sounds coming up from the first floor—scuffling feet, the sharp bang of something hitting a locker, and a boy shouting, "How you like it, pig?"—told him, *Bad idea.* He turned around, retraced his steps, and found himself confronted by an entirely new riot landscape in the very same hallway he had left only a few moments earlier.

Evenly spaced down the corridor, three different crowds of gang-bangers were mauling white boys: the closest getting stomped in the alcove of a classroom doorway, another being smacked and tumble tossed like he was caught in a mixing drum, and the third hard for Simon to make out through the mob engulfing the boy. *Keep moving.* Simon swung around to the next flight of stairs and had only climbed a few steps before the rumble of dozens of feet storming down from the floor above made him halt. Again he about-faced, retreated, and then paused to review his no-win escape options. *This is it.*

He plowed forward, managed to sneak past the swarm of gang-bangers attacking the boy trapped in the alcove, and was hugging a wall to avoid the mob that was swallowing up the second victim when someone blocked his path. The hand pressed to Simon's chest insisted that he go not one step farther. He immediately recognized Frank Tucker's groomed looks and a hardboiled rage just underneath the surface of his gaze. That same helium lightness that Simon had felt when Tucker had placed a board squarely on his head seemed to tug on his arches. And then the gangbanger made a series of moves that completely baffled Simon. First, he shielded Simon from harm's way by waving off several friends who appeared only too eager to assist in jumping another honky. Next, he reached under his front shirttail and pulled out a chrome-plated snub-nosed pistol from inside the waistband of his baggy khakis. He held the weapon flat in his open palm to give Simon time to carefully consider the consequences that the lethal weapon implied. Before Simon could make up his mind whether he should run, miraculously float, shit his pants, or simply kiss his life good-bye, Tucker shoved the gun back inside his khakis and concealed the handle under his shirttail again. He grinned bitterly, stepped aside, and with a sarcastic, salaaming flourish of his arm, let the white boy pass.

Survival mode carried Simon forward. *He could have killed . . .* Sweat had drenched his taupe button-down shirt and soaked through to the lining of his heavy coat. In the intersection just up ahead, gangbangers scattered, frightened off by something or someone not yet visible to Simon around a corner. They left a white kid behind on his hands and knees, hawking up blood. The urge to stop and help the boy off the floor slowed Simon, but his legs, sticking to a practicality all their own, took him down the other corridor. As he picked up speed again, through the dreamy smoke he saw who had caused so many gangbangers to flee. Clark moved in Simon's direction like a man whose every step was a game changer. He must have been the only cop at Dexter that day who hadn't thought it necessary to trade in his uniform hat for a riot helmet. As they passed each other, Clark winked at his protégé before continuing on toward the more immediate needs of the injured boy. Simon nimbly took a short flight of stairs down and barged through one of the swinging doors that led to the old building. Before it shut behind him, he heard Clark's booming voice, "Come on, kid, upsy-daisy."

The fire alarm bells went off again, but despite the real threat of fire this time around, everyone in the school seemed to think that the possibility of burning to death was no worse than evacuating into the full-scale riot outside. It wasn't until after Simon had zigzagged through a couple of sharp corridor turns and left the smoke far behind him that the cop's wink and Frank Tucker's free pass suddenly clicked for him. *Oh.* His mouth curled into a pleased grin. A few steps later, it bordered on smug.

The rest of the long hallway in front of him stayed empty, and Simon almost believed that Clark's larger-than-life shadow had cleared a path for wherever he chose to go. He thought, *Fuck my world history class.* And he decided to aim for the biology room, hoping to find John Lange. Passing one closed classroom door after another, he relaxed and began to feel something new, formidable, and loose in his groin. It was power.

25

Frog Genocide

"I'M TELLING YOU, Gary dropped like a rock, nothing but a blur going by. My guess is the cops scraped him off the floor and took him to the hospital."

"Wow," John said. "Lucky he's not dead. And what did a socially conscious kid like him ever do to deserve . . . gangs. You think uneducated thugs like them don't play right into the hands of racist school administrators?"

In the lab storage room—about the size of a walk-in bank vault just off the biology classroom—Simon made himself at home by sitting on a black countertop with his feet dangling over one of the cupboards. Here, sealed off from the riot and under John's mentoring eye, he quickly shunned any vicarious power he'd felt because of his friendship to Clark. He watched John snatch another frog from a tall plastic bucket in the sink. Wearing a chef's apron to protect his powder-blue turtleneck, the teacher leaned with his pelvis against the counter's edge, clamped the creature's head in a pair of forceps, and gave it a sharp, lethal twist. It wasn't the frog's last spasmodic shudder or the blood that bubbled up from its gaping mouth or even how its long, thin legs looked strangely human once they'd gone lax that made Simon have to fight off the urge to cringe. No, it was the audible crunch of vertebrae and the frog's saucer-eyed expression of stupefied acceptance that gave him the creeps.

"Gross," Simon said.

"Believe me, you get used to killing these suckers in graduate school." Hamming it up, John cackled like the Wicked Witch of the West, snapped another neck, and then flopped the new carcass onto the already heaping pile on an aluminum tray. He nudged the bucket's lid open just enough so he could stick his hand in and fish around for his next victim without allowing any of the remaining overcrowded frog population the chance for a great escape. From within the bucket, Simon heard the pitter-patter scraping of every-amphibian-for-himself pandemonium. "When we dissect these guys for class tomorrow, their organs will still be nice and fresh. Want to make yourself useful? There's an extra pair of forceps in that drawer over—"

"No thanks," Simon said. "I believe in the discipline of nonviolence."

"Just like your old man, Gandhi, and Martin Luther King, eh?" John secured another frog tightly in his fist. "As for me, I'm more of the Machiavelli and Malcolm X type. Know what they had to say about the political struggle for power?"

"What?"

"That the end justifies the means." *Snap.* "I mean," continued John, tossing another limp frog onto the stack, "the ruling class has the police, FBI, CIA, National Guard, and Armed Forces at its disposal, not to mention nuclear weapons, so why the hell should the working class limit itself to turning the other cheek?"

Simon wasn't in the mood to get drawn into one of John's complicated revolution discussions. Instead, he reached across the counter, picked a dead frog off the tray, and started bobbing him around like a puppet, singing in falsetto,

Getting to know you
Getting to know all about you

"Ah, yes," John said. "Rodgers and Hammerstein's *The King and I.* Good old-fashioned ruling-class propaganda." *Snap.*

"Huh?" Simon dropped the dead frog back onto the tray and slumped against the cabinet behind him. "How so?"

"*Think*, Simon. It's a story about a potentate who threatens to beat his subjects, but we're supposed to like him. TV shows and movies brainwash us into sympathizing with the ruling class."

"If you ask me, girls love *The King and I* because they've got the hots for Yul Brynner," Simon said. "That bald-headed dude is built."

John asked, "Why not cast the king as a fat slob? He's so lazy, he has his servants carry him from place to place in a goddamn chair. Just flip on your television, and it's the same propaganda every time."

"Even a show like *Bonanza*?" Try as Simon would, he saw no connection between the ruling class and cowboys the likes of Hoss and Little Joe.

"Especially *Bonanza*." John huffed dismissively. "It's about a supposedly kind-hearted, capitalistic rancher who owns a billion acres and has three privileged sons. No hidden message there, I suppose."

"OK, what about *Star Trek*?" As far as Simon was concerned, the heroic Captain Kirk could do no wrong.

"A show about a captain and his starship crew spreading the Federation's imperialist rule throughout the galaxies," John said. "Gee, what's the analogy?"

"*The Beverly Hillbillies*." Simon was confident that imbeciles like Jethro, Ellie May, and Granny were in no way instruments of ruling-class oppression.

"A show where a bunch of hicks just happen to accidentally strike oil in their own backyard," John said. "It perpetuates the myth that poor people are going to miraculously become rich overnight and join the ruling class. Dream the fuck on."

"*Hazel*," Simon challenged. A show about a happy-go-lucky housekeeper could not possibly come with any sneaky political messages attached.

"That's an easy one," John said. "Hazel works like a dog, earns a shitty wage, and never complains about having to take care of her employer's kids morning, noon, and night. If that's not a modern-day slave-master relationship, I don't know what is."

Simon was tempted to bring up *Bewitched* and *The Flying Nun* but decided against it, figuring that he had better start learning how to identify the ruling class's manipulative propaganda for himself. Still, he found himself wondering exactly what the brainwashing intent was behind a sexy witch who casts spells by wiggling her nose, or a nun who uses her starched hat as a hang glider. For a moment, he listened for any telltale sounds of rioting beyond the locked biology room door, but he heard nothing happening in that tucked-away corner of the old building.

"If only we could have kept the boycott going and held the board of ed.'s feet to the fire a few weeks longer. They'd have caved in to our demands soon enough." John braced himself against the counter and stared at the bucket's lid. Behind the dignified glasses and bristly, thick mustache, the man's usual confidence appeared to Simon to have been snuffed out. "After all those damn caucus meetings, it's back to square one."

Like most boys, Simon did not want to know his heroes' limits. He suddenly felt uncomfortably sorry for John and distracted himself by glancing around the cramped room. Microscopes lined up higgledy-piggledy on top of cabinets, counters, and a mini-refrigerator were in need of organizing. Finally, John opened the cabinet under the sink, pulled a second metal tray off a shelf, and let it bang onto the counter next to the one loaded with frogs.

"Just remember one thing, Simon. Opportunists always swoop in and exploit any community that can't stay united."

"Yep. Like gangs and the school administration." Simon wanted John to know that he'd been paying attention, that all was not lost. He briefly got the urge to confide in his teacher about how Clark had taken him under his wing and protected him from further Cobra Stones harm. *No, better keep that quiet,* and reasoning that he could juggle contradictory worlds just fine, he hopped off the counter, gave his adult friend a pat on the back, and held out his other hand for the forceps.

"Take a break, John. I'll do the rest."

————————

Left alone in the supply room while John graded quizzes at his desk, Simon stood at the sink wearing the apron, his first sacrificial frog held snug in his fist. As he clamped the forceps around the animal's head, it seemed to take one last, desperate gulp of air.

"Sorry, dude." Apology aside, Simon felt like he had something to prove to himself that he'd already put off far too long. Ignoring the queasy tickling in the base of his throat, he silently counted: *One, two, three.* Then scrunching his eyes shut, he did the deed. Ten frog executions later, he realized that killing had become old.

He stayed with John for the remainder of the school day, performing odd jobs. After stowing the filled trays in the refrigerator, he consolidated the microscopes on a single countertop by lining them up in neat rows of threes. Out in the biology room, he wiped down student tables with a soapy rag, drained and cleaned the aquarium tank, and began cataloguing hundreds of jars of miscellaneous chemicals in the many storage cabinets along the walls—a task that would take days to complete and give Simon a legitimate reason for excusing himself from study hall in order to work as John's "lab assistant." Not one other student showed up for biology throughout the rest of the afternoon—the result, he would later learn, of Principal Jursak having office messengers circulate a memo that ordered teachers to either keep students locked in classrooms or let them go home. And as would become more of the norm on "riot days" at Dexter in the weeks and months ahead, those who continued to do battle with the police called it quits around eighth or ninth period, put down their rocks and bottles, and swarmed south through neighborhood streets to their home turf, the Cabrini Green Projects.

At four o'clock, well after the tenth and final period, Simon left the biology room and found the school's hallways deserted. Only a silver-haired janitor came around a corner, shoving a couple of push brooms side by side to make his path wider. The apathetic glance he gave Simon implied, *Another day, another dollar.*

There wouldn't be much in the way of homework that night. Stopping off at his locker on the second floor, Simon snatched his English textbook from the lower shelf and swung the door shut harder than he meant to. The unintended bang echoed throughout the old building, and then there was only the nearly silent patter of his gym shoes on the tile floor as he made his way toward the main doors of the new building. Once he was back on the first floor, approaching the library, he noticed several colorful splashes of paint that had long since dried high on a wall—temporary riot scars for a building that had seen students come and go since the end of the last century. He listened to the hushed silence and thought, *Should always be like this.*

Instinctively, he kept an eye out for gangbangers coming from all angles, but Dexter was empty except for the night help in the office, John in his biology room, and the janitor sweeping steadily.

He saw no one else on Orchard or the playground. Thunderheads—a roiling, dark soup closing in fast over the city from the southwest—popped flashes of lightning, rumbled, and sent winds gusting through the swaying canopy of neighborhood trees. Broken or smashed classroom windows still needed boarding up, and pages of a basic math book that someone must have thrown into one of the school's fenced-in yards fluttered back and forth, like a ghost couldn't make up his mind which assignment to concentrate on.

Simon cut across the playground, lost in a daydream. Assault rifle in hand, he led a troop of dedicated revolutionaries on a suicide charge under withering fire from the ruling class's pig army. With John, Clyde,

Dia, kids from the white caucus, and radical members of Students for a Democratic Society fanned out on either side of him, he urged his troops, "Forward! Power to the people! The streets belong to the working class!" In cinematic slow-motion and to the beat of Led Zeppelin's "Whole Lotta Love," they returned fire at rooftop machine-gun nests and never flinched under the hail of bullets spitting up tracer dust all around them. "Take cover!" he muttered to himself, and pumped a fist-salute into the air. "Off the ruling—"

"Interrupting anything, Liberal?" The familiar voice traveled from one side of the playground to the other and bounced off Washington Upper Grade School's brick gymnasium wall. Startled, Simon stopped in his tracks, looked up, and saw Louis resting on his hip, high atop the baseball backstop's chain-link overhang. His grin said it all: *Caught'cha.* Simon thought, *Like talking to yourself is a crime?* He quickly changed his defiant salute into a laid-back wave, and yelled out, "Where've you been?" Guiltily, Simon could only hope that Louis hadn't seen him that day in the hallway when Louis had gotten jumped by gangbangers— seen that Simon had chickened out on coming to his aid.

"Just pulling my pud," Louis said, showing no sign of holding a grudge. "You?"

"Getting an education." Simon's tone insinuated that Louis might want to try doing the same sometime.

"Academic or political?"

"Both, you dumb-fuck."

Louis gave Simon a mocking fist salute of his own. "To the barricades! Or we could skip the revolution, go to my house, and"—he wiggled his eyebrows suggestively—"check out the *Playboy* I got. You ever see Ursula Undress's titties? Whoa."

Simon weighed his options. A peek at model/movie star Ursula Andress's breasts? Tempting. Then he remembered what John had said about staying away from people hooked on drugs. "Nah, can't," he lied. "Too much homework." As he moved on, the drizzle changed to a downpour, his gym shoes and bell-bottoms getting soaked. That's

when Louis yelled "Hey!" The boy got up on his knees at the edge
of the overhang, started waving his arms like the blackface performer
Al Jolson, and belted out a Negro spiritual popularized by the civil
rights movement, as well as ingrained in Simon since early childhood.

Ohhhhh-ohhhhh freedom
Ohhhhh freedom over me

He might as well have jabbed a finger into Simon's chest and said,
No place to hide, PK.
"How about this one, Liberal?"

We shall overcooooooome
We shall overcome someday

"Speed freak!" Simon shouted, but the wind and driving rain seemed
to steal the insult's teeth. A wriggling snake of lightning lit the sky
directly overhead in search of a lightning rod. With almost no delay,
a cracking boom of thunder made him jolt and duck for cover. *Fuck!*
Had a fissure in the earth's crust suddenly opened up between his
feet and glowed with molten magma from within, it would not have
surprised him. *Wants to get killed, be my guest.* And Simon took off jogging
for home, his fellow PK's hoarse voice fading behind him.

Deep in my heart
I do believe that
We shall overcome someday

26

Hail Mary

"DIA'S NOT TAKING ANY CALLS."

"But is she all—"

"Sorry." *Click.*

That was all the information Simon could pry out of Dia's mother when he phoned on Friday evening. He'd gone straight home from Juan's house to call Dia after having learned that she had been jumped by gangbangers in the alley. Now he loathed and mentally whipped himself. Why the hell hadn't he made it his number one priority during the riot to go find and protect Dia? *Coward!*

The following week, Dia didn't show up for school, and by Wednesday there was a rumor that she had transferred. Simon thought, *Gone, just like that?* He could easily walk the seven blocks from his house over to hers on Belden Avenue, but Mrs. Grossinger's sharp tone hadn't exactly given him the green light to drop by. On Thursday of the next week, the phone rang just as he got home from school. Still in his coat, he snatched the receiver of the desk phone in his father's study.

"Hello."

"Meet me at my basement door as soon as you can."

"I knew it was you! Where the fuck have you—"

"Gotta go." *Click.*

"Daaarling!" Whether Dia was mimicking the sex-kitten flamboyance of Hungarian actress Zsa Zsa Gabor or just overreaching in her teenage attempt at being alluring, Simon didn't care, letting her pull him out of the blustery March cold snap by his coat sleeves and into the den. She shut the door behind him and immediately started peppering his lips and cheeks with kisses.

"*Mmsk, mmsk, mmsk*, missed you." When she'd finally given the kisses a rest, Simon asked, "So, you're all right? I heard you got jumped and almost . . ."

"Raped," Dia finished for him. "Fucking asshole niggers."

It was the first time Simon had ever heard Dia use a racial slur, but under the circumstances, he let it ride.

"Talk about scary," she said. "If it wasn't for Mr. Lee screaming out his classroom window . . ." she leaned in for a hug, and Simon gave her one for what seemed to him a long time, so long that he wondered if all was right with her. Finally, he said, "I'd have gone ape-shit on those fuckers."

"You're a sweetheart," Dia murmured, her cheek pressed hard against his chest. She took a deep breath like she was luxuriating in his scent, and then as she let it out and let go of him, she said, "Oh well," sounding like her usual bubbly self again.

Simon thought, *Oh well?* Had he ever heard of the phrase *in denial*, her tone may not have struck him as odd. But odd or not, if she wasn't going to burst into a crying jag about her rape close call, who was he to insist she should?

"Like an idiot I go and tell my mom and dad what happened," Dia continued. "They freeeeaked! Just look at me." She stepped back so that Simon could get a load of her school uniform—pleated blue wool skirt that fell well below her knees, plain white blouse, and matching knee socks. Aside from her new straitlaced getup, she still looked as pouty-lipped, doe-eyed pretty to him as ever.

"They put you in a Catholic school?"

"Yep, Saint Bonnie's, and it's all girls. You've never seen so many two-faced sluts in all your life—genuflecting to the Virgin Mary during morning mass and then going to the bathroom to sneak a smoke and brag to each other about the boys they picked up at Rainbow ice rink. Here I've been raised a Unitarian, but now I'm supposed to get down on my knees and pray to some chick who lied about how she got knocked up? Besides, even if I were to buy into the whole Immaculate Conception thingamajig, it's been a while since I thought being a virgin was any great shakes."

"You're saying you're not a vir—"

"Shhhhh." Dia put her finger to Simon's mouth. "Don't be rude." She peppered his face with kisses again, and he tried to give as good as he got but kept thinking, *Saint Bonaventure High School?* His number one incentive for rolling out of bed each school day—flirtatious encounters between classes with the girl he had a crush on—had just taken a nosedive. Dia tiptoe-danced more than walked across the den to the couch and fell into it.

"Why don't you hurry up and take your coat and boots off? My dad's at work, and Mom took Benny to his judo class. That gives us maybe half an hour. I'm not allowed to . . . all of their new goddamn fucking rules. Ugh!"

Simon wondered, *New rules?* But before he could ask her for the lowdown, she patted the seat cushion next to her and singsonged, "*I'm waaaaaaiting.*" She didn't need to tell him twice.

An album was spinning on the stereo's turntable, and from the twin speakers came the muted voice of Jim Morrison crooning "People Are Strange." Dia scootched closer to Simon on the couch, took hold of his hands, and deposited them in her lap.

"So, did you miss me, too?"

"Yes, terribly." Simon's own use of the word *terribly* sounded a bit Zsa Zsa Gabor to him as well.

"Thought about me every night before you fell asleep?" Dia asked.

"Except on Sundays."

"Smart-ass!" Dia slapped Simon's face lightly. It tickled him to have gotten her goat, but he protested, "Hey!"

"You'll live," she said. Then getting the conversation back on track, she asked, "Do you want to go steady? You can't say yes if you don't love me."

"Yes, yes, yes." In case Simon had left any room for doubt, he drove his point home. "Quadruple yes."

"Ooooooo," she squealed, and dropped her eyes shyly for a moment, only to look dreamily up at Simon again. She gently raked her fingers through his unruly nest of hair. "My handsome blue-eyed boy."

After a short make-out session, during which Dia gave Simon pointers on how to shape his lips during French kisses so that he wouldn't keep slobbering on her, she brought him up to date. Apparently she'd gotten over her initial upset a few days after the attack, but by then her parents had decided that their permissive lifestyle was as much to blame for their daughter's brush with serious harm as anything else. "Like because I'm allowed to wear miniskirts, I'm asking to get raped?" From now on they were, as her father put it, "Getting their act together." That meant no more Dexter for Dia and definitely no more boys coming over to the house to, as her mother called it, "sniff around." Dia complained about the unfairness of Benny not having his life turned topsy-turvy, too, but at the tender age of nine, their parents must not have deemed him to be as morally corruptible as his big sister. "They should at least take the brat's magnifying glass away," she said. "Last summer the sadistic little fuck got his jollies frying ants with it in the sun. Are my parents worried he's going to turn into a mass murderer? Noooooo."

A free pass for Benny or not, the Grossingers' new leaf did not begin and end with Dia. Mrs. Grossinger swore off her habit of drinking a glass or two of wine during dinner, and Mr. Grossinger voluntarily flushed his stash of pot down the toilet.

"You're kidding me," Simon said. "Your father smokes dope?"

"Like a chimney." Then Dia added, "But only on weekends. I've got a nose that can smell a fart someone cut in Florida, so what makes him think I can't smell his pot smoke in the bathroom just because he stuffs a towel under the door and opens a window? Once upon a time, my parents were beatniks. They've gone from bongos and grass to ordering me to get rid of clothes that look too *hippy*. Bell-bottoms or anything mod? Gone. My mom takes me shopping in the prissy department at Marshall Field's. I mean, *saddle shoes?* Now we go to church every Sunday instead of just on Easter and Christmas Eve. Between that and the holy-roller nuns calling the shots at Saint Bonnie's, my ass is chapped from all the time I spend on pews. It's not fair!" She huffed, folded her arms across her chest, and stuck out her lower lip in a way that Simon found irresistibly cute.

"In other words, I'm up shit creek if your parents find me here."

"Unless," Dia said, "you're looking forward to spending a few years in jail."

Simon sprang off the couch in a show of terror. "Gotta go!" But now that he'd survived several riots at Dexter, sneaked undetected into Dia's basement twice, and been rewarded by her each time for his daring, operating under the threat of parents catching them red-handed seemed easy enough to deal with. He felt her tugging hard on the hem of his gray sweater, stretching the wool behind him so taut, he was able to lean forward at a forty-five degree angle without falling flat on his face. Hamming it up, he began to windmill his arms, demanding, "Lemme go!" Then, "She's lying, Your Honor! That is not my baby!" His clowning made her giggle as she managed, with a little less struggle from him, to pull him down onto the couch beside her again.

"Really, Simon. Like I'm not worth the risk?"

"Depends," he teased.

Dia took his right hand into hers and placed it, as solemnly as one who is about to pledge allegiance to the flag, onto her left breast. His fingers roamed, squeezed, and roamed some more.

"Thought so," she said triumphantly. And as they leaned in for another smooch, Simon felt himself crossing that great divide between the confines of childhood and a new world of adult bliss.

Dia was the first to hear a key jiggling in the front door lock upstairs.

"Shhh, is that . . ."

"We're hooooome!"

"Go!" Dia frantically pushed Simon off the couch. Even in the danger of the moment, they did their best to suppress fits of laughter. She hustled him across the den to the door, and before he knew it, he found himself out in the freezing cement stairwell.

"But my—"

His coat and boots came flying out the open door after him.

"Take the backyard gate to the alley so that my mom or Benny don't see you from the living room windows," Dia whispered. "Bye." And after a wink, she shut the door, the bolt lock clicking.

————————

Halfway down the cobblestone alley lined with garages, Simon realized that going steady meant new responsibilities. For starters, he'd have to get a job to pay for dates. Grocery stock boy? Maybe Clyde could put in a good word for him at McDonald's. Date scenarios flashed through his mind: splurging on Cokes and a sausage pizza in a booth at Roma's Pizzeria; watching *Night of the Living Dead* at the Three Penny Cinema, his arm draped protectively around Dia's shoulders in case she gets scared by the cannibal zombie hoards on the screen; or skating hand in hand round and round Rainbow ice rink, so lost in their own private world that the crowded flow of other skaters seems to always magically part and give them extra space. *Like a normal couple that goes to a normal high school.* And as for the discipline of nonviolence? *Sure, unless someone so much as even thinks the word rape around*

Dia ever again. Then Simon would do like Juan and crack a few skulls with his Louisville Slugger. *Push my nonviolence at your own fucking risk.*

Simon continued past a telephone pole and a couple of garbage drums, stopped briefly just for the hell of it to do a bossa nova two-step that his mother had taught him years before during a church social, and then went around a corner toward the mouth of the alley on Belden. A part–German shepherd mutt rushed up to a chain-link fence and kept pace with Simon for the length of a backyard, growling and barking bloody murder.

"Shut the fuck up!" Simon screamed, and to his amazement, the dog did just that, trotting away toward a porch, his bluff called. Simon moved along, a cushion of pride beneath his boots. He veered around a large patch of black ice, and, sick of winter, he longed for spring. *Melt, motherfucker.* All things seemed within reach. Dia Grossinger was his girlfriend.

27

Dreamer

"I TRIED, REVEREND. Tapped out all of my politico channels. The word is you got some rotten apples around here."

It was weird. Adam thought, *Drops in for a visit to the Body Politic on a Saturday? Out of uniform, no less.* Clark's explanation of "happened to be in the neighborhood" just didn't add up, even smelled of harassment. Not that Adam had ever fully believed a beat cop assigned to Dexter would have the kind of political pull it would take to stop the city from putting him out of business.

"Rotten apples, huh?" From behind his desk strewn with publicity announcements, headshot photos of cast members, utility bills, and more, Adam slowly rotated in his high-backed swivel chair, measured the man sitting across from him with a sideways glance, and then rotated back again. "If you're referring to struggling actors, puppeteers, modern dancers, muralists—"

"Not the artsy types." Clark's frown implied that Adam should stop playing dumb. "The rabble-rousers."

"Like I already told you. Rising-Up Rage pays their rent on time."

"Look, alls I'm saying is that you might want to reconsider whether or not it's smart to mix art and politics."

"The two often go hand in hand," Adam said, "historically speaking."

"How's about prehistorically?" Clark asked. "Ever hear of any cave drawings that show people clubbing their chief—the dude who could hunt rings around everyone else—because they didn't agree with how much meat he kept for himself? Nope, cave peons stuck to drawing antelope. Now fast-forward a few thousand years. Guess whose name keeps popping up on the Red Squad's intelligence reports?" The cop's tight smile said it all.

"Didn't know renting out an office was the same as clubbing a chief," Adam said.

"Let's just call it poor cave judgment." Then Clark added, "Like when you went down to Lincoln Park last summer and joined in with the rioters at the Democratic Convention."

"Protesters," Adam corrected. "Antiwar protesters."

"And you had to go and help organize that student boycott at Dexter, align yourself with those Che-loving Young Saints and that card-carrying pinko John Lange. Can you see how some folks might start to connect the blips you're making on their radar screen?"

"Only if those same folks are looking for an excuse to violate my constitutional rights," Adam said. "And by the way, I've heard that John Lange is an excellent teacher."

"In what subject?" Clark smirked. "Biology or Bolshevism? Don't it bother you just a teensy that the man's giving your boy an earful of propaganda?"

"I'm sure Simon can figure out his own political views just fine."

"Whatever you say, but from what I've heard, Lange never shuts up with his goddamn brainwashing. If he spent half as much time doing what he was hired to do at Dexter instead of telling coloreds they should run the zoo, maybe we wouldn't have had that riot last week. What a mess: sixty-three arrested for disorderly conduct."

The total parroted what Adam had heard on the evening news, but if they were indeed accurate rather than inflated, why, Adam wondered, had Simon stonewalled any attempts to pry information out of him about the riot, even stormed away from the dinner table, yelling, "You think I can't handle myself?" Adam had chalked up Simon's defiance to typical teenage orneriness rather than to his son hiding his feeling that he was failing miserably at his given mission: to thrive in a racially integrated school. And so Adam and Helen had decided that until Simon communicated otherwise to them, he had learned how to fit in at school.

"Whatever the hell happened at Dexter, you can't blame it all on John Lange. My son didn't have a scratch on him, so how bad—"

"Who do you suppose made sure of that?" Clark asked. The way he slowly eased back in his chair seemed to imply that there could be but one honest answer. "Trade places with your kid or me for a single day, and you'd drop all the do-gooder bullshit. For example—"

"I never asked for any special treatment for Simon," Adam reminded Clark. "And you can spare me your example."

"What's a matter? Afraid I might turn you into a law-and-order Republican?"

"The trouble with you, Officer, is that you can't recognize a lost cause when you see one. Now, if you'll excuse me, I have work—"

"You're telling me your boy's safety is a lost cause?"

Adam squashed an impulse to flare up. Then aware that as a responsible father he had no other choice than to take the cop's bait, he shrugged. "If it'll make your day . . ."

"Indulge me," Clark said. "A few years ago, we had this child molester locked up down at the station, a real perve, if you know what I mean. Here he is pushing forty and still living with his folks. First time I laid eyes on him, he was getting fingerprinted in the booking room. That fucker deserved to be executed on ugly alone—cauliflower ears and a honker so big, I'll bet you could have shoved a Trident sub up each one of his nostrils. Had that shy, namby-pamby, wouldn't-hurt-a-fly way about him. Little girls, though, he considered fair game. Used to wait until his mother was doing something like grocery shopping, his father was still at work, and all the kindergartners from Agasse Elementary were coming down his quiet side street on their way home from school. All it took was a 'Hey, wanna come into my house for some peppermint ice cream?' and it was game over."

"Your point?" Adam's asked.

"Long story short, charges are pressed, we make an arrest, perve signs a confession, and it's as good as case closed, right? Not in the real world. The arresting officers who kicked in perve's door also dropped the ball on reading him his rights, a technicality that allows his hotshot lawyer to bitch and moan that his client's confession is inadmissible evidence. One by one, the parents who pressed charges start to think twice about putting their kid through having to testify in court and instead want to keep things hush-hush. The DA's office takes a closer look at the hand they're dealt and decides they don't have a strong enough case. End result? Perve goes free to molest again, except now he's learned his lesson about leaving kindergartners behind for witnesses. He manages to keep his dick clean for about a month, and then we find a girl who's been sexually violated in more ways than I care to count, strangled to death, and dumped naked in the woods by the north branch of the Chicago River. She lived right around the corner from you-know-who. Coincidence? We pick up our prime suspect for questioning, make damn sure this time around to read him his fucking rights, but can't get him to admit so much as his zip code. Meanwhile, forensics—whether they just screwed up royally or namby-pamby wore a Trojan and gloves—draws a blank on any hard physical evidence. It doesn't take long for hotshot lawyer to start squawking about habeas corpus. We can stall and keep his client locked up a couple of more nights, but after that . . ."

"Sounds like the moral to this story is to follow proper procedure the first time around," Adam said. "Everyone's entitled to due process. Live and learn."

"Yep," Clark returned. "But tell me, would you be singing the same tune if that was your kid dumped in those woods?"

Adam's long pause admitted, *Fair question.* Then he asked, "Your point? If you don't mind getting to it—today."

"Almost there. A couple of pals and me decide that enough's enough, and we pay namby-pamby a visit in his cell. Fucker's sleeping with the covers over his head, but not for long. He starts blubbering about mercy. Like the mercy he showed that little girl? Let's just say that his belt and an air vent on the ceiling came in handy. I'm the lucky one who got to grab him around his waist and tug. Ever hear a man's neck snap? Justice served. The first round of beers was on me that night.

"My point, Reverend, is this: when I have a job to do, I make sure it gets done for the *good* of all. Right now, one of my jobs is to keep tabs on John Lange. You've got some radar blips that could use erasing and a son who needs protection. How's about a little trade off, like asking Simon to keep me posted on what Lange's up to every now and then? Just a little dad-nudge, and you and him can live happily ever—"

"Let me get this straight." Adam tilted upright in his chair. "You want me to ask my son to snitch on his teacher so that you can help the Red Squad build a file and maybe get John fired down the road. Is that it?"

"Exactly."

"What makes you think . . . how about I go to the authorities instead and tell them that you admitted to murder?"

"*Authorities?* Funny," Clark said. "Besides, did we ever have this conversation? Didn't think so." He let Adam hang on the meaning of his grin and slowly got up from his chair. "I just stopped in to see how things were going with you and your Body Politic. No offense taken I hope."

Adam's silence spoke for him. Then he watched the cop take his time leaving, pausing in the doorway and glancing about at the bare-bones office with a look that bordered on wonder.

"Pity to see everything you've worked for go down the drain. Minus the Rising-Up Rage idiots, I kind of like what you're trying to do around here. You won't believe me, but once upon a time, I wanted to be an actor. Got to play George in *Our Town* during senior year. All that applause and two curtain calls. I changed from a nobody and into a chick magnet overnight."

"Why didn't you go into acting?" Adam was aware of the strange turn in the conversation and his stranger still impulse to take Clark at his word about having considered a career on the stage. The cop gave a look of buried regret and began zipping up his leather coat.

"Not exactly practical."

"Never too late," Adam suggested, his tone split between sarcasm and a ministerial belief that all human beings are salvageable.

"Sure, I'll give up my badge for the life of a starving thespian first thing Monday morning. Just remember that *never too late* is a two-way street." Clark waved so long. Then, stepping out the door, "See you at the barricades."

Adam realized how on guard he'd been, and his shoulders slumped. He couldn't get the image of a man, his neck oddly bent and chin buried against his collarbone, twisting to a dangling halt. And Adam knew one thing for certain: if Clark had indeed been responsible for Simon's well-being of late, Dexter was not the culturally diverse panacea that he'd naively hoped it would become—not for his fourteen-year-old, anyway. He and Helen would have to find their son a new high school, but where? Because the board of ed.'s desegregation plan . . . *Joke's on us.* He considered private school options. But without a scholarship like the one Francis Parker had given to Beth? *Can't afford it!* Adam reached up and rubbed his fingertips hard against the furrows in his forehead. *Stupid mess!* Trading one predicament for another, he flipped open the Community Arts Foundation's ledger book on his desk and then opened the checkbook spiral, too. First he wrote a check to Commonwealth Edison. Next, Peoples Gas. *Pay half and pray for a warm April.* Illinois Bell? *Bastards already cut off my phone service once.* Water bill? *Deal with it next month.* He pegged the roofer who had tarred over a leak as a decent enough fellow to let him slide on the bill for a while. That left the $58 for a new toilet in the women's bathroom, $364 on the equity loan from Aetna Bank, $531 on the mortgage from First National, and the lawyer's bill—$1,480 and counting—for fighting city hall. *Got me by the balls!*

Almost five minutes later, Adam was still staring at the line items in the ledger book, wishing he could will the figures into juggling themselves balanced enough for him to write in a token dollar amount on the line reserved for his salary. His rising anxiety began to merge with the rhythm of clapping—someone keeping time for modern dancers rehearsing in a studio. He glanced at his wristwatch. *Fuck it.* He got up and went over to the coat tree to grab his army-surplus trench coat. Time to go home for lunch.

He locked his office door behind him. Then he heard a floorboard creak somewhere in the upstairs theater. Stepping around the corner of a stairwell wall blocking his view, he thought he saw someone standing perfectly still in the inky darkness and at center stage only twenty or so feet away. *Still here?* A dim exit light in a far corner wasn't much help. Whether Adam's eyes were playing tricks on him or not, the phantom appeared to have Clark's hulking stance, only minus the gut, like this shadowy version of the cop had magically shed the padded wear and tear of middle age. *Tell him to get the hell out?* Then he thought of suggesting that Clark pick up a flyer at the box office, one that listed the schedule for acting classes offered at the Body Politic, but he quickly vetoed that idea as nothing short of insane. Neither he nor the phantom spoke a word, both waiting for the other to break the ice. Finally, Adam slowly backpedaled until he'd gone behind the stairwell wall again. He reached for a doorknob, turned it, pushed, and stepped out.

Looking down into the lobby at the bottom of the stairs, Adam saw the overcrowded leaflets and posters on a wall used as a bulletin board for upcoming arts-related events of all sorts. Across from that, Bonnie, the promising young actress who worked a couple of shifts in the box office to make ends meet, sat on her chair behind the counter, reading a novel in her lap, the reservations phone obviously not ringing off the hook. Chilled by the weird experience he'd just left behind, Adam started down the stairs and thought, *Fine. Might do the man some good to regret what might have been. Let him dream.*

28

Gun Diplomacy

MR. LANGE MUST HAVE BEEN RUNNING LATE from the teachers' lounge to his biology room for the start of class. Unsupervised, students goofed off, someone yelling at someone else, "Your mama so poor, she live on the second floor of a vacant lot."

Amid lots of slapping five and hooting, little Floyd Murray crowed, "Damn, that one so old, Moses use it to crack on Pharaoh." Simon, already seated and tapping his Bic against the edge of his textbook, just happened to glance a few tables up the row to see Frank Tucker leaning closely over a girl in her chair. The Cobra Stone must have slipped into the room between classes to lay the rap on her. All dimples and redbone skin, she kept shaking her head *no* but grinning *yes*, skilled at making Tucker work hard for her affection. And then the inevitable happened, and Tucker's gaze landed on Simon. The boy's flirty smile immediately dropped to . . . what? Anger? Dominance? Regret? Simon had already quickly flipped open his textbook to the unit on evolution and begun to pretend he was studying before the gangbanger's expression clicked for him. Indifference.

The bell rang. Tucker gave a wink at the girl, pimp-walked out of the room, and must have just missed bumping into Juan coming through the same doorway only a few seconds later. Dressed in a gray suit and carrying a briefcase, Juan would have looked like the epitome of a Wall Street banker had he not also been wearing combat boots. As he made his way halfway down the first row of tables to the one that he shared with Simon, many students stopped whatever they were doing to whistle at him or clap.

"Looking *clean!*"

"What?" Juan feigned surprise. "Haven't none of you ever been around someone high class?"

"*Faaan*-cy," Simon said, shaking his hand like it needed cooling off. "Did you get lost on your way home from church?"

In a dignified manner, Juan straightened the knot in his tie, slipped into his seat, and waited a moment longer for the rest of the class to resume suspended conversations before he told Simon, "This is my stomping suit. I wear it whenever I think I might have some business to take care of."

"Business?" Simon asked.

Juan lowered his voice, whispering, "Want to see something?" Taking his briefcase off the table, he placed it on the floor in between their chairs, flipped the latches, and opened it up just a crack so that Simon could peek inside. Light from the overhead fluorescent bulbs bypassed a few folders and books and reflected dully off the stunted barrel of a sawed-off shotgun.

"Baby, meet Simon."

There had been close to a month of on-again, off-again riots at Dexter, and for the last couple of weeks, it was a known fact that every black and Latino gang on the North Side of Chicago had declared war on Corps. A half dozen Black Disciples pulled one Corps member right out of his seat in the middle of Miss Herta's Spanish classroom. Dragging him into the hallway, they ignored the teacher's hysterical protests and inflicted a "whupping" so severe, there was talk of brain damage. In another incident, a group of Latin Kings stabbed a Corps member twenty-four times with switchblades and left him for dead on the sidewalk in front of Nick's Vienna.

Staring at Baby, Simon thought, *That's a gun, a fucking gun.*

"Are you nuts?" Even as Simon said it, he couldn't resist reaching a hand down, wanting to run his fingers along Baby's stock and trigger. Juan slammed the briefcase shut and locked the latches shut again.

"Not here," he told Simon. "But stick around. First nigger or spic that fucks with me, I'll blow his motherfucking head right off. Told you Baby was for real. Didn't believe me, did you?"

And then Simon knew. Whether it was carrying a gun, the sheer safety of numbers, or having a cop like Clark looking out for you, all was fair in an unfair world.

Soon John Lange whisked through the doorway and to his desk at the front of the classroom. As he took roll, the students' chatter died down.

"OK, everyone turn to page 204 in your textbooks. The immune system. Can anyone tell me what that is?"

For the rest of the period, Simon thought about Baby in the briefcase at his side, pretended that the gun was his, and felt unafraid.

29

Higher Consciousness

MEANWHILE, LOUIS HAD DISAPPEARED from Dexter again. Days turned into weeks. Then one evening at the tail end of April, as Simon lay on the couch watching reruns of *Superman*, the phone rang. When he picked up in the study, a voice on the other end of the line asked, "Wanna get stoned?" Louis explained that he was babysitting for a "hippy" divorcée mom. On the hunch that she liked to get high, he'd scoured the loft apartment and found her stash—a vitamin C bottle half filled with pot—tucked behind pairs of pajamas and jeans in her bottom dresser drawer. "She won't notice we borrowed some." He assured Simon that you can't get addicted to marijuana, and no, it doesn't kill your brain cells or turn you into a schizophrenic. "Seventeen-o-three Armitage, third floor. The name on the buzzer is Maher."

Simon thought it over. *Maybe just this . . .* "OK." He hung up the phone and yelled out, "Going to meet Louis!" Already streaking down the stairs to the front door, he heard his mom calling to him from in his parents' bedroom, "Home by nine o'clock, and not a second—" *Slam.*

———————

He climbed the last of the three-flat's entryway stairs, saw Louis grinning down at him from the top landing, and immediately noticed the wicked shiner anchored under his friend's left eye socket.

"Damn, man. What happened to your—"

"Compliments of the brothers," Louis said. The way he moped back into the apartment sent the clear signal that he preferred not to go into detail. *Fine*, Simon thought, familiar with the shame.

The four-year-old was already fast asleep in her bedroom. Simon took in his surroundings: a bare brick wall adorned with a neon-bright poster for the musical *Hair* and an American flag that had a peace sign where the fifty stars should have been; the leftover smell of incense, Tiger Balm, and patchouli oil; and an eclectic array of shabby and makeshift furniture, some of which served as testimony to the many utilitarian and stackable uses of milk crates. *Definitely hippy taste.* He followed Louis across the loft's rough planks to the living room area, peeled off his windbreaker, and fell onto the couch. Through an open window came the drone of traffic on Armitage, the dying light of dusk over the city, and the breezy scent of an awakening spring.

"So where is it?" Simon wanted to hurry up and smoke before he got cold feet.

"Easy, Liberal." On the other side of a coffee table made out of an industrial-sized wooden spool, Louis sank into an overstuffed chair, reached into his shaggy hairline, and plucked a joint from behind his ear. "Smoking pot takes a sense of grace, a sense of culture, a sense of cosmic dignity, all of which we're going to have to work on in your case."

Scattered on the table were back issues of *Evergreen Review* and a *Black Panther* newspaper with a front-page photo of Huey P. Newton sitting in a tall throne-like wicker chair, a harpoon in one hand and a shotgun in the other. Louis produced a book of matches from one of his khakis pockets, lit the joint, and took a long, deep toke. Holding in his breath, he passed the cigarette to Simon. Back and forth it went between the boys, with Simon determined to match his friend's druggy finesse by never gagging on the raw smoke. Louis solemnly ate the last of the burnt roach. A standing reading lamp rigged with a round Chinese paper lantern cast them both in sinister shadows.

"Are you stoned?" Louis asked.

"Nope."

"It always takes longer the first time."

"It better happen before nine o'clock," Simon said. He'd expected to feel like he could float and dematerialize through walls.

"What's your rush, honky?"

"Fuck you, asshole," Simon said. "Look who's calling who a honky."

"Sheeeeeeee . . ." Louis stretched the word until the *it* on the end might as well have been silent.

"Only honky I sees round here be you," Simon said. Two could play this game.

Louis popped up from his chair, Simon did the same, and in less-than-smooth pimp-walks around the table, they met halfway. Squared off in belligerent stances, each tried to out-black the other.

"Loan me a dime, honky." Louis began to frisk Simon down. "All I find, all I keep."

Simon gave his friend turned gangbanger a hard shove. "Keep your mothafuckin hands off me before I dot your eye and wipe some of that white off your ass."

Louis doubled over laughing.

"What the fuck you laughing at, honky? Not me unless you ready to joust. Think you so beau-coup bad?"

"Awww, scrub," Louis said, "be cool."

"I ain't no scrub, and I ain't no honky." Simon set the record straight. "I'm Stone to the bone."

"Right on, brother." Louis beat his fist proudly against his chest and then held it out in a stiff-armed salute, the same way any gang member of the Peace Stone Nation would represent his club. "We's partners."

"Partners?" Simon's black hearing must have been playing tricks on him. "With a honky? I ain't your mothafuckin partner. I ain't even your mothafuckin associate, much less your mothafuckin blood. And if you calls me your mothafuckin brother one more mothafuckin time, I'm going to whup you upside your mothafuckin head. Is that moth-a-fuck-in clear? Now, this here be my brother."

Simon snatched the *Black Panther* newspaper off the table and held the cover photo of Huey P. Newton next to his own face.

"See the family resemblance? I taught Huey P. everythang he know; just ask any soul brother on the South Side. Go ahead and laugh, honky, 'cause that's what I be doing all last night when your mama be sucking on my dick like it a Popsicle stick."

"Don't be talking about my mama," Louis warned. "Last honky talk about my mama found his dick hanging from the gotdamn antenna on de Prudential Building. He done fucked his last hammer."

"His what?" In Simon's need for clarification he'd turned white again.

"His hammer, honky! There he be walking down the street, leaning hard on his hammer, when I drives by in my Cadillac and says to myself, 'Ain't that the honky who been signifying on my mama?' Sho-nuff it him, so I's jumps out my car, push the hammer flat back on her ass, and then takes out my blade that always come in handy for slicing off honky dicks."

"Sheeeeeit," Simon said, hitching up his jeans, but now it was he who couldn't stop laughing, and he threw himself down onto the couch.

"So the honky be laying there bleeding and shit, screaming, 'Gimme back my dick, mothafucka!' I's about to jump back in my Cadillac when I notice that the bitch just naturally spread her legs after falling flat on her ass on the sidewalk. Might calls it a ho reflex. So I drop my pants and drawers and start getting me some. The dude ain't saying boo, 'cause he know damn well he can't no way satisfy her pussy no more. He just start crying and shit, and she be groaning and shit, and I'm a humping fool."

Simon sprawled out on the couch and started kicking his legs like a kid throwing a temper tantrum. "Will you shut up!" Beginning to have second thoughts about the game, he wondered, *Racist?* He grabbed a small throw pillow and held it down over his face in an effort to smother his laughter.

"Four or five hours later, it time to zipper up," Louis continued. "I drives off, go straight downtown to the Prudential Building, and take me the elevator to the observation deck. Sheeeit, I give them honkies something to observe, all right. I sneak up the stairs to the roof, climb on up the antenna, and sticks the honky's dick over the top. Had to stretch it a little, 'cause them white boys' dicks only be about three inches. Then I look out over the whole gotdamn Chicago skyline with all them big-ass skyscrapers where rich honkies give orders and make money off a black folks' sweat, and I say, 'That what you get for talking about my mama.' Ain't no one get Channel Nine tuned in for quite a while with that honky's dick ruining the reception and all."

Simon slid the pillow off his face, in control of himself just as long as he stared up at the ceiling. He took a deep breath, looked over at Louis, and said, "That's not funny."

Louis's bone-weary expression implied, *Give me a break.* He went over to his chair and dropped into it.

"So tell me this, Liberal. You don't take acid, you don't drink, you don't fuck, you don't read, and you can't even imitate blacks without feeling guilty. What exactly is it that you like?"

Simon shrugged. He supposed he could tell Louis about Dia, but in truth his going-steady romance with her had hit a few snags. None of his job applications—one to become a McDonald's server, another for a stock-boy position at a Certified grocery store, and still another for an usher opening at the Biograph Theater—had so far amounted to an actual job offer. His lack of money to pay for dates, his and Dia's now going to different schools, his extensive baseball game and practice schedules, and the fact that Dia's parents watched her like a hawk and wouldn't let her stray from their house after dark, even on weekends, had left their relationship reduced to little more than marathon phone conversations. Besides, he didn't want to risk giving Louis an opening to tease him about not having "gone all the way" with Dia. Then, sure that Louis would make fun of his second *like* choice, but having no third, he said it anyway. "Baseball."

"Well, golly-gee-whiz. The liberal likes to play baseball."

"Yeah, that's right." For once, this was something Simon knew how to defend. "I like the feeling you get when you're out in center field and you can smell the grass and there's all these dandelions and the sun's real hot. From there you can see the whole game in front of you, and the infielders are chattering, 'Hey-batter-hey-batter-heeeeeeey, swing!' It's weird, but you get to where you know a batter's going to hit the ball in your direction before the pitcher even throws it. Everything gets real quiet inside your head, and then *BAM!* There's that crack of the bat, and you're already off and running. You follow the ball as it comes over your shoulder, and just when you think there's no way you're going to get there in time, you dive for it. You're flying, every muscle straining, and like a miracle you snag the ball in the top of your web. Then as you slide through the grass, you know that this is what you play baseball for, this is what you always want, 'cause it's cool, man. It's fucking *cool!*"

"Baseball," Louis said impassively, but now his facade of boredom seemed forced, his undivided attention on Simon.

"I mean, did you ever hit a baseball?" Simon asked. "Really cream one solid?" He stood up and assumed a batting stance, his hands gripping an imaginary bat. "You're up at the plate and the pitcher goes into his windup and you're already stepping into the pitch before the ball even leaves his hand. You can feel the power in your body uncoil right up your legs and into your hips and then your arms start to come around and just at the moment when your bat meets the ball you flick those wrists and *BAM!*"

For a few seconds, Simon visualized the trajectory of a ball sailing over the heads of fielders and beyond.

"See, no one thinks I can hit a ball far 'cause I'm skinny, but all it takes is quick wrists and timing. There's that solid crack, and the ball takes off like a bullet down the left-field line. Watching it only slows you down on the base path, so you let the coaches do your watching for you. If the first-base coach waves you around, you go for two, and if the third-base coach yells at you to keep on coming, you head for three, and if he waves you around, you barrel for home. The other team's relaying the ball in and the catcher's getting set to take the throw and your whole team's up off the dugout bench, yelling, 'Slide! Slide! Hit the dirt!' The ball beats you to the plate, so you plow into the catcher and jar the ball loose from his mitt. The ump calls 'Saaaaaafe,' and your team goes wild, everyone cheering and slapping five 'cause you just hit a home run."

The look of stoner boredom in Louis's bloodshot eyes contradicted how he was pressing himself into the chair, hands gripping armrests. "To each his own." Then he cracked, "If a coach didn't mind me toking off a joint between innings, I'd be all in."

"You know," Simon continued, and slowly sat down on the couch again, "the first time my dad took me to Wrigley Field, I was seven. For some reason I thought it was going to look black and white, the same as on TV, but jeez! The outfield grass was so green and the infield dirt looked like gold dust and there was all that thick ivy on the outfield walls. Ernie Banks came to the plate and smacked the first pitch onto Waveland Avenue, and everyone started cheering and shit. I knew right then and there I wanted to be a major leaguer. I mean, when I lived in Oriole Park everyone played baseball. First you start out in the Peewee League, and then you move up to the Midgets and then Pony. I was an all-star for three straight years! You get to where you play so much baseball, you know what to do before it even happens: man on first—play's at two; bases loaded—force at home; watch out for the bunt—third base and first base pull in; steal sign on—shortstop cover second; full count—runners going; sacrifice fly—tag up and dig for home. And when you win, rub it in. Two! Four! Six! Eight! Who do we appreciate? Yankees! Yankees! Yaaaaay!"

Simon had leapt to his feet, his hands above his head like he'd just thrown his baseball mitt into the air to celebrate his team's victory. And then the words were just there in his mouth. He looked at Louis, lowered his arms, and said, "I know how your father died."

Louis's expression subtly changed from disbelief to grinning to anger and back to disbelief. "So." His jaw twitched, his lips a tight, flat line as he stared at Simon. "What do you want, a fucking medal? It's not like front-page news on every newspaper in the country is any goddamn secret." He looked furious, furious with Simon, with his father, with anything and everything. Simon plunked down onto the couch, uncomfortable with the advantage he felt over his friend, and said, "Sorry. I just wanted you to know I know." Then, trying to disarm Louis, he asked, "Why do you hang around me, anyway?"

Louis looked on the verge of saying the nastiest, foulest, going-for-the-jugular thing he could think of, but then he seemed to relax and consider the question. Finally, he said, "Because you're so normal."

Simon didn't know whether to take Louis's opinion of him as a compliment or a put-down. *Normal?* This was 1969, the age of the flower child, underground rock, "Power to the people," and "Off the pigs." Somehow *normal* just didn't seem to cut it.

They avoided looking at each other for a while, nothing to break the silence but the rattling hum of a refrigerator at the other end of the loft. Trying to lighten the mood, Louis asked, "So do you feel it yet?"

"Feel what?" Simon was still preoccupied with digesting his new title of Normal.

"The grass, Liberal, the grass."

"Nah." Simon stared across the loft at nothing in particular. "I don't feel shit."

30

Mistaken Identity

"WHERE'S YOUR HALL PASS?" At the start of third period, Clark had just topped a staircase in the old building, rounded the corner, and nearly bumped into the boy.

"Awww man, the bell just—"

"Your pass?"

Except for the two of them, the long corridor was deserted, with classroom doors already shut. The kid explained, "I had to go to the baf'room."

"Must have been one hell of a slow piss." As Clark folded his arms across his chest, he scrutinized the student and thought, *Dark as Africa. And how the hell does he breathe through a nose that flat?*

"Maybe if you got to class on time, you could learn stuff, like how 'baf'room' isn't in the dictionary." Something vaguely familiar about the boy made Clark ask, "Haven't I seen you in front of school wearing a black beret?"

"Naw, I don't—"

"Jive, jive, jive," Clark repeated. After a month and a half of on-again, off-again riots, Dexter had been relatively calm for almost a week, and he intended to keep it that way. That meant no "strays" wandering the hallways, itching to pull a firebox alarm to get the riot-ball rolling again.

"Last chance. Are you or are you not a Black Assassin?"

"You gots me mixed up with—"

Before the kid could finish his sentence, Clark had grabbed him by the scruff of his neck and slammed him up against the green lockers that lined the wall. The boy's folders and textbooks that he'd been cradling under one of his arms spilled with a paper-strewn crash onto the checkerboard floor.

"Spread 'em."

The boy kept his cheek pressed against a locker's air vent, spread his legs, and placed his palms high against metal doors. Clark frisked him from top to bottom. Nothing.

"Turn around and empty your pockets."

"Awww man."

"'Awww man' me again, and you'll find out what real trouble is, punk."

The kid sullenly did as he was told, digging into the front pockets of his trousers and then pulling out his hands to show the dollar or so in coins he held in one and a strand of lint in the other.

"Rolled some white kid for chump change, huh?" Before the boy could deny the accusation, Clark smacked the bottom of the kid's open hand so that the coins sprayed and ching-a-linged onto the floor. A quarter fled the farthest, took a step down the stairs, and then gyrated to a stop. "Next time you think about lying, think twice. Now get your Black Assassin ass out of my sight."

While the boy squatted to collect his strewn belongings, a drawing, done in ballpoint pen and hanging halfway out of a powder-blue folder, caught Clark's attention. "What the hell's that?" He pointed and snapped his fingers a couple of times. "Fork it over."

The boy slid the piece of artwork the rest of the way out of the folder and offered it up to Clark, who noticed that the sheet of lined notebook paper was shaking because of the boy's trembling hand. *Good.* He snatched the drawing and held it raised for closer inspection.

"You drew this?"

The kid gave a minimal nod.

"You're shitting me. Pretty damn good. You some kind of Rembrandt?"

"*Rembrandt,*" the boy said, standing up straight again, "don't know nothing about no comic books. That my character."

"Superman with an Afro?"

"He called Supersoul," Clyde said.

"What the fuck is he doing?"

"He tunneling through rock and fiery lava on his way to the center of the earth. That where his arch nemesis Nucleatron done stashed a few hundred mega H-bombs. Supersoul got thirty seconds to get there, deactivate them, and save the planet."

Clark kept scrutinizing the drawing's intricately shaded details. "Where did you learn . . ." Something just didn't compute, seemed beyond the realm of possibility, but despite that, the cop had to ask, "Does he get there in time? To save the world?"

"Ain't decided yet. Won't know till after I've started the next drawing."

Creative license aside, Clyde's response sounded intentionally smug to Clark. He crumpled the drawing in his bearlike mitt and then let it drop.

"Noooooo." It came out more of a moan than a word, and Clyde stooped to try to catch the falling paper ball on its way to the floor, only to flub it.

"Next time have a pass," Clark said, and strolled away boldly, refusing to look back even as he heard Clyde trying to smooth out his drawing. He fought an itch to second-guess how he'd treated the kid. *Fuck it,* he thought. *Protects my rep. No real harm done.*

31

Maxwell Street

DAWN. LOUIS SWUNG HIMSELF out of his twin bed. From the floor he picked up the same dirty Levis and faded tie-dye T-shirt he'd worn for the last couple of days and dressed as quietly as possible so as not to wake his mother, whose bedroom was on the other side of a wall. Outside his window, birds were already making a racket with their chirping and competing songs. He moved across the tiny room, pulled his *Webster's Dictionary* off a bookshelf, and opened it to a page in the *Ms*. There he'd stashed a hundred bucks of profit from dealing pot. He put the book back in its slot on the shelf, wadded up the bills, and shoved them deep into one of his jeans pockets. Good to go, he suddenly remembered to feed his tropical fish and picked up a small tin shaker of food from the table where his ten-gallon aquarium sat. The other half of the table served for what he called his "pyro lab," complete with a dozen or so jars of chemicals and an empty mortar and pestle that permanently gave off the tangy reek of homemade gunpowder and other flammable concoctions. From the tin he sprinkled a gluttonous amount of dried flecks into the water, watched his diverse school of exotically colored pets dart straight for the surface to feed, and felt a pang of responsibility. Who would periodically clean the tank, jiggle the finicky air pump whenever it stalled, and check the thermometer to make sure that the heater was keeping the water temperature at seventy-seven degrees? *Add it to the list*, he thought, and whispered to his pals, "Bye."

He began to hunt through the deserted neighborhood side streets for a VW Beetle with an unlocked door. It was already mid-May, and the rising sun would undoubtedly burn off the chilly haze in no time flat. A few blocks from home, he found what he was searching for parked near an alley on Bissell Street. Stopping on the sidewalk, he took note of the car's color, grinned, and thought, *Perfect. Black.* He checked up and down the block for any witnesses in the darkened windows of the two- and three-flats, spotted none, and then cut across the dew-soaked curb lawn. Once he'd opened the driver's door and climbed into the bucket seat, he reached underneath the steering column, pulled an electrical switch out of its clip, and yanked a couple of wires loose. He sparked them together to hop the ignition. The engine purred. A few minutes later, he was pushing the speed limit south down Halsted Street.

He hit one green light after another. As he passed the sterile high-rises and grounds of the Cabrini Green Projects on his left, he cranked the window handle down, felt the rush of wind against his face, and screamed, "Yeeeeeee-owwww!" Time for some music, but all he could find after scanning through commercials on the AM radio dial was the bubble gum song, "Yummy, Yummy, Yummy." *Fucking top-forty teenybopper bullshit.* Out of self-defense to his ears and hard-rock sensibilities, he clicked the radio knob to off again and wondered how much longer it would take for car companies to start adding FM to their factory-equipped tuners. *Idiots.* A mile to the east, the downtown Chicago skyline was magnificently backlit by a sliver of crimson sun already peeking over the lakefront.

On Randolph Street, dock workers were unloading crates of produce from trucks, and in Greektown, Louis passed by a strip of closed restaurants, then crossed yet another bridge that spanned the Eisenhower Expressway, and continued on past the University of Illinois' new Chicago Circle campus. He reached the Maxwell Street outdoor flea market—better known as Jew Town to blacks—where people came from all over the city looking for good deals on anything from hubcaps to laundry detergent, antiques to overcoats, toys to knives. Arriving just as most of the vendors were finishing with unloading their merchandise from pickup trucks and vans, he found the last parking spot still available on that block of Halsted and swerved his "borrowed" car right into it.

The rich deep-fryer smell of french fries and grilled Polish sausages escaped in a smoky cloud from an exhaust vent atop a Vienna hot dog shack where bargain hunters were already lining up. Louis checked his watch. *Twenty-five minutes to kill.* Shoving his hands into the pockets of his gray hooded sweatshirt, he headed down the middle of Maxwell Street and worked his way into the throng. There were Jews, blacks, Latinos, WASPS from the suburbs, hustlers, panhandlers, wheeler-dealers, the legal, the illegal, and the simply curious. On Sundays, everyone and everything had a niche on Maxwell. Tables loaded down with merchandise lined the curbs in front of shops, vacant lots, and rundown tenements. The market spilled over into several blocks of side streets. He passed a table strewn with used pipe wrenches of all sizes, another piled high with hand towels, and still another stacked with brand-new boxes of Barbie, Ken, and GI Joe dolls. A man, dressed in overalls and looking as calloused and roughly hewed as his salvaged goods, sat on a folding chair surrounded by claw-foot bathtubs, pedestal sinks, oak doors, mantels, and lead-glass windows. Some of the items had no doubt been recycled from condemned buildings, but others, Louis suspected, had probably wound their way from burglars to shady middlemen to Maxwell Street. Next to that collection of interior decorating fixtures, a woman and a young girl were hanging an array of used clothes all over a chain-link fence that fronted a vacant lot, and farther down from that, a man hawked, "Socks! Five pairs, one dollar!"

A teenager, his long stalk of a body topped by the overabundant bloom of his Afro, fell in step beside Louis, pulled up the sleeve on his maroon windbreaker, and showed Louis the half-dozen watches he was wearing on his forearm.

"Thirty-dollar watches for twenty dollar, my man." Then he whispered, "Hot off the truck." Louis waved him away, and the boy, stopping in the middle of the street, called after him, "Ten dollar. Can't beat that price with a stick!"

Louis wandered over to a table loaded with rows of record albums and began flipping through them just for the hell of it. Soon an old man with a steel guitar strapped to him came up to the other end of the table. Craggy-faced, stooped, and wearing a sports coat that had seen better days, he gave Louis the impression of being the real blues McCoy. With a tip of his fedora, the street musician gave a joyous smile to any and all in the market and then began to strum his instrument with an intensity that bordered on abuse, wailing:

Well I wish I was a catfish

In a matter of seconds, Louis found himself surrounded by a pack of scruffy-looking street urchins, boys no older than eight or nine. They tapped their feet and slapped their hands against their thighs in time to the Muddy Waters song.

I would have all you good-looking women fishing after me

The vendor, a squat man whose swarthy persuasion Louis could only guess at and whose singular expression seemed aimed at assuring others that he was nobody's fool, leaned over his table toward Louis, gave a quick nod in the direction of the blues man, and said under his breath, "It's a setup. The old guy distracts us so that his little sidekicks can pickpocket you and steal me blind."

Louis thought, *Playing me for a chump?* Amused, he decided to turn the tables by upping the ante on fate. As discreetly as possible, he took the wad of bills out of his jeans pocket, slipped it into his shallow sweatshirt pocket, and then shifted his weight even closer toward one of the boys. If the kid had the balls to try to pinch his money, Louis would let him get away with it scot-free, and take it as a sign that he should never have come to Maxwell Street to buy a gun in the first place. But if the kid chickened out . . . To keep the bet absolutely fair, Louis even tried to tempt the urchin by fully extending himself over the table and feigning interest in some Frank Sinatra albums. With the stakes so high, he had to squelch an attack of giddiness to keep from laughing. The boy, maybe scared that Louis was a young *Mod Squad*–type undercover cop setting him up for a bust, didn't bite. Instead, he glanced at Louis, must have seen something in those dark and cratered eyes that struck him as dangerously off, and backed up a step. He nudged another boy with his elbow.

"C'mon."

The pack scrambled away down Maxwell and melted into the crowd. The old man played his guitar for a little longer and then cut his song short with a burst of finale strumming. He tipped his hat at the vendor, grinned as if to say, *Can't blame me for trying,* and shuffled away to probably go try his luck elsewhere.

Louis continued on his way down the street. *That's that.* But having won his own wager, a sudden doubling of gravity seemed to press down on him, and the act of putting one foot in front of the other became as laborious as it did aimless. Slowing almost to a standstill, he reminded himself to breathe just as he had on that day his mother—temporarily shaking off the trauma from which she would never fully recover—had sat him down on the living room couch to tell him the devastating news. Suicide or statement? Did it really matter? To a boy of nine, a dead dad equals forever. Louis hadn't cried then, at the wake, or even at the funeral, but several weeks later he took the miniature pool table that his mother and father had given him for Christmas and dropped it out of his bedroom window. He watched it twist, drift, and plummet two stories to the yard below, where it shattered on impact. Later, when his mother had come home from her secretarial job and found him lying on his bed, facedown and sobbing, he told her what he had done but couldn't explain the logic in needing to break something he loved, and break it beyond repair.

Louis forced himself to pick up his pace again, passing a table with enough boxes of Chiquita bananas on it to ensure that no one at the flea market need go bananaless. Noticing a few straw cowboy hats on some of the Latino customers, he thought, *Wetbacks*. He'd always considered the term *illegal alien* to be far more derogatory, like the US government had categorized Mexicans as a criminal life-form from another planet. He checked his Timex. Nearly seven o'clock. Better double back. When he reached the designated spot next to the hot dog shack, he scanned the crowd and wondered, *Where the hell is he?* Louis was supposed to meet a junkie friend of a friend who he'd been introduced to at a party. Across Halsted and just a little ways east toward where Maxwell dead-ended at the Dan Ryan Expressway, another musician—younger and with more meat on the bone than the first one, but looking every bit as much Delta sunbaked—was jamming on an electric guitar in front of a porch stoop. The cord to his portable amplifier trailed up the cement steps and through the open window of a first-floor apartment. Louis dodged traffic and crossed the street, drawn to the music.

The gypsy woman told my mother

On a whim, Louis took out his wad of bills, peeled off a one, and dropped it into the guitar case left open by the curb.

I got a boy child's comin'

He went into a loose-legged dance, humping his shoulders, dipping and wagging his head, his arms snaking upward and then back down, the sum total of his awkward movements pulling together into a style of expression that was his alone. A small crowd of spectators, drawn to the red kerchief and dancing teenager interplay, began to collect on the sidewalk. A matronly Latina threw a couple of quarters into the guitar case, and a biker dude—all sunglasses, blue kerchief bandana, and hands the size of mallets—dropped in a few more. The day was turning muggy, and as Louis kept right on with his slide-steps, hippity-hops, swoops, and gyrations, he peeled off his sweatshirt, tossed it without a care into the gutter, and closed his eyes, losing himself in a buttery guitar riff.

"Yeeeah!" shouted the blues man into his microphone. Then, encouraging Louis, "You doing it, boy!" He went right back to singing in a gravelly voice that to Louis seemed as loaded with heartbreak as it did with inexhaustible perseverance and ultimate triumph. Louis knew that if he could just keep himself locked in this space, time, rhythm, and beat . . . But with a sensation of free-falling, not wholly unpleasant, he opened his eyes and immediately saw his connection—a young man maybe a year or two older than Louis and who, even from across the street, looked a little grubby around the edges. He had a shoebox tucked under one of his arms, and with a subtle wave down low by his side, he invited Louis to come over and transact their business. Louis stopped, his oneness with the blues shattered. He snatched his sweatshirt from the gutter and, neither dawdling nor in any great hurry, started back across the street, squinting from the blinding sunlight reflecting in shop windows along the west side of Halsted. *Yeah*, he thought. *I'm doing it.*

32

Game Over

"YOU CALL THAT A STRIKE, MR. EVANS? Lemme tell you about my daddy, the eye doctor."

"Leroy, just bat and stop wasting time!"

"Let's go, batter up."

Early June. The day sticky-hot, overcast, and still undecided about rain. They were having gym class—a sixteen-inch softball game—in the vacant lots, where there was enough of a clearing in the weeds, chunks of brick, and other pulverized debris to fake a baseball diamond. Playing third base, Simon occasionally picked up a stone or a piece of broken lath and lobbed it beyond the foul line. He tried to convince himself that he didn't care if he got his chance to bat or if the class pissed away the entire forty-minute period. *Dumb-fucks.* From where he stood, he could watch a huge mob of students swarming up and down the block on Orchard Street in front of Dexter. They fled from reinforcement cops who, having already arrived in a dozen or so squad cars and paddy wagons, seemed content to keep the lid on things by slowly patrolling and staying spread out. Windowpane glass shattered somewhere, and everyone in the gym class looked off toward the school, transfixed for a moment, only to go back to their game. Riots had become strangely routine.

"Damn, boy," Moe yelled at Leroy from his second-base position. "The next time your mama wanna suck my dick, I'm going to make her wait." Apparently Moe was unhappy with how the other boy kept stepping out of the box and taking his sweet time between pitches. Leroy, proving just how fast he was, hauled the bat back and flung it spinning toward the infielder. Moe ducked, and the piece of athletic equipment turned lethal weapon sailed just inches over his head before landing in a patch of tall grass out in right field.

"Aww, scrub. You gone and done it now!" Moe scrambled over to the bat, snatched it up, and charged at Leroy. The two boys chased and dodged each other in a semiserious display of bat and fist swipes, ignoring the pleas from the rest of the class to stop messing around. People pushed complaints only so far, because everyone had recently seen Leroy and Moe around school wearing bright-red Cobra Stone berets. Virgins or not, they must have gotten drafted.

"You guys are just wasting time," Evans said, umpiring behind a rubber plate. He glanced at his watch. Simon flipped another stone underhanded into some weeds. He thought about how easy it would be for him to wander over to the riot, let the crowd swallow him up, the stinging blows raining down on him until he went numb, dropping to his knees, hands, the asphalt street oh-so-soft against his cheek, and just at the moment of blacking out, he'd think, *Big fucking deal.*

Pow! Simon got his hands down an instant too late to field the hot grounder. It deflected off his fingertips, scooted through his legs, and hugged the left-field line. "Son of a . . ." He stared at his traitorous palms while Leroy galloped safely around the bases to third, stomped with both feet on the bag, and began to gloat.

"Ahhhh, honky. And you on the baseball team? What position you play, bench? Let a pussy softball go right through your—"

In truth, Simon had no memory of how he ended up straddled on top of Leroy, two fistfuls of spongy Afro in his hands as he kept bashing the other boy's head against the ground, screaming, "Motherfucker! Motherfucker!"

"Get this, honky—" Try as Leroy did to claw, flip, or whack Simon off him, he failed, his wild punches having little effect even when one caught Simon flush in the jaw.

"Dang!"

Then someone else: "White boy gone craaaazy. Tee-hee!" Simon heard dirt crunching under the quick approach of footsteps, then felt an arm crook around his neck from behind, tighten against his windpipe, and begin to pull.

"Don't just stand there!" Evans yelled. "Help me!"

More hands grabbed at clumps of Simon's white T-shirt and blue shorts, his elbows and wrists suddenly restrained, fingers getting pried open. He was peeled off Leroy, stumbled to his feet in the process, broke free, and lunged to attack again, but a wall of several boys seemed to instantly assemble and blocked his path. He tried to shove them apart, but they kept brushing him away, one of them saying, "Be cool." A yank to Simon's collar whiplashed him backward, and before he could recover his bearings, Evans had him by the shoulders and was in his face, shouting, "That's enough!"

Simon stopped, suddenly aware of his aching lungs gasping for air. Through gaps between boys' legs and torsos, he saw Leroy rocking on his knees, cradling his head in his arms. A long scratch on one of his thighs was oozing blood.

"Think this over, honky? Best think again!"

"Awww, Leroy." The matter-of-fact response came from Conrad, whose head spiked above the others in the wall. "You gots to fight, go to Vietnam." A boy in the circle of spectators was pantomiming an instant replay of Simon's maniacal head-bashing technique, telling classmates, "Like he think pro wrestling for *real!*"

Evans nudged Simon away to arm's length and ordered, "Somebody take tough guy here to the locker room."

"I'll do it." Threshing his way through knee-high grass, Clyde stepped in to take charge of his friend. By pure coincidence, he must have been passing by the vacant lots on his way to the riot.

"Let's go, Hotdog. You just full of surprises."

Evans gave a nod in Leroy's direction. "He stays." The teacher must have preferred to handle the situation "in house" rather than have the boys suspended from school. Besides, Simon would realize later, with the baseball team's record a lousy one-and-eight, Evans could ill afford to lose his star center fielder for the remaining three games of the season.

Leroy sprang to his feet, jawing more threats, but Simon drowned him out with an "Asshole motherfucker cocksucker pussy!" Clyde tugged him along by an arm toward school, Simon resisting only hard enough to save face.

"Put a cork in it, both of you," Evans said. Then to Leroy, "You're safe on third. Move it or lose it."

The team that belonged on the field began to drift to their positions again, and someone reminded everyone else, "I'm up."

"Damn, Hotdog." Clyde had broken the awkward silence between them as they crossed Dickens Street, heading for a rear school entrance on Howe. "Don't you know that boy a Cobra Stone?"

"Fuck Leroy!" But despite Simon's brave front, he didn't know if he could count on Clark's protection after yet another run-in with the gang. Clyde, looking as exasperated as he did puzzled, asked, "Why you go to Dexter anyhow? Lane Tech's more your speed."

"Because . . ." The answer seemed too complicated for Simon to articulate, so he left it at "To be with the community."

"Even if the community is fixing to kill your white ass?" Clyde cupped his hand around his mouth like a megaphone. "Now hear this. The brothers is rioting and the Cobra Stones crazy. You in danger. Go home!"

"Fuck no." It had become Simon's mission to stay. "This is my school, too." Unknown to him, his parents—who had instilled that mission—had been frantically weighing alternative high school options for their son, and Lane was now among them. The two boys climbed the cement steps and reached the door that Evans had left wedged open with a gym beater.

"OK," Clyde said, and his shrug suggested that there was no law against acting stupid. "Later."

Simon pulled the door open. "Aren't you coming with me?" From beyond the dark vestibule, he heard the rowdy noise of students and judged, from its volume and tenor, that chances were good he could make it the twenty-or-so feet to the locker room without getting jumped. There he would change back into his street clothes. "Naw. I gots to go riot."

"What?"

"You deaf, honky?"

"Oh, so now I'm *honky*?" An itch to retaliate by calling Clyde a nigger was almost too much for Simon to resist, but instead he told Clyde, "Have fun with your uneducated friends."

Clyde got nose to nose with Simon. "What you know about black folks' education, fool? Pigs make the rules, not us. You don't tell me where I belong. I wants to play baseball, I play baseball. I wants to flip burgers at McDonald's, I flip burgers. I can draw Supersoul, do my ROTC thang, and riot, too. You just too gotdamn ignorant to know who I really be!"

In the nasty, glaring standoff that followed, Simon wondered if they were about to come to blows, but then Clyde was already on his way down the stairs, muttering "Uneducated." He wasted no time following the sidewalk toward Dickens and never looked back as he disappeared around the corner of the building.

Fine, Simon thought. *Go riot.* For an instant, he longed for the balance of rules, physical skills, and the teamwork that often took place between the chalk lines of a baseball diamond. Then he slipped inside Dexter.

33

Lunchroom

Mama come here quick and bring that lickin' stick

Like it was the sureness of the next beat that counted more than the music itself coming from the PA, the sureness that James Brown was right there with them, a soulful black man's scream screeching through the lunchroom.

Mama come here quick and bring that lickin' stick

Simon had only ducked into the lunchroom because he'd judged the hallways too full of gangbangers to make it safely to his homeroom locker at the far end of the old building. A girl sitting at a table screamed, "Gimme back my quarter, mothafucka! Gimme back my quarter before I bust your mothafuckin head!" Her boyfriend just grinned, and then she grinned, too, trying to slap his face, but he caught her wrist and held it loosely. She didn't seem to mind. Everywhere dudes threw fake punches as they yelled, "You a lie, boy!" or knocked someone's hat off or took a couple of steps back from a friend and shadowboxed, shuffling like Muhammad Ali. Black girls bobbed their heads in time with the music, and some of them stood on their chairs, jerked their hips, and looked mean as a motha, because you got to look mean to be bad, and you got to be bad to be cool.

A Coke bottle crashed against the back wall. Simon, sitting alone at a table over near a window, looked up from the history book he'd been pretending to study. He stared straight ahead and let his hearing scan the room to tell him what he needed to know. The crowd's voice rose as one, "Ohhhhh," then sporadic singsong voices, *Who did iiiiit? Who did iiiiit?*

Black dudes walked around whistling shrilly with their fingers in their mouths. Others pounded on tables, any kind of noise so that what wanted to happen would happen. Simon leaned farther over his history book and flipped pages faster. Adrenaline pumped through his temples, and his feet sweated in his gym shoes as he curled his toes in and out, digging into the soles. Already it seemed like years since his fight during gym, and he kept telling himself, *How stupid can you get? Fucking with another Cobra Stone. Now the whole Peace Stone Nation is probably after my ass.*

He heard the chair across from him slide out. He tensed, looked up, saw Louis, and thought, *Calm down.* Louis's face was unshaven, and there were dark bags underneath his eyes. He wore an oversized white dress shirt with the tails untucked. He plopped down in the chair, didn't even look at Simon, and gazed out the window into the barren courtyard that was enclosed on all four sides by the school.

Defying everything that had and would happen that day, Simon tried to sound cheerful.

"Say, Louis, what's going on?"

Louis just continued to stare out the windows, his face pale, legs sprawled, and the rawhide shoelaces in his boots untied so the ends were all black from being walked on. He took a long snorting sniff through his clogged nose, then let the air out through his mouth.

"Why do you mess with that shit?" Simon asked, Louis sitting there, once again strung out on some drug or other, but Louis just looked at him with an expression that seemed to say, *Not now, man. Don't start that shit on me now.*

Fuck him, Simon thought. *He comes in here, sits next to me, and then doesn't say a word, looks out the goddamn window like a jagoff.* But underneath his anger, Simon wondered, *Why do people always get tired of me? Well, fuck him. Fuck the whole goddamn place, fuck every—*

"Say, man." A tall, skinny black dude stood over Simon. "Loan me a quarter."

Simon glanced up, his anger erased just like that. He raised his eyebrows as if to say, *Who, me?* and *Sure, man,* all at the same time. He dug his hand into one of his pants pockets and rubbed a couple of quarters hard between his fingers in his pocket, then released the coins without letting them jingle. He would risk it—no, don't be a fool—yeah, risk it, risk it. He took out a dime, his voice sounding black as he said, "Ah thought ah had a quarter, man, but ah guess ah just got a dime."

The gangbanger glared theatrically. "What you mean, you guess?"

"Really, man, come on, it's yours. That all ah got. Take it." Simon held his hands up to his shoulders. "All you find, all you keep."

The boy gestured with his hands for Simon to rise to be frisked. "All right, mothafucka. If you a lie, you a dead lie," and then the boy mumbled something about how he didn't take no shit from no honky. Simon stood, and from another table where a group of students sat, someone yelled, "Dig, Jackson. What you gone do to that white boy, Jackson? If he ain't give it, dot that honky's eye, my man."

A nervous grin glued itself across Simon's face. Three quarters lay at the bottom of his pocket. That's the kind of stuff people get killed over, trying to hide seventy-five cents. It didn't take long for Jackson to find them. He pinched the material of Simon's pant leg and held one of the coins sandwiched inside.

Oh fuck, Simon thought, a simple *Oh fuck.* So this was what everything had been building up to all day; he was going to be the *Oh fuck* of the day. For the benefit of the lunchroom audience, the boy looked all around with a smirk. Then his eyes came right back around to Simon's grin. The boy glared even more. With a couple hundred black students around him, Simon couldn't swallow his fear and knew he would just stand there and do nothing. Just then Louis leaned forward with his fist clenched on the tabletop. He ran his nose close along the table and sniffed like a bloodhound.

"Damn. Where's it coming from? Damn. Do you smell it, Simon? Damn!"

Jackson still pinched the quarter inside Simon's pocket. "What you call this here, honky?" He moved a step closer so that his warm chest smashed against Simon.

"Like maybe you didn't hear me, nigger," Louis yelled. "I said, damn, it fuckin' stinks! Stinks of niggers! Yeah, Jesus Christ, there's just too many fucking niggers in here!"

James Brown alone didn't have sense enough to shut up.

Say it loud
I'm black and I'm proud

Everyone in the lunchroom stopped what they were doing and turned toward the white boy's screams of "nigger." The weight of all those eyes pressed down on Simon like he was in a feverish dream.

"Louis," he whispered, yet his words seemed uncomfortably loud, "what have you done?" There wasn't a teacher or another white student in sight, not even the German canteen lady: funny how people can always feel what's coming and split. Jackson glanced up to check if . . . yes, the whole world, at least his world, was watching. His hand fell away from Simon's pocket. He turned to face Louis sitting across the table. Jackson's lips moved, but the words wouldn't come quickly enough or accurately enough to express whatever he felt. For the first time, Simon saw blood rise in a black man's face, and Simon's chest quivered with each breath, his uneasy grin just now disappearing. He looked around, wondering why the hell his mom and dad hadn't just let him go to Lane. He backed away until his ass pressed against the next table just behind Jackson, leaving Louis to stand on his own. Louis just gazed up at Simon with a calm look that Simon interpreted as a half-assed attempt to release him from the guilt one feels when ignoring the responsibility of friendship.

And then Jackson couldn't move fast enough. He bent down and sprang back up almost in the same instant, with a pearl-handled switch-blade in his hand that he had pulled from inside the top of one of his combat boots. The blade flashed open and gleamed clean. As he reached back for the first slash, people knocked over chairs to get closer to the action, girls screamed with their hands over their faces, and other students jumped up on tables to get a better view.

Just as Jackson swung his arm around and started to dive across the table for Louis, he inadvertently caught the blade on the inside of one of Simon's nostrils as Simon stood pressed back against the table directly behind Jackson. A fast, sharp, lacerating pain pulsated through Simon's face, and in a rush his body both plummeted and rose into shock. With a thrust of his legs, Louis scooted back in his chair as Jackson swung down with his knife, stabbing the air where Louis had been. Jackson didn't quite make it over the table and lay stranded on top of it, kicking his legs and waving his arms. That's when Louis reached under his shirttail and pulled from the waistband of his khaki pants a short-barreled .357 Magnum. He pulled it out like he'd rehearsed that smooth draw all night. He placed the barrel of the gun right up against Jackson's forehead and cocked it.

"Move, nigger."

Jackson's arms and legs froze stiff in the air, and the crowd stopped dead in confusion. He dropped the knife, and it clicked on the floor.

"How about that?" Louis said. "You're not as stupid as you look, are you?" He uncocked the gun and took it away from Jackson's head. He looked the other way, pretending he was about to get up and go attend to other, more important business, but when Jackson started to move, Louis sprang from his chair, grabbed him by the Afro, and banged his head down on the Formica table top so hard, his jawbone must have cracked. Before Jackson could say or do anything, the gun was again cocked and pressed against his head. Thick, warm blood was running down Simon's face and dripped onto his shirt in deep-red splotches. He reached up to feel his slit nostril as it throbbed.

The crowd stood still, amazed at Louis, the crazy white boy. Simon picked up his books, which felt so heavy, and slung them under his arm. "Come on," he said, sure that Louis would follow. But Louis just stood there grinning down at Jackson.

"Let's go!"

"What's the hurry, honky?" Louis said. The crowd laughed, and the multitude of their numbers became painfully clear to Simon. It was like suddenly Louis had the power to turn the crowd on Simon, to say, *You want a honky? Here's your honky,* just for one of his jokes. Or maybe underneath all that coolness, Louis was really scared and wanted to save his own skin. He laughed, still holding the barrel of the gun to Jackson's head.

"Relax, Liberal. Have a seat. The show's just beginning."

Simon came back to his chair and sat down. As long as he stayed near Louis, near the spell his friend held over the crowd, he was safe. Louis took the gun away from the gangbanger's head and, stepping around beside him, placed the barrel right in the crack of his ass.

"Excuse me, ladies and gentlemen," Louis addressed the crowd, one and all, "but does this nigger have any relatives out there? Sheeeeeit, I hear you're all brothas and sistas. Come on now, no relatives? Let's be honest. This nigger had a busy mama working late nights. Why, I bet all thirty of his brothas and sistas go to school right here. Sheeeeeit, I bet they're all in the same grade, too!"

Some students giggled.

"Sheeeeeit, I bet his mama's related to the whole fuckin' neighborhood. Do you know his granddaddy still hasn't graduated—fucker's been going to school here for forty-five years. Oh, man, come on now, don't be laughing. We shouldn't talk about his relatives, especially his mama, since none of us, including him, know who his mama is."

Louis shoved the gun barrel harder into Jackson's ass. "Anyone could be this boy's mama." Louis pointed at a boy in the crowd. "You

there, sir, are you his mama? Don't be shy now. Are you his mama?"
The boy mumbled something, and Louis aimed the gun right at him.
"Tell me you're not his mama again."

Just like that, the crowd stopped laughing and parted away from
the boy, who backed up, waving his hands in front of himself as he
said, "I'm his mama, I'm his mama. Come on, man, be cool."

Jackson started to ease himself off the table, but Louis shoved the
barrel of the gun back into his ass, and he froze. The crowd laughed
and slowly gathered around again. It seemed like Louis was becoming a goddamn soul brother the more he talked. He stamped his foot
and yelled, "I knew it! I knew this nigger's mama was a brave man."

Simon's wound had started to numb. Louis laughed with the
crowd as he flipped open the gun's cylinder, and whereas maybe
seconds before the crowd might have rushed him, now they just
watched. He hit the gun against the heel of his palm, shook most
of the bullets out onto the floor, and pranced up and down the
aisle, shuffling his feet in an awkward dance step, always trying but
never able to stay on beat with James Brown telling blacks to be
proud over the PA. As Louis passed by students, he'd show them
the nearly empty cylinder.

"See? One bullet. See? One bullet." The shoestrings of his boots
flew every which way, and there was a drip of dried mustard on his
white shirt just above the pocket. The shirt was so formal compared
to Louis's usual grungy clothing, Simon would later decide—on nothing more than a hunch—that it had belonged to the boy's father,
Terrence Collins. Louis stopped, snapped the cylinder shut, and put
the gun to his head. Squinting, he pulled the trigger real fast three
times—*click, click, click.*

Girls nearby gasped, but they and everyone else wore something
between a smile and an expectant wince on their faces. Even Simon
smiled against his will. Again Louis shuffled up and down the aisle.

"See? One bullet. See? One bullet." He stopped, spun the chamber,
put the gun to his head, and *click, click, click.*

While Jackson had the chance, he wormed off the table and didn't seem to notice Simon. If he had, he probably would have wished he had never asked for a goddamn quarter. *Where the fuck are you going, nigger?* Simon heard his mind ask, and then, just as quickly, he blotted the thought out—yes, he was above thinking such thoughts.

Louis pranced back over to Simon, put his arm around his friend's shoulders, and hugged him tight. The fact that the hug felt comforting made Simon goddamn uncomfortable as Louis looked at him seriously, eye to eye.

"White men aren't afraid to die," he told Simon, and kissed him on the cheek, a kiss Simon could not deny, no matter how uncomfortable it made him. Louis looked out at the silent crowd.

"White men aren't afraid to die."

The grin fell from his face. "I said, 'White men aren't afraid to die!' How about you?" and he whirled every which way, pointing the gun at the crowd and pulling the trigger again and again. "Or you or you or you!"

Girls ran with their hands clasped over the backs of their heads, a useless attempt at trying to protect themselves from a bullet, and other students kicked chairs aside. Tables crashed to the floor, and one boy stumbled and fell, a friend dragging him by the arm so he wouldn't get trampled. Louis squeezed the trigger one too many times, and a bullet went off, the noise from the blast ringing in Simon's ears. A pair of fluorescent light tubes exploded overhead, sprinkling stardust down on the crowd as it streamed through the back exit door, which banged again and again against the wall in the hallway. And then the lunchroom was empty except for Louis and Simon. Louis laughed his ass off, bending over forward and slapping the table.

James Brown gave another soulful screech. The person running the record player ran off and left the forty-five to play over and over. Finally, wiping his tearing eyes, Louis sat back down in a chair and stared out the windows into the small courtyard the way he had before it all started. He let all the air out of his lungs. Simon looked at the floor. He wanted to say something, but he wasn't sure if it was a thank-you, fuck-you, or maybe both. Or maybe it was best not to say a thing. Yeah, he had to keep moving, keep thinking. What was he going to do next? Where was it safe to go? He picked up his books, still not looking at Louis, because there was something so strong between them that he wanted to try to ignore. He started down the aisle.

"Come on, man," Louis called out. "Stay awhile. You're always in such a fucking hurry. Whaddya running from, me?"

Simon spun around. "Stay for what?" He threw his hands up, then let them fall. "Fuck, man, you're crazy. You're absolutely positively a banana!" He looked up at the ceiling in total disbelief as the whole scene replayed in his mind: Louis with a gun, with a gun on Jackson, on the crowd, on himself. A shiver ran through Simon.

"Well, this banana's asking you to stay, OK?" Louis smiled at Simon for a long time, then laughed softly. "This won't take long." The fact that his voice was so calm and sincere as he sat slumped in his chair pulled Simon back to his seat across from his friend. Louis propped his feet up on the table. "Good," he said, nodding in approval. "Good." He didn't have any socks on, and his hairy legs showed. Simon sat stiffly in his chair with his back straight, his feet flat on the floor and his palms flat on the smooth tabletop. He rubbed his fingertips—a couple of them bloody from dabbing at his wound—against the Formica, leaving red streaks. Louis pulled handfuls of brass-cased bullets from his coat pocket and flung them on the table, where they scattered like beads and rolled in little circles, spilling to the floor. He flipped open the cylinder and began plugging the chamber with bullets, then snapped the cylinder shut. His easygoing expression turned hot and explosive and—"Christ!" He pointed the gun back over his shoulder and aimed at the PA speaker above the back door, firing again and again, and no matter how hard Simon tried, he couldn't keep from flinching with each deafening shot. At least one of the six bullets drilled a hole right in James Brown's vocal cords.

"Never tell a nigger he's black and proud more than three times a day, or it goes right to his head and he hears black is better," Louis said.

"Don't start that shit!" Simon's ears rang so badly from the noise of the shots, he heard his voice like it came from someone else. Both he and Louis had to talk a little louder than usual just to hear each other.

"What shit?" Louis asked.

"You know what shit, that—that *nigger* shit."

Louis slapped the gun melodramatically over his heart. "Oh, excuse me. I mean colored, I mean Negro, I mean Afro-American, I mean black. Don't give me that liberal shit about how that nigger I almost wasted not being a fucking nigger! Like he doesn't know any better 'cause he's uneducated. Is that what you're going to tell me? I don't need it, man. You want to know what's racist? That's racist! Saying he hasn't got the brains to know better. He can kiss my white ass."

Simon listened beyond the silence. Out in the hall, he heard the light tapping of street shoes running, and at the other end of the lunchroom, a teetering lunch tray clattered from a table to the floor.

"Would you really have shot him?" Simon asked. "If he'd moved?"

"I don't know. I had the right to, but I don't know if I would have. Maybe I don't have the right. Maybe no one's got the right. Fuck, yes I do."

"But Jesus, Louis!" Simon tried to make him see the seriousness of the situation. "What would you have done if the gun went off when you were dancing around?"

"Uh, I guess I would have fallen down and acted dead. Does that sound about right?" Louis slid his feet off the table and leaned forward. "I don't think about those things anymore. I really don't. You know, I hear when people die violent deaths, they have an orgasm. Can you believe it? The ultimate fuck, a sweet, succulent death."

Simon, still on another train of thought, pointed out the windows across the lunchroom where the street lay outside. "Just because in here—" and then he finally realized it. "Just because in here we're the niggers, it isn't like that out there, and out there is always, man, out there is—"

"We have the right to stand up for ourselves no matter where we are," Louis said. "Man, I'm here five hours a day, five days a week. You're fucking crazy, Liberal. Just listen to what you're saying—that you're a nigger, and you haven't got the right to be anything else because of out there. Jesus, the ultimate in guilt. Jesus, I just can't fucking believe it."

"Don't put words in my mouth," Simon said, glaring at Louis.

"You said it, man. I'm not putting anything in your mouth. I can't. It's too full of donkey dick. Just listen to me a second, OK? I say, you have the right to say 'screw you' when someone cops a dime off you, 'screw you' when six of them jump you, 'screw you' when you're scared to fucking walk into a school bathroom to take a fucking piss. I mean, if you're still going to try to apply right and wrong to this shit, I suggest you give yourself the benefit of the doubt and live your life. Don't you ever get sick of politely asking someone why he's shitting on you when it's dripping down your face? You telling me you can't because you're white? You don't think like that, man; you just react. I mean . . . oh, fuck, I don't know what I mean. All I know is it sure felt good to see those niggers run, didn't it?"

Just then the back door opened. First a pistol stuck through the door and then a cop's head in a riot helmet. "What the hell's going on in here?" The cop said it like he hoped the harshness of his voice would intimidate Louis and allow him to take control of the situation, but before he could say anything else, Louis spun around in his chair and pointed the empty gun right at the cop's head. The cop disappeared, the door slammed shut, and Simon could hear a lot of commotion out in the hall.

"Damn, Louis, what's the matter with you? Those are cops, man, real cops!" But Simon could see that his words went right through Louis, who couldn't have given a shit if it were fucking President Nixon himself out there. Someone called to them from a bullhorn out in the hallway.

"This is Sergeant Garzato. Come out with your hands up."

"*Dragnet* is your next door to the right, greaseball!" Louis yelled back. He rubbed his hand over his face.

"I repeat, with your hands up."

Louis still rubbed his face. "Five minutes, greaseball! Five minutes and we come out and no one gets hurt and life can go on beautiful like a fart rising between your legs in the bathtub, OK?"

There was a pause from the hallway. "OK, son, five minutes . . . as of now."

Simon scooted his seat away from the table, about to get up, a trapped expression on his face. "Come on, Louis, let's go."

"What for? He said it was OK for five minutes, and he's a reeeeeal po-lice-man."

"Let's go. They're going to put your ass away, so why make it any worse?"

"Five minutes. Goddamn. You're always in such a fucking hurry." Louis shook out a cigarette from a soft pack of Marlboros and started to light it.

"What the fuck are you doing?" Simon pointed at the cigarette.

"What's it look like I'm doing?" Louis took a drag.

And then Simon realized how silly what he was about to say would sound, but he said it anyway. "You can't smoke in here; you're in school."

Louis laughed, gobs of smoke spewing from his mouth, but Simon shook in spasms, his chest quivering with each breath. Louis flipped open the cylinder of the gun and put one bullet inside, then spun the cylinder again and again, waiting each time until it clicked to a halt.

"You know," he said, "I can honestly say that none of my best friends are black. I have never met a nigger in this school who felt comfortable with me unless I hated him or felt guilty because of him, and when I'm neither, he's scared shitless of me. Now that is sad." He spun the cylinder again.

"Damn. As soon as I toked off a joint and copped a buzz this morning, I knew something was going to happen. I mean, I knew this was the day. Can you understand that, Liberal?"

"The day for what?" Simon asked.

"What do you think?" Louis's eyes glazed over and, talking to himself, he said, "Shit, I wouldn't mind another quick buzz now."

He flipped the cylinder of the gun shut. Simon stared at Louis and felt so young, so incomplete. He picked up one of the bullets off the table and rubbed it between his fingers, trying to stabilize his shivering body. He wiped at the dried, caked-on blood on his lips, and then said, "Yeah, I did enjoy watching them run. I really did."

Louis laughed, "Dig the liberal now. The truth speaks."

"Quit calling me *liberal*! Come on, Louis, how come they can't see I'm trying to mind my own business?"

"Because there isn't anything more racist than a nigger. They must wake up in the cold morning and say, 'Hello, honkies. Do unto you just like you done screwed unto me, except I'm going to do it ten times better.'"

"Yeah," Simon said, "blacks are racist. You're fucking right, they're—"

Click.

Louis had the gun pointed at his own temple.

"Quit fucking around, Louis!"

"Just keep talking," Louis said calmly. "Let's see, where were you? Oh, yeah, they're racist. Sounds good." *Click.* "Almost promising, Liberal." *Click.* "Don't stop now."

Simon raised his hands, wanting to do something with them but not sure if he should cover his eyes or reach across the table and try to wrestle the gun away from Louis.

"Goddamn it, Louis, you're fucking crazy, fucking positively crazy," and from out in the hallway came a loud, scratchy "Time's up, son. Whaddya say? Come on out, huh?"

Simon rose to his feet, still not knowing what to do with his hands. "Why, Louis? Just tell me why."

"Why the fuck not? It's time to try something new." *Click. Click.* "Damn! That's five. Can you believe it, Liberal? Five times! Guess I'm just a lucky motherfucker."

Louis scrunched up his face like it was going to really hurt. The blast picked him up as though he was shot out of a gun more than with one, and he flew down the aisle, ricocheting off chairs until his back smashed against the edge of a table. Blood showered down over Simon like millions of hot, tingling freckles. Louis's feet slowly slid out from under him, and he fell into a sitting position with his arms hung up on chairs to either side of him. His eyes were bugged out, and one side of the top half of his head was missing, like someone had dug in with an ice cream scoop—blood, bone, and brains splattered all over his body.

Simon deaf except for the ringing, the constant ringing. Blood everywhere, on his yellow pinstriped shirt, on the table he leaned on, the floor, the ceiling. Louis hung like that on the chair, *Dead, dead, blew his brains out with a gun, at least that's what they'll say—yeah, that's what they'll say, all right, because he's dead, dead.* Simon reached up and began to massage his temples. He couldn't feel his head—his fucking head!—and now he rubbed violently with both hands, scratching his scalp. *Goddamn you, Louis.* "Goddamn you!"

Suddenly he realized he wasn't alone—no, wait! Spied on. He looked up across the courtyard at the black faces lining the windows of the classrooms on all three floors, and he couldn't tell if they were satisfied or disappointed, all of them watching. They had seen, seen everything. But still Simon could almost believe Louis might walk through one of the doors with a big grin on his face and a cap gun in his hand, saying, "Fooled your ass, boy."

Gotta . . . gotta keep moving, Simon thought. *What to do now . . . what . . .* He started slowly down the aisle toward the back door, his teeth chattering, eyes wide, mind wired. Refusing to look back to where Louis sat hung up on the chairs, his steps quickened.

Every door in the lunchroom crashed open, and cops burst in, crouched down with their guns drawn. Before Simon knew it, someone was frisking him. Then he heard someone else yell, "He's not the one!" A far off "It's OK, son," let him know he could come back into the real world if he wanted to, because he was free and white, even if not proud. *Yeah*, he thought, *it's OK. Yeah, big fuck.*

A cop held his limp body up on either side with a firm grip. They took him back over to where Louis hung on the chairs. Someone whistled as if to say, *What a mess*, and other cops reached up to adjust their riot helmets, having nothing better to do with their hands, and all was quiet. Until Simon took a breath, the first breath he could remember taking in a long, long time. And now, as he stared at the hulk that used to be his Louis, his crazy Louis, breath came to him in loud, sobbing gasps. He'd have to learn how to breathe all over again.

"I'm taking this boy outa here, OK?"

Simon recognized Officer Huntly on his right, a huge black cop who, like Clark, was permanently assigned to Dexter. Respected by students, Huntly was an approachable, if not also reserved, man who patrolled hallways and broke up fights with no more brute force than was absolutely necessary. Simon figured that maybe after a couple of more days like this one, Huntly would recognize him, too, just maybe.

"Yeah, take him to the hospital," said another cop who sounded in charge.

Goddamn you, Louis! They marched Simon out of the lunchroom. Things were becoming clearer to him now.

"It's OK, son. It's OK," Huntly kept saying. "It's all over now." But the sobbing would not stop.

34

Arrest

EVERYONE KNEW IT. John Lange had been pushing his luck all year. His participation in the boycott. Openly admitting that he was a member of the Progressive Labor Party. Telling anyone who would listen that Donald Jursak should be fired and replaced with a principal elected by the community. And now Lange had decided to hold a "Smash Racism" rally in his biology room. "Flushing his whole career down the drain," fellow teachers would say, or "Talk about a man with an authority problem." A few admired him for his social activism in general but dismissed him for having "a few loose Communist screws."

By midafternoon, somebody must have snitched to Jursak about the unsanctioned rally. As John, alone in his classroom, collected beakers of bromothymol blue solution that had been used for respiration experiments, Clark and a partner strolled through the door.

"Sorry to put the kibosh on your revolution, Lange, but I'm afraid you're coming with us," Clark said. "Principal's orders."

"Excuse me?" John went back to collecting beakers, only to realize that acting normal under abnormal circumstances could be easily interpreted as conspicuous. Then, with his hands so full of glass containers that he had to press some against his chest to prevent dropping any, he began making his way to a sink along the room's far wall.

"Where's all your loyal disciples?" Clark asked. "You were expecting thousands?"

"I'm afraid I'm not following—"

"Your rally?"

Switching tactics, John offered, "You're welcome to stay and join us if you like, officers. It's still a few minutes early. Better grab a seat before everyone starts pouring through the—"

"You won't be here even if they do," Clark interrupted again. He slowly moved a few steps farther into the room, leaving his partner—a man who was making up for his lack of size by folding his arms over a chest puffed up for business—in the doorway. His riot helmet, a size too big, rode level with his eyebrows.

"Dr. Jursak," Clark said, "wants you in his office, pronto."

Face suddenly hot, throat turning dry, John tried to bluff with a look of *You've got to be kidding*. "Don Jursak had to send two police officers to tell me that? Am I under arrest? What's the charge?"

"Brainwashing America's youth," Clark said, and grinned. "Haven't you heard? Nixon just made that a federal offense."

The other cop—thin-lipped and pockmarked on his jowls—cut loose with a laugh that exposed a set of small teeth, the top ones looking almost like they'd been filed to more closely mirror the bottom ones. John carefully lowered the beakers into the metal sink so that none of them would slip from a finger too soon and shatter.

"Either of you officers ever hear of First Amendment rights? Tell Don that I'll stop by his office after—"

"Do me and Officer Crawford here look like messenger boys, Lange?"

"If the shoe fits . . ."

"Hey, hey, hey!" Crawford wagged his finger at John. "Show some fucking respect. Think we got time to burn? Because of people like you, we got us a riot to deal with."

"People like me?" John snatched a dishtowel off the counter and began drying his hands. "Maybe if you didn't stop me from showing students how to voice their grievances in a constructive—"

"Suuuuure," Clark said. "And maybe, if you and your so-called community ran things around here, you'd make Zulu dancing a class requirement instead of English. Now enough of the chitchat. Your boss would like a word with you."

There was a long pause during which John still maintained a presumption of choice. Then, with a smile of pleasant ridicule, he extended an arm toward the door across the room. "After you." As he trailed behind the cops, a brash impulse to slam the door shut and lock himself in the room once they'd already stepped out into the hall suddenly seized him. He reached the open doorway, found himself going out voluntarily to join his escort, and then fished into his pants pocket for his key ring. He closed the door and locked it, unsure whether he had chickened out or taken the high road. *Would only put off the inevitable.* If this was the opening salvo to his getting fired, he knew that he could count on the party to get him a pro bono lawyer. *The board, Jursak, these two blowhard pigs . . . sue their fucking asses.*

It didn't exactly turn out to be the showdown of political wits that John had been mentally rehearsing for over a year. Just as he and the two officers reached the main office door off a first-floor corridor in the new building, Jursak came all but flying out of it with Vice Principals Tanana and Kahara in tow behind him. As he whisked right by the biology teacher, Jursak said, "Go home, John. I've got my hands full."

"Am I fired?"

Still on the move, Jursak tossed over his shoulder, "That's for the superintendent and board to decide."

"And the union," John countered, knowing his employee rights.

Jursak, already passing the trophy case and about to round a corner of the floor's main intersection, stopped so abruptly, his two subordinates nearly did a comical pileup behind him. "Oh, really?" Then, slowly retracing his steps back to John, he came to a halt a little too close for the other man's comfort. Refusing to feel bullied, John held his ground and noticed how the shiny bald dome of Jursak's head seemed to have soaked up the same florid hue as his pinched-nose face. What hair remained, trimmed to military standards, was as white as an arctic fox.

"Always stirring up students with your rabble-rouser agenda. When the superintendent gets back to me on whether or not you still have a job, I'll give you a call. Until then, a sub can cover your classes, one who damn well knows the difference between biology and communism. Now if you don't mind, I've got a student suicide to deal with. You see what getting these kids all worked up with your antiestablishment rhetoric leads to? Happy?"

A shocked pause later, John repeated the word that refused to sink in. "Suicide?" His logic scrambled for a foothold, his own predicament trumped, and he immediately wanted details. "Who? Where? Why would you think . . . You're blaming *me?*" But Jursak was already rushing off again, disappearing around the corner and down another hall that led to the lunchroom. Tanana, the school's only black administrator, had avoided directly meeting John's eyes during the entire exchange, behavior that John thought of as cowardly and proof of Tanana's Uncle Tom guilt. But Vice Principal Kahara, a man so short he might as well have been chopped off at the knees, gave John a self-satisfied look of winner's contempt. It slashed the teacher's ego to the quick. Then the vice principals were off, chasing after Jursak around the corner. John thought, *That's it? Banished? Fuckers!* Behind the windowed wall of the school's office reception area, he saw several matronly secretaries typing away on their IBM Selectrics, heads bent down as they seemed focused on pushing the speed of their fingers without making typos. Their obliviousness to the up-for-grabs world around them left John feeling all the more ruined. Clark gave him a light pat on the shoulder.

"Be sure to send me a postcard from Moscow, Lange."

"Nah, Peking," Crawford suggested. "He can get some cosmetic slant-eye surgery and make his living selling Mao's little red book."

"Hardy-har-har," John said. Then, resisting the urge to waste any more breath on a couple of racist bozos, he thought, *Save it for the lawsuit.* He wondered whether or not they would allow him to go back to his room to get his jacket and briefcase, but a firm nudge from Clark made him start for the building's main front doors. He'd go home, make a phone call to PLP headquarters, and line up a lawyer. *Fuck this place, this country.*

Before John took more than a couple of steps, students coming from outside on Orchard Street flooded through the doors and clogged up the intersection. Another wave of them began trampling down a staircase, and still a third crowd converged from the other hall. People shouted, "Power to the people!" "Pigs!" "This *our* school!" Whether he was witnessing a preplanned revolutionary protest or simply a coincidence of timing, he couldn't be sure, but as he found himself suddenly treading in a colliding swirl of mob current, his surging optimism seemed to keep him afloat, and he thought, *Finally!* By the trophy case only a few feet away, Sheri, the girl who had tried but failed to chair the boycott meeting at Saint Matthew's Church by Cabrini, was holding a megaphone up to her mouth.

"Organize yourself! This ain't no riot! Don't give no pigs no excuse to—"

Later, when John tried to piece together the exact sequence of events that followed, he would have only intermittent links to his memory chain. A glimpse of Clark's billy club poised high and then John's spontaneous decision to step in and shield Sheri from the blow. Terrorized screams, a close-up view of the checkerboard tiled floor, and a forest of legs scattering. He's somehow on his feet again and aware of what feels like a throbbing hot spot glued to the crown of his head as much as he is of Clark screaming in his face, "*Now* you're under arrest!" Something tickly crawls out of his hairline, meanders down his forehead, gets trapped in one of his eyebrows, and then drips to his cheek. He wants to dab at the wetness but discovers that his hands are caught behind his back by sharp rings cutting into his wrists. The secretaries have all stopped typing to stare at him through the windows, stare at something horrifying, and where did Simon come from? *What's with the bloody . . . he's under arrest, too?* Muddled talk between Huntly and Clark takes on the semi-edgy tone of negotiations until Clark brings it to a close.

"I promised the kid's father I'd look out for him."

The next thing John knows, he's in the backseat of a squad car parked in front of the auditorium. He can't decide whether he's woozy or fully alert, but the jumble and gaps in sequential time have vanished. Directly in front of him, the nape of Simon's neck is only a growth spurt shy of manhood. The Plymouth Fury dips under Clark's weight, and the last door slams shut. Keys jangle as Officer Crawford, behind the wheel, reaches for the ignition.

"One big happy family," says Clark. The engine stutters and revs alive. "Stitches, anyone?"

News of a suicide takes time to travel. As Crawford threw the squad into a tight U-turn right where Orchard dead ended into the vacant lots, the whirling image of Evans's next gym class playing softball in the weeds flew past outside the windshield. Simon wondered, *Don't they know?* Everything pre-Louis's death seemed distant, untouchable, and a century ago. Since being ushered out of the lunchroom, he'd had to keep clinching his jaw to stop his teeth from chattering. The distorted, squawking voice from a dispatcher came over the radio, but the only words that stuck in Simon's brain were "Proceed" and "Do you copy?" He noticed that the solid sheet of cloud cover had turned darker and soupy with the threat of rain. Then as the squad started back down the block, passing by the auditorium on one side and the deserted playground on the other, Clark said, "Fasten your seat belts, folks. The natives are restless."

There was no mistaking the target of Clark's wisecrack—a crowd of a few hundred students loitering about on the sidewalks and overflowing onto Orchard at the other end of the block. For now, no one, including the dozen-or-so helmeted cops scattered throughout the crowd, seemed interested in ending a riot time-out. Crawford laughed and looked across the bench seat at Simon, obviously expecting the boy to show some appreciation for Clark's white humor, too. Then he must have misread why Simon was smushing himself against the passenger door, and he said, "Relax, kid. You're safe with us."

"*Safe?*" Apparently John was alive and well.

"Yeah," Clark said, "Simon here knows who looks out for him. Don'tcha?" From the backseat, a hand nearly the size of an oven mitt gave Simon's shoulder a couple of hard pats, and he sank with each one like a nail being driven in. He kept his nod as quick and closed to interpretation as possible.

"Attaboy!" Clark said. Then, "No offense, Lange, but you look like a pussy on the rag."

"Now, now, Harry," Crawford said. "Not in front of the kid."

"You telling me this scumbag piece of commie shit don't have it coming?"

Crawford jabbed his foot on the brake, the squad car coming to a halt in the middle of the block. "I mean it, Harry." They were dead even with Jursak's office in the new building, but still a few car-lengths away from the outskirts of the mob up ahead. "No funny business. These guys are going straight to Augustana's emergency room. Then the kid gets a ride home and Lange gets booked. *Capisce?*"

Clark mimicked, "*I mean it, Harry.*"

"I'm just saying . . ." The way Crawford's voice trailed off implied that he would appreciate it if his partner nipped a familiar tendency in the bud.

"We should at least clean Lange up," Clark said. "Wouldn't want one of them fine young nurses to lay eyes on him and lose her lunch."

"Fuck you."

"Fuck *me*, Lange? Oh, I get it. Handcuffs cramping your style? Here, lemme give you a—"

"Touch me with that comb, and I'll sue your ass to kingdom—"

"Harry, we aren't moving until you—"

"Get your fucking comb and pig hands—"

Later in life, Simon would always wonder if his memory loop had creatively added the blast's sideways nudge to the car's suspension, but he never doubted how a tremor in the floor had gone straight up through the soles of his feet. The *KA-BOOM* had thrown him into a survivor's duck, his head shielded by his arms and level with the glove compartment. Then he and Crawford, in stunned sync with each other, slowly straightened back up again to look out the driver's side of the car. Two glittering runways of glass carpeted the patch of lawn beneath Jursak's office. In either window frame, a set of long, fluttering curtains, remarkably undamaged, caught on what was left of splintered sashes. Smoke, plaster dust, or a mixture of both drifted up and made a run for the cloud cover above. *A bomb? In Jursak's office?*

Shrieks from secretaries in the outer office, a spontaneous cheer from the mob, and Clark's "Holy shit" ended a hiccup of lost time, the earth starting to spin again. On the sidewalk close to the yard's tall chain-link fence, Simon saw a cop down on his knees and covering his right eye with the palm of his hand. Whether he'd been blinded or only gouged near the socket by a piece of glass shrapnel, blood—lots of it—began to leak between his fingers, dripping onto his blue shirt just above the nametag and badge. Another cop, not more than twenty feet away, was the first to come running to his fellow officer's aid, while still others started attacking students, using their billy clubs to hack, waylay, and ram. From different parts of the school, fire alarm bells went off one after another, forming a shrill chord, and youths, quick on their toes, started dodging, sprinting, ducking, scattering, regrouping into clusters, and nimbly scattering again. They slipped between parked squads and paddy wagons—the blue-and-whites handy for roundabout escape routes—and made it difficult to impossible for cops to land anything more than glancing blows. From Simon's safe-haven view, the spectacle erupting all around him looked as much like a choreographed riot ballet as it did brutal pandemonium. He kept mistaking boys for fleeting glimpses of Clyde—getting choke-held and shoved through the open back door of a paddy wagon; skidding on his hip over the trunk of a parked squad; twisting middash into a rubbery contortion to avoid a club to the ribs, and another breezing past the tip of his nose. *Fucker*, Simon thought, still angry at Clyde. Then, contradicting himself, *Hope he's halfway to Cabrini by now.* He heard a door handle click in the backseat, felt the rock of shock absorbers and the car's bounce in relief.

"Harry! Where you—"

But Clark, ignoring his partner, was already on the trot in the street, swatting wildly at any blacks darting past him within arm's reach. Several close misses later, he finally managed to clip a girl just hard enough to make her yelp and cup a hand over her ear as she shot past the front bumper.

Crawford muttered, "Serve him right to just leave him here."

"Fine by—"

"Zip it, Lange. That your bomb that went off?"

"Not my style, Officer."

"No, you just brainwash kids to do your style for you, that it?"

"I don't brainwash anyone," John said, "and I certainly don't do *bombs.*"

Crawford glanced at Simon with a look that seemed to say, *Can you believe this lying sack of shit?* Simon, trying to limit the meaning of his shrug to *Not for me to judge*, stared out his window at the drawn shades along Washington Upper Grade School's library. He half expected the cop to dig for a more committed response, but the backseat door handle clicked again, and Clark, out of shape and huffing, was piling into the squad. The entire vehicle tilted his way.

Crawford asked, "Done?"

"Fucking coons are like jackrabbits." Clark laughed low at his own joke. Then, "What are we waiting for? Move it!"

"Yes, sir, whatever you say, sir." Crawford jerked the stick on the steering column into drive, adding, "Will you be dining alone or with a guest this evening, *sir*? I'll need to inform the butler if he should set another motherfucking plate."

Whether Clark was amused by his partner's sarcasm or not, Simon didn't know, because the officer was already asking John, "Make you feel good to see a cop go down? He's got a name, you know. Lester. I'm his daughter's godfather."

From nearby in the neighborhood, Simon heard the approach of a siren drawing even in volume with Dexter's fire alarm bells.

"Hey, look at me when I'm talking to you, Lange!"

The car was lurching, braking, and lurching down the street, Crawford playing a game of chicken with any kid who didn't snap to and leap out of harm's way fast enough for his satisfaction. The closer they got to the end of the block, the more the crowd thinned out. A rock ricocheted off the roof with a booming noise that resounded inside the car. Simon heard a skin-on-skin slap in the backseat, followed by the scuffling of bodies on vinyl. A kick or a knee—one that Simon felt through upholstery springs as a sharp poke to the small of his back—brought the short-lived skirmish to an end.

"They hit us, I smack you!" Clark yelled. "Like these niggers give a shit about your ass?"

"Big man," John spat. "Takes real guts to hit someone in handcuffs."

"Harry, wait until the kid is—"

"Drive!"

Just as they reached Armitage Avenue, a fire truck whipped around the corner and came barreling at them. Brakes slammed, and Simon, thrown forward, braced against the dashboard. In that heart-thumping moment when the screech of tires seemed to go on and on, he watched the truck's toothy chrome grillwork closing in on the windshield. Then as vehicles skidded to a stop just shy from kissing bumpers, he was flung back into the seat again. An ear-splitting siren now topped the alarm bells and made Simon feel like he was about to evaporate into sound. Crawford, bending low to peer up at two firemen high in the truck's cab, flipped them the finger.

"Assholes!"

Beams from a red mars light atop the truck's roof streaked across the pavement, the grid of Washington's aluminum window frames, and the set of towering iconic pillars that fronted Dexter's old building. The firemen were waving frantically for Crawford to back up in the narrow street and let them pass, but before the cop could even think about blinking first, a hand clamped down on his shoulder.

"Ain't no fire-fucks telling us what to do!" Clark, stretching so far over the front seat he almost toppled into it, pulled out a white knob on the dashboard. Beams of blue light from the squad's rooftop mars flasher started playing a roving game of tag with the red beams from the fire truck. He flipped a toggle switch and then reached across Crawford to push down on the steering wheel's horn. Instantly, another siren went off—*wha-ooo-wha-ooo-wha-ooo!* Simon used the tips of his index fingers to airlock the cartilage flaps over his ear canals, but the standoff seemed like it would last forever. Finally, it was the firemen who caved in, and the truck did a slow reversal into the intersection, jamming up traffic on Armitage. Crawford stepped on the gas, and the squad car's sudden thrust flung Clark into the rear seat again. As the car lunged and then squealed on a tight axis to head west, Simon spotted a white woman leaning out of a third-story apartment window to snap pictures with her Polaroid camera.

A half block later, as the world's volume dialed down, Crawford pushed in the mars knob and flipped off the siren toggle. Simon lowered his hands, heard Clark's chugging, derisive laughter and the leveling-off whine of the Plymouth. Ironically, the car was the exact same Fury II model as the one his family owned. He grabbed the armrest on the door beside him, fingers in a stranglehold, and pressed his other hand flat against the vinyl seat, trying to cling to his emotional balance. *Yeah, let the fucking school burn to the ground.* John had gone silent, his null-and-void authority leaving Simon to feel like he'd slipped a dependable mooring and was drifting toward consequences. It hadn't occurred to the boy yet that they were heading in the exact opposite direction from Augustana Hospital.

Maybe it was payback for Lester's injury. Maybe when the fire engine had blocked the squad's direct route down Armitage to Augustana Hospital, destiny, too, had taken a detour. Maybe Clark simply weighed the risks of overstepping against the regret of missing a golden opportunity. For the next several blocks, the cops' conversation took on the minimalism of a code.

"Keep driving, Joe," Clark said. "Good idea. All the way."

"Huh?"

"You know what they say about great minds."

"Harry, what the fuck? Not with the—"

"Relax. Got it covered."

"Covered?" At the very least Crawford sounded skeptical.

"Trust me."

"I'd rather—"

"Think I'm stupid?"

"I'm just saying   "

"Pussy."

"Who you calling—"

"*Pu*-ssy."

"That's the thanks I get for all the times—"

"Heeeeeere pussy pussy pussy."

Crawford banged his fist on the steering wheel. "Jesus H. Motherfuck!" His breathy snort reminded Simon of a bull psyching itself up to charge. "Fine!"

They'd already blown through a red light at the Halsted intersection, passed the corner Rexall Drugs, gotten the usual dagger-eyed, coming-and-going stare from the Che banner hanging from the Armitage Avenue Methodist Church, and then gone under the El station viaduct just as a train roared by overhead. They float-stopped at the Sheffield Avenue crosswalk long enough for Simon to catch a snippet of the Cubs game on a pedestrian's transistor radio: "Foul tip, full count. Banks on deck." As a means of escape, Simon yearned for the score, his faith in Mr. Cub as unshakable as the popular slogan Ernie had coined for the season: THE CUBS WILL SHINE IN '69.

They hung a right onto Racine, but it wasn't until two blocks later, when they took a left onto Webster and swung past Oscar Mayer Grade School's softball diamond that Simon could no longer ignore his sense of déjà vu.

"If we're not going to Augustana," John piped up, "we damn well better be taking a roundabout way to the People's Law Office. I know my rights."

The sound of another hard slap in the backseat.

"Fucking son of a bitch!"

"Tell you what, Lange." The contrast of Clark's cool and calm to John's rage sent a chill down Simon's vertebrae. "When it dawns on you that you're wrong about your rights, be sure to let me know."

Simon looked over at Crawford, thinking, *Do something!* But the cop, keeping his eyes fixed on the road, shook his head in a way that implied regret as much as it did for Simon to *Deal with it.* Sweat, already starting to bead, tickled Simon's upper lip. He wiped his hand across it, careful not to pull too hard on his throbbing nose. He stared down at his moist palm smeared with clotted blood, but there was no way to read what he should do next from it. *This is bad.*

It was a long, decelerating glide past the used tire dump with the barbed-wire fence, left onto Wayne Street, followed almost immediately by a right into the alley. Tucked between those brick factory buildings, the squad had already slowed to an idling crawl by the time it reached the middle of the block. Simon noticed raindrops, few and far between, splatting on the windshield. Then Crawford tapped on the brake and killed the engine.

———————

"I want you to do me a favor." With each step they backtracked toward the mouth of the alley, the log-like weight of Clark's arm draped over Simon's shoulders seemed to grow heavier. They'd left the squad car far enough behind so that Simon could hear only the tone of Crawford and John's conversation—weirdly closer to that of friendly debate than to heated argument.

"Keep walking," Clark told Simon, "and when you get to the street, holler if you see anyone coming. Got it?"

"Please." Even to Simon's ear, his own begging sounded on the edge of pathetic. "He's just a biology teacher. John didn't do anything to deserve—"

"Whooooa there." Clark brought them both to an abrupt halt, withdrew his arm, and faced the boy. "Fucker lets you call him by his first name? Like you're pals? Tell me, does *John* keep the niggers from jumping your ass, from stealing your lunch money or dragging you into a bathroom and banging that pretty white face of yours off a toilet bowl? Whose fucking side you on, anyway?"

"*Side?*"

"You heard me. Save the phony nigger-lover act for your old man."

Not sure why Clark had sprung the dad reference on him, Simon skipped to borrowing a piece of street philosophy he'd heard from Clyde.

"I don't take sides. I'm the fence."

Clark, not buying it, erupted with a guffaw. "Like hell you are."

Simon mentally scrambled for another tack and asked, "You really have to do this? With me here?" Then, pushing his luck, "Not the smartest move."

Instead of flaring, Clark seemed to soften, his expression a complex blend of frustration, vulnerability, and justification as he explained, "There comes a time when a man's got to know if he's making a difference or just shoveling other people's dumps. Don't you fucking appreciate . . . you're just a scrawny piece of the puzzle that I'm supposed to serve and protect every day I roll out of bed. You owe me, friend. *I'm* your fence. No free rides. Time for you—hell, time for America—to either pay the piper or learn how to speak nigger and Russian." Any trace of Clark's vulnerability had submerged again. "So go right ahead and tattle. See how fucking long you survive at Dexter without me to wipe your nose. That's your idea of a smart move?"

A choice of *yes* or *no* left Simon tongue-tied.

"Uh-huh. That's what I figured." With a pat to the boy's back that ended with a gentle shove, Clark sent him on his way. "Don't look back. Just keep a sharp eye out for any snoops. I'm counting on you."

Simon had to consciously think about the mechanics of putting one foot in front of the other. *Out of my control.* He passed a row of rusted oil drums used for garbage cans. Rain, still hesitant but gathering courage, had stuck enough marks on the red paving bricks to become official. *Run home?* Not like he could beat a squad car seven blocks down Webster Avenue. He thought of Louis. What would he do? The boy who had climbed out a music room window during the middle of class, who had screamed "beat your meat" at the top of his lungs on a busy downtown sidewalk, stolen a VW and taken Simon on a joy ride, knelt on a baseball backstop in the middle of a thunderstorm and sung "Oh Freedom." *White men aren't afraid to die. How about you?*

Simon reached the side street and stopped. Deserted. Across from him, the mountain of worn-out car tires peaked above the barbed-wire strands. *This is fucked!* From down the alley behind him, he heard the raised tenor of familiar voices.

"Hold him!"

"Knock it . . . no!"

"Slippery fuck!"

"Joe, if you can't even—",
"I'm trying!"
"Help! Heeeeeeelp!"

There was a thud. Then a piercing scream flushed the air out of the alley and flushed the strength out of Simon. He turned around to see Clark pinning John from behind in a half nelson, facedown over the car's fender and trunk. The teacher's left arm was bent into the open back door, and through the rear window Simon could see one cuff still locked on his wrist and Crawford kneeling in the backseat, holding onto the empty cuff with a double-handed grip. And as Clark struggled against John's writhing to slam the door on his elbow for a second time, there was a brief moment when Simon's vision went fuzzy and dense, only to clear during the middle of his flat-out run—"Nooooooooo!" The cops—distracted by another awful scream—didn't notice him charging toward them with the smooth grace of a center fielder. And then suddenly he was there, braking momentum with hard-pressed stutter-steps, his next move a mystery to him even as his arm stretched for the holstered revolver on Clark's hip. He yanked on the butt hard enough to unsnap the leather safety strap and pulled the gun free. Its heft served as a wake-up call. Too late. Instantly, Clark slapped his hand over his empty holster.

"What the—" He jerked around to find his own gun pointed at his face. John slid down the side of the car, eyes shut, face drained of color, chest heaving as Crawford, having let go of the handcuff, leaped out of the backseat on the passenger side, his gun drawn, too. Simon, recognizing his hideous mistake, his own mortality never more real to him, dropped the weapon like it was scorching his fingers. He backpedaled, hands high in the air, just as Crawford drew a bead on him over the roof of the car.

"I didn't mean—"

"Don't fucking move!" Crawford ordered.

Simon's heels struck brick, and as he pressed himself against the wall, he started to sob.

"You didn't *mean it*?" Clark stooped to pick up his gun. "Why you ungrateful little cocksucker." With the gun pointing down at his side, he slowly came over and scrutinized Simon like he was baffled by an odd and impossible-to-identify species.

"If you were a nigger or just a little bit older, I'd fuck you up but good." The silver badge pinned to Clark's blue shirt rose and fell with labored breathing. Finally, he slid his gun back inside his holster, grabbed the boy by the scruff of the neck, and flung him stumbling toward the squad.

"Get in, asshole!"

Simon tripped, fell, ripped a hole in the knee of his gray bell-bottoms, and almost ended up in a pile with John. Scrambling to his feet, he did exactly as he was told, moving quickly around the car's hood to the front passenger door.

In his seat again, he felt a strong urge to magically shrink. Crawford had already gotten in next to him, in his hand now a set of keys instead of his revolver. He reached for the ignition.

"Dumb, kid. The absolute dumbest thing you ever did."

Simon heard the creak of a rear door's hinges. Then after a few grunts and groans, bodies were sliding over vinyl, the car sagging. The door shut, and before anyone could say another word, Crawford gunned the car down the alley. Relief swept over Simon and began to calm him. *I did it.*

35

Détente

THE DESK PHONE RANG.

"Community Arts."

"Reverend?"

"Speaking."

"I got your boy here at Grant Hospital. He stuck his nose a little too close to a Cobra Stone's switchblade."

"What?" Adam tipped forward in his swivel chair. "Who is this?"

"The man who looks out for your punk-ass son, that's who."

"Officer Clark?"

"Yeah, listen up. He needs a couple of stitches. And by the way, a friend of his committed suicide. Besides that, Simon's just fine."

"What are you talking—*suicide*? Is this some kind of—"

"Do you hear me laughing? Kid by the name of Louis Collins. Blew his brains out right in front of Simon. Nice, huh?"

In the speechless moment that followed, Adam felt the blood drain from his face. A steady drizzling rain outside of his Body Politic office windows was falling in a straight sheet, and with the room shrouded in shadows, he'd had to turn on his desk lamp, giving him the look of a man adrift on his cluttered raft.

Clark asked, "You still there?"

". . . Yeah."

"Don Jursak didn't call you already? Wouldn't take it personally. He's stretched kinda thin lately—a suicide, race riot, the arrest of your pain-in-the-ass biology teacher buddy."

The bad news just kept getting worse for Adam. *John arrested? What the hell?*

"I'll be there in five minutes."

———————————

Grant Hospital was only a block down Lincoln Avenue and around the corner on Webster. In close to a jog, he made it through the emergency room doors just as the rain had begun to soak through his navy sports jacket. Wiping his drenched face and hair with a handkerchief, he passed a couple of empty wheelchairs and then went into the reception corridor, where a cocktail of disinfectant smells screamed *hospital* in his nostrils. At the counter of an office behind a glassed-in wall, he caught his wind while he filled out a stack of insurance, liability, and other forms on a clipboard. Then, signing and dating his signature with the pen for the umpteenth and last time, he handed the board back to the pert nurse behind the desk and asked, "May I see my son now?"

She recommended that he wait until the doctor finished with Simon's stitches. "I'll let them know you're here."

It must have been a slow accident day, because Adam found only one other person seated in the waiting room.

"Look at what the rain washed in." Clark tossed a well-thumbed *Sports Illustrated* onto a corner table among issues of *Time*, *Life*, and *Sweet Sixteen*. "Didn't know you had that kind of *quick* in you, Reverend. Wha'd you do? Use one of them *Star Trek* transporters?"

In no mood for chummy talk, Adam slipped into the chair on the other side of the table from the cop.

"I love that show," Clark continued. "Ever watch it?"

"Religiously," Adam said, keeping his irritation in check.

"Hah! That's a good one, you being a man of the cloth. The way Captain Kirk gets all the babes and wanders the galaxies whipping evil aliens into shape . . . sounds like a pretty good life to me."

"So about Simon and today," Adam said, anxious to get the conversation on track. "From the beginning if you don't mind."

Clark's smile slid but didn't completely fall. "It's complicated. Better hold on tight to your Bible." In that same chummy tone that only served to underscore Clark's chilling version of events, he started with the riot.

"In other words, your run-of-the-mill day at Dexter." Clark went on to explain that Simon's nose had gotten slashed by a gangbanger's switchblade. "Just some underprivileged negro practicing his turkey carving for Thanksgiving. Strictly white meat." Next up, Louis's suicide. "Sprayed his brains all over Simon and half of the lunchroom. Must have been psycho, like the kid who shot up Dexter's auditorium a while back. And get a load of this rumor that the nut-job's father was a preacher and a suicide in some other city. No doubt we'll get all the nitty-gritty on the five o'clock news, but if you ask me, the whole thing sounds just a little too loony to be—then again, there's shrinks out there who claim that hara-kiri can get passed on from one generation to the next. Call it an off yourself chromosome. Say, you being in the preachers' club, did you ever know a man by the name of Collins?"

Adam, unable to tell whether or not Clark was toying with him or only digging for information, shook his head, seeing no point in voluntarily connecting the dots between himself, Terrence Collins, or any of his other associations in the civil rights movement. "And if the rumor is true," Clark continued, "how'd you like to be in Mrs. Collins's shoes right about now?"

"I can only imagine," Adam said. For a moment, he took on the guilt of the deceased minister, which weighed almost as heavily as his own. A part of him wanted desperately to revisit the logic that had led to his and Helen's mutual decision to send their son to Dexter. Now that their search for a new high school had narrowed to two possibilities, they still hadn't been able to bring themselves to choose between what they considered to be equally inconceivable options: Saint Michael's, a Catholic school with affordable tuition, or Lane, the all-boys vocational school with a streak of military discipline to it. They'd also hoped that Simon could finish out the last few weeks of his freshman year at Dexter before making a clean break to a new school as a sophomore.

Clark wasn't done with his highlights. He told Adam about Lange's unsanctioned rally, followed by the man's arrest, and how Simon had ended up in the same car with the teacher due to a "shortage" of available squads. "I promised you that I'd look out for your boy, and that's exactly what I did. Things get messy in the heat of a riot. Like it's my fault Lange took a swing at me, tripped, and broke his damn arm?" Here, Clark allowed himself a brief smirk. "If I'd known communists were so clumsy, I could've stopped worrying about us winning the Cold War a long time ago."

"John just happened to trip, huh? Interesting."

"That's my photographic memory of it," Clark said. Now Simon might have a different take on things, but could you blame him after . . . wouldn't be the first time trauma played tricks on a boy's mind."

Before Adam could raise any objection to that convenient theory, Clark added, "One more thing. Your kid pulled my gun on me."

Adam's expression went from shock to dismissal.

"No way."

"Yep, pointed it right at my face. In case you haven't noticed, I'm still shaking."

"Hold on a second," Adam said. "You're telling me . . . *Simon?*"

Clark leaned forward to where his unofficial space ended and Adam's began.

"My partner's a witness."

Had Adam matched Clark's move, the men would have been bumping foreheads. Instead, he straightened up taller and asked, "Why the hell would Simon ever do something like that?"

Clark shrugged. "Feel free to get the why and other details from him, but if I were you, I'd start thinking more about the crime. Ever hear of Audy Home?"

"Rings a bell," Adam said coolly, but he'd also more than caught the cop's drift. As a young seminary student, Adam had done social work at the Audy Home on Chicago's Near West Side and remembered the incarcerated, streetwise, and swept-under-the-rug kids there. He listened as a Doctor Norwood was being paged over the hospital's PA.

"I'm just saying"—and here Clark eased back into his chair again—"that Simon doesn't seem like the Audy Home type. His new juvey delinquent friends will be busting his booty morning, noon, and night. By the time you and his mommy get him back . . . then again, some kids are more resilient than others. It's your call."

"Can we cut the bullshit?" Adam's urge to smash and break things nearly consumed him. "What is it you want exactly?"

"Want?" The look on Clark's face implied that he hadn't much thought about it. "Since you ask, for us to call it a draw. There's blame enough to go around for why we're in this room, don't you think? You should have never sent your son to a nigger school, and you damn well know it."

"Fuck you," Adam said.

"I think," Clark replied, "this is when I'm supposed to say, 'Just like I fucked your mother,' but can we skip the pissing into the wind contest? Tell Simon to keep his mouth shut and get him the hell out of Dexter. Is that really so hard after all you've put him through? Because if I ever so much as see his candy-ass again—"

"Let me make sure I'm hearing this right," Adam said. "You want me, a civil rights minister to . . . and even if I agreed to do that, how do you propose I get around the board of ed.'s antisegregation residency rules."

"Jesus," Clark said. "You are about the dumbest smart man I ever met. Lie! Take your boy over to Senn, Sullivan, or some other white high school and use a false address. Responsible white parents do it all the time, or haven't you noticed?"

"We'll see." Instinct told Adam to play his hand close. "First, I need to talk to Simon. You have any problem with that?"

"None whatsoever. The bond between a dad and his boy—I've got nothing but respect."

Adam was curious about another missing piece of the puzzle. "Where's John? Locked up in some cell?"

"Soon," Clark said. "My partner's got him over at Augustana. I thought it best to split him and Simon up—bad influence on a kid and all. But rest assured, Lange's getting separate but equal medical treatment."

Just then the reception nurse stuck her head through the archway. "Mr. Fleming? You can see your son and the doctor now. Would you follow me, please?"

Adam welcomed an excuse to get up and start out of the room. From behind him he heard, "Think it over."

As Adam followed the nurse down the corridor toward a triage room, he told her, "Sorry, but I have to make a quick call." Though he could not help but question whether or not his own priorities were out of whack, a gnawing, ministerial obligation demanded that he act fast before a window of opportunity closed.

In the emergency room foyer, he dialed 411 on the rotary pay phone to get a number from Information. Then after reinserting his dime into the slot, he dialed a second time. The line seemed to ring forever on the other end.

"Progressive Labor Party."

"Yeah, please listen to me very carefully," Adam said. "You need to get a lawyer over to Augustana Hospital."

EPILOGUE
National Pastime

May 20, 1969

This is your friendly neighborhood dead man talking to you. Though my possessions are now as worthless to me as the shit stains I used to leave on my underwear, I thought it might be appropriate to give what little I have to what few friends I have left behind. To Gail Hopkins, who taught me what a hard dick is all about and whose tits I still covet even in the life hereafter, I leave my aquarium, fully equipped with pump, filter, gravel, and stocked with exotic fish of all kinds that I have given such exotic names as Sam, Bob, and Joe. It is the soft, steady gurgling of my aquarium that has always reminded me of the nights I would sneak you into my bedroom after Mom was asleep, and we would silently fuck our brains out and speak only in whispers and never tire of such poetic lines as "I love you" or such soul-searching questions as "Do you love me?" Gail, set this aquarium up in your bedroom, and when you are alone in the house, when it is dead quiet and all you can hear is the peaceful gurgling of my aquarium, know that I am with you.

To Steve Jorgensen, my bosom drug buddy, who, quite frankly, was beginning to bore me, I leave my thirty hits of speed, four hits of blotter acid, half a dime bag of dope, and five Valiums I stole from my mother's purse, all of which are wrapped up in the aluminum foil in the far left-hand corner of my closet inside the toe of my right cowboy boot. Steve, if you can get to them before my mother flushes them down the toilet, they're all yours.

To my mother, I leave you with the fact that I will spare you all of the half-assed explanations such as the ones you tried to feed me when Dad died. I no longer hate Dad for what he did, because no man can judge whether it was right or wrong, strong or weak; it was simply valid, just as who I am and what I did was valid. How did I do it, anyway? Did I slash my wrists and let my blood drip down over the Venetian blind in the bathroom, or did I yell "Geronimo!" and take a flying leap off the top of the Prudential Building so that when I hit the ground, my guts splattered all over everyone's spit-shined shoes? Maybe I hung myself in my closet with my belt that has a peace sign for a buckle, or maybe I blew my brains out with the gun I hope to buy off a junkie on Maxwell Street tomorrow.

Mom, you may also have my stereo.

To Miss Davis, my English teacher, who just sent me a failure notice—to you I leave a copy of this will just so you know that even if you did threaten to flunk me, I could have written rings around your ass if I had wanted to.

And now, last of all, there is the ridiculous business of disposing of my remains. Though I'm sure that my cosmic soul will be long gone from my physical body after death, there is something claustrophobic in knowing that what used to be me will be buried under six feet of dirt. Therefore, do not bury me but cremate me instead and rent a small airplane from which my ashes may be sprinkled down over San Francisco, Gail's neighborhood preferably.

Well, that just about wraps it up. In the name of the Father, the Son, and Jimi Hendrix, amen.

Louis Collins the Terrible

P.S. I almost forgot. To my friend, Liberal, better known as Simon Fleming, I leave you all of my books so that you may know that man does not live by baseball alone. I envy your stability.

The decision was made. Simon stayed home, a boy without a school. Sleep spilled from night and into naps crammed with vivid dreams at all hours of the day. In one that kept recurring, he'd find himself scaling straight up an outside wall of his house, fingertips clawing at the rough and crumbling mortar between bricks. He'd reach the flat tarred roof, allow himself only a short breather, and then driven by a lack of choice, step off the edge. Tumbling into a headfirst dive, he'd see the grassy yard below racing up to meet him, but just before the moment of impact, time would skip a beat, and he'd be inching his way up the wall again.

He cut himself off from all things Dexter and refused to answer phone calls, even ones from Dia.

"It's her again," Helen told Simon from his bedroom doorway, but though it was nearly noon, he just stayed in bed and pulled the comforter over his head.

"She sounds really concerned about you. Awfully sweet, too. Can't you just come to the phone and—"

"Maybe later," Simon mumbled from under the comforter, but he planned on there being no *later*. In some warped way that even he couldn't fathom, he'd judged himself as unworthy of Dia, and after several more days, her phone calls ended, leaving him lost in a conflicted mess of relief and disappointment.

Unable to face Louis's closed casket, Simon let his parents pay their respects to Margaret Collins at the wake and funeral without him—missed opportunities to grieve that he would later regret. From his vote on what prime-time TV shows the Flemings should watch to who got the very last scoop of banana pudding to dibs on the Zenith radio, privileges were his without complaints from Beth or Dawn. At first he thought, *Cool*, but by the end of two weeks, their abnormal kindnesses had begun to itch at him even worse than his bandaged nose. Just before Beth was due home from her prep school, he returned the radio to the top of her dresser along with a note on a scrap of paper that read, "Your turn. Thanks, asshole." Then, wondering whether or not the tone of his note was nice enough, he thoroughly crossed out "asshole" and replaced it with "retard." *Perfect.*

Dinner table conversations often stalled, got jumpstarted to new topics, and stalled again. Once when Helen and Adam had questioned Simon too closely about what had happened in the alley with the cops and John, he burst into tears and screamed, "I didn't know what else to do!"

"Shhhhhh," Helen said soothingly. "That's all over with now." Then from Adam, "We're proud of you." Outright apologies from either parent for having insisted that Simon go to school at Dexter would not come until long after the mindset and political dust of the '60s had settled. Until then, there would just be the shared, sobering family vibe that something had gone terribly wrong.

With twelve days left before the start of the summer vacation, Adam told Simon, "Your mother and I have decided to enroll you at Senn."

"But don't we live in the wrong—"

"You'll be moving in with your aunt," Helen said.

"Huh?" Simon was slow on the uptake. "Don't my aunts all live in Texas?"

"Not your long lost Aunt Gertie." Adam kept a straight face. "She moved to Chicago yesterday. Says she's looking forward to all the snow and frostbite."

"Yeah, suuuure." Simon smirked. "Like anyone is ever going to believe—"

"You let your father and me worry about that," Helen said. Sitting at the kitchen table, she extinguished the butt of her Parliament cigarette into an ashtray with a bit more force than seemed necessary.

"You live at 1430 West Argyle. Memorize that until you can say it forwards and backwards."

Each morning, Simon traveled with Dawn on the El train from the Fullerton station to one farther north at Bryn Mawr Avenue. Willowy, never short of boyfriends, and already looking forward to leaving the confines of high school for the hallowed halls of college, she had made tolerating her little brother a new priority, which he in turn greatly appreciated. After less than a mile walk through the Edgewater neighborhood, they'd reach Senn, a school nearly double the size of Dexter. With its cream-colored bricks and decorative columns, it reminded Simon of an Olympian temple. Because Dawn had enrolled at Senn before the board of education's desegregation residency rule had gone into effect, one Fleming always stepped through the school's main doors as *legal*, and the other as *illegal*.

Teachers, whether under instructions from a counselor or just because the withdrawn new boy gave the impression that he was marked FRAGILE, went easy on Simon, sometimes keeping him for a few minutes after class to go over an assignment. So long as he showed effort on his work and didn't make any behavioral waves, he was good to go. During lunch in the cafeteria, he adopted an empty corner table amid the swirl of friendships already cemented. *Fine*, he thought, content just to *be*.

The overwhelming majority of Senn's students were white and Jewish, with a sprinkling of Asians and blacks mixed in. The blacks—transfers looking to escape from far rougher high schools on the West and South Sides of the city—mostly kept to themselves, and whenever they didn't, Simon had long since learned the difference between bluster and real bite. There were a couple of white gangs, but it took only the one that proudly went by the ironical name of Ridgeview Fuck Offs, or RFO for short, to keep race on Senn's front burner and blacks on the short end of the riot stick.

Ninth period ended at 2:40. Simon would leave the building and head down Glenwood, passing modest brick two-flats and apartment buildings on his way toward the El. Dawn always met up with her friends after school, so he often went it alone on the sidewalk with a small herd of black students in front of him as well as trailing behind. At first he thought it weird that not one of them ever challenged him for chump change or gave him any grief more than a suspicious glance, but soon he reasoned, *Different school, different blacks, different rules.* The more convenient Thorndale Avenue El station was closed for repairs, so everyone would have to reverse migrate the mile or so through the neighborhood in order to hop on the train at Bryn Mawr again. He didn't think twice about why these kids all stuck close together, until the day he crossed a busy intersection at Clark Street, and the stones and bottles began to fly.

One bottle skittered past the front chrome bumper of a parked Ford Fairlane and then shattered to bits in the gutter. He heard the terrified screams from girls, felt the squeeze and bloom of panic in his chest, and lunged with others to hug closer to the plate-glass window of a dry cleaners and a shoe repair shop. Across the heavy flow of traffic on Bryn Mawr, thirty or so RFO greasers were on the opposite sidewalk, all of them dressed in baggies and dago tees. They shouted taunts and gave the finger.

"Go back to Africa!"

"Banana-eating niggers!"

In front of a currency exchange, an RFO used his thumbs and index fingers to pinch his lips and make them appear fat. Then, upping the racial insult another notch, he romped about grunting and mimicking an ape.

"Stay in your trees!"

"If God can burn niggers, so can we!"

Simon kept pace with those all around him. *This again?*

"Stick together, y'all," someone said, close behind Simon. Then someone up ahead of him with gallows humor—"Best call animal control before these crackers gives us rabies."

Simon saw an RFO—shadowed under the Bryn Mawr Theater's marquee advertising a double feature of *Midnight Cowboy* and *True Grit*— wind up and chuck another bottle. It flew in a propeller spin across the street. *Poosh.* Granular and sparkling glass sprayed on the sidewalk among feet and ankles, but no one slowed, sped up, or showed any sign of injury. *Steady.* Up ahead and toward the middle of the block, where the El tracks bridged over the street, commuters had already gathered in a bunch at one end of the southbound platform to gawk at the action down below.

A black girl with arms so skinny they reminded Simon of bicycle spokes, fell into perfect sync beside him, mirroring his every stride. She kept her head low, the top of her Afro never peeking above his shoulder. He thought, *Hey, do I look like a shield to you?* But then the fear verging on terror in her huge eyes jogged his sympathy. *Fine. No skin off my—*

A chunk of something whizzed past, nearly clipped his chin, and punched a jagged hole through the front door window of a flower shop. He flinched, recovered, and glanced inside the store just in time to see the gray-haired crown of someone's head disappear beneath a counter display of bouquet arrangements. *Too fucking close for—*

He noticed that the girl, after jolting from the near miss, must have fallen behind. *Not my problem. Would she have cared about . . .* But he hesitated, questioned if doing so made him a sap, just long enough for her to catch up to him again, and they moved on, their forward progress calibrated by necessity, convenience, pride, and even a baffling unity. In an instant, the sum total of his experience clicked. He was older.

The sun's midafternoon rays turned the windshields on parked cars into blinding mirages of rippling flames—infernos that Simon masochistically felt tempted to touch. Instead, he reached up to put an arm around the girl's bony shoulders, only to think twice. *Better not.* Whether at Senn or Dexter, there were limits to what the "brothers" would tolerate. Just as the crowd began to veer toward the swinging doors to the El station, he heard the screech of tires on the street behind him and saw blue beams from a police mars light streaking over the girders supporting the train tracks directly overhead.

"You! Drop it! Go home!"

"This neighborhood is my home! Whose side are you—"

The screeching of another set of tires, followed in quick succession by a third.

"Move it!"

"Nigger-loving pigs!" And then the sounds of a scuffle that ended with the drumming thud of someone being slammed against the trunk or hood of a car. Simon never looked over his shoulder for the details, took his turn through the station's doors, and was immediately stepping past a newspaper stand trimmed in tabloids and girly magazines. *Safe!* The crowd split in two, his partner peeling off to join the queue of people at one ticket booth while he joined the queue at another. On his own again, he dug into his pants pocket for his twenty-cent fare and tried to squelch a feeling of abandonment. The girl and he hadn't spoken a single word to each other.

Mid-July and a sun-drenched day at Wrigley Field. Cubs and Dodgers. Adam called it "a boys' day out." Simon still couldn't believe it: *box fucking seats!* Fifth row, down the left-field line, and dead even with the Cubs bullpen. A sea of color mesmerized him: the vibrant green of the manicured outfield, the golden clay of the infield, and the Cubbie blue of hats and T-shirts throughout the packed stands. Lush ivy covered the outfield wall. Beyond the right-field bleachers, across Sheffield Avenue, and up on one of the neighborhood's many flat rooftops, a lone, shirtless man in a lawn chair nursed a longneck bottle of beer and watched the game for free. Farther still toward the horizon and out over Lake Michigan, a neat stack of thin clouds, as serene as a patch of lily pads, kept their distance.

A vendor hawked, "Peeeeeee-NUTS!" Then another one, "Heeeeeey, cold Budweiser here!" Pennant flags high atop poles on the center-field scoreboard let Simon know that the wind was blowing straight out from home plate and over the left-field bleachers—perfect weather conditions for home runs—but so far Don Drysdale and Fergie Jenkins were locked in a pitchers' duel after six and a half scoreless innings. With "sweet swinging" Billy Williams at the plate for the Cubs, Drysdale shook off a signal from his catcher before going into his windup. There was the collective pause in the breathing of forty-one thousand fans, and then *crack!* They roared to life as Williams smacked a hot grounder straight up the box and into center. The organist played, and the crowd responded with "Chaaaaaarge!" Pat Pieper, the age-old field announcer with the iconic nasally voice, spoke in his usual slow cadence over the PA system.

"Next batter . . . for the Cubs. Ron . . . Santo."

Out in the left-field bleachers, a couple of self-proclaimed bleacher bums, easily identified by their trademark yellow hardhats, unfurled a banner with a huge target on it. The bull's-eye had been cut out, and just as another bum stuck his head through the hole, Adam read off the banner, "Hit the pizza bleacher bum." Puzzled, he told Simon, "I don't get it."

"Jeez, Dad." Did his father live under a rock? "It's a joke. Santo owns a pizza restaurant, so the bleacher bums want him to aim a home run right at that guy's head."

At a glance, Simon studied his dad. A few days earlier, Adam had said, "Time for a change," and switched from his Lincoln beard to stylish muttonchop sideburns. There were the light wrinkles, creases, and puckers of early middle age; the Fleming-straight eyebrows that had gone from thick to tangled and flecked with gray; the long, steep nose that on a man without Adam's seasoned blue eyes would have overshadowed all else. And Simon saw not what others did when they came up their aisle and by chance compared the adult-teenager tandem—two different-stage peas in a family pod. No, he saw only his indomitable dad.

Santo dug into the dirt with the toe of his spike for so long, he seemed to be telling Drysdale, *I own this batter's box.* The Dodgers' ace must have thought otherwise, went into his stretch, and tucked the next pitch high and tight right under Santo's chin. The ninety-eight-mile-an-hour message sent the perennial all-star into a spinning dive for the ground. Fans voiced their overwhelming opinion.

"Boooooooooo!"

"Coulda killed Ronnie," Simon complained.

"Just part of the game," Adam said. "If a batter can't take the heat . . ."

Santo popped back up off the dirt, dusted himself off, resumed his stance, and began slicing the air with a few practice cuts of his bat. Someone a few rows back from Simon heckled, "You're a looooong ways from Hollywood, Drysdale! Chicago don't scare none!"

A fastball, nothing but smoke down the middle of the plate, did Drysdale's talking for him. Santo swung, missed, and nearly cork-screwed himself into the earth. Before hope could deflate out of the Cubbie faithful, a bleacher bum, taking rally matters into his own hands, climbed up onto the ledge of the left-field wall and began to dance back and forth along it in a precariously drunken hop, jig, and shuffle. Fall to one side, and he would soft-land into the laps of other bleacher fans; fall to the other side, and it was doubtful whether or not left fielder Manny Mota would risk injury to himself by attempting to break the fool's ten-foot drop to the warning track below. With thousands cheering, egging the bleacher bum on, and the ballgame suddenly upstaged, the home-plate ump called time-out.

"For your own safety"—and Pieper went on to announce that violators of Wrigley Field's rules and regulations would be subject to a hundred-dollar fine and escorted out of the ballpark. The bum's only response to the public address warning was riskier twirls, shimmies, and one-footed balancing acts. Andy Frain ushers in their blue-suited uniforms and cadet hats converged down from the bleacher catwalk and into aisles, on a mission to apprehend the daredevil. Fans, anticipating a confrontation, whooped it up even more. Adam leaned in closer to Simon and said, "Some people push things too far."

The words *too far* lodged in Simon's ear. Exactly what else, he wondered, belonged in that category? Louis's suicide? John's communism? Clark and Frank Tucker's brutality? Juan's gangbanging? Dia's miniskirts? Clyde's claim to all sides of the fence? Simon's mom and dad insisting that he go to Dexter instead of to Lane? The racism that sometimes sneaked into his thoughts? Ashamed, he could only rationalize that he was not the only human being with a breaking point.

Two of the Frains snatched the bum in high and low hugs around his knees and waist while several others reached for any shred of his CLUB POWER T-shirt they could grab and helped in gang-tackling the drunk off the ledge. High above the melee, Simon saw a small prop plane doing a flyby with a red-stenciled message trailing behind that read SUE WILL YOU MARRY DAVE?

Time in. The game delay must have rattled Drysdale.

Crack! A low-liner off Santo's bat grazed the outstretched glove of the first baseman, brought fans to their feet, and hit smack dab on the foul line, sending up a puff of chalky lime dust.

"Fair ball!"

Santo, all power and no speed, held at first, runners on the corners. The box on the manually operated scoreboard that showed how many hits the home team had changed from 4 to 5, and Simon could taste the potential rally in the air.

"Next batter . . . for the Cubs, Ernie . . . Banks."

In the twilight of a hall-of-fame career that had started in the Negro American League, Mr. Cub moved with such slow deliberation from the on-deck circle to the batter's box, Simon vicariously imagined the arthritic throbbing in his hero's knees. Kids in the stands demanded runs by collectively banging their wooden flip-up seats against the metal frames below—*Clack! Clack! Clack!*

Ernie went into his stance, right elbow cocked high and those fingers staying loose by moving on the skinny bat handle like he was playing scales on a piano. And as Simon looked from Banks to Drysdale's long, drawn-out stretch and back to Banks again, something caught in his throat by surprise, tightened, wrung, threatened to close his air passage altogether, and then broke loose with the confusing tears of permanent loss. He did not want to let go of Louis, not ever. He stopped his hands from shaking by rubbing his thighs, rocked ever so slightly, and felt his upper lip quiver and go calm again. Blurred vision reduced Ernie to a smear of pinstripes against the facade brick wall of the golden box seats well behind the batter's box. After a few rapid blinks, Simon witnessed the two-time MVP's hitch and fluid swing and then heard the faint *pop* of the fastball against the catcher's mitt.

"Steeeeeee-rike!"

On the next pitch, a foul tip straight back to the upper deck rooftop put Ernie deep in the hole but still alive at the plate. Simon wiped at his burning, wet cheeks, felt an arm slowly slip around his shoulders and a larger-than-life hand give him a gentle pat and squeeze. Not a word passed between father and son for a good minute, their mutual understanding for this moment better left unspoken. Finally, Adam said, "It's going to be all right. You'll see."

Santo and Williams took their leads off the bases, Drysdale paused before delivering the pitch, and Banks, having worked the count even at two-and-two, got set to swing again, the ballpark and everyone in it suspended for that deliciously tense moment. Who cared if Ernie's batting average had recently dipped to 253. *Yeah*, Simon thought, *we can win this game.*

Except for the drugs bequeathed to Steve Jorgensen, Margaret Collins honored all of her son's last will and testament wishes. Then she broke her apartment lease, disappeared into the American landscape, and was never heard from again by family or friends.

A combination of luck and parent finagling got Simon accepted to Metropolitan, a brand-new experimental high school promoted by the board of ed. as a "school without walls." Starting sophomore year, he transferred from Senn and felt like he'd rematerialized in the land of milk and educational honey with classes at businesses and institutions all over Chicago: marine biology at the Shedd Aquarium, ceramics at the Hyde Park Art Center, animal and human behavior at the great ape house in Lincoln Park Zoo, and evolution at the Field Museum. He'd still run into people from his Dexter days in the neighborhood and hear things.

Julio knocked up his girlfriend and was forced by his parents to "do the right thing" and marry her.

A couple of Latin Kings ambushed Juan just as he stepped out onto his back porch. The dual blasts from sawed-off shotguns blew him right through a wooden railing, and paramedics arriving on the scene couldn't tell what had killed him—the buckshot that tore through his gut, lungs, heart, kidneys, and spleen, or the three-story fall to a backyard covered in cement.

The following April, Simon had a chance encounter with Dia on the lakefront bicycle path near Oak Street Beach. Two days later, he lost his virginity in her basement, and less than a couple of weeks after that, she got expelled from Saint Bonaventure's for smoking pot in a bathroom. Her parents wasted no time shipping her off to a boarding school in Colorado. Romance over. Years later, he'd heard a rumor that she'd become a stripper at a gentleman's club, but he preferred to always remember her as the girl who had once picked a bloom off a lilac bush growing wild in the vacant lots and held it up to his nose.

"Smell."

For the rest of his life, he would always associate lilacs with Dia.

In October of '71, John Lange's defense lawyer bargained two counts of alleged aggravated battery and one count of inciting a riot down to a sentence of probation. In exchange, his client agreed not to bring a civil suit against the Chicago Police Department and waived his right to due process for his termination of employment at Chicago Public Schools. Court adjourned. The last Simon heard, John had moved with his wife, Cynthia, and their one-year-old son to Atlanta, Georgia.

During the summer that bridged high school and college, Simon was hoofing it down the sidewalk on Broadway when he spotted Clyde through the plate-glass windows of a McDonald's and pulled up short. Behind the serving counter, his old friend was demonstrating for a novice coworker the correct way to lift and dump a basket-load of piping-hot french fries from the deep fryer to a tray for salting without getting burned by splattering grease in the process. Besides the tamer Afro, a few extra pounds of muscle, and the assistant manager's white cap that he wore straight instead of cocked, Clyde looked about the same. *Go in and say hello?* But something made Simon think twice about interrupting the former Black Assassin's corporate ladder climb. *Maybe next time.* He continued on his way to the North Shore Theatre to see *The Godfather*, never to cross paths with Clyde Porter again.

While Simon was away at the University of Wisconsin–Madison as an English major, his parents divorced. A few years later, and shortly after Helen had settled into a teaching career at the Art Institute of Chicago, Adam resigned from the Body Politic. He returned to the ministry and became the head pastor at Bryn Mawr Community Church, located in the predominately African American neighborhood of South Shore.

Hairdos kept getting shorter. In '84, Simon caught a glimpse of Clark cruising by in a patrol car on Halsted Street. In that snapshot of a moment, he saw not a man whose aged and bloated face exuded satisfaction or proud legacy. Instead, it was the resigned and cynical look of someone who felt shafted by an ungrateful world.

The '90s came knocking. One day, while riding the Ravenswood El train to go teach a European literature class at Roosevelt University, Simon was listening to the grinding metal-on-metal screech of wheels at a tight bend in the rails just south of the Sedgwick station platform. By the time the train began to clickity-clack accelerate toward a downtown skyline spiked by the Sears, Hancock, and Amoco skyscrapers, and just as he stared past his own blank expression reflected in the window, over the rooftops of side streets, and beyond to the Cabrini Green high-rises, where so many of his Dexter classmates had once lived, he put two and a long delayed two together. A grin that he feared was more wrong than right slowly spread in his adult reflection. *You did it, Louis. You rigged a homemade time bomb and planted it somewhere in Jursak's office. Fucker should thank his lucky drawers that he'd just stepped out to go investigate your suicide.*

ACKNOWLEDGMENTS

In writing *Hey, Liberal!*, I owe thanks to so many: to my mother, Betty Shiflett, who taught me by example that writing is a discipline; to my father, James Shiflett, who braved so much in life; to John Schultz, who was the first one to tell me that the bits and pieces of scenes I was writing were in fact the beginnings of a novel; to my son, Cole, and daughter, Maggie, for reteaching me about the struggles and joys of youth; to Eric Charles May, whose generous laughter during my readings of *Hey, Liberal!* excerpts gave white folks in the audience permission to laugh, too; to former police chiefs Ray Pelleteir (Broadview, Illinois) and Mike Holub (La Grange, Illinois) for their forthright answers to my many questions concerning police procedures; to Nate Blackman for advising me on administrative procedures in the Chicago Public Schools; to Anita, Jordan, and Eric Miller at Academy Chicago for choosing my manuscript for publication; to Cynthia Sherry, Lindsey Schauer, Mary Kravenas, Geoff George, and the entire supportive Chicago Review Press team; to Mort Castle for his kindness and timely help; to Carl Larsen for forensic expertise; to Columbia College Chicago for granting me a sabbatical to work on *Hey, Liberal!*, as well as to my literary family in the Department of Creative Writing; to Beverlye Brown and Adrienne Clasky for keeping the faith; to Camille Blinstrub for finding the letter that Dr. Martin Luther King Jr. wrote to my father, along with Elaine Hall and Eric Tidwell at The King Center; and to Sarah, without whose love and patience I could never have found the courage to finish this novel.

Finally, thanks go to Rupert Kinnard, whose character Superbad (see illustration below) partially inspired the character Supersoul.

AUTHOR'S NOTE

Hey, Liberal! is a work of fiction. However, I would like to share a letter with readers that Dr. Martin Luther King Jr. sent to my father, the Reverend James Shiflett, shortly after my father participated in civil rights demonstrations in Albany, Georgia. While in Albany, my father was arrested along with forty-five other northern clergymen for holding a prayer service on the courthouse steps to protest the Jim Crow laws of the southern United States. To further their protest, the clergymen went on a hunger strike that lasted until their release from jail six days later. This key moment in the civil rights movement helped to transform King from a regional leader into a leader with national prominence.

October 9, 1962

Rev. James A. Shiflett
5444 Oriole,
Chicago, Illinois

Dear Rev. Shiflett:

For several weeks I have intended writing to express my personal appreciation to you for your marvelous witness in Albany, but the accumulation of a flood of mail has stood in my way. The smoke is gradually clearing from the non-violent battle in Albany, and as we assess the results of our summer long effort we all agree that one of the high points of the summer was the contribution rendered by our brothers from the North who came to share with us in the fight against injustice.

A non-violent campaign toward social change is at least a year-long effort and in the deep South, probably longer. Albany is now in its ninth month. We have amassed a nationwide protest, and the world knows through Albany, exactly what the Negro's situation is in the South and the nature of their grievances. During the next few months we will be working toward reconciliation. The first opportunity for which is the coming election, on October 26th. We have been successful in adding another 2000 voters to the rolls, and are prepared. We now must depend on the moderate white community to join with us in creating an opportunity to establish a community of Justice. Your witness certainly did much to raise the right moral and religious questions for them. Let us hope that they have been sensitive enough to at least express an opinion for Justice in the privacy of the voting booth.

Your continued help and prayer will be greatly appreciated. You have now become sensitized to the problem in a new way. We are counting on you to discern some methods of action which will contribute to our national problem on race relations. Our nation suffers when Churches are burned or when mobs kill and ravish in protest of a single person being admitted to an institution of higher learning. Certainly this is the responsibility of freedom loving, religious people everywhere. We thank you for being sensitive to these concerns and giving of yourselves that we may walk together as sons and daughters of God one day soon in these United States.

I hope our paths will be crossing again in the not too distant future. I will certainly be keeping in touch with you.

With warm personal regards, I am,

Sincerely yours,

Martin Luther King, Jr.

MLK:wm